DEATH OF A COAST WATCHER

Australian author Anthony E_____ _____ _____ _versity lecturer in international _____ _____ ___ a civil servant and development _____ ____ _____ New Guinea, Kiribati, Australia___ ___ _____ ___anka and New Zealand. Previou_ _____ _____ __ _____ism and academic articles. His non-_ _____ ___ _f War: The Tension Concept and the Art of Inter_____onal Negotiation (2010) analyses international negotiation in hostage release, diplomacy, trade and business. Death of a Coast Watcher is his first long work of fiction.

Praise for *Death of a Coast Watcher*

'*Death of a Coast Watcher* is a gripping and ambitious novel that ranges across time and space, exploring the distant ramifications of a seemingly minor act of violence on a remote island during WWII. Deeply atmospheric and with a firm command of local cultures, it plays with the misunderstandings that form part of all human relationships and lays them bare as key to the human condition itself.' Nigel Barley, author of *The Man who Collected Women*

'After an incredible opening and a brutal account from WWII New Guinea, readers are kept guessing as to where they will go next in the islands of the Pacific. They are then spun sideways to Australia and to Japan to revisit the scene of wartime crimes. I found myself on a complex journey that I did not want to stop.' Tim Page, author and photojournalist

'English tackles tough questions about war … the question whether those who survived will ever cease to be haunted is left open.' Susan Blumberg-Kason, *Asian Review of Books*

DEATH OF A COAST WATCHER

ANTHONY ENGLISH

monsoon

First published in 2020
by Monsoon Books Ltd
www.monsoonbooks.co.uk

No.1 The Lodge, Burrough Court,
Burrough on the Hill, LE14 2QS, UK

ISBN (paperback): 978-1-912049-70-7
ISBN (ebook): 978-1-912049-71-4

Copyright©Anthony English, 2020.
The moral right of the author has been asserted.

All rights reserved. No part of this publication may be reproduced,
stored in a retrieval system, or transmitted, in any form or by any means
without the prior written permission of the publisher, nor be otherwise
circulated in any form of binding or cover other than that in which
it is published and without a similar condition being imposed on the
subsequent purchaser.

Cover design by Cover Kitchen.

A Cataloguing-in-Publication data record is available from the British
Library.

Printed and bound in Great Britain by Clays Ltd, Elcograf S.p.A.
22 21 20   1 2 3

For Linda, always tolerant and supportive.

Who's this presumes to interfere?
What means the forward fellow here?
Goethe, *Faust*, 1808

One's sensibility seemed to grow finer, more acute,
whilst at the same time it became somewhat distorted.
Frederic Manning, *The Middle Parts of Fortune*, 1929

Contents

PART ONE

Bougainville Island,
Territory of New Guinea, 1943

Death of a Coast Watcher

Sunday 21 February 1943. Bougainville. Half an hour after sunrise, a blend of sweat and gore had already pasted the prisoner's shirt and shorts to his skin. The young Caucasian barefoot and gaunt; not much taller than the squat Japanese guard who forced him to his knees. Hugh Rand spat a bubble of blood onto the sand. Strange—it didn't absorb. How long would it take to dry? He drooled another globule and tried to hit the first; missed. Sand greyish here, darker than Sydney beaches.

Rand's elbows were roped hard against his waist and pulled back towards his kidneys to ensure torment as well as restraint. The rope gnawed at skin and muscles, tried to dislocate shoulders. A roundish burn on his forehead, like a Hindu *tilak* dot; blood from his scalp matted his blonde hair and beard into clumps; his left cheek puffed out blue within the serrated oval of a human bite. His testicles ached from kicks. Three fingernails ripped from each hand; a stab-wound festered in his left palm. Several teeth smashed out with a rattan club. Three broken ribs, two in front and one behind, grated and agonised at his most feeble movement. His back and buttocks shrieked from rattan thrashings and the branding iron; still a whiff of barbequed pork. He refused to even murmur against pain that should have made him scream.

Four minutes later, Hugh Rand's cheeks stung from slaps delivered by a village woman. Her wad of fresh spittle slid down his forehead and clung to his right eyebrow. An officer had permitted her and a teenage girl to approach the captive at the end of the few minutes the Japanese had given him to ruminate before they masked him with a rag that stank of coconut oil. He had spent most of that time meditating on his embryonic son, David; but in another more conscious stream of thought, about fear and courage, he wondered why he was unafraid. Perhaps because he could no longer exploit the adrenalin of fear to steel him for flight or fight, both impossible for a hogtied man almost beaten to death. In a passive way, perhaps he was brave in his calm wait for death, but he had always associated bravery with an intelligent choice of danger when relative safety was an option. No choice now, so probably neither brave nor cowardly; detached, more like it.

Before the Japanese captured him he killed two of their hunting hounds and one soldier with no time to wonder if he should fight or flee, or both. In the first skirmish he fought because he was inclined to do so, and fled because he won; in the second he fought on impulse, lost the fight and could not choose to flee. No considered choices in either case, therefore no bravery? After his capture he had no choice as to whether or not the Japanese would torture him. He had behaved well under torment, but because neither the killings nor the torture were choices he would not claim courage.

Rand was sure the Japanese thought him brave, but to him their concept of courage did not include choice and was therefore less refined than his. In their naivety, they were about to behead him with honour rather than shoot or bayonet him as a pig, their routine ways of killing prisoners who, unlike him, had surrendered, or had wilted under torture, or both. Cowards, to the Knights of Bushido. If they wanted to turn him into a bogus hero in Australia and perhaps Japan, let them behead him. They might have decided to lop his head as a warrior but to present the method as a gesture of honour for courage was spurious, delusional; a cultural cloak for ritualised murder as theatre; an entertaining break from routine sadism.

No, he did not think himself courageous, just defiant. How about 'dignified' as he faced death, a few minutes away? In his current hell, as with a victim of cancer or some other terminal disease, dignity was a display of self-control, of emotional and intellectual power, when taking the consequences of not being able to choose or spurn safety, or opt for life over death.

To make the victim contemplate separation of head from body was the ultimate assault on dignity, a ploy to taunt the victim, to make him and the audience focus more on his total loss of choice than his looming loss of life. Would the Japanese bury his head and body together or apart, or bury the body and cast the head into the sea, or vice versa? Or cast both into the sea, in the same place; or far apart, to compound the indignity of dismemberment?

Now was no time to indulge in semantics and scrambled philosophy, or speculation about the disposal of his body, and no time to explore courage or dignity in military and other contexts, or to assess the motivation and other forces acting on people who were said to be brave or dignified. His killers and the gallery could label him as they saw fit. No matter. They would see his defiance and feel his scorn, and would know he could still influence the script.

The woman slapped Rand out of his musing; spat, scolded and sneered; showed him something in her cupped hand and something about the girl that she needed to show him; grabbed the girl's elbow and hauled her back to the rear of the audience.

The guard masked Rand. He fought to stay on his knees but had to sink his backside onto bare heels to prevent a forward topple. Rested his beard on his chest, both pasted with vomit and blood. Fifty Japanese soldiers jeered at his assault by a black woman and his surrender to gravity and pain; when an officer chided them they shuffled and calmed. A hundred Bougainvilleans murmured. Soldiers silent. Rand listened to the wash of the sea and tasted the salt in his blood and in the air. A plane took off from the airfield nearby. Sounded like a Zero.

To his left, Rand heard an officer's knee-boots stomp and squeak to his side. He focused on the wheeze of his own breath; remembered the snub nose of his mother's bulldog slavering at a bone. Smelled leather and alien sweat beside him, through the stink of his own body—in this dreadful humidity the main ingredient in a soup that simmered harder as the sun rose higher.

Someone else wrote this part of the script. Maybe not. He had accepted the assignment even though his minders in Townsville warned him how it might end. Perhaps he alone had anticipated and created this finale, led himself and the other players to it step by step, always the flexible playwright and director.

"If the Japs get you, keep away from their cutlery," Rand's estranged father, a damaged veteran of the Great War, had joked during a rare meeting just before the Bougainville posting. Rand said he would be safe in the navy.

He heard a sword scrape from its scabbard. For three seconds the blade vibrated and sang at a lowering pitch as it dipped on the practice swing to the juncture of his C4 and C5 vertebrae; went dead when it tasted his skin for an instant, light as the wing of a passing butterfly. Sword as tuning fork, heart as metronome. The butcher splashed water. Blade lubricant? New Irelanders would wet knives to slaughter pigs.

Rand calm, shudderless. With chin still heavy on chest he conquered agony and rose to kneel in triumph, pleased that his groin muscles were too cramped with pain for him to piss, his bowels too vacant to erupt.

His mother, much too young, struggled to reach him through fog; tried to promise she would take care of David, but could only sigh and brush her son's cheek with a forefinger before the fog sucked her back in. He dwelt on her touch in a futile attempt to override what the village woman had said to him and shown him after she smacked his cheeks and spat on his face.

Why was this woman a turncoat? Wait. No, impossible. Courageous? Brilliant? Yes, yes; both. Of course. Under his inspiration, at great risk to herself, she had performed a perfect act of cunning in public to fool the Japanese into thinking she hated him when they had suspected the opposite. Now they would ignore her and the girl; his son would be safe.

The Zero now the hum of bee on the horizon he could not see. Rand the pilot on a routine hunt in his mobile *axis mundi*. Food in the cockpit for a mid-morning snack. Rice?

The officer's boots creaked as he raised the sword and sucked in air. Rand held his breath and locked his sphincter. Tried to see David in the cradled arms of his own mother in Australia; but the beloved village woman's fake sneer would not let him. So brilliant, so loyal.

The butterfly returned as a wasp and the sneer span into oblivion.

* * *

Eight days earlier, on Saturday 13 February 1943, Rand stumbled up a ridge along a bush track still wide enough for only one walker after centuries of wear by human soles, tough as tyre rubber, and the trotters of wild pigs. The pursuing Japanese hound had little stamina and barked less often, from further away and without the confidence of an hour earlier when it halted its run at him, a hundred yards ahead of its masters, in the village far below. He had shot its companion, the sprinter, the leading dog-missile of the usual Japanese pair. The sprinter yelps—an idiot—as it races after its quarry, then grabs and holds it until the slower, more muscular growler arrives to tear at arms, legs and buttocks; to terrify but not kill, to paralyse the victim while the handlers jog to catch up. When they arrive, they enjoy the spectacle until their panting subsides; then they stop the dogs.

Rand did not need to shoot the growler. Attracted by the dying sprinter's screams and the delight of an exploded gut, it pounced on its partner and let Rand flee through the village in the opposite direction from his familiar track into the bush. Flight; now no need for fight. He waved his pistol at a babbling old man who hobbled towards him. Everyone else had retreated into houses when the dogs yapped and growled as their handlers released them to chase him down and make him squeal like a pig.

The growler could not catch him now. He fled further up the ridge, made sure he avoided the track to his hideaway. He thought about the woman in the village an hour earlier, where he stood trembling and indecisive at the sound of the surviving dog and its handlers. She had called to him in a low monotone that would not carry far: "*Yu go long dispela rot!*" Go that way. Her hand with fair palm pointed to the scrub from a doorway. Her arm shone black from wrist to shoulder but he could not see her face within the shade of the hut. He took a sharp turn towards the tangle of green and shadow and found a gap. At mind's core he knew he might die soon; in more peripheral thought he wondered about her. How old was she? Was she pretty? Did she speak any English? If so, where had she learned it? Why did his mind bother to extract the pattern of her European dress, white hibiscus on dark background, from the dusk behind the pointing hand?

Rand also wondered who had told the Japanese his name. Before the handlers released the dogs, one of the men called out to him in a fake Australian accent from the scrub in the direction of the track from which he had entered the village after descending from his refuge on a mountain ridge, beyond the scrub and deep forest. "Stop mate! Wait for us." Too shrill and flat. "Stop! Who? Who?" He listened harder as he ran. Again, "Stop! Who?" Not "Who?" but surely "Hoo!"—as far as he knew, the best a Japanese tongue could make of "Hugh!"

Someone had betrayed him. Neither he nor anyone else had used his name on his two-way radio, hidden in a mountain cave not far from this village, and due for a move in ten days to frustrate Japanese attempts to trace it by sight from the air and with direction finders on land and at sea. A Japanese radio operator had taunted him but seemed not to know who he was or where he hid. Only Simeon, the village head, knew his name.

If Simeon had told the Japanese Rand's name, later they would have discovered from abandoned government records in Rabaul that he was 26 years old, born in 1917 at Nyngan, New South Wales, six months after his father went to the Great War; estranged from his father since his parents split when he was ten and his mother took him to Brisbane; an arts graduate, and from 1938 to 1942 a government patrol officer and magistrate in the New Ireland District, 100 miles northwest of Bougainville. What else might they know? They had spies in universities and other institutions in Australia.

He let his mind run. Did the Japanese know his memory stored almost every telephone number he had ever dialled? That he had instant recall of names, addresses, photographs, paintings, and a lot of other things, including Greek mythology and long sections from Shakespeare's tragedies? That his IQ score at fourteen years of age was 170 in a test that could not deliver a higher score? When the psychologist told him with awe and solemnity that he could do anything in life he chose, his reply puzzled her: "All I want to do is never get bored. And never have a god or any other boss." She wrote it down, so it was on file somewhere. Did she make a note of his high-pitched voice? At 26, it was still far too high and he preferred not to say much to anyone except his mother.

Simeon must also have told the Japanese that Rand was a naval lieutenant. His superiors in Australia had given him an officer's cap to prove it, and advice on how not to get shot while wearing it. The more senior of the two men who gave him final instructions said: "Don't wear it unless you're trapped and have just surrendered, otherwise the white crown will make you an easy target, even for a long shot. Don't underestimate the Arisaka rifle or the little prick who points it at you. It's too long to manoeuvre in dense bush but it will get you from a distance if you stick your head up. Cracks like a stockwhip. It doesn't flash or smoke so you probably won't see its position unless you are looking straight at it. In which case it won't matter."

The second minder continued the speech: "Stick to the scrub and forest during the day. If they go for you there they'll try to sneak up and whack you with a Nambu pistol. It's inaccurate and has a one in six chance of misfiring. A sort of reverse Russian roulette. If you see someone point one at you, run like hell because it has low muzzle velocity and won't do much damage beyond about 30 yards unless it gets you in the eye or throat, or an Achilles tendon. Maybe a knee. Hope that makes you feel better. By the way, the Japs can see at night and not many of them actually wear glasses like the arse of a Coke bottle."

Military fatigues and the authority of the naval cap would convince the Japanese to abide by the Geneva and Hague Conventions on the treatment of prisoners of war, and not kill him as a spy if they caught him. When they caught him, thought Rand; not if.

The senior man finished off the tandem speech as if he were an actor and Rand the audience, and the curtain about to fall: "The locals on Bougainville are looking more and more pro-Japanese but they still haven't turned on us where you'll be dropped, at a small village of about two dozen houses, near Cape Nehuss on the northeast coast."

How long did they want him to stay on Bougainville? The two minders silent for a few seconds; then the senior man nodded deference to his colleague, who said: "You may be the last man we put in place. It might be only a month or so before we pull you and the others out of the northeast. It's getting damned hairy there and some of our blokes have to move camp every day. Just do what you can while you can."

"By the way," said the senior man, "you don't have to tell anyone your name. It's up to you. But if you do, make sure you give your real name. If you use a false name and the Japs hear about it, they'll use that to claim you're a spy if they get you, regardless of the name on your navy ID. Well, that's about all.

Goodbye and good luck."

Rand would decide when today's curtain should fall. "I know the Japanese have signed those conventions but I don't think they've ratified them? Is that so?"

"Well, no, they haven't," said the senior man. "But they should do the right thing, even though their record is not squeaky clean. Take risks as needed to get information but don't try to be too brave. It's not an intrepid adventure from *The Boys' Own Annual*. You'll be useless to us if they get you. Anyway, good luck, and keep your head."

"Here endeth the lesson," thought Rand. Anonymity suited him, so he decided he would keep his name to himself. The Bougainville locals could call him whatever they wanted.

When the Japanese did catch him, how much could he take? Would he scream and beg them to stop when they shoved a water-hose down his throat to bloat him, and jammed bamboo slivers under his fingernails, or pulled out his toenails with pliers? At best he hoped to control the drama by stretching the denouement, the chase that would follow his detection; by delaying his death—the inevitable finale if the war were to last more than a few months.

* * *

At 2am on Thursday 11 February, ten days before Rand's execution, two sailors from an American submarine paddled him ashore at high tide on an overcast night; the moon intermittent, almost a quarter. They left him on the beach, not far beyond the wash, with six metal boxes containing his radio, a generator, fuel, a large battery for the radio and small ones for his flashlight; a few cans of food, maps, a compass, ammunition for the pistol on his right hip, matches, cooking and eating utensils, a water canteen, a machete, a short spade, clothes, spare socks and canvas boots; a thin blanket, a mosquito net, binoculars, a medical kit including quinine and a few condoms; and thirty kilograms of stick tobacco, twisted like rope, tacky with molasses, to pay for carriers and food.

Against orders not to take books because of their weight, he had packed the first volume of a two-volume edition of Shakespeare's plays.

On his left wrist an American Bulova A-11 military watch with nickel casing and black face; a leather cover to hide the luminous hands and numbers by night and prevent the glint of sunlight off glass by day; ultra-precise for the perfect timing of radio schedules. A bayonet in a webbing sheath on the belt of his shorts, on the opposite hip to the pistol.

He wanted to bring American cigarettes but did not do so because Japanese dogs might smell them; so, on the submarine, he relished what he thought might be his last feast of Lucky Strikes. Ashore he would smoke stick tobacco as he had done when desperate on patrols into the wilderness before the war.

Whispers of good luck; firm handshakes that took too long. Farewell to a man on death row.

Rand sat on a box and waited in the gloom. Solitude did not bother him, which was a criterion for the job he was here to do. Seclusion was the pith of his life and everyone else's, even though few people were game to even think about it; even capable of doing so. A hermit in the desert was no more secluded than someone living in Calcutta or New York. Rand was alone wherever he might be, or imagine himself to be: sitting in a classroom listening to teachers prattle in Latin, leading a patrol into mystical country, drinking and laughing with friends in a city bar, mating with a stranger or a friend. To be alone was not to be aloof or reclusive. It was more the opposite, about being at the centre of your own stage and everyone else's in your orbit; about being in control and making hordes of other acts subordinate to yours, whether or not the other players knew it. He dismissed a vision of himself floating at sea without a lifejacket, surrounded by mockers, secure in their jackets, who begged him to take control of their rescue.

Two minutes after the submarine merged back into its refuge but still lingered as a whiff of diesel, the blur of a man glided towards him from the darkness above the beach. In a Pidgin English whisper the phantom said he was Simeon, the village head. Rand found the man's hand and shook it with more muscle than he had applied to the retreating submariners. "I'm a naval officer," he said. He had expected the village head but also another man, a loyal policeman who would live and work with Rand. "Where is Sergeant Ampa?"

After a silent ten seconds, Simeon whispered that a few Japanese with two dogs were based ten miles away and would not visit this village for at least a week because they had been there three days earlier. They had captured Ampa a month ago and said he now worked for them. Rand grunted, did not speak. If that were so, Japanese soldiers would have waited for him here, and the submarine would have been attacked from the sea and air. Ampa was probably dead and had died without betraying Rand, whose name he did not know; but he did know a coast watcher would land from a submarine on or about 11 February, not far north of Cape Nehuss. He would get by without Ampa, who might have been a burden anyway.

Simeon confirmed Rand's intelligence that the village asleep beyond the beach was loyal to Australia; even though, said Simeon, still whispering, most of the white masters fled by air and sea from Bougainville last year, six months before the Japanese ambled ashore to claim Kieta, the district headquarters. "Why in hell are you whispering?" said Rand in Pidgin, their sole common language. No reply.

Simeon's rider to the pledge of loyalty annoyed Rand. Like his counterparts on Bougainville he fled New Ireland, just to the northwest, when ordered to do so; heard mockery from Simeon that he could not confirm by sight in the darkness. Simeon only a blur and an occasional whisper, belch or insolent fart in the darkness.

The smell of sweat and chewed areca nut, sweet with slaked lime and leaves of the betel vine, defined him a little more; but he had no body or face for Rand to read.

Rand was fair of head and skin and wore pale khaki, so he wondered how well Simeon could see him in the weak moon that shone through sporadic rifts in the cloud. Melded with the night, did other people watch him in silence? Had Simeon sent anyone to inform the Japanese? Perhaps Sergeant Ampa had talked and they waited nearby until they could see Rand at dawn. He yawned to disguise a shiver, invisible anyway, that did not match the warm air.

Without a light, the two men took fifteen minutes to move the boxes away from the beach to a tree that would be an umbrella to the Japanese pilot who Simeon said flew over the village every morning an hour after sunrise.

For fifty sticks of tobacco, Simeon agreed to supply twelve men at 7am to carry the gear inland through the bush, away from the well-worn tracks favoured by Japanese patrols. He recommended a cave about 1500 feet above sea-level, known only to men of this village, with a view of the shipping lane along the northeast coast, and on the main Japanese flight-path between Rabaul and the Solomon Islands. No clear track for much of the second half of the journey; rain would soon wash away the party's footprints. The entire walk would take as long as it took a man to smoke ten cigarettes. Rand calculated about three and a half hours, an acceptable distance from the coast, which the Japanese would hug for fear of the inland, a haunt of spirits and barbarians—more animals than men—with silent arrows and a taste for human meat. Simeon would supply him with food and news, and let him know if Japanese patrols changed their pattern.

Rand must trust this man, must accept his word that the carriers dared not betray him because the Japanese would kill them for carrying the gear, in particular the radio that would report intelligence for relay to Allied aircrews and submarine commanders.

Rand refused an invitation to sleep in Simeon's house. He wanted to listen and watch and taste the air for Japanese until dawn. The two men sat on the shelf of the beach; they said little, stung alert by mosquitoes trying to feast on their blood and inject malarial parasites and dengue fever into the stream. Simeon sat with his back to the land; Rand side-on to the sea and land to watch the form of Simeon and listen for Japanese or other treachery that might come from the coconut grove beside them. Every few minutes Rand heard Simeon spit betel chew.

The cycle of the tide fed Rand's sense of exile. The peak washed away all evidence of the landing and the wane dissolved his hope, absurd as he knew it was, of hearing the dinghy come back with orders for him to return to the submarine. He forced himself to deny that his protectors left him to rely for his life on a cocksure native who would have been servile a few months earlier, before Rand's administrative colleagues fled across the beach the other way.

Rand flinched when a tree cracked and crashed far away on a ridge, a stalled tsunami dark and rigid in the gloom. Otherwise the mountains were silent. On intermittent puffs of a breeze, the stink of pigs and household smoke. He would survive because he was used to patrolling in the sort of wilderness waiting for him up there; parried thoughts about the difference between living alone in a cave—with no authority in Japanese territory—and leading a pre-war patrol of twenty carriers and ten policemen armed with shotguns and .303 rifles.

How well would he sleep in the cave? Would it be damp? Bat-musty? Pigshit to skid on? No venomous snakes here, so he could walk at night without a strong light. He remembered the stealth and savagery of the wild boar, and his thick Pig File of coronial inquests into the deaths of New Irelanders gored to death and sometimes gnawed to the bone by this most vicious of beasts. Water supply? Springs and creeks, water stored in live vines and green bamboo, and waterfalls for showers. Women? In the whimsy of dreams, if he could sleep. Safe to light a fire?

No squelch and spit of betel chew for twenty minutes. Simeon dozing, by the sound of his breath. Rand more alert to the night; now only one set of senses in play.

Unlike Rand-the-child, blankets grasped to chin in fear of darkness, the adult Rand wanted the night to linger despite the scourge of mosquitoes; to be a womb from which he might emerge when he chose. He had not wanted to leave the submarine. Perhaps when the engine stopped he would feign collapse so the commander would forbid him to disembark. He had vanquished the temptation and carried on for fear of seeing himself as a coward; but now, separated more than usual from humanity by the night, doubt churned him. The fraud of feigned illness had tempted him, so was he inclined to be a coward? Would it have made more sense to accept his cowardice and withdraw from the mission by fraud? If he had done so, would he still be a coward or would he be some sort of hero by default for confessing his cowardice to himself and passing his role to a man more suited to the task ahead?

The crew of the submarine and his superiors in Melbourne might think him courageous but that was because he was here and they were elsewhere. They would define any other man in the same way if he were in Rand's boots.

As advised by his father Dave, a veteran of the Great War, Rand would be brave only if he had to be. "Listen Hughie. Let's say you know you're going to die with your mates if you don't run. You might as well bugger off. And it doesn't make any sense to get a posthumous VC by trying to save one of your mates who's not in fighting shape, or won't be for much longer. Don't try it unless the odds are against your escape and your mate might have enough left in him to add firepower that could help you and your mob survive."

Behaviour in field battle or commando raids was a pragmatic issue, not a moral one. "Hughie, listen to me. If you're in a fix, ignore right and wrong. Some of the bravest diggers I met were real bastards with no morals. Criminals before the war and after it, if they made it through. Adventurers with no interest in right and wrong. Bloody brave, for sure, but with a lot of common sense when the shit hit the fan."

Hugh Rand concluded that to take even minor risk because a minder in a safe place expected him to be brave but not aggressive was to relinquish control of his life, and might leave him dead for no good outcome, like too many soldiers who died on the Somme as their generals drank champagne in chateaux well behind the front line.

Rand's father saw bodies with stiff arms raised, if they still had any, imploring some unearthly power to drag them to glory out of the blood and shit and mud, the funereal quagmire created for them by lords and knights and generals and politicians, all safe elsewhere. "If we got to bury them, we dubbed the poor bastards 'landowners'. Knighted a few of the lads on His Majesty's behalf. Rich at last, 10,000 miles from home. Glorious. Heroic. Yeah."

A pause, a tremor of the jaw, an eye wiped dry with the back of a leather hand to forestall a tear: "Gave their lives, did they, the poor bastards?" said Dave Rand. "Bullshit. No choice about giving. Their lives were taken from them, more like it. Doesn't say that on the memorials, does it? Must respect the lads for what happened to them. No triumph in it though, unless maybe you look at the big picture and don't dwell too much on the individuals. Stopped the Huns, didn't they?"

Hugh Rand thought of the studio photographs on lounge-room walls in every Australian town: perpetual heroes, cocky in slouch hats and new uniforms fitted by blind tailors. About 60,000 of their names carved into cenotaphs or embodied like New Guinean spirits in trees lined up as a guard of honour on the main road leading into town; or out of it, depending on your attitude to the town. His father said many such heroes went over the top of the trench to almost certain death because the alternative was an officer's bullet in the back. With that sort of choice, who was heroic? Once the lads were conned into the adventure there was no way out.

"One night in a village behind the lines a few of us cornered three pompous little Pommy bastards who did that to some of our blokes. Two snivelled but the other one was a bit more dignified. We sent them for a swim downstream with their guts hanging out. Their posh mates got the message. The blokes still went over the top when the whistle blew because they didn't know anything different by then. A few of us enjoyed the killing and were bloody good at it. We watched out for our mates like guard dogs but I don't think too many of us thought we were making any sort of brave choice. Or doing any particular good for the world. We didn't think too much about what the Huns might do to us. Just went for the buggers. Not bad blokes, some of the Huns we captured if we were in a good mood. Yeah.

"This New Guinea thing's a lot different, Hughie. Not a con job like the last war, nowhere bloody near home soil. No threat to Nyngan back then but there bloody is now, with the Japs coming right at us. Darwin bombed. From what the papers say, and a couple of young blokes back here wounded, the Owen Stanley thing a few months back was for real. Kokoda and so on. The Japs on their way here for sure. A lot of real heroes there, mate, dead ones and a lot still alive, don't you ever doubt it. Could have backed off but chose not to, for you and me and your Mum and everyone else. Nothing to do with a bloody adventure. No con-job like my war. Different story altogether. Yeah."

Hugh Rand contemplated his own position as his father talked to him at length for the first time in his life, as if it might be the last chance. Maybe, maybe not. Unlike the puppets and compulsive killers on the Somme, the young Rand saw himself as a free agent who would operate more or less alone. His minders would be thousands of miles away. He would take as little risk as possible as he gathered and transmitted intelligence to the Allied forces;

would give the Japanese hell by proxy. Although no optimist, he wanted to be alive and forgotten at war's end, having done a good job and behaved with courage like the Kokoda men if necessary; not immortalised on a lump of rock that might wring tears out of wives, girlfriends, mothers and school-kids on Anzac Day.

* * *

Thirty minutes before Rand saw the dawn, Simeon said the village roosters would crow soon. Rand was pleased when a bush-cock, distant but clear, got in first. The village roosters replied; the scrub and forest threw back screeches and songs that did not always match the ugliness or beauty of the birds that Rand could identify. He ducked when a paddle bumped against the hull of a wooden canoe. Something splashed. Perhaps an overnight fisherman jumped from the canoe into shallow water, or dropped a stone anchor.

Rand wanted to lie where the beach met the grass and probe the dawn for Japanese. Instead he stood and watched Simeon's face emerge from the darkness as a portrait develops on paper in a photographer's darkroom, red-lit. Frizzled hair came first, then eyes, staring at Rand, who searched for contempt and thought he found it. In the fast retreat of darkness at this latitude, all of Simeon's features soon developed. Familiar. Rand had seen him two years earlier at the courthouse in Namatanai, New Ireland.

Rand watched him now with much more interest than in Namatanai. He saw a typical Bougainvillean man of about fifty; blue-black, of medium height, barefoot, dressed only in a laplap—a New Guinean sarong—held up by a leather belt pulled tight beneath a distended belly. Tapped his machete against his calf every ten seconds or so. Three short, vertical parallel lines tattooed on each cheek; two lightning bolts on his forehead. Teeth tanned by betel pulp, chewed with open mouth. He spat russet drool onto the sand. Rand thought it was aimed closer to him than would have been wise before the war.

"Hugh Rand? I heard your clear voice in the dark but I thought perhaps there was another white man with that sound," whispered Simeon.

"You were in the crowd at a trial in Namatanai when I was the magistrate," said Rand, searching for a way to revise the script.

"Yes. My brother was accused of rape. You saved him from gaol."

Rand wrote a test of treachery for Simeon. "You know my name but do not call me by my name, and do not tell it to anyone else. Okay? I have no name. If I hear that the Japanese or any villagers say my name, I will know I cannot trust you. That will be a big problem for you."

"Yes. Only you and I will know it but we will not say it."

Pigs snorted and shit-wallowed in their sties near the village. Dogs whined and threatened one another. A woman coughed nearby; another giggled inside a house; a child started to sing and a baby cried further away. Pots clattered, water sloshed. Rand smelled smoke from twigs piled on embers almost extinguished by the night. Life normal; no Japanese here or nearby. But don't relax.

A bird he could not see, and had not heard in New Ireland or anywhere else, cried out once from the scrub in a staccato series of five even yelps, a pup learning to bark: "Ha-ha-ha-ha-ha." Rand heard it as mockery. Simeon whispered: "Bougainville special crow. Lives here. Nowhere else."

They went to the edge of the village and sat on metal boxes under the umbrella tree. Rand watched a woman dandle a naked baby on her hip. Two teenage girls with bare backs that shone black as eggplant wheedled a fire to life nearby. He watched them bend, squat and roll their weight from foot to foot as they prepared sago and tea for his breakfast. Grass skirts rustled. Simeon collected the breakfast from them for Rand but did not eat or drink.

At 7am Rand checked his watch, gulped his tea-dregs and waved his empty water canteen at the more enticing teenager, whose black mop of curls radiated in an even tangle from crown to earlobes and from forehead to nape. "Put boiled water in this." Most of the women wore the same hairstyle but hers was longer than most. She looked at Simeon; he nodded. Rand scanned the tattoos on her cheeks, hips and breasts as she dawdled towards him on broad feet with callused soles. He ignored his atheism and thanked God that girls had returned to bareness because the missionaries had gone; apart from two triumphant Huns at Kieta, who no doubt swilled beer and *sake* at night with the new Japanese friends who made the Australians flee like chickens from the island they took from Germany in 1914.

He tried to attract her eye; she raised her chin and stared past him as if he were air. When close enough for him to smell her she snatched the canteen and swung her breasts away from him; hissed annoyance at Simeon as she returned to the fire, watched all the way by Rand. More than a year since he had gnawed such breasts and tasted the sweat-salt on such a back. Maybe he had no more chance of enjoying those pleasures again than of smoking another Lucky Strike. The girl filled the canteen and gave it to Simeon to pass to Rand.

Rand could feel other eyes. He told Simeon he wanted to go: "Where are the carriers?" Simeon said they could not risk any unusual movement, even for the few minutes it would take the party to move the boxes from the umbrella tree to the cover of the jungle. The Japanese pilot had not made his run. The carriers would arrive when they were needed. Rand did not like Simeon's way of turning his right ear to him and looking at the ground; the schoolteacher quizzes a dim child and gauges the reply.

Simeon eased off his box and lounged on a mat to wait. Rand watched him pare a wart on the palm of his left hand with the machete. When he spoke to Rand, which was not often, he still whispered. Every few minutes he spat betel juice onto the sand between them, a yard from Rand's feet. Rand wanted to object but said nothing; for the sake of diplomacy he would not let his eyes meet Simeon's. Sort him out later.

* * *

No plane. At 7.45 Rand offered Simeon another five sticks of tobacco to get the carriers to move the gear. Simeon lost his whisper and asked for another ten, his voice baritone. Too pointed, you bastard. Rand opened one of the metal boxes and gave him the fifty sticks agreed the night before, and seven more. Simeon gave him a small package as if it contained diamonds: "*Sikispela kiau.*" Six chicken eggs. Rand nodded and put them in a metal box.

Simeon shouted into the village. Twelve barefoot men with bamboo poles sauntered from behind a house. Pairs lashed one pole to each box and raised the load to their shoulders.

The carriers followed Simeon in single file towards the scrub, with Rand at the rear. He always led patrols but did not know the route of this one; so he hurried to the head of the column to assert himself for a few seconds, then dropped in behind Simeon, where he could see the machete. Sensed the carriers' gaze, thought he heard them snigger; decided not to look back. Petty annoyances must not distract him from his task to set up a base from which to report Japanese movements. Too many sailors, soldiers and airmen depended on him.

After two hours they were out of the sun and into primary forest suffused in mist and doused by squalls that roared like surf as they tore across the canopy. The men climbed hard now. Little undergrowth or clear light after they moved off the coastal trail into the trackless forest, away from the grass and scrub eight hundred feet lower, two miles of climbing behind them. Rand told Simeon to ensure no one marked the forest route with machete blazes on tree trunks, or by any other method. No vines were to be slashed for drinking water. The carriers could drink if they came to a stream or could open their mouths to catch rain. Rand would drink from his canteen, filled by the girl with the perfect back and breasts.

An hour before they had left the scrub and disappeared through the forest wall, they stopped at a fenced garden near the village for Simeon to put vegetables and fruit in a sack. "When you see the owners, pay them with a couple of the extra tobacco sticks I already gave you."

Off the marked trail the smells changed from sweet grasses and flowers to pungent mould and slime. Flying foxes roosting in the canopy screeched and spattered shit onto the forest floor around imperial trees, gripped by liana cables and steadied by buttresses that radiated from the trunk. Simeon's sweat and betel drool made the stench worse to Rand, even after he stretched the gap between the two men. He cut it back when Simeon started to melt into the mist.

Rand tried to breathe the wet air only through his mouth to dilute the miasma, fouler than the aphids his mother crushed with pliers in her vegetable garden; but his lungs burned for more oxygen than his mouth could deliver and forced his nose to inhale as well.

The forest cooler than the scrub but still an oven that cooked soil dampness into steam. His new boots were stiff and did not hold ground well; the pistol, bayonet and water canteen grew heavier on his hips. He must rest, so told Simeon they would not go on without the cargo; they would wait for the carriers, hidden somewhere behind them in the mist. Simeon quizzed him with his teacher's ear. The habit by now an annoyance; deliberate insolence, provocation.

After twenty minutes he heard the carriers' chatter; they arrived three minutes later with the cargo intact. Rand allowed them to rest for ten minutes, until his own lungs were comfortable. As he sat on a log and waited he could smell the filth of pigs and hear them scurry, then stop to sniff him through the mist, and scurry again. Invisible in the canopy above the mist, birds reported him with low, infrequent squawks; the ones he heard whenever he read Poe's 'Raven'. He could not hear the distinctive mockery of the Bougainville crow. Above the twitter and carol of small birds boomed a robust green pigeon, his favourite wild food in New Ireland, where he would blast pairs of romantics from their branch without having to worry about who might hear his shotgun.

An hour later they hauled themselves out of the murk into sunshine and tall kunai grass on a ridge curved like the hip of a reclining woman. A sea breeze rustled the grass with the wash of foam across sand on a calm day. Before the war Rand would have experienced this eyrie and the deep forest from which he had just emerged as sanctuaries to absorb and revere. Now they menaced him. He sensed danger in the open but could no more retreat into the forest mist than to the submarine or to the beach lit by stars and the quarter moon.

Rand demanded silence while he listened for planes and stared northeast at the ocean, two miles away by sight, several more by foot. He heard no planes and saw no boats, so told the party to move fast. No clear path here. Simeon chopped at the grass with his machete as he led them along the curve of the ridge to scrub that hid the cave. Trying to leave a swathe for a pilot to see? "Stop slashing! I told you not to cut anything."

A stream five yards wide flowed past the cave. A knee-deep path of pebbles crossed the stream to the entrance; deeper pools each side of the narrow path. The path irregular, not evident to a pilot unless he flew too low and slow to survive.

Rand stood at the mouth and stared into the gloom; sniffed hard as he waited for his pupils to adjust but could smell no bats or pigs. "No pigs here?" he asked. Ear-quiz me and I'll clout you.

"No," said Simeon. When his pupils adjusted he pointed to a carved head about two feet long, on a high shelf five yards inside the cave; a mask lit by shimmers reflected from the stream. "We put that mask here to scare pigs and women so this place is clean for men's rituals every three years. Women know that if they see the mask its spirit will destroy their mind and attack their men."

"The pigs wouldn't see it if they came in at night."

"Pigs are smart. They know it is here."

"What about the women?"

"They know it is in a cave somewhere in the bush. They don't know which one. There are many caves. We tell them it is much further away than this one, near the top of the highest mountain. If they come near this cave by mistake and see the mask they will go crazy and die."

"Why am I allowed to see it and sleep in its home?"

The interrogative ear, the thorn. "Because you are a man, but not a mission man or trader who might try to hurt the mask or take it away." Yes, you bastard, a doomed man with a voice like a girl, yet still a man. A man who is not going anywhere else but here.

Simeon told the carriers to put the cargo inside the cave, well away from the mouth. Rand sat on a box and watched them make a bunk, table and chair from bush materials. They put them a few yards within the cave, lit well enough by the daylight that filtered through the scrub and glittered off the stream onto the roof. To Simeon he said: "If any Japs come to the village, come back here alone and tell me. Otherwise, bring the carriers back to move my camp in ten days. Bring taro and green bananas. Don't worry about anything else. I can live off the bush. And don't tell anyone my name. Okay?" He held out his hand. Simeon shook it, nodded and led the party back through the stream towards the forest, swinging his machete at air.

Rand watched until long after their chatter faded and no heads bobbed above the kunai grass. He returned to the cave and looked into the mouth for half a minute to adjust his pupils again, then went deeper, into the cooler air; sniffed smoke above the mould.

The submariners had left diesel fumes to torment him on the beach in the darkness; here the carriers left a whiff of smoke from stick tobacco rolled in leaves. Someone had made a fat cigar and put it on the table for him. Or had forgotten it? He found matches in one of the metal boxes and sat on his new chair to smoke; stared out of the cave at a cloudburst spattering on the stream. After a few draws that cut into his throat and sinuses, he threw the cigar out of the cave and decided not to smoke again. He might degrade his sense of smell.

When the rain stopped he lay on the bunk and tried to think of nothing as he listened to the rhythm of the stream and watched its reflections dance on the mask. Lime-paste skin crumbled off wood. Painted red tattoos shaped like those on the cheeks of the girl who snatched his canteen. The mask female—none of the men wore such tattoos. The dead eyes were sea-snail valves stuck with sap inside circles of black paint. Hair of orange-red coir fell from a pointed crown onto square ears like wings, more than half as long as the head; these ears intended to warn that nothing goes unheard.

The ears symmetrical in shape and size but not decoration. On the left one, four white squares separated by a black cross. On the right the bottom half of a red sun curved down from the top of the ear into a field of black. From the lower edge, in some sort of challenge, another half-sun almost met the first to form the profile of an hourglass. The thin nose and lips of black paste—sap, perhaps. The mouth open as if its owner had died with a last whistle-in-the-dark through decayed teeth.

Rand had studied masks and other carvings in New Ireland where the style and finish were more refined. They had troubled him because they were said to capture the souls of the wandering dead, malign until lavish ritual forced them to become benign and join like-minded ancestors in another realm, somehow still part of this one; no clear distance between them. This face was passive compared to others he had seen. It might warn women away because they knew about it, never having seen it, and feared the penalty for letting it see them; but how could it scare wild pigs, more heartless than crocodiles?

The cave and mask, like the forest and the night beach, made Rand reflect on esoteric matters, mostly grim; distracted him from his purpose as a coast watcher; triggered his recurrent demand for self-analysis and dissection of others. To erase the intrusion he opened all the cargo boxes and took out what he needed for that day and night. Just outside the cave he stretched a wire aerial between two trees and linked it back to the radio in the cave. Put the mosquito net over the frame built for it on the bunk but changed his mind and repacked it. He wanted to rest that night but not sleep. Needed the mosquitoes.

At 4pm he tuned the radio to the secret coast watcher frequency, opened his codebook and key-tapped a message to tell his fellows in New Guinea and the Solomons that he was in place. Waited; heard voice and Morse messages but no reply to him. Tried voice contact, saying only his codename, Eve, the first three letters of his mother's name, Evelyn. Nothing.

Fifteen minutes later he turned up the volume, took a small spade and went a few yards into the scrub to shit. He removed his shorts completely so that he could react without tripping at the ankles if he were threatened. To reduce the discomfort of the heat and humidity, and to impair the growth of fungus, Rand wore no underwear.

A lizard and Rand watched one another as he tried to relax in this most vulnerable of positions. A veteran of the First World War had told him in a Sydney pub: "The best part was when I sneaked up behind a fat Hun having a shit. '*Kamerad kacken*', I said, real quiet and sweet. He yells '*Bitte! Nicht! Bitte!*' I said '*Auf wiedersehen, kamerad!*' then bayoneted him right under his left ear as he tried to get his pants up. Came out his right temple. Had to put my foot on his neck to pull it out. Lots of nudge in the old 303 rifle. The Huns hated cold steel." Rand had chuckled because the raconteur expected him to do so. Now he pondered his own bayonet stuck in the ground beside him. He knew how to use it if he could not follow the order to gather intelligence and avoid direct combat; to adhere to the strategy of the Ferdinand Group, named after the Disney bull that chose to sniff flowers rather than fight.

This was the fruit of a rejected life in which 'superiors' would tell him what to do and watch him all day to ensure he did it. Not for him. As a patrol officer he had infrequent contact with supervisors, enough power and adventure to satisfy himself, and plenty of space between him and the boredom of life in Australia. By the time the war started he was too used to autonomy to leave New Guinea, enlist in one of the services and bear the annoyance of officers who came from elitist schools and had never been off their own dunghill. While he stayed with his mother in Brisbane after his escape from New Ireland in 1942, and tried to decide on a wartime role that would not earn him a white feather in the mail, a naval officer came to see him. Over a cup of tea, Rand agreed to become a coast watcher.

A patrol officer could create and recreate much of his role. Now, as he squatted in the twilight on his own dunghill and watched a lizard watch him, he wondered how far he could write, rewrite and direct his coast watcher's script. Much of that day and the previous night was out of his control.

"We know you there," said the Morse message from the cave in plain English, at full strength and therefore sent from a radio not far away. Only bespoke radios for coast watchers had the crystal for this frequency. A ship? His buttocks cramped. Was it for him? From whom? Japanese? Morse has no accent. Had he heard it wrong? He left his shorts beside the hole, grabbed the bayonet and pistol and ran back to the cave. He was about to tap out his codename but thought better of it and sent, uncoded, "Who is the message for?" Then again after a minute, and again five minutes later. No reply.

He took his binoculars onto the ridge to scan the sea, placid and flat as a lawn cemetery beyond the surf that pounded on the reef with the crash of distant artillery; or the din of a thunderstorm, the saviour and dread of his father's post-Somme life at Nyngan on a farm always parched.

The tide on the rise. A few birds and fading light out there; and hidden fish that played their game of eat and be eaten below the surface, broken now and then by prey leaping to freedom before plunging back into the hunter's lair. He could not see the hunt but knew it was just below the grey glass; and probably above it, because somewhere up there in the last light a sea eagle watched a shoal and waited for a molested fish to splash about without a tail.

Rand laughed at his nudity from waist to canvas boots; looked far sillier than if he were nude from head to foot. He returned to his bog-hole and put on his shorts, filled in the hole to quell the stink that might wander on the breeze to Japanese dogs, and went back to the cave to send and listen for signals while the night closed in. No one replied to his messages and he heard none for anyone else. Might try again later.

When it was too dark for smoke to betray him, he lit a small fire of almost smokeless wood, far enough inside the cave to hide the glow that might otherwise filter through the scrub to eyes at sea or in the air. The breeze sucked out the occasional feathers of smoke and whisked them up the mountain, away from the nose of anyone who might climb through the forest from the coast at night to search for him.

In the firelight he ate boiled taro mixed with a can of beef as he listened to the radio. Reception poor so he switched off the set, against orders to leave it on all day and night, and went into the stream; sat naked with his bayonet in one hand while he rinsed his clothes with the other. He did not use soap as someone might detect it downstream tonight or in the morning. A few fireflies landed, inquisitive spirits on a nearby shrub, and started to switch on and off in unison; he moved a few yards upstream to evade the glow, however weak, that could reflect off his bayonet, eyes and skin.

He put out his tongue to taste the air; listened to the night through the ripple of the current. He was an antelope at a soak, testing the breeze every few seconds for scents and sounds that should not be there: sweat, dogs, food, other people's flatulence or shit or urine, stirred up mud, coconut oil, smoke, soap, toothpaste, crushed grass, rifle grease, boiled rice, whispers, laughter. Occasional rustles made him grip the bayonet harder and probe the darkness with wide eyes, acute by day but wanting by night. No matter. The more time he spent away from artificial light the better his night-sight would become.

He eased back into the caresses of the stream and wondered what his mother was doing. Was she thinking of him? The girl who had cooked his breakfast soon displaced her.

A plane flew above the cloud, far out to sea, too far to worry him; but it magnified his isolation and reminded him of his purpose. He settled back again and allowed the current to free his mind to wander among the smells and tastes and chatter of restaurants, where women diners directed Act One as they steered themselves and their men, who thought themselves in charge, towards or away from Act Two on another stage—a bed, a sofa, a mat or a beach.

For an hour Rand fast-forwarded three pairs through their entire play as he wrote and revised the script, sometimes letting the female players think they changed it by offering to substitute him for their man; but he was always sure who wrote and directed and revised. He had never had a relationship that lasted more than a few days; could not accept the common female need to control his script.

Rand made a lissom Ethiopian catch his eye over her partner's shoulder. Rewound them, deleted the man, too old and languid for the girl, and wrote himself into the finale in a luxurious apartment; tried to draw the scent of her skin and hair and breath into every cell of his body as he took pleasure from her but did not try to give much in return. She whispered a cryptic remark that he chose not to decipher: "Are single men like that because they are single, or are they single because they are like that?"

The silk flowing over Rand's skin turned to ice slurry when the stockwhip cracked, close enough for him to recognise the signature shot from an Arisaka rifle but much too far away for him to be a target, even in daylight. The crack came from the coast, perhaps from a ship at sea.

From the rock beside him he picked up his flashlight but did not switch it on; stumbled barefoot to the glow of the coals within the cave. They popped and steamed and hissed as he pissed on them. He felt his way to the bunk, put on his socks, boots and clean clothes, and sat there for the whole night with pistol in one hand and bayonet in the other, staring through the vague oval of the cave mouth. Mosquitoes kept him awake.

At dawn on Friday 12 February he lay down in the scrub away from the cave, close to the forest wall, and tried to doze. Fervent birds, elated to have survived the night, would not let him rest. Again he heard a crow's derision and wondered if the same bird had tracked him from the beach to retaunt him. A hornbill high in a ficus tree at the forest edge showered shit at his feet, rasped for ten seconds like the starter motor of a car with a flat battery, and beat inland on tired wings; to Rand a weary sawyer ripping into the day's last log.

He slept for an hour after the birds settled at about 7 a.m. When he woke he scanned for danger, found none, then went back to the cave to listen to the radio and eat. No messages for him and he did not try to send any. Nothing to report, and he wanted to conserve battery power so he would not have to start the charger until ready to move camp. On that day he would pack his gear and then charge the battery for an hour within the cave, rather than outside, to reduce the chances of anyone hearing the motor on the coast, or closer.

At 5pm, after a fruitless day of scanning the sea and sky for boats and planes that did not come, he switched on the radio, voiced his call-sign once and waited for a response. "You hear shot last night? Bang! Stop you sleep? We know you there." Then a chortle, pitched high. He switched off. They must have captured a coast watcher's specialised radio, with or without the coast watcher.

They knew he was here somewhere; but if they knew exactly where, they would have been to the cave by then. Therefore no one in the village had talked. As he had decided on the night of the dark beach, Sergeant Ampa must have died without telling the Japanese about the imminent landing from the submarine. Otherwise, Rand would not be here.

No one in the village had talked, yet. Rand decided to go back there next morning to warn Simeon about the consequences of betrayal for him in particular and the village in general. On Saturday 13 February, after a night of broken sleep in the scrub near the cave, Rand walked through the kunai grass along the ridge and entered the forest. Three hours later, the white palm of the woman in a European dress would direct him away from the Japanese soldiers and their surviving dog, without his having a chance to talk to Simeon or anyone else.

* * *

Rand fled for an hour after he shot the sprinter hound. For the first fifteen minutes a few rifle shots slapped through the scrub around him; cut and splashed sap from tree-trunks, and released puffs of honey and lime and sourness from the foliage. The bullets close at first but became scattered as their target drew away. He left the Japanese and their dog far behind, well down the mountain, and knew they would return to base for the night. He paused to subdue the agony of barbed wire that tore at his lungs and throat. No sense in continuing to scamper away from the direction of his cave into steeper terrain, so wet and slippery that three steps were worth one.

His face and neck bled from snares by thorny vines and whacks against branches seen too late in the rain and mist; his body and legs ached from trips on roots and limestone outcrops.

No gardens up here; no matter, as Rand could survive on bush food for a few weeks. His best hope of survival, if the Japanese did not yet know the site of his cave, was to get back to it and use the radio to arrange evacuation before they could get the village men to talk even more than someone, probably Simeon, had done already. The alternative was to run, to climb higher with a deluded sense of freedom that could last only until Japanese patrols homed in from different directions to trap him on a peak or seize him when he left it to seek food or water or freedom. A legendary colleague, a veteran of long patrols in the 1930s into isolated mystery on mainland New Guinea, always pitched camp on ridges or peaks if possible; but he and his police had superior firepower and plenty of food. The Japanese had more than arrows and stone axes, and if a submarine did not pick him up they would get him in the end, peak or no peak, perhaps nearby and soon, perhaps a hundred miles and a month away. Would get him for sure.

To buy time for evacuation he would go back to persuade the villagers not to double-cross him again. Too late in the day to return to the cave so he went from the scrub into the forest and made a shelter of branches hewed with his bayonet. The rain stopped. He ignored hunger and slept well until an animal tripped over his feet in the middle of the night and scooted off in a fury of snorts and growls.

At dawn on Sunday 14 February, Rand wished a painful death on the taunting crow and worked his way through the forest towards the track that had led him, Simeon and the carriers from the coast to the forest edge two days earlier. At 7am, as he was about to break free of the forest, he heard the daily reconnaissance flight over the village. A few minutes later he found the permanent track that led to the garden from which they had taken fruit and vegetables on the first day. Outside the pig-fence, on the opposite side of the garden, an old man slept under a tree.

A girl hummed as she worked alone in the garden, rump towards him, grass skirt riding high as she bent down to dig earth with a short stick. He recognised the legs of the teenager who had cooked his breakfast. When he crept up to her and hissed, she jerked upright, turned to him in terror and covered her breasts with her arms in a gesture of fear that enticed him to stand even closer. Her self-embrace squeezed tufts of damp hair, tar black, from her armpits. "Relax, sweetheart. You don't need to wake up your watchman. I haven't got time for you."

Even though the fresh and canned food at the cave would last for a couple of weeks, and he knew he would be in Australia or dead before it ran out, he took a hessian sack from the garden fence and told the girl to half-fill it with sweet potatoes and bananas. "Wait here. I'll be back soon. Any Japs stay near the village last night?" She raised her chin to agree with his order and shook her head to answer the question.

He left her and walked until near the village, then left the track and hid in the scrub for half an hour to watch, sniff and listen. He could not detect Japanese soldiers, nor hear or smell their dogs, easy to distinguish from the village mutts. He strode into the village through the same gap by which he had exited, but now with the aplomb of a peacetime patrol officer who intended to arrest a criminal, hold court or shoot an unfenced pig.

He sat on a drum carved from a log and shouted for the men to approach him, and for the women and children to keep their distance. Simeon ambled to him last, delayed by a limp; bandages on both legs. He waved his machete and spat betel juice almost in Rand's direction. Rand ordered the other fifteen men to stay where they were and told Simeon to come away from them for a private discussion. Behind the men, a geriatric simpleton marched on the spot and prattled to himself.

A few women and children gathered in the background. Rand saw no one in a European dress, hibiscus-patterned. Heard the women snigger at the white buffoon with a eunuch's voice, mad and reckless for returning to danger. They galled him.

Rand pointed his pistol at Simeon's forehead. Simeon raised his machete, jerked his head away and turned it to expose the left ear, not the one he had used to quiz Rand. This left ear had only a semblance of a canal; a mere dimple, at best a normal canal blocked at the portal by membrane. Rand fired at it. The bullet, trailed by a splatter of blood, bone and pinkish scraps of brain, tore through Simeon's head and smacked into the trunk of a coconut palm behind him. He dropped into a tangle of body parts, a marionette with cut strings; pitched onto his back with his feet jammed under his buttocks. A knee cracked. His life exhausted in a gasp. Eyes of a stunned fish stared at nothing; his arms, covered in welts and bruises that Rand had not noticed when last they met, shivered for a few seconds, then twitched three times, the last twitch much weaker than the two before it. Blood and betel juice leaked from the corners of his mouth, locked open; his right hand still gripped the machete.

The women screamed and scattered with their children into and under houses and behind trees. The simpleton marched faster and prattled louder. Other men groaned and shuffled. They would stay where they were without protest and would not meet his eye, each for fear of attracting singular attention. "Listen! You know why I shot him. Say nothing about me or the cave to the Japs. Tell the women and kids they saw nothing. Plant him now. If they ask about him, say a heart attack or a dose of the shits killed him. Got it?"

Rand jogged from the village—a Japanese patrol might be close enough to hear the shot. At the garden, neither the shot nor the girl had woken the watchman. She did not ask Rand what had happened. He told her to pick up the sack of potatoes and bananas. When she held it in front of her breasts he said: "Put it on your shoulder. Lovely. That looks a lot better. Keep quiet and follow me.

Don't call out or try to run off or I'll catch you and pull your ears off."

She hesitated at the edge of the forest and gestured, mute, that the load was too heavy to carry far. He cupped his hand on the back of her neck and pushed her ahead of him. Wanted to watch her walk, to see her back and leg muscles flex, to hear her skirt rustle.

A formation of four moles prominent on her right shoulder blade; the Southern Cross minus the fifth star, the smallest. What's it called? Epsilon Crucis. Caught up with her and stroked his right hand twice over the cluster. She did not falter. He stopped for a few seconds to sniff and savour the mix of coconut oil and sweat on his palm.

She stopped often. To Rand, a slow trip while he studied her with eyes and nose and ears was better than a fast one with her behind him, where only the sound of her skirt and her panting under the load would engage him. He would walk her far into the forest until she was too tired to go on without a rest, or until he could smell a higher level of fear than she now exuded. When she displayed one state or the other, he would tell her she could have sex with him and go back, or keep on walking until she did agree to have sex with him. This might be his last chance to couple and he wanted to have unambiguous control of her. Too often he had wondered, after his partner was asleep or gone, if she, not he, had authored the script in which he seduced and dominated her.

There was little mist and no rain to delay them. Within an hour they were more than halfway through the forest. He did not want to take her any closer to the cave. She did not seem to weaken, nor did she smell as if she feared him. So resigned to her fate that fear was pointless, as it was to the automatons on the Somme, once they were over the top? Sweat ran down her legs to her feet of leather and down her back into the calico waist-band of her grass skirt. Perfect rump. He would insist on sex now, before she could see where the forest ended and the ridge began. Then he would send her back.

The crow, veiled in foliage, derided Rand from the canopy. As soon as she heard the caw, the girl stopped and threw down her load. Without covering her breasts, soaked in sweat and wobbling from her exhaustion, she turned to glare at Rand. For the first time he heard her voice, monotonous and sibilant, as she spoke to him in firm Pidgin English.

A few weeks earlier, when her father hunted pigs in the bush, she said the Japanese crushed a hot pepper and put it inside her mother when they searched for Sergeant Ampa. "They knew he was her cousin. She said she did not know where he lived. She screamed and cried but did not tell, even though she knew where he was, far away. Then some soldiers pointed guns and made the men watch other soldiers push pepper inside five other women. But not me. I was in the garden." She said they grabbed a young girl and threatened to rape her if someone did not say where Ampa was hiding. The people did not know where, nor did they know that her mother knew where he was. "The girl cried like my mother. Then a fat soldier took her into the house and raped her. Then they went away." Her voice quavered. "Now you want to ruin me like her."

Rand stared at the girl as he wondered for a few seconds why Simeon had kept this detail from him. She gazed over his shoulder and walked at him. He stepped aside to let her pass, so close that he saw tiny bristles mixed with sweat and grime on the back of her neck, below her mop of black curls. Her back flashed through a ray of sunlight that filtered down from the crow's hideout. She soon vanished into the forest. Why golden hairlets, not black? Just before she vanished, he called out to ask her name but she ignored him. Then he yelled "Do you know my name?" She called over her shoulder: "We do not care about your name!"

Rand sat on a buttress to eat two bananas from the sack. She was at least a pepper virgin. What was her name? No matter. He dismissed the nuisance of the foiled sexual script; put the sack over his shoulder and walked for an hour to the cave, the last five minutes through the grass in heavy rain that would rinse his spoor from the forest mulch and the ridge.

He crept up to the cave from the side and sat in the scrub, three yards from the mouth, searching for the sights and sounds and smells of danger. When satisfied there were none, he covered his eyes with his left hand for a minute to dilate his pupils and held the pistol in the right. Took the hand from his eyes, peeked into the cave. Everything in order so he holstered the pistol, went inside and emptied the sack. The light from the stream danced on the mask. Its dopey stare irritated him; he stood on tiptoe and threw the empty sack over it.

Rand reported the betrayal in encrypted Morse for relay to his minders; he would stay on the island or evacuate, whichever suited them. No reply; or at least he could not detect a clear response. He fine-tuned the dial but heard only muffled voices and muddled Morse blurred by electrical shrieks and whines that seemed to plead for mercy from a torture chamber on another planet. He switched off before the Japanese could taunt him again.

* * *

At dusk Rand lit a fire and burned his codebook after memorising the keywords for the next two months, against orders intended to prevent him from divulging the code under torture. He ate three boiled eggs and a can of beef stew, doused the fire, stripped bare and waded into the stream to sit and ponder the girl.

She needed a name. 'Maria', of course. A virgin for sure—a symbolic ray of light from the forest canopy had beamed on her, only her, that day. Now he watched two bare-breasted women in Gauguin's painting, 'Ia orana Maria, Hail Mary', pay homage to a Tahitian Madonna in a scarlet sarong; on her left shoulder she carried a naked boy, lighter of skin than her, who rested his haloed head on hers and contemplated Rand.

Rand summoned his image of Maria to join him in the stream; took off her grass skirt and assessed her; made her a little taller, pruned her pubic hair, trimmed her thighs and daintified the feet he could see through the darkening water. Breasts already perfect. Satisfied with his sculpting, he told her to kneel behind him and scrub his back with bare hands. When it suited him she pressed her breasts against his shoulder blades and reached around his waist.

The distant, continuous cry of an injured bird or animal expunged Maria and cut through the babble of water, louder and faster this evening after late rain. To hear the cry better, he left the stream and walked naked under the clouded moon towards the ridge of grass, woman-curved. The lament rose and fell in volume, and wandered between soprano and contralto in pitch, as a fitful breeze blew it up to him from the coast. Mezzo-soprano?

The clouds released the moon. Rand studied the grass with eye-ear-nose. Savour of a wheat field; rustle louder than Maria's skirt in the forest; rhythmic shine of tall grass in the moonlight breeze. He tried to make his senses rout the chorus of women who mourned for Simeon.

The plaint would go on all night but would not penetrate the cave enough to bother him. He unfurled the mosquito net over the frame of the bunk and slept until the crow's mockery invaded the cave at dawn. Poured a cup of cold tea and went outside; no women's wail; the breeze as dead as Simeon.

He cleaned his pistol, filled his pockets with bullets, switched on the radio and settled into his bush chair. He would stay there to watch the cave mouth; stay alert all day for radio messages and signs of danger in the air and bush around his refuge. The cave was safe enough; anyway, if he could not be evacuated he must stay in or near it for a few days until the funeral rites for Simeon were over. Until then the village men would not be available to move his camp to a more secluded eyrie.

Few Japanese in this part of Bougainville, he knew. Resources thin. The bastard Simeon had certainly betrayed him, had told them he was in the bush somewhere but not exactly where because he didn't want them to find the mask and the cargo. Maybe said he just saw him near the garden or in the bush and recognised him by name from Namatanai. Too afraid to follow him. Told the Japs no one else had seen Rand. Maybe that's what he said.

The betrayal a mystery. Stupidity. What could Simeon gain from it? Nothing now, that was certain. Forget it. His motivation irrelevant. What mattered was that the Japanese did not know exactly where he hid, and no one in the village would betray him after yesterday's lesson.

Rand's mind an eddy churning into a whirlpool. The village men might think the mask engineered Simeon's fate in revenge for betraying Rand. They would not want the Japanese to find it in the cave. They were known to damage such artefacts, even piss on them, and the men would fear that if the Japanese were to find and desecrate this mask its vengeance would be worse and more enduring than any terror the soldiers might inflict.

Rand safe from the carriers; not about to dob themselves in, and therefore not him. Even if the Japanese were to pepper the girl she could not lead them to him and would not betray the carriers. But maybe Simeon gave directions to the Japanese. Left deliberate spoor? Liked to chop at things with his fucking machete. The Japanese, short on manpower, afraid of Rand, waiting for backup from Rabaul? Maybe. Maybe on their way to the cave already.

Get your head out of the whirlpool, now, before it becomes a maelstrom.

* * *

At 10am on Monday 15 February he picked up the pistol and went to piss outside the cave mouth. Started, stopped. Went further away;

Jap dogs might come straight to it. Ammonia fumes from his puddle made him squint. He stopped buttoning his fly to concentrate on the distant warble, above the murmur of the stream, of a scale sung full-voice up and down unbroken for ten seconds at a time, with a ten-second break between cycles. In other parts of New Guinea, this type of call warned of a government patrol on its way to a village. The voice did not struggle up to him from the coast like last night's lament. Closer. Clearer. Female. Maria? Had she returned to the forest to warn him of a Japanese patrol? He might investigate after he listened to the radio for a few minutes.

Rand could not go to higher ground until he knew whether or not there was a plan to evacuate him, so he switched on the radio and tapped out a coded message to say he had been betrayed and must have orders right away. After ten minutes, no reply. Then a strong Morse signal in plain English: "You coming to Cape Nehuss tomorrow at night ten on the spot. No worries. We rescue, mate." Good. The Japanese did not know the precise location of the cave. Simeon's directions flawed, the fool. Rand still director and star player.

He went outside but stayed within earshot of the radio. The warbler continued to practise her scale; an occasional answer from a distant crow perched somewhere near her. Damn the radio. He switched it off.

He strode along the ridge and crept down through the forest for thirty minutes until he saw her. Maria. She knelt much closer than the spot from which she had stormed away the previous day. A scarlet laplap bound her from armpit to knee. She was exhausted and had stopped her song a few minutes before he saw her. He scanned the forest for ten minutes; sniffed and listened for dogs, watched and tasted until sure she was alone, then drew his pistol and approached her.

Unperturbed, she said she had thought about him all night. This morning she went from the village to the garden for her usual day's work but could not stay there because she could not stop thinking about him; must find him. Her voice clear.

The crow above them gave up its insolence and flew away. In the same tree an invisible nuisance went on and on with a piccolo trill. A hundred yards back along the route to the garden, the crow squawked in crude contrast. This time not crowish mockery or insolence or derision. Warning? Rand's eyes cut sharper through the gloom as he sniffed for Japanese sweat and dogs. No sense of them; only the scent of Maria challenged the miasma, the stink of natural forest.

No, wait. Two scents, variations on female sweat. His sense of woman-smell through any other—jasmine, the stink of garbage, of sheep dead in a drought—was prodigious from infancy; the woman-smell, delicious in his youth and young adulthood, ruffled him now in the forest of fear.

Rand put the pistol to the girl's forehead and told her she would die in five seconds if she did not summon whoever was with her. She would not look at him; her eyes half-closed, wet. Palm down, she beckoned at a regal tree fifteen yards away. A tall woman stood up behind a buttress and walked towards them with hands on her head of stubble. She wore a scarlet laplap like Maria, bound from armpit to knee. Rand thought her face attractive despite her cool eyes; her body built well for a woman near forty. With breasts and belly like hers, this beauty had not borne a child. He pointed the pistol at her. She stopped three yards behind Maria and stared at him, eyes loaded with fear and defiance that belied her smile. Rand mocked her with wide eyes and bared teeth until she blinked.

"This lady is my friend from the next village. She owns the garden. We worked together this morning. Don't shoot her," begged Maria, chin on chest. "She saw me walk away towards the forest and followed me because she was worried. I will stay with you and she will go back."

Rand must shoot both of them. No, that would impair his

control of the game. At the moment, fear of him cowed the men and they knew the Japanese would retaliate if they were to find out the village supplied carriers to him. If the men were to direct the Japanese to the cave the question would arise as to how the cargo got there. He cringed—argument unsound. The Japanese knew he was in the area, so they must know someone carried the cargo. How could Simeon tell them Rand was there but not tell them about the cave? As deduced earlier, he would have told them. And maybe they got the directions wrong. Maybe. And why did they not force Simeon or someone else in the village to admit they carried the cargo? Why not pepper the women? Forget it. Confused and confusing. Don't speculate. Deal with the here and now.

He banished the complications. In New Guinea too much logic killed the intuition that was often a more reliable guide to reality. He did know that if he were to harm these women the men would summon enough courage to kill him. They could not blast him with shotguns because the Japanese would have confiscated them on their first visit to the village. With infinite patience, downwind men would watch him through the shrubs and grass until he was off-guard, pistol out of reach; then they would club him to pulp from skull to toes, or butcher him with machetes.

Even if he were to kill the women and hide the bodies where they could not be found, the villagers would suspect and despise him and he could not recruit carriers to help him move camp; nor would they let him reach the coast for an evacuation if he could arrange one, which was unlikely. He could elude the Japanese if he were to slip away to more remote, higher ground and work his way southwards along forested ridges to another coast watcher; but the young village men would hunt him down before he could consume even half the food he could carry.

Another consideration—to kill the traitor Simeon was reasonable because he endangered other people, including his own kinsmen, and would have been shot after the war anyway; but it would be rash to kill these women. They were naïve extras who did not intend to harm him. One wanted sex with him and was too besotted in his presence to look him in the eye or get off her haunches without his permission. The other was her shepherd, probably unwanted. He would keep one as hostage, the one less likely to distract him, the one he trusted less, and send the other, the one who needed him, back to the village with his threats and orders.

If the navy could not rescue Rand he must soon dissolve into the mountains. Two more days in the cave would be a sane risk. He put the pistol to Maria's forehead again and held open her right eye with his left thumb. "Go back to the garden and work there for the rest of the day. Pretend your friend is with you to protect your arse. At the normal time, go to your village. Send a child to this woman's village to say she is sleeping with you and your family tonight and tomorrow. She will come with me. If anyone comes to look for her tonight or tomorrow I will shoot her. Tell the new village head to bring ten carriers here in two days, as long as there are no Japanese in the area. Then I'll release your friend. Understand? Now get moving." The longest statement he had made to anyone since he last saw his mother.

The woman told Maria to go. When she had disappeared into the forest he cut a thin vine with his bayonet and tied the woman's wrists together at her belly. Pushed her ahead of him towards the ridge. When she hesitated he shoved the pistol into the small of her back. After five minutes of awkward gait she learned how to balance with immobile arms, and strode with grace that Rand had never seen in a New Guinean woman. Whiff of sweat in her wake.

Fifty minutes later she faltered where the forest opened onto the ridge of hissing grass. He shoved her so hard between the shoulder blades with his fist that her laplap came loose and slipped until she jammed its top edge against her waist with her elbows. His knuckles surveyed the taut muscles along her spine as he sniffed her fear through the bird-shit, pig-turds, leaves and other matter composted on the forest floor. Gazed at the skin where her concave back started to become buttocks, clenched bare beneath the laplap, damp with sweat. A pig snuffled and scurried ten yards behind them.

This woman was not supposed to distract Rand, so he holstered the pistol, hauled the laplap back into place and fastened it under her left armpit with the tuck he knew well from performing the task in reverse with New Ireland girls. Shoved her onward.

The crow flitted from hide to hide and laughed them all the way to the cave. If he could see the bastard he would shoot it and worry later about who might have heard the shot.

They stood in the stream to drink and rest. A squall climbed up from the forest, over the trees like a wave and across the ridge towards them, laundering their path so well that no eye could see it and no dog could sniff them out. He was amused by the fear with which she watched the rain approach, as if it were an avalanche or tsunami about to annihilate her.

Despite the cold rain, the woman wanted to wash her laplap and bathe. When she began to lower herself into the water, into a deeper pool beside the submerged path, Rand grabbed her by the wrists and hauled her out of the stream into the cave. She tried to sit on the bunk; he told her to sit on the floor, so she squatted on her heels to avoid the mud created by water dripping from her legs and the lower hem of the laplap. In Pidgin, she spoke to him for the first time since her capture. "This is not the cave of the mask?" she implored, in a more timid voice than he expected.

"What mask? No!" From where she was she could not see the ledge on which it rested; anyway, it was hidden under the sack.

Rand sponged some of the rain from his clothes with a towel and turned on the radio; watched the woman as he tapped out a message and waited ten minutes for a reply that did not come. He shut down the radio and went back to her.

The woman glared at Rand too long before she blanked her face. "You bitch. Don't look at me like that." He peeled two bananas and force-fed her until her cheeks bulged and she could no longer plead that she was not hungry. "I don't know your old name but your new one is Mrs Banana. Right?" She nodded and started to choke. With the pistol still in his left hand, Rand pushed her forward with the right until her face was near the floor; smacked her between the shoulder-blades until she hawked the slop.

She stopped spitting and tried to sit up; Rand put his fist on the back of her neck to hold her down. When she no longer resisted he released the pressure and stroked his palm across her bare shoulders to confuse her. The heel of his hand steered tiny waves of sweat across her back until the edge of her laplap sucked them in.

Rand sniffed his hands. A trace of coconut oil in the mix. He had smelled less alluring concoctions behind the ears and between the breasts of women clothed by the couturiers of Paris and Sydney. Whether a woman was on a catwalk or a train or anywhere else, he graded her garments by the strength of his urge to remove them, no matter how complex or simple they might be. The energy of the laplap's style and fragrance alarmed him. The woman must wash herself and the garment.

He stepped back and told her to sit up. "What's your name?"

"I am Mrs Banana," she panted. She said she needed to piss. He cut the vine from her wrists with the bayonet and told her to go into the stream.

"Do it there while you wash your lovely red laplap. Pick up the banana spew and throw it outside. I'll shoot you if you try to get away." She wanted soap; he refused for fear of detection downstream.

The rain passed into the mountains above them and back down to the coast, well to the south where the Japanese were based. Rand hoped his clothes would dry in the breeze as he stood on the bank to watch the woman. She washed the banana slop off her hands, settled into the stream up to her armpits and took off the laplap underwater; as she sat, raised it high with both hands and whacked it hard on a protruding boulder to loosen the grime. The noise startled Rand but he let her continue the beating because her breasts heaved from the water and resubmerged in a rhythm of slaps and splashes.

The laplap clean, she washed her head and body with it; stood up to beat the cloth again on the rock. The water came halfway up her thighs. Rand had never seen a New Guinean woman bare her backside like this in the open. She was getting in his way. He fondled the holster. Shoot her in the back or the head?

"Get out of the water and go back into the cave." She wrapped herself in the laplap, water-darkened from scarlet to venetian red, and dawdled out of the stream into a patch of sunlight. She stopped to stare at Rand. There again in her eyes were fear and defiance and insolence, ill-masked by a fleeting smile. The laplap stuck to her, painted on. "I want to stand here to dry." Perhaps he could forbid her to move and watch her dry. It would take about twenty minutes. His clothes were still damp from the rain, so he could stand and dry off with her. Hawk-eyed near and far, he listened for planes and sniffed the air; shook his head at his stupidity. Allow her to stand in open sunlight to dry? He might as well perch his white naval cap on a pole above the mouth of the cave. Put it on his head and dance a jig if a plane flew over.

"No. Go inside."

"Have you another laplap so that I can hang this one to dry?"

"No. Go inside." She stomped into the shade of a tall tree near the mouth and wrenched off the laplap in anger; with the poise of a ballet-dancer, cast it like a fishing net over a low shrub near the tree-trunk. With her back to Rand, she ruffled the water from her hair and brushed it from her arms, buttocks and breasts until she was calm; ignored him, turned a perfect turn on her toes and walked naked past him into the cave. He must neutralise her nudity. He retrieved the laplap and followed her; offered it to her; changed his mind for no clear reason and spread the cloth over the table to dry.

Too erotic for Rand's good. Shoot her inside the cave to muffle the sound. The bayonet too messy. To protect his own ears and ensure the noise did not carry far, he would wrap the pistol in the sack he had thrown over the carved head.

When he entered the cave behind her he looked at his watch, kept an eye on her and turned on the radio. It spluttered for a few seconds and died in a stink of burned electrical wiring. A shudder from the back of his knees to his crown, to the unruly whorl that made his mother laugh when she combed his hair before school.

Rand drew the pistol from its holster. The woman pressed her arms and back against a stack of boxes and stared at him. Light from the stream flashed her eyes; sculpted her with ripples on damp skin. Her feet heavy, her manner distant; but the woman carnal to Rand's eye and nose, and to the limited touch he had experienced with her.

To shoot her now would be to admit he could not control her. He holstered the pistol and picked up the longest piece of the cut vine. "Put out your hands," he ordered. He tied her wrists, palms joined and fingertips together as if in prayer; held her shoulders from behind and steered her to the bunk. Her skin greasy; should have given her soap to cut through the coconut oil. "Kneel on the bunk. Keep your backside up and lean right down on your elbows."

When she was in place he rummaged in the medical kit, then took off his boots, socks, clothes and weapons and put them on the chair, with the pistol at easy reach; stood behind her and put on the condom. The carriers had built the bunk low, so the position suited his short stature. "Pretend your husband has come to visit you while you dig with your stick in your garden."

For the first few seconds Rand balked at what he was doing; at most, she was ten years younger than his mother. He focused on the back of her stubbled head. Doubtless her body eager to gratify him; yet a sense of her mental struggle against her own pleasure. "Mrs Banana! Look at me." She could turn her head only far enough to glance at him from the corner of her right eye, the glance as detached as the stare of the mask when first he studied it.

A fool to bring her here. Made no sense and reduced his chances of survival. What was he thinking? More apt, what wasn't he thinking?

No, his impulse was well-founded and he was still in control. All about survival. He backed away from her and removed the condom. The deadness of her eye affronted him because she must know he had chosen her body to process what might be his only chance of living on, now that the radio was kaput. To foster survival by proxy he had chosen her instead of Maria, who might be more fertile but was too young to refuse the hibiscus tea that her parents would pour down her throat to make her abort.

Rand resumed his task. The hair on the woman's head was too short for him to pull, so he gripped her pubic hair and twisted it until she whimpered. In pleasure? Yes. Entitled to it. Sweat pooled in a hollow at the small of her back and overflowed into the channel of muscles along her spine; trickled down to her lowered neck and shoulders. Some sweat escaped the pool the other way, onto his belly.

Cooler inside the cave than outside but too hot for prolonged intimacy with someone who did not want to make the most of it. At least her eye now had some life in its occasional backward glance but not the sort of life he wanted; rather, he saw the frightened eye of the girl who lay belly-down and glanced over her shoulder in Gauguin's 'Manao tupapau, The Spirit of the Dead Watching'.

This woman absent-minded; too inert, despite his grip and twist, for such an august event. Make her participate a bit more in mind and a lot more in body. He let go of her pubic hair, stepped away and told her to roll onto her back. "I'm putting my shirt over your face, Mrs Banana. Leave it there." He once saw a vet paralyse a zoo crocodile by laying a piece of wet canvas over its head. Later he pulled the canvas away with a long string; the beast vaulted into a paroxysm of menace and potency.

When sure she could not see through or under the shirt, he took the hessian sack off the mask. Ripples of light that had shaped the woman's body when she stood naked in fear of him now gave the mask a life he did not see before. Its eyes seemed to wake up, to wonder in half-sleep who in hell he was, like a girl he once picked up at a bar and nudged awake at dawn to oust from his hotel room.

He bent the woman's elbows and propped her hands under her chin, with her fingers now clasped bloodless in a more ardent semblance of prayer. Remounted her with dead weight, crushing most of the air from her lungs; told her to keep her eyes shut under the shirt, not to open them until he said so. With the bite of coarse sandpaper, her callused feet scraped hard along his thighs and dug into the backs of his knees as she fought to breathe. "That's better. Keep your eyes shut." He jerked the shirt off her face and was vexed that she still looked dispassionate, nothing like his ideal, Bernini's sculpture of Saint Theresa in blind ecstasy. He raised some of his weight so she could gulp air, and whispered close to her mouth: "I'll make you squirm even harder for the final bit. Open your eyes. Look over my shoulder."

At first mute, she then stunned him with yelps, amplified and multiplied off the rock walls and ceiling. Fuelled by fear of the mask, which Rand knew was animated by mere light to him but ancient and lethal malice to her, the woman beneath him thrashed and kicked, and battered his face with her bound hands. He could not subdue her any more than he could have subdued the crocodile.

Just after he peaked, the knot in the vine on her wrists failed. She heaved him off her onto the floor, leapt at the chair and grabbed the pistol as he tried to scamper to it on hands and knees. She smacked his temple hard enough with her knee to daze him for a few seconds.

Mrs Banana pointed the pistol down at Rand with both hands and jerked at the trigger; he smirked—she did not know about the safety catch. She snatched her laplap from the table and fled from the cave in a horror of shrieks; threw the pistol into the stream and disappeared out of the frame, to his right. What a clown; not the pointiest arrow in the quiver. It would take him half a minute to get the pistol and one minute to dry it; then, a hound at hunt, he would go after her.

Ten seconds later she dashed past the cave mouth in the laplap, dried back to scarlet from venetian red, and hurtled through the stream into the scrub on the other side. Bleats of a sheep mauled by wild dogs.

Rand trembled, still supine on the floor. Oh, Christ. To stuff bananas down the woman's throat; to dub her 'Mrs Banana'; to threaten her, terrify her, hurt her, his last hope of survival. Where did his beast come from? More than aberration. Madness. Why do this to the incubator of his son? His mother moaned something indistinct from deep within a well, far away. Rebuke? Plea? Warning?

Oh, shit. The red laplap she wanted to leave spread across the shrub under the tree would have been invisible from the air but would have marked the cave and told the Japanese on the ground that their naked bait was inside doing her work; her fake orgasmic racket to be timed for his climax, for the ecstasy that would shroud him in torpor for a lethal minute. No, these addenda too fanciful for his script. He edited them out.

He must get the pistol, pack some food and bullets and bolt for higher ground. No time to chase the woman. There it was again, the bloody crow that stalked and mocked him. As he stooped to pick up his shorts he halted half-way, snap-frozen. Could he smell a wet dog or was it a blend of him and the woman? Perhaps it was only his shorts and the shirt on the chair. No one visible within the frame of the mouth but he could feel eyes trying to see him in the dullness of the cave. Out of sight, did someone hiss above the murmur of the stream to restrain a dog? No. Must have been his own hiss of annoyance, as if to dismiss a black cat; a curt soliloquy to chide himself for conceding too much of the script to other players.

The radio. The crystal. He threw his shorts back onto the chair, removed the bespoke crystal, threw it on the floor and pulverised it with the back of the spade. Jammed the spade into the radio again and again to scramble its innards beyond repair. He stopped. Why bother to smash the radio or even the crystal? The Japanese had gibed him on air, so they must have captured another set.

The wet dog plunged through the frame and launched itself at Rand with a rolling growl, a load of coarse gravel dumped from a tip-truck. He swung the shovel in an upward arc, a cricketer belting a full-toss over the bowler's head to the boundary. The blade smashed through the jaw and flipped the dog onto its back. It lay stupid for a few seconds as it shat and pissed, slobbered blood. The canine wreck agonised back through the frame with tongue flapping and most of its lower jaw dangling by a strip of mangled skin. Rand was amused that the dog did not clamber with tail between legs but curved it high in a furry question-mark, dotted by the anus. With cold interest, he watched the brute whimper and die a few seconds later at the entrance, eyes puzzled to match the question of the tail.

Shrewd bastards, the Japanese. They had come with an attack growler—always silent until upon the victim—and with no sprinter to yelp and give him a few seconds of warning. Of course; he had shot their sprinter two days earlier. Two days?

Someone's eyes drilled him now. The pistol must stay where it was or they would shoot him as he tried to get it; and with or without it he could not run before dark.

The bayonet, cold steel, would put him back in charge. He must stay deep within the cave and attack the Japanese if they entered. There would be no more than a few of them, and his training in close combat as part of his induction was probably better than theirs. He might have another gun or grenades, so they could not stand at the mouth and wait for their eyes to adjust. At their invasive rush he would pounce with the bayonet before they could see him.

There was only one soldier. With grenade in hand, he spat at the dog and stomped into the gloom of the cave with histrionic purpose, invincible. "You not come I throw you die!" Before he could prime the grenade Rand knocked it from his hand. As they rolled on the floor the soldier clasped Rand by the throat with one hand and held his wrist with the other to keep the bayonet from his ribs.

Rand knew he had an advantage apart from the bayonet and a bit of extra weight. Naked, so no clothes for the soldier to grab; Rand's skin still slippery with sweat and oil from the woman, the nameless lover who would give him a son. Why was she not here to help him? He lay on the squirming soldier and twisted his collar to throttle him, to cut off the oxygen that gave him the will to keep the bayonet away from his body. The man groaned as if constipated, let go of Rand's throat and gouged his left eye.

Rand's shock at this bantam's strength and resolve gave way to smugness as the challenger's stamina flagged a little, then a little more. The bayonet tip crept towards the border of ribs and belly. Control of the script would revert to Rand. In superior position, flushed at the pleasure that burgeoned with the man's weakening breath and a sense of victory, he tried to knee his opponent in the testicles, to get it over with, but could not generate enough momentum and accuracy to cripple him.

A loose hand cupped the back of Rand's head and jerked him forward to crush his nose against the soldier's forehead. Rand swooned long enough for teeth to snap onto his left cheek, barracuda tearing at bait in a spatter of saliva and vomit.

In tears and rage, Rand shook free of the bite and rammed the bayonet too hard for the victim to hold or deflect with only one hand. The point struck the lowest left rib and skated off to spike three inches into the belly. The soldier squealed, a pig; mustered his last energy to grip Rand's wrist with both hands and curb the stab which tried to burrow deeper into the gash that pumped out blood and stank of shit. Rand slid his left hand along the ground behind the small of the soldier's back and horse-bit him hard to make him arch towards the spike; then leaned on the bayonet-hilt, just as he had applied all his weight to the woman before she opened her eyes to the mask.

The prey's eyes quizzed Rand and started to resign; the grip on Rand's wrist relaxed as the stab went deeper. Rand lifted his body a few inches and pounded it so hard onto the bayonet that it plunged through the conquered body and impaled the palm of his own hand, still at the soldier's back.

Rand pulled the bayonet back only far enough to extract it from his own palm. Angry at his pain, he twisted the blade in the squelching hole like a screwdriver until the soldier's pupils dilated and there was an end to screeches, throat gurgles, flailing of arms, spasms of legs; now only the venting of gore, urine and dung.

The victor shivered; lay naked, exhausted and filthy on his kill.

The stream burbled a concert. Light dapples danced on the wall and mask in harmony with the burble. Foul-sweet fragrances from the dead soldier baffled Rand—he had thought his nose was broken.

Nausea engulfed the victor. He leaned over the dead man's shoulder to vomit on the floor. The crow warned him too late. From the corner of his eye he saw a shadow hurtle through the frame of the cave mouth. A blow to the back of the head plunged him into what he took to be death, the realm of the numb, where senses did not function.

* * *

Saturday 20 February 1943. Rand had a vague memory of being carried and dragged for hours, and of swooning in the hold of a boat that rose and fell on ocean swells. He did not know how far or for how long he had travelled from the cave before he was dumped punch-drunk in the dank room with concrete floor and walls, and roof of pandanus thatch. He found out where he was when someone hauled him upstream in the dark into a waterfall where some demon kicked him in the groin, shouted at him and struck his head with a bucket.

That was probably less than a week ago. Who knows how long? Two Japanese interrogators had tortured him, still concussed, to the threshold of death many times but he had hauled himself back as if going into and coming out of anaesthesia. At each return he pretended to know things he would not tell; then tell them a lie that could induce undue confidence or cause them to divert soldiers and materiel to inappropriate places: for example, that the Allies had not broken any Japanese message code; that Australian naval officers spoke of an Allied invasion of Bougainville within a month. They wanted his radio code system but could not agonise it out of him with nail-pulling, semi-drowning, hours of kneeling in the sun, dehydration, starvation and the worst of beatings. His body might be putty but not his mind. Much of the script was still his to write and direct.

Late afternoon. He squatted on the floor with head on knees and lower back against the wall, its concrete cooler than the air. The nearby airfield busy. Urine reeked from the furthest corner of the cell. His bowels not loose so no need to shit there. The Japanese jostled him to a latrine every morning to void the Lilliputian scat refined from his daily bowl of rice and gruel. The journey and the shitting became a worse ordeal as each day's torture inflicted new injuries. To clean his backside as they watched and laughed, the guards made him rip pages from the volume of Shakespeare's plays they found in his cargo at the cave. The entertainment over, they would shove him back into the cell for his daily torment.

The taller and sturdier of his two interrogators entered the cell and strode up to him; this man the senior officer, with refined bearing and good English. He had only once mispronounced Rand's name as Hy-oo Rando—the pronunciation always used by the junior officer, who knew almost no English. The senior man, the less savage foil to his partner, had inflicted no physical assault worse than occasional slaps to the face; had delegated sadism to the troll with squeaky boots. The aristocrat would ask questions, always calm; the sadist would say little but try to inspire capitulation, usually after the senior officer left the cell.

The foil once ordered the thug, exhausted, to take a break for an hour, and tried to chat with Rand about European art as if prompted by blood as paint. "When my subordinate tries to persuade you to answer me, and you become less alert, you sometimes mention artists with names familiar to me. We have a common interest, it seems. Botticelli. Mantegna. El Greco. You mention portraits of St Sebastian. I do not know those works. Tell me about them." Rand ignored him. The aristocrat left; sent the sadist back.

In this late afternoon session the aristocrat had no interest in art. "We will kill you tomorrow, Hugh Rand. A waste to extinguish a man with such aesthetic sensitivity, is it not? But you are a spy. And you murdered and tried to rape our soldier when he came to talk with you. You killed two dogs, expensive ones. Killed your friend Simeon in the village. The headman."

"Rape the soldier? What? Why raise such a stupid accusation now?"

"Yes, Hugh Rand. You were wearing a wrist clock. A watch. No clothes. Why were you not wearing trousers? You were still aroused. We saw some stain on his body, on his uniform, that told us you much enjoyed your contact with him. We know why you told the black lady you did not want her. You prefer men. Maybe your captured her as a hostage to stop us from arresting you. A stupid plan. If we must kill her to get you, no problem for us."

"All bullshit. Anyway, you can't shoot me. Can't you get it into your potato head that I'm a naval officer? A lieutenant. I've told you about 50 times. The Geneva and Hague Conventions protect me as a prisoner of war. And where is my fucking wristwatch?"

"Forget about the wristwatch. Your time left is so little you do not need it. We will not shoot you, I promise. We will bayonet you or cut your head off because we do not want to waste bullets. It is difficult to get ammunition because the American navy has recovered enough strength to disrupt our supply lines. We found papers in your cave, we read your name, we checked from Australian records in Rabaul and Kavieng. Patrol officer—*kiap*—not military. Like we have to remind you every day, you are not a real navy officer. You are a spy."

"All that's bullshit. You knew my name before you captured me. The soldiers in the village called out my name when I was escaping."

"No, they did not. They told me they called out to ask 'Who are you?' but you shot the dog and ran away. We did not know your name until we got your papers in the cave camp. False navy papers. Not a real officer. Then we first knew your name is Hugh Rand."

"Simeon told you."

"Simeon? The head man of the village near the cave? He and all the other black people lied to our soldiers. Said they did not know your name, did not know you were at Bougainville until you came to the village from the jungle, the day you shot the dog and ran away. Soldiers hurt and beat Simeon but he said he did not know your name, where you stayed, how you got here. The stupid soldiers believed him. We knew already you were near Cape Nehuss because the captain of our ship for listening heard your radio strong near there and said hello to you. On our special radio we can hear all the spies talking and sending Morse messages. A few days later we followed two ladies who came to tell us they heard a white man sing in the forest and wanted to show us that place, maybe near where he lives." Today, this bastard is much more talkative than usual.

"All bullshit. I never sing. And they did not know where I lived. If you followed them, why didn't you shoot me in the forest?"

"We knew from before, when we get close you will trick us and our dogs and run away up the mountain. Also, we could shoot you but maybe we and the dogs would not find your radio and cargo because any heavy rain washes footsteps and smells away from the ground. We wanted to catch you where you sleep. The villagers would not tell us. We believed most of them did not know. Also if you are dead we cannot make you tell secrets, can we?"

"What happened to the two ladies?'

"We protected them because they said some village people might kill them."

"Why?"

"Too many questions, Hugh Rand. My officer and his soldiers and dog followed the ladies into the forest. You are stupid if you do not want to believe that. It would be too much coincidence without the help of the ladies, don't you see? The soldiers were a bit too slow so the girl came back to find them and say you captured her companion for a hostage. Later we knew it was her mother."

"Mother? What the fuck are you talking about? They are friends, from different villages."

"Ah, Hugh Rand. Sometimes I think you are a smart man, sometimes a stupid one. I do not know their names but I do know they are the family of the headman you murdered. We did not know that until after we captured you and they came to us for protection and told us. Didn't you ask the girl for her name? Her father's name would have been part of it, no? Simeon, I think."

Rand knew her name was Maria. As New Guineans do, she would have mentioned her father's name, which Rand must have forgotten. Anyway, it was not Simeon.

"My officer and his soldiers were a little stupid too, but not for such a long time as you are. They should not have believed the story about a white man singing in the forest. They should have asked why the ladies wanted us to find you but no one else would help us."

"Look, whatever your bloody name is, you're making up

a lot of crap because you don't like the women's loyalty to me. They wanted to find me for personal reasons and your patrol just happened to follow them. As you said, coincidence."

"My bloody name? Sorry I have not told you before. Major Yuki, a short form of my name. You can call me Yuki because we have come to know one another well and are good friends, are we not? Do you want to hear the rest of what happened that day in the forest?"

Rand said he had heard enough fantasy for one day.

"I choose to finish anyway. After the girl came back to the waiting soldiers they went quickly with the dog, back along the way she came. They soon found the cave and caught you after the older black lady ran out when you did not want her and screamed to guide them. Our soldiers found your cargo. So we knew the men from the village lied to us. As we suspected already, only they could hide you and carry your cargo from the beach. One crazy old man wanted to be our friend, so he agreed with us that the men carried your cargo. My officer later shot some but not him."

"Where are the ladies now?" No answer.

"Then we made twelve strong men go to cave, get the cargo, the day after we caught you and put you on the Kieta boat. But outside the cave the men said they must not go inside because a black lady had been there and maybe saw the spirit mask for men only. The spirit might be angry and kill the men. Our soldiers went in, brought out the body of the soldier you murdered and tried to rape the day before. No pigs or animals hurt the body at night. Strange, yes? The men saw something from you on his uniform. A stain from excitement."

"I asked, where are the ladies now?"

"You don't care about the black men, Hugh Rand? A funny thing happened."

"What funny thing?"

"After the black men buried our soldier and the officer held a

69

ceremony for heroes, our men entered the cave again and brought out the godly mask. They threw it on ground. Old rubbish wood. They made a fire. My officer said the black men cried out like the howling monkeys from South America in Tokyo Zoo. They tried to run away, so our soldiers shot them."

"Shot them? Jesus! How many?"

"Eight. Needed only a few bullets. About one for each target, maybe a couple extra. Then the soldiers changed to bayonets. Ha! Maybe the black men were right about the spirit causing them to get hurt."

"How did you move my cargo if you shot all the strong men from the bloody village?"

"You ask too many questions, Hugh Rand. Okay, I'll talk now because you will be dead tomorrow and we will no longer talk or listen to one another. Not all were shot. I already said we shot eight, so kept four. My officer said the dead men smelled bad as soon as they died. The soldiers piled wood on them and used your petrol to make a strong fire. A very evil spirit mask, yes? Ashes now, like the eight men."

"Yes, yes, yes. Very bloody evil. And thank you for a very funny story."

The interrogator, a non-smoker, glared at Rand for a few seconds. "Enough questions. Want a cigarette?" He took a packet of American Chesterfields from his shirt pocket and slid one through blood into the left corner of Rand's mouth; gentle as a new mother giving a nipple to her firstborn. Too good to spit back at the bastard. Not as sweet as a Lucky Strike, clear to Rand even through the blood and vomit.

The interrogator lit the cigarette; allowed one deep draw, seized it with thumb and forefinger and stubbed it on Rand's forehead. Not ready for the pain, he screamed the first scream of his life.

"Not so strong as you want me to think. Want yourself to think? Goodbye Hugh Rand. You will eat water tonight. Boiled so your health will not suffer. We will not waste food on a homosexual spy who will have his belly bayoneted or head cut off in a few hours."

"What's the date today, you fucker?"

"February 20, my good friend. The date should not matter to you. Do you want bayonets in your body or would you prefer to have your head cut off? Bayonets would be good practice for our men. And more like St Sebastian for you."

"Oh, a choice of cutlery. You Japanese are so refined. Bayonet, please, if you don't mind."

"No. We'll cut off your head. More frightening. Good for people to watch and learn, like the theatre of your beloved Shakespeare. I ask you one more time. Tell me how other spies have got here. When? Where? How many? You tell me and I promise to shoot you if you want, not cut off your head."

"They were born here, like me. They're all over the island. Too many to count."

"So, smart man. One more question. Why do you speak like a girl, Hugh Rand? Not deep down like other white men?"

"Mock all you like, you bastard. My father was a eunuch, like you."

"I know what a eunuch is. Okay, smart man. We'll cut off your clever head. Tonight, a moon eclipse. A strong English word, is it not? Tomorrow, your eclipse."

An eclipse. That's right, it's 20 February. The sub commander told me.

After the interrogator left, Rand saw a spark on the floor; picked up the crushed cigarette and coaxed it to life, just as Maria revived the fire to cook his breakfast in the village. The Chesterfield became a Lucky Strike.

A weak attempt by that Yuki prick to break him with the bullshit about Maria and her friend. Ignore it. Let him believe it. Maybe a good cover for them and the baby after Rand was gone. Best if the Japs did not suspect the real connection with him. The opposite of what the blockheads had decided. Laugh's on them.

* * *

Rand saw himself as dignified rather than brave, but Maria would not see the difference and would be proud of him for being so heroic that he could make the Japanese behead him. No matter what the interrogator might say about saving bullets, Rand had forced them to apply their code of honour by making them think he was brave. Maria would raise the boy incubated by her older friend; they would both inspire him with tales of his father's courage and power under duress. Spurious, but better than having his son think him gutless and weak. They would live in bliss with the boy as they waited for Rand's mother to adopt him after the war.

In another Gauguin painting, 'Te rerioa, The Dream', Rand watched his son sleep in a cradle tended by Maria, cross-legged on a pandanus mat, near naked, wistful, chin resting on left hand, other hand on the cradle. Her skin of burnt umber, much lighter than Bougainville black but darker than his child's. Caramel gloss on the umber sculpted her face and body. Rand could smell the luxury of the paint. The incubator, relaxed but alert, cocoa skin a shade short of black, guarded Maria's back.

A few minutes before sunset, when mellow light still gleamed into the cell through the tiny eastern window, mosquitoes launched from the roof of thatch to attack Rand in squadrons of buzz and jab, the drill of a mad dentist. Ten or so days ago he relied on loathed mosquitoes to keep him awake and alert. Now he wanted them to inflict mild pain and annoyance to distract him from the mental and physical fruits of torture. This evening the mosquitoes were more frenzied than ever. To prove they could not pierce and suck at whim, he selected a group of arm-guzzlers and slapped them into red paste flecked with petite wings and legs. He writhed and moaned at the slap—he had used the hand, now rotted green, impaled at the cave when his bayonet passed through the soldier's gut.

Rand wiped the green-red hand on his shorts and dialled telephone numbers to kill the agony. All engaged. Last night he memorised a sequence of a hundred random digits to blunt his pain, and two nights ago calculated a Fibonacci series to 9,227,465—the thirty-fifth number.

As the sun faded the glow in the cell brightened when it should have diminished. With his better hand, minus three fingernails, Rand hauled himself up to the window ledge and peered out at the full moon. Its crown had emerged from the sea and cast a path of lustre towards him. No cloud. The pain too great for him to stay upright so he settled back on his haunches and redialled his mother.

Women in the nearby houses and a village half a mile away began to wail for him as they had for Simeon. The Japanese must have told them he would die the next morning with honour; so they wailed to lament his death, to say they revered him for the courage that forced his captors to behead him as a warrior, not shoot or bayonet him like a black man or annoying dog.

Rand's mother asked about the background noise. He explained the tribute the women sang to him as he spoke; told her about her grandson, David, and where she could find the boy after the war to collect him and take him to Australia. As he talked and she listened, the moon-glow into the cell started to fade when it should have brightened. The wailing grew higher in pitch and volume; the dominant tone shifted from tribute to him to horror at something else. Men shouted as they did when chasing wild pigs out of a garden through a breached fence.

Rand rang off and hauled himself up to the window again. The whole moon had broken away from the sea. A translucent shadow, a ginger bruise, curved at the edge like a bite taken out of a wafer by perfect teeth, had captured a large section of the moon's base, close to the sea. The section was shaped like the bottom half of the hour-glass painted on the right ear of the mask in the cave.

The light waned as the bruise grew, a slow cancer. The women wailed harder. The men bellowed louder, and on the beach Rand could see and hear two boys beating a wooden canoe with paddles. The moon climbed higher with eyes frantic as it tried to escape its slaughter.

The bruise conquered almost half of the moon, then started to heal as the moon pulled away, snail-paced, from the arc of the bite. The women's lament now a paean that melded victory with relief at deliverance from evil. The men howled contempt at the loser as it sank back into its lair; cheered the prey now free to gleam deliverance. Cheered Rand?

Rand moaned and slid down the wall through smears of blood and sweat, back onto his haunches. What was the right name for his son? Probably David, perhaps Alexander. Gideon? Samson? No, not Samson. David. Yes, David. Tomorrow morning telephone his mother to confirm it.

Someone played a flute nearby. Japanese? Bamboo? Wood? Not metal. With the women's tribute and the men's shouts of encouragement still fresh, he let the flute ease him into sleep, his mind relaxed, unworried about his going to oblivion next day as a physical individual with conscious mind. A personal return to the nothingness from which we came. We don't worry about that first nothingness so why worry about the next?

The Japs could control his physical here and now, could snuff out his consciousness, his self-awareness; but not his survival in human memory, at least in the oral tradition of Bougainville and beyond, perhaps even in Japan. Also, the Japs did not know about David, and no one was likely to tell them. Moses hidden from Herod. Rand would survive in David and endure through him and his progeny. The 'abstract me' immortal, eternal. And in the near future, 'the idea of me' still around to the Japs when they get shot up and realise it's because they made decisions based on bullshit about Allied plans and firepower. Still the director. They don't know it.

A dreamless night on sacks stuffed with coir and grass; calm, unbroken until the crow, far away, cawed the laugh Rand had first heard on the day the submariners marooned him. As his last sun rose on Sunday 21 February, he crawled to the corner of the cell and tried to piss away the pain in his bladder. Not a drop. Rand dialled his mother for advice; engaged signal.

Two guards and the aristocrat—the non-smoker who carried Chesterfields—entered the cell, the guards with cocked rifles. "You want to shit before we cut off your head, Hugh Rand?" asked the interrogator. Was that a touch of compassion? A new script waiting for an editor.

"No food, no shit, you cretin. Tell the intrepid Knights of Bushido to point their rifles somewhere else. Wouldn't want to waste bullets, would they? They look like they're about to shit instead of me. Do I scare them that much? Do they reckon I'll sodomise them?"

"What is a cretin?" hissed the interrogator. Heels snapped together.

"An idiot like you. Small brain like Emperor Hirohito." A kick to the chest broke a fourth rib and hammered Rand to the floor in wretched pain, but satisfied to have wrecked again the aristocrat's attempts to present as refined, to see himself in a white hat. Now close to the death-point, Rand was satisfied to checkmate the king in a hitherto one-sided game of human chess.

The interrogator taunted down at his kill: "Good news for you, Hugh Rand. I am leaving now. You will not have me for your companion again. My officer will kill you now, Mr Smart Man. Man? With a girl's voice and fear of sex with women?" Bowed low twice and left in anger at himself for letting Rand make him lose composure; shameful for an aristocrat bred to control every aspect of his being, to restrain all impulses.

The guards roped Rand's elbows, shoved and agonised him into the sunlight; allowed him to hesitate for fifteen seconds to take in the reality of his stage and audience; dragged him close to the beach. To Golgotha without having to carry the cross? Good of them. The crowd of soldiers and villagers surprised him. He had not heard anyone or anything that morning apart from the guards and the interrogator, and the tide; and that fucking crow.

The gnome with mad eyes, the cocksure lunatic from Maria's village, dribbled betel juice and muttered gibberish as he marched on the spot in front of the gallery. He wore Rand's naval cap. More wrinkles than flesh or muscle on the geriatric moron. No one else from Maria's village? Where was she?

The squat guard forced Rand to his knees on a patch of soft sand. The other one said in bad Pidgin: "Hy-oo Rando, we will give you five minutes for thinking. Maybe say goodbye to yourself. Then mask. Then goodbye from us."

If this place was near the Japanese headquarters at Kieta, Maria's village was a long way north. Was she here, at the back of the crowd? Had she come all this way to see him defy the Japanese, so that she could tell his son, David, about witnessing his father's courage? She would tell the story again and again, and David would do the same, until Rand became better known after death than he was in life, like a Viking hero. Again his monotheme, his obsession: But what were courage and heroism? And where was his fucking wristwatch? David's wristwatch.

The swordsman troll—the junior interrogator—squeaked leather boots up to him and sniggered in Pidgin, loud enough for the audience to hear: "Two black ladies want to talk with you, Hy-oo Rando!"

The two women stood in front of him, the older gripping the arm of the younger. Rand saw the incubator and her friend Maria, each in a European dress, white hibiscus on cobalt background. He knew they would come; admired their courage and loyalty. To prove their love and respect and compassion for him they must have confronted the Japanese officer; insisted they console their hero, hear his last words. The incubator would want to forgive him for mistreating her in the cave. If she did so, he would apologise.

"David. You must call him David," he instructed, in Pidgin. Maria did not react, but he knew she loved him and would comply. He asked the incubator to bend down close to him. "Take Maria back into the crowd now," he whispered, "or the Japanese will beat you and her for comforting me. The baby will get hurt. Go back!"

The incubator stood up and slapped him twice on the face, hard, once on each cheek; cupped the back of Maria's head with her left hand, pushed her down until her face was so close to Rand's he could smell the flowers of her breath, and she the stink of his. She closed her eyes. There were no tears but he knew she still pined for him, as she did when they met in the forest, the day he recruited her friend as incubator.

The incubator sneered and spat an oyster on Rand's forehead. She lifted a clump of Maria's hair and twisted the girl's head to expose her left ear to him.

"*Pikinini meri bilong mi*," snapped the incubator. "*Nem bilong em Bos Simeon.*" My daughter. Her name is Bos Simeon. "*Mi katim dispela samting long diwai kokonas long ples bilong mi.*" I cut this thing from a coconut tree in my village. She held a cupped hand close to his eyes; showed him the bullet that mashed her husband's brain.

What's she on about? Bos? An empty palm? "*Em Maria, pren bilong yu.*" She is Maria, your friend. He asked her to bend down to him again, and whispered. "*Lukautim em na pikinini man bilong mi. Bai mi luklukim yu.*" Look after her and my son. I'll be watching you.

PART TWO

Bougainville Island, Papua New Guinea, 1971

Bos Simeon's Notebooks

Translated from Melanesian Pidgin
by Charlotte Millar, Tarawa, Gilbert Islands

Notebook One

8 August 1971. Masta Peter Millar at Tarawa in the Gilbert Islands, this is Bos Simeon from Bougainville in Papua New Guinea. I surrender to you at last. If I do not write to tell you what I know about Masta Hugh Rand, I cannot hope to forget the dark past because I will always expect another letter from you, or even worse that you will come here to my village to question me again about his death and what happened in the forest and other places before the Japanese killed him. That would send me crazier than I am already.

I shivered and cried when the first of your four letters arrived from Tarawa one year after your last patrol here on Bougainville. On that last visit my mind and stomach calmed when you said you would leave Papua New Guinea and go with your wife, Missus Sharlet, to another country. Your first letter from Tarawa made me so ill I could not breathe well or eat for two days. The second, third and fourth letters made me hate and fear you more and more, almost as much as Hugh Rand, for your power over my mind and gut.

I did not reply to your letters until now. I did not know about Tarawa, so after your second letter I asked the new patrol officer, the new *kiap*, when he came to do the census, hold court, and to complain about the shit of loose pigs in the village. He pointed out to sea: "Tarawa is about 2000 kilometres that way. Why do you want to know?" I told him I had no reason. He shook his head and did not ask me again. Unlike you, he did not care if I did not give a straight answer, or any answer.

Your Pidgin is still good so I will write as if you are still here listening to me talk. If you cannot understand some things you can ask your wife, because Missus Sharlet's Pidgin was always stronger than yours even though she used to say much less than you.

You ask me to remember too many things about Rand and the Japanese that are hard to remember, not because so much time has passed but because I have spent over twenty-five years trying to forget them. You tormented me by asking the same questions, again and again, during your five patrols to my village in the three years before you left New Guinea. I was relieved when you left for the last time. Each time you asked questions I refused to answer and had to battle with myself to defeat my memory's attack on my soul. You could not see past my face to my secret pain.

It has taken me a long time to suspect that I cannot defeat memories by trying to deny them. That idea reminds me of your wife saying she cannot fix sores unless people agree they have them, and show them to her, even the ones in the most secret places on the body. Most sores, she said, become worse if people hide them. On the fourth day of her second visit with you the women began to show her all their sores and injuries, and those of their children, and tell her about their illnesses. She and I laughed together behind your back when she told me you were annoyed because she made you add a day to your visit instead of going back to Kieta to drink beer.

I do not know or care if your wife told you about our secret laughter. I do know and care about another thing she told you, that caused you to make my life worse. When village women talk to one another they do not tell their husbands everything that we talk about. That is one small thing we women can control in our lives. Your wife did not know that rule because she is white, and so she made an innocent mistake, a bad one for me. The two of us would sometimes talk about nothing important. One day as we talked while she packed your things to leave for home, we saw you walk back into the village from the beach and stop to talk to children. I said to her, "Masta Peter is a gentle man, the only kiap or other white man since the war who did not scare me when I first saw him arrive here." She asked me why the others scared me for so many years. I told her it was because whenever I saw a white stranger my memory would suddenly bring back my fear of one who came from the sea in the Japanese time and hid in the forest until they caught him and cut off his head in Kieta. But soon I would relax and be unafraid of the new white men, who did us no evil.

Just then, you came to me and Missus Sharlet, and she left with you right away, with the carriers and police. That was good because I did not want to tell her more about that man.

The next time you came here she did not come. You shocked me when you said, "Missus Sharlet told me you met a white man here when you were a girl, and the Japanese cut off his head in Kieta." I could not deny it or you would think your wife was a liar. I told you I did not know the man's name and knew nothing more about him. You asked if his name was Hugh Rand. I said again that I did not know his name. You looked as if you did not believe me but you did not ask more. I felt ill and you now scared me for the first time and always did so on every visit after that, whereas other white men scared me a little on their first visit but not on later ones.

I did not know how to say his name until you told me what it was, and I could not write it until I saw how you wrote it in your first letter from Tarawa. Now I can write it in this notebook to you when I write about things he did long ago. I will put in his name even though I did not know it then.

On your next visit you tried many ways to make me answer your questions. I always said I knew no more. You knew I lied, I could see that. I did not think I should have to tell you the truth about private matters. Most of your questions told me you knew little about Rand's behaviour here, or his fate.

I realised it had been a mistake to talk too much in trust to a woman as a woman.

The next time I heard you were coming here with Missus Sharlet I told a big-man you asked too many questions about Rand

and the wartime. He said the last time you visited you also asked other people, who said like me that they knew nothing much. The big-man said I should go through the scrub to another village you would visit before ours, when you were already walking here from that place. I would stay there until you went away. People here would say I was in Kieta. I did as the big-man told me but refused to do it for your later visits, because this was my village, and not yours to control in every way, because you were a kiap.

Your fourth letter is the same as the first three. This one has forced me to reveal my sores, which cannot be cured but may become less painful if I do not continue to hide them from you. When you were here I should have told you everything I know, to save my mind and maybe the mind of Missus Sharlet. Even so, you are shameless to persist after I told you when you were last here that your questions cut holes in me. Even Missus Sharlet asked you to stop. Yet it is true that my sores worsen each time I tell myself not to reply to your letters.

To reduce the hurt you caused me here and in your letters from Tarawa, and to convince you to leave me in peace forever, I will now tell you things about the Japanese time that only I know. You might not understand me well. If Missus Sharlet is still your wife I do not mind if you ask her to explain as she will feel my pain and see my purpose better than you. Will she convince you that you have already caused me too much trouble for one lifetime? I hope so. The women in this village know there were some sores and illnesses she did not understand but she always understood the people who had them.

The way I hope to stop you is to tell you what you want to know. Perhaps I will tell you because I like your wife and hope you are kinder to her than you have been to me. As I write in this big notebook I borrowed from the mission school this morning while I was cooking for the children, I will pretend that you and Missus Sharlet are here, in the village guesthouse. That will make it easier for me. I write slowly and always whisper to myself while I write. Tomorrow night I will pretend you are here. I will watch your house until I know you have eaten and the village complainers who always bother you at night have left you in peace. Put your lamp on the step when you are ready. Then I will come to talk while you and your wife listen. Do not ask questions. Say nothing. Also the next night and perhaps the next, until I finish my story.

* * *

9 August 1971. May we sit inside your rest-house away from other human eyes? There should be no mosquitoes in there as this house and all the others were sprayed a few days ago with liquid made from the sweet smelling white powder in the bags stored underneath. The spray has dried and you can see the powder it left on the bamboo walls and the pandanus-leaf roof. You and Missus Sharlet sit in your chairs and I will sit on the floor. When I talk I will look at the lantern behind you. Please do not ask me to repeat or explain anything as I do not want to think too much.

Some things I might forget to tell you. Sometimes you will have to guess my meaning if I am not smart enough to be clear. I tried to draw a writing plan on a big sheet of paper but could not do it without confusion and a spider web of changes, so my pencil will take me where it wants to go, just as a fisherman who gets blown out to sea in a storm, who loses his paddle, must go where the current and winds take him, perhaps to destruction, unless there are two men, so that whoever dies first in one way or another will relieve the hunger of his companion.

The mosquitoes were savage the night Hugh Rand came from the submarine and sat on the beach until sunrise with my father. That is one of the few things I told you when you were here. I will tell you things about my mother which I would not discuss with you before. She died long ago and did not have any children apart from me. Before the Japanese came, when I was a small child and not yet old enough to be a real girl, I asked my mother why I had no brothers and sisters. She cried a little and said she wanted more but could not make any, no matter how hard she tried. Perhaps she tried not to have any because she thought they would be deformed like me and my father, with our useless left ear. Do you know about my ear? Did you notice? If so, did you care?

Once I saw my mother make and drink hibiscus tea. I did not think about it again until a few years later when my aunt, her sister, told me that if I was made pregnant by a young man named Titus, who liked me a lot, she would make hibiscus tea for me. She said he came from the wrong clan and I could not marry him. Later I will tell you about Titus.

The way time passes is sometimes unclear to me so I might tell you a more recent story, then one that went before it, then another that happened in between the two. Maybe I will mix them.

I told my mother I was pregnant about two and a half moons after the Japanese cut off Rand's head on the day after the full moon fought a monster from the sea. She pulled out pieces of her hair and shouted my name as she ran into the sea. "Bos! Bos! Bos!" The tide was low. She stood there in the sun for most of the day as the tide rose above her ankles, up to her waist and back down again. Many times I hugged her and tried to sweet-talk her out of the water but she pushed me away. She refused to eat or drink. After the tide sank below her knees, two men dragged her from the sea to our house. She did not look at me or speak to anyone. The sun was about to set and most villagers did not care about her. They thought she was insane.

Until now I have never told anyone else what I told her. You want to ask me about my father and the father of my baby. Wait. When the men brought her out of the sea she ignored me, rested on her mat for a little while, took her machete and gardening stick and walked out of the village in the dusk with her dog, along the path towards our garden. She did not come home that night. When her sister came to see her I said she wanted to sleep in the garden shelter. The dog was small but savage and would protect her.

My father, Simeon, used to beat my mother because boys and men of all ages liked to look at her, even when she was no longer young. I think Rand shot him for beating her. You did not know Rand shot him or you would have asked me about it. Before, I did not want to tell you Rand did that, and I still do not want to tell you because old people here want it to remain a secret for reasons I still do not understand, so long after the murder.

I do not know how Rand knew about the beatings. Maybe one of the carriers who took his cargo from the beach to the mountain told him. Soon after the Japanese captured Rand they took them to the mountain to get the cargo from his camp. When Rand came down to the village a few days before the Japanese got him, my mother saved him from them when they came to the village with dogs. He did not know where to run. She told me she pointed him onto a safe path. Maybe he admired her and wanted to repay her, so he came back and shot my father Simeon for beating her, although he had never seen him do it. He had no other reason to kill him. Rand told the men that the next time the Japanese came to talk to my father they must tell them his heart stopped and he fell dead.

You are dry but my sweat is staining my laplap. Usually we are dry and you are wet, which gives us another reason to laugh at you after you leave. That and your awkward shoes. We also laugh when Missus Sharlet does not wear shoes. We have never seen another white woman who walks shoeless. The boys and men also like her skin and eye colour, and her hair and the shape of her body. And her polite voice when she talks to them. Along the coast the wives of white and Chinese plantation managers yell at our men like nasty bitches that bark at strange dogs.

The night my mother went to the bush I worried sleepless all night about her and my baby. I intended to talk to her next day about how to stop it. She did stop the baby but never knew she had done so.

I went to find her when the first light filtered through the thatch before sunrise. I cried out her name when I reached the garden. She was not there, nor was her dog, so I bit the back of my hand to make it bleed. Later I will return to that story about my mother. First I will tell you something else.

Before that day, the last time I was so afraid was also at the garden. Rand came from the forest to the garden where I was working and told me to put bananas and sweet potatoes in a sack. He would return to get them soon, he said. Soon after I heard the pistol shot that I did not know had murdered my father, Rand came back and took me into the forest to rape me. He made me carry the sack of food. Don't worry. He changed his mind and did not touch me. I do not know why. You did not know until this letter that he captured me. It was none of your business before and even now.

At first he walked ahead of me, and although I was terrified I smiled to myself at his silly shoes made of rubber and green canvas, and tied with long brown strings. My feet were strong and did not need protection. I could feel the forest floor with my toes as if they were fingers. My grandmother told me that when I grew old my feet would feel the footprints of my ancestors, good and evil, who still walk there but leave no visible tracks. My feet and nose and eyes and tongue-tip and good ear told me other creatures lurked there, the evil ones we call *maselais*, and spirits that live in trees and other things, but I felt no ancestors that day. The ancestor souls and the *maselais* flit about in the forest and only let you see them from the corner of your eye, but not clearly. Sometimes, not often, they come in front of you and you can see if they are man or woman or neither. Maybe we saw no spirit ancestors that day because they feared Rand.

His steps were awkward and I wondered how he could walk in those hard-soled shoes without falling over. He did not fall but was always clumsy, with no rhythm in his legs, and I knew he would soon slip whenever my toes felt the earth get softer or muddier. When we got to a hard dry spot he would trip like an idiot. His shirt was wet and his shorts became dark around the arse. He could not sweat that much, so I think he pissed himself in fear of the forest. He seemed afraid of things I could not always identify. Some bird-calls made him nervous and even more likely to trip.

He must have felt embarrassed because he made me walk ahead of him so I could not see him stumble. I could still hear his clumsiness and decided to focus on it to push my fear of him to the back of my head.

Fear came back to my forehead when he told me to stop. I have not told you he had a voice like a small boy or maybe a girl. I cannot remember what I said to him but I was surprised to be so brave. He must have respected me for that, so he told me to go home and did not molest me even though I expected him to do so. I did not know his name then and he did not know mine. Even if he did know my name he did not say it. He must have had a name for me in his head if not his mouth. A man cannot spend that much time alone with a grown-up girl and not ask her name. Maybe he knew it already. I was too afraid of him to ask his name or make one up. I first heard his name a few days before the Japanese killed him with a sword.

Sometimes it is safer if a dangerous person does not know your name, otherwise they can use it to harm you with sorcery. If he had asked mine I would have told him the name of a pretty girl I did not like who lived in the next village. She used to look at the young man, Titus, who would watch me from a distance in the day and whisper close to me at night through the house wall. Rand also protected his name. In the morning after the night he arrived on the beach I asked my father, "Who is the sour-faced white man who does not like women?" He said the man would not tell him his name.

As I struggled through the forest with Rand's bag of food it occurred to me that I would be embarrassed if any ancestors or other spirits saw him rape me. Although I still feared him I decided to argue with him about his plan. I saw his alarm when a crow squawked at us, so I thought the time was right to defy him. I threw down the bag and told him some things that I cannot remember now. Whatever they were, they caused him to step aside and let me go when I started to walk back the way we had come. Maybe I am not telling the truth to myself. Perhaps the words had no effect, and he let me go because he hated me too much to bring himself to fuck me.

On my way home through the forest, I thought for the first time that it was my good luck to have parents who gave me a good body but not a pretty face. I was much shorter than my mother, whose body was perfect even though she was no longer young, and I did not have her prettiness. She had no tattoos and her hair was short because her ears were normal. My skin was a bit lighter than hers, which was not as dark as my father's. I was strong like him but my face was not his.

I wondered if Rand would have been more dangerous if my parents had given me a pretty face as well as a good body, or a pretty face and not such a good body. Did he like pretty faces and not care if a girl's body was good or bad? Maybe it was simpler than that. Perhaps he did not like tattoos, or black girls. When he came to the village from the sea and watched me in the early morning as I made tea for him, he looked at the tattoos on my breasts and face like a missionary disgusted by a bush kanaka. My dead ear could not have repelled him. He could not have seen it because my hair was long, unlike my mother's, and I kept my head straight. My father used to twist his head to one side to hear well. Did you know I had a deaf ear like my father? I call it 'dead'. I think not, because you did not tell me, and you like to say everything you know.

Until I got back home after I left Rand in the forest I did not know he had killed my father. When I think about it now I wonder if he let me go because he felt guilty or maybe sorry for me because

I no longer had a father. But I do not know if he knew Simeon was my father or that my mother was the one in the village who waved him to a safe path and saved him from the Japanese and their second dog. They had two dogs. Before he ran from the village along the path my mother told him to follow, he shot one dog with the hand-gun he would use to kill my father next morning.

On the day of the murder, when I was close to home after Rand did not want to fuck me, my mother and her sister met me on the track and told me what he had done to my father. My aunt cried but my mother did not cry and seemed more upset about me than her dead husband, my father, even though she saw his terrible death from our house.

She did not believe my story about what happened in the forest and said I seduced the white man even after he told me he killed my father. "You were pleased when he told you, because you hate the dead ear your father gave you." She said 'white man' because we did not know Rand's name. My aunt agreed with her. I cried in fake shame at what she said but I am not sure if my performance made them believe me. They took me to my father's body. Everyone except my mother cried for him.

Enough for tonight.

*　*　*

10 August 1971. Tonight I will tell you more about my search for my mother after Rand's death, after I told her I was pregnant. Later, maybe tomorrow or the next day, I will return to the time when he still lived, when I was with him in the forest a second time and my mother was there too.

The mist swirled around me as I went deeper into the forest to search for my mother. I passed the place where Rand decided on the day he shot my father that he did not want me and let me go home. I expected to feel Rand's spirit but it had not yet wandered back there after his death to be close to me and others he wanted to harm. Even so, I was afraid as usual of the curls of mist that hummed as they hid the path and revealed it and hid it again. The deeper I went into the forest, the thicker and noisier the mist became. No one else ever heard the mist hum, nor did they hear as many sounds in the forest as I did, even though everyone else apart from my father had two good ears that many of them were too stupid to use well. I could also smell and see better than most people but if I closed my eyes to listen, or if the night was dark, or the mist in the forest was dense, sometimes I could not detect the direction of a particular voice or other noise.

I thought about the spirits of the carriers the Japanese shot on the mountain, not far away. The mist moaned their fear and pain. By now we knew their fate because some of the village men had gone up there to look for them, and had buried in one hole the ashes they found there, scattered by pigs. No bones, only ashes.

I will tell you later why no one harmed my mother or me after the villagers said I lied about what the young man called Titus said to me, when the Japanese brought him down from the mountains after they killed most of the other carriers. They herded Titus and the other three survivors through the village like pigs, or like bush kanaka slaves on a coconut or cocoa plantation.

As I searched for my mother I tried to stay calm by listening to songbirds but it was impossible not to shiver at the warning of the evil crow and the snorts and grunts of hidden pigs, and the hisses and whispers of troublesome ancestors and other vengeful spirits who always watched me. As they still do now, they hoped I would make a mistake in something I did or said, so they could punish me or someone close to me. When I say 'ancestor spirits' I usually mean the invisible but sometimes visible part of people, if they want to be visible, that never rots away or gets turned into shit by sea or land creatures. Other spirits are the *maselais* I already mentioned and the countless invisible but sometimes visible beings that live in trees, waves, water, vines, orchids, bamboo, and everything else, including rocks. Some are good, most are not.

You do not always know your mistake, but if you get punished you know you did something to annoy ancestors or other spirits. The Bougainville people gave Jesus a try because they thought he might be strong enough, if the missionaries were right about his power and benevolence, to stop nasty spirits from continuing their vengeance. Each spirit has limited, special power. The missionaries said Jesus could control and eventually destroy them because he was stronger than any one of them, and the spirits seemed to do things alone, not together to make themselves stronger, even when many gathered in one place to make trouble.

The people and the missionaries were wrong. The nasty spirits of ancestors and places and things were real and there was no escape from them. Jesus and his enemy, Satan, were added to the many hundreds of spirits that lived among us here, not in some other place like heaven or hell. They could punish us now and after we died. Even if Jesus was too strong for Satan and other spirits to get inside his church when the Catholic priest or Seventh Day Adventist pastor was there, those spirits still waited for us outside in our houses and gardens and canoes, and in the sea and forest. They still do. Some people said Jesus wanted to cooperate with our old spirits, so he became more like them and punished us now instead of waiting until we died to let Satan drag us down through the earth to burn in the fire of hell. Together, Jesus and Satan could terrify and control us like the old spirits could do, and maybe more. They worked together so well to control the villagers that I used to wonder if Satan was really a friend of Jesus, who could have no power without him.

As you will see, the ancestors and other spirits punished me and others many times and never did any good thing for us. It did not matter how much people prayed to Jesus like idiots, it did not protect them from the old spirits. You could pray and pray but you still had to do ritual things every day to try to stop the spirits from harming you. Sometimes they harmed you anyway because they could, and you could not harm them. They made the Japanese come to punish us for going to the church of Jesus, who was white but even so could not control Satan or our old spirits. The spirits also made Rand punish us. Now they use you, Masta Peter Millar, to hurt and punish me.

Back to the search for my mother. Two hornbills laughed together up the mountain with joy that denied the crow's warning. At the place where Rand left me the second time and took my mother away, which I will tell you about later, I saw the shit of her dog, so I called out to her for a while with the up and down yell we make to attract an answer and locate someone in the forest, or on the sea at night. She did not call back. I knew she was nearby because I could smell the dog and thought I could smell her sweat and hair in the mist that today hummed around me like a swarm of giant mosquitoes.

I bit my wrist when the dog scampered to me and jumped into a clear space at my feet where the mist hovered just above the ground. Before I saw him I expected a pig to ram its tusks into my groin and twist them until I bled to death. I could usually smell pigs and spirits above any other smell, and often confused the two. Those smells were always most pungent in the forest when there was mist.

The dog, which had no name, folded back his ears, whimpered, wagged his tail and twisted and turned to show he was happy to see me. That was a surprise because I used to beat him with a stick or throw stones at him when I was annoyed about things that had nothing to do with him. Most times it was my dead ear that annoyed me, if someone talked to me and I was not alert enough to keep my head straight instead of turning my right ear to them, like my father used to do.

After a short time, about three puffs of a cigarette, again I heard the crow we dislike, the one that mocks us, follows us, hides, goes silent, and mocks us again when we do not expect it. A vile bird. Perhaps a wandering soul that searches for small trouble to make it big. My mother said there is always only one alive, and I have never seen a dead one, or eggs, or even a nest, so it must come from an evil place that we do not want to find. As one dies its replacement comes to life somehow. My mother once saw a crow feather fall like a leaf from the canopy but the crow caught it and took it away.

The crow that mocked me now was in a tall tree, the beautiful one where my mother hid behind a buttress when we met Rand in the forest a week or so after he took me into it the first time, when he did not make me go as far as this tree. I will tell you soon about the second time. I ordered the dog to take me to my mother or I would hit him with a stick my feet found on the forest floor beneath the mist.

I wonder if Missus Sharlet will read this long letter at night and yawn, as she used to do when we three would talk, or you would talk and we would listen, until it was time to put more kerosene in the lamp or go to sleep. From your questions that I would not answer long ago, I know you will want to hear about the second meeting with Rand, so I will tell you about it before I tell you, tomorrow or the next night, what happened when I found my mother in the forest. I imagine you are here and we have decided we are too tired for me to tell you more tonight. Tomorrow night I will write more as I pretend you are here and it is early enough for Missus Sharlet to be alert after dinner while the village sleeps. Maybe you do not want to know more, and will burn my letter in this book, in which case I will talk to myself.

* * *

11 August 1971. Last night I told you too much and I am exhausted from pain in my gut and a sleepless head. Throughout the night I wondered if you ever noticed my dead ear. I always tried to keep my head straight when I talked to you.

Tonight I cannot talk for long so I will tell you about the second journey into the forest with my mother, and answer a few questions with which you pestered me when you visited my village and later in your letters from Tarawa. Now I know how the men feel when they are at sea in a small canoe and a large shark comes again and again and bumps them on one side, then the other side, then on the bottom, as it tries to work out how to get at a big fish they have caught and do not want to give up. Sometimes, if the shark is big and persistent, the men must give up their fish to protect themselves from mutilation or death.

I still wonder why Rand shot my father. No one in the village knows for sure. Some people said it was because he thought my father had betrayed him to the Japanese, who then came after him with their dogs, the time my mother saved him by pointing to the safest path. The spirits in the forest made him think that way, so he would harm us because too many people talked too much to Jesus. The spirits made Rand and the Japanese work together to punish us even though they hated one another. The spirits were angriest against our big-men, who got money and tobacco for telling the villagers to do what the Jesus missionaries told us. My father was one of the biggest of the big-men and had a lot of influence. That may be why Rand shot him, under the spell of the spirits. I know the old people would not tell you anything about that matter when you asked, many years after it happened. Maybe they know a lot about it, maybe nothing.

The village men decided not to bury my father. The Japanese, like Rand, thought Simeon was village headman, which he was not, and might come and tell them to dig him up to see if he had injuries inflicted by Rand or someone else. They would not believe the heart attack lie instructed by Rand. The men's worry was not about the stink. If the Japanese saw the bullet hole they would know the white man who shot their dog had come back to kill my father and would begin to ask a lot of difficult questions. To get an acceptable story they might kill some of the men and hurt the women. The Japanese were persistent like you have been to me, Masta Peter.

A young man said the best protection was to tell the Japanese, before they asked, that the white man came back to the village and shot my father because he had refused Rand's demand for food the day before, the same day he came from the forest and shot one of the two Japanese dogs. They must say that day was the first time we saw him or even knew about him. The Japanese would think Rand hated the villagers for not helping him. If Rand hated both the villagers and the Japanese, the Japanese would think the villagers must be their friends. Even the Japanese did not shoot their friends.

The older men did not listen because he was young. If the village went through a traditional funeral and told the Japanese a white man had killed him, the Japanese would soon discover, by beating the men and pushing crushed pepper into the women, that the first time Rand came to the village from the forest was not the day he shot their dog, that he had come from the sea a few days before and we had not told them, and our men had carried his cargo to the mountain. The young man did not argue.

That night the men tied a chunk of coral to my father's waist with thick line used to catch sharks. Four men from his clan paddled him a long way out to sea in our village's strongest canoe. They dumped him overboard out from the reef, where the green and blue water gives way to bottomless black in the daytime, where the biggest sharks sleep during the day and emerge at night to hunt along the steep wall of coral.

My mother could not go with the men and her dead husband because it was a fishing canoe and she was in her last day of menstruation. It destroys forever the power of a canoe to attract fish, unless the men later conduct expensive ritual to satisfy the evil spirit that does not want menstruating women in canoes. Anyway, I do not think she wanted to go. She and I held burning palm-fronds to light the men's way as they carried my father to the canoe. We walked beside him and watched him for the last time. In the flame I looked at the mud plastered across the bullet hole on the entry side of his head, near his useless ear. Thicker mud, a lot more of it, was packed on the other side. He had cuts and bruises on his legs and arms. My mother said, "The Japanese hurt him the day before the white man shot him."

For a while he looked as if he had never lived. Then I noticed, but maybe I didn't, a hint of surprise on his face. But no fear. He probably did not have time for that. Nor was there any of the loneliness you see in some people if their death is gradual, over a few hours or days. They get more and more lonely. Right at the end they are loneliest, even if many people are with them as they go away.

I cried because my father was kind to me, if not always to my mother, and I tried not to think about the damage he did to my life because he gave me an ear without a hole and another that listened and heard too much for my own good, especially in the forest.

When I watched my mother's face twist in the light of the flame I could see she did not cry much. She held her mouth open wide with a surprised look and breathed hard. Maybe she saw an evil ancestor. She looked like she had wandered by mistake into a secret men's meeting in the forest and was about to have her head smashed in with a rock. She said, "I hope he can return to his stingray family in the sea instead of to his other ancestors in the forest."

After the body was gone and our palm-frond flames were also dead, she said to me in the darkness, "No more bruises and hard words unless I marry again." She did not like my father much. Even so, she seemed a little angry about his death. She said, "The Australians ran away from the Japanese. That white man should not pretend he is still our master. When the Japanese catch him they will kill him if they find out he killed one of us. Only they can now kill us and get away with it." Until she spoke I thought she was relieved Rand shot my father, and that she probably thought it happened because someone told Rand that Simeon used to beat her, the brave woman who rescued the white man from the Japanese when she told him where to run into the bush.

For most of that night we and all the other women wailed together to calm my father's spirit, perhaps on land, or in the sea in the form of a stingray. We did not say so, but we all knew he could be already in a shark's belly. I wondered if Rand could hear us as he hid in the forest near Jesus and Satan and the other spirits. We all agreed to make the men run to tell the Japanese straight away if another white man came from the sea or the forest.

The next afternoon five Japanese soldiers and a dog on a lead came to the village. The officer's boots squeaked like a rat. He was a few years older than the others and could speak Pidgin well. He was skinny and his eyes so narrow I wondered how he could see. They made me think of a tired turtle lying on its back in sadness as it waited to be chopped up alive for roasting on coals or hot rocks. Later I would see his eyes become spears, like the left eye of Rand, whose other eye seemed to watch faraway things that no one else could see. Maybe my mother's eyes also peered at such things after her time in the forest with Rand and the officer. Soon I will tell you about that.

The officer stayed quiet but his eyes became more and more hostile, which never happens to a turtle. He said he wanted to talk to Simeon, my father. An hour before, a boy who watched the path for strangers ran back here and said the Japanese were nearby. Before they arrived, ten men dashed to five canoes and paddled them across the lagoon, through the reef passage and onto the open sea, as smooth as rainwater in a puddle.

An old man, my mother's father, told the officer Simeon was not in the village. The officer slapped him on each side of his face and screamed that he was a liar. The old man would not fall over, nor did his body shake. He pointed to the canoes at sea. "Simeon went fishing yesterday and did not come back. They are searching for him." The officer punched him so hard in the throat that he fell over, then he kicked him in the stomach. The other villagers watched. The dog wanted to get involved but his handler held him back. I used to think the Japanese were vicious because they were embarrassed by their fear of the *maselais*, even if they said they did not believe in them. They liked to march near the forest but did not go into it unless they had to. Maybe they became vicious to protect themselves but I soon came to think they brought most of their evil from Japan, an unhappy place, to add to what was already here.

I went back inside the house to my mother. She splashed water in her eyes and wailed like a widow as she ran outside and sat on the bottom step. She called to the officer. "I am Simeon's wife. The old man is my father. He is telling the truth." The Japanese were near the tree where Rand shot my father. From the top step I could see the bullet scar on the trunk, and the blood stain. The Japanese did not notice these things. Twice the dog stared at the tree and whimpered and moved his feet from side to side but did not bark.

The officer saw me and told me to make tea for him and his soldiers. A boy brought a dish of water for the dog, which did not drink until the handler told him to do so. The officer gave me the tea powder, green as the slime on pigswill in an old canoe, and told my mother how to prepare the drink. The soldiers sat on coconuts. The officer sat on a log and yelled at the other villagers to go away. *Raus! Raus!* He was close to where Rand sat on a box when I made breakfast for him the day he looked at my breasts and face and hips as if he did not think I was female. Maybe he was tired after staying awake all night on the beach.

The officer took some long eye-glasses from a leather bag that a soldier gave him and hung them around his neck by a strap. I did not know it then but now I know they were binoculars, like the ones the Australian and American soldiers had when they came to kill the Japanese. Through them he watched the men in the canoes for a few minutes until I brought his slime tea. He did not bother to look at my breasts. He opened his eyes wider, even though they were still narrow, and told me to look through his glasses at the canoes. He held them to my eyes, with the strap still around his neck. I was so close to him that he could have touched me anywhere. I could hear his heartbeat. He sniffed a few times and breathed like a pig with its nose in mud. I think his lungs were sick. He had some broken teeth and his breath smelled like the guts of the dog Rand shot in the village. His body stank like rice with rotten fish in it. This did not surprise me as all foreign people smell like their food. The strange food of Chinese on Bougainville stinks and so do they. Many white people stink because they eat too much stale meat from metal cans, and drink too much beer, especially the men.

When I tried to look through the officer's glasses I could not see clearly until I closed one eye. Then I could see that the canoes had grown and the men in them were giants. The officer snatched the glasses from my eyes and shoved me back towards my mother. He hurt my ribs. His stare was cold black.

Soon after he pushed me away my mother bowed and spoke to him from a few metres away in her quietest voice, the smooth one she used when she thought my father was about to beat her. I heard her say, "Can I talk to you so that only you can hear?" She knew the power of my right ear. He waited a long time, then beckoned her with his palm down. White men never do that. They always do it with the palm up, which makes young girls gasp and hold their knees together. Older women laugh and men scowl. He said something to the soldiers. They drained their tea-mugs and walked with the dog to the path by which they had entered the village.

My mother stood in front of the officer with her hand near her mouth so I could not read her lips, a skill she knew I had, even though I did not rely on it much because my right ear was so sharp. After she said a few words he opened his eyes wider and stood up to move closer to her. He listened hard without talking until I saw him say, "Early tomorrow. Be ready. Tell no one." After a few minutes of secret thought, without even a finger-twitch and maybe without a heartbeat, he left to join his men and the dog. The officer screeched and they marched back along the path towards their base.

I asked my mother what they had discussed. She said, "I once saw a white man with big glasses like his. That man used them to make birds big and easy to find. I told the officer, and asked him if he also used the glasses to look for birds. He said yes. I told him there were many unusual birds in our forest and that we could show him if he wanted. It was too late to go today. He will come early tomorrow. We will guide him and his men, and maybe their dog, into the forest until we find the mocking crow. If we are with them, they will not fear the forest as much as usual. Maybe we will find a pair of the hornbills that tell jokes to one another in the canopy, the ones with the long, slow chuckle." We call them *kokomo*. We gave that name to a white patrol officer with a long nose, but he did not know about that.

My mother said we should find birds for the Japanese if they wanted to see them. We should do anything we could to make them happy so they would not hurt us as they did once before, when they pushed hot peppers inside us to make us tell them things we did not know, then came back a week later and did it again when they realised the stories we told them to make them stop were untrue.

As the afternoon shadows grew long I watched my mother's face while she prepared our evening meal. No one came near us, even her old father. She did not look at me and did not want to talk. I thought she kept a secret from me but I could not say so because she was my mother. Later she cried a little in the night, long after the dogs and pigs and babies were quiet and she thought I was asleep.

The next morning we put on our best laplaps, the red ones. She said we should wear them because the Japanese liked red and it would put them in a good mood. Even if we did not find the crow or hornbills they might not get angry with us. All this did not make much sense but I could not question her.

Goodnight. You can listen to me again tomorrow.

* * *

15 August 1971. The nasty officer came early next morning with three different soldiers and the same dog on a leash. I knew they were different soldiers because they were even younger than those who came the day before. I feared the dog. It looked insane, and drooled spit from the sides of its mouth, half open, as it panted and growled with the clatter of a dying geriatric whose throat vibrates when he sucks air to delay death. It stopped panting and looked at me with the evil of a sorcerer who would murder me when I least expected it, as I slept. Its tail curled higher than usual as it flattened its ears against its head and squatted to shit. It did not take its gaze off me. In a few seconds the stink hit my face like something solid, like the officer's breath the previous day. We teach our dogs to shit on the beach like us.

I looked for the bird glasses around the officer's neck. He had forgotten them or maybe one of the soldiers had them in the canvas bag on his back. The officer refused our tea and told my mother to lead the way to the forest. He did not let us take food, nor would he let my mother carry a machete to cut vines and bamboo for water. He said, "The soldiers can do that if there is no stream."

My mother made me walk ahead of her, and the officer came behind. I thought a noisy bird chirped as it followed us, until I realised the officer's long boots of leather squeaked louder than the day before. He stumbled along like Rand, but a bit smoother. The junior soldiers wore short boots also made from leather. No one talked. The dog panted to delay his death. When we were past our garden and through the forest entrance the officer started to wheeze like the dog. Three boot squeaks separated each wheeze from the next one. He would be an easy target for the *maselais* if they saw his weakness. I thought he might collapse and die when the climb became steep, but he didn't. Later I would wish he had died.

We stopped just inside the forest for the Japanese to drink water from their metal bottles. The soldiers looked away as the officer ate some tiny white thing that he took from his shirt pocket. Each soldier splashed a bit of water into the dog's mouth as he slobbered with his head back and jaws open. After he drank he was silent until we started to walk again.

The dog from Satan's hell did not like the forest. He stopped many times to whimper and sniff the earth along the unclear track. When the dog barked the officer slapped the handler on each side of the face, which made the handler punch the dog hard on the nose when the officer turned away. The monster did not howl. If I had been told to punish him I would have flogged him on the head and body with a stick or rock until he started to scream, and maybe a bit longer.

My mother and I enjoyed the shade of the forest but the Japanese, especially the officer, could not breath well unless the ground was flat, which was rare. They took slow steps. The officer's noisy boots annoyed me. The other three, with boots a lot like Rand's but leather, were not as awkward as the officer or Rand. They were all awkward compared to my mother and me. We did not look back to watch how they walked. As with Rand, I could hear their uneven steps, their slips, their stumbles, their gasps, their fatigue, and their filthy farts. The dog also farted from time to time. The one other time I heard Japanese laugh at a fart or anything else was at Rand's execution.

Over my shoulder I whispered to my mother, "I am worried that we cannot hear the crow." She ignored me. When we stopped for a long rest near the place from which Rand let me go back the first time, she and the officer had a quiet talk that I could not hear. Then she came to me and said he had told her to go ahead with me to look for the crow by ourselves for the time it would take a resting man to smoke four cigarettes. The Japanese would follow after that time had passed.

Perhaps the crow already watched us from the canopy. My mother said it was sometimes silent if it could see or hear more than one person. I had not heard that before but believed her because she was my mother.

Before we left the Japanese we drank water that poured down from the vine a soldier cut with a knife attached to his rifle. When we were out of sight we unfolded our laplaps from under our arms and refolded them at waist level to keep our breasts and back cool. After we had walked for a while I asked her, "What will happen if we cannot find the crow?" She said, "The crow will find us. If we sing it might come to investigate." I had never heard of such a thing. Then I heard the crow laugh a single warning from far away. After we listened through all the birdcalls and other sounds of the forest, she told me to kneel and sing the notes we sing to warn our people a long way off that intruders are in the forest. The song is beautiful so the intruders will not know it is a warning. I sang up and down, and back up and down, and up again.

At first I sang for ten breaths. No crow. My mother said it might want to reveal itself to just one person that day. She hid nearby in the roots and gloom of a tall tree so the crow would not see her. I heard her beg the spirit of the tree to make her invisible. When she was hidden I sang louder with more control and beauty than ever. I wanted to attract the crow and please my mother, and the Japanese officer, who might otherwise punish us for making him stumble so far for nothing. I soon tired and my song was not as loud as I wanted. I wondered if Rand heard it, maybe only a cigarette away on the mountain somewhere. Maybe the crow had gone to warn him about us.

"Sing louder!" called my mother from behind her tree. I leaned back my head and waved it from side to side in pain as I sang and sang until my lungs could not draw enough air to go on. I do not know how long I sang. My mother told me many times to sing again, louder. I was so exhausted I had to collapse to my knees to rest my body and lungs so I could continue.

My eyes were still closed when I smelled Rand beside me and saw his boots. Why didn't I smell or taste him in the air sooner, or hear him slip and slide like a wounded pig? Had he learned to walk well? When I looked at his face his eyes still hated me. I closed my eyes again when he put his pistol against my head, the pistol that killed my father. He spoke but I could not hear his words through the terror and cries that took over my mind and body. I had seen my father's head a few hours after Rand shot him.

Rand knew my mother hid among the tree-roots, which meant the spirit of the tree did not want to hide her. Maybe the crow warned him. When he told her to stop hiding I said she was my friend. If he hated me as much as I thought he did, he might hurt her because she was my mother. We were not much alike and she looked much younger than her age, so he would not guess the truth. I cannot remember much about what happened after he ordered her to come forward. In our native language, not Pidgin, she told me not to mention the crow or say anything about the Japanese who would soon approach behind us.

Rand said things I did not hear. In panic I ran back down the way we had come so he could not shoot me simply because he hated me. I did not think he hated her as much as me but if he shot me he would probably shoot her, so I ran away to save her life. I knew he would not want to rape her because she was attractive to black men but too old to arouse a white man.

Many times I slipped and fell in the mud. I ran too fast, tried too hard to skip over the earth instead of feel into it with my toes. They were numb anyway, like the rest of me. After I ran for the time of a cigarette I lurched through the mist and collapsed at the feet of the Japanese and their dog. As the dog tried to escape his leash to attack me, the handler staggered against the monster's strength and laughed at the mud on my breasts. The officer slapped the handler on the cheek. Many times I later saw officers slap their soldiers. If other soldiers watched they did not worry because it happened to most of them and so they were used to it.

The officer looked down at me to ask if we had found the white man my mother and I often heard sing in the forest. I did not know what he meant. Rand did not sing. We usually understood the Japanese better than we understood Australians or Germans. I wondered if he saw the crow as human in some cunning disguise. "We could not find the crow." He was puzzled at what I said but did not reply.

By now I hated Rand at least as much as he hated me. I told the officer my mother was two cigarettes away in the forest with an ugly white man we did not know and certainly had never heard sing. I said he might be a spirit who knew where to find the crow. Maybe he was the crow. The officer looked at me with turtle eyes and did not speak. The soldiers laughed at me. The dog sat on his arse in silence as he held his breath for a while and stared at my belly with a plan to tear out my guts when he got the chance. He was all the more evil for the patience that replaced his earlier ferocity.

Good night. The lamp kerosene is low and I cannot see the paper well enough to continue. There are a few pages left in this notebook but I will start a new one tomorrow.

Notebook Two

19 August 1971. The big-men left you and Missus Sharlet early tonight, Masta Peter, so here I am already.

In the forest the officer watched each of the soldiers eat a small white thing he gave them from his shirt pocket. Then he sent them with the dog in the direction from which I ran out of the mist. Now there was almost no mist and the sun shone down through a few gaps in the canopy.

When the soldiers and dog were gone the officer sat on the log again and told me to sit at the other end of it, where the dog handler had sat with the brute at his feet. I did not want to sit there so I sat a bit closer to the officer, about two arm's lengths from him. He smoked a cigarette until it was almost finished, while he stared at me from the side of his face, with his head bowed and his eyes almost shut. He did not blink. He leaned towards me and offered the rest of the cigarette, which I puffed twice and returned to him with my muddied fingers. He inspected it as he moved it towards his mouth. When it touched his lips he became angry, threw it into the bush and spat near my feet. "Pig," he said.

I told him there was a stream nearby and I wanted to wash the mud off my body and my laplap. He said no and looked up into the forest canopy, maybe to see if the crow was there. Soon he changed his mind and told me I could wash. He would guard me and would kill me if I tried to escape. I could feel him stare at my body as I walked ahead of him. When we were about ten of my longest steps from a shallow pool I turned and raised my hand to ask him to stop where he was. He stood and watched me as he lit another cigarette with a smooth, slow movement. Rand was never smooth or slow.

The officer pointed to the pool and told me to go there and not go out of his sight or I would soon be dead. He put his finger a little way down the cigarette and told me to finish my bath by the time he had smoked that much. My mother and other women had told me the Japanese did not think black women were attractive so I was not too worried that he would see my bare body. I had no choice. The laplap must come off within his view for me to wash. If I tried to hide behind a rock or bush he would shoot me. I could stay filthy but he might shoot me in anger because I disgusted him more than I might if I washed.

I turned my back to him, unwrapped the laplap from my armpits and breasts and fastened it around my waist. When I began to sit he shouted for me to stand and wash. He annoyed me so I snatched off the laplap and threw it into the water at my feet. Only white men, most of them, care about breasts, and the officer was not white so I assumed he would not care about them, and that if he did not care about them and did not like black women he would not notice my arse, even though it was strong.

I looked over my shoulder and saw that he watched me but seemed absent, and therefore did not seem to care if I was naked. Maybe he worried that the mist would return and I would try to escape if he lost sight of me. I decided to bend over and point my arse at him while I rinsed the laplap. We sometimes do it to insult one another. A Japanese man would not know about that and I could enjoy my insolence. I bent forward for a long time as we do in the garden and did not even glance at him again.

When the laplap was clean I put my foot on it in the current and washed all over. When I finished I leaned forward to pick up the laplap. An almost complete cigarette and some spit floated past as tiny fish nibbled at them. I looked upstream about ten steps to another pool, almost in front of me and easy to see through the mist, which had returned calmer and thinner, its hum silenced by the stream. I had pointed my arse in the wrong direction and had not noticed because my head was down near my shins.

The naked officer scooped water into his cap again and again and tipped it over his head and body. The cap had a metal star on the front, shiny with water. His gut was fatter than it looked when he was dressed. His body and legs were light yellow, much lighter than his face and arms. Unlike most of our men, he had no hair on his chest or legs but did have some, not much, where his belly and cock connected. His cock was stiff and I drew a deep breath because it was the first time I had seen a man like that, although my mother's sister had told me a lot about it. Since then I have seen few men in that condition, most times a patrol officer, one of them an old one who said he loved me. I loved Titus and have never wanted to marry anyone else and see a cock any more often than I have since the war. Also, my mother was safer when her husband died, and my fear of Japanese, Australians and local thugs during the war made me wary of all men. Apart from the old one, the kiaps did not love me but they all liked me more than Rand did. For a little while, not so many years ago, I thought the old one made me pregnant.

You, Masta Peter, made me feel a little better about white men until you started to throw questions at me like rocks at a dog. When you came here without Missus Sharlet and we searched for birds and animals in the forest, you were interested in my tattoos. When I walked ahead you said you admired my bare back and strong legs. But when we got back to the village you were not stupid enough, like some other kiaps, especially the old one, to invite me to come to your bunk while the village slept.

The officer pretended to ignore me but I know he watched my belly from the sides of his eyes. His cock was stiff for a few of my breaths, then went soft, pointed down and shrank into his belly hair. I looked away. Had he made any children with that baby sea slug? Could any woman enjoy it? Was Rand's slug bigger? Would it have given me an angry baby, or a calm one who could learn to walk without a stagger? My mother's sister told me a girl in the next village who used to sleep with patrol officers said they were big enough but too quick because they did not like the heat of women's bodies. Missus Sharlet knows if that is a lie. I think it is true.

He dressed and told me with gestures but no voice to put on my laplap and run ahead of him back to the log. His boots made me think of rats my mother's dog tortured under our house.

We sat silent for a long time while he listened for the crow or something else. Thick mist had returned and he did not like to wait in this place. Although he tried to look fierce and brave all the time, he feared something, maybe the spirits I could feel all around us that lived in birds and animals and insects and plants.

White men and Chinese and Japanese fear the forest because they always fear things they do not understand and therefore cannot control. We fear the forest because we do understand it and know its spirits will always control us by making us say and do the things that appease them. You might say we control them by doing so, but that is wrong because they are the ones that require us to meet their demands.

Sometimes I could see spirits when they showed themselves for an instant as creatures I cannot describe, then vanished like the spray of waves on a windy day, or sank into the earth like piss into sand. They have no age. One spirit would go into and out of a tree trunk many times. Others hid in creepers, vines, orchids and moss, all of which were grey but became green when the sun shone through the canopy for a few seconds like streaks of yellow rain. When that happened, not often, the creatures would all vanish from the corners of my eyes and leave behind a stink of rotten fish.

I am sure the officer did not see or smell these creatures, nor could white men or Chinese. Maybe he could feel them. More likely he feared Rand, as I did. If so, that was about all the officer and I had in common apart from arms and legs and a head. Perhaps we were the same in one other way. I was an animal to him, and to me he was no better than his devil-dog, maybe worse.

To convince the spirits not to harm me I whispered to them, the same words again and again, exactly as my father and aunt had taught me. If you make a mistake they will punish you now or later, maybe many years later. If you get it right, they will do no harm for a few days but they never do anything good for you. If something good happens to me it does not mean any spirit has rewarded me. It means I have not made a mistake. You cannot escape these things by going to the white man's church and singing to Jesus. Inside the church, you might not think much about them. When you come out they are waiting for you.

While I whispered to the spirits, the officer smoked another cigarette. My laplap started to dry and return to its beautiful redness. I tried to think of a way to get the spirits to harm the officer but not me.

A howl from far away made the officer jump up from the log and pull his pistol from the leather bag on his hip. I said it was a dog and he told me to shut up. He listened for a while and sat down again. I heard the crow and saw it in the canopy through a hole in the mist. I smiled and pointed to the bird. The officer saw only me, a crazy girl, crazier than my crazy uncle. I sat in silent shame. The crow skipped on its branch, ruffled its feathers and flew away without a second call.

An animal shrieked louder and louder as it hurtled towards us from the direction of the mountain. The shrieks were long and shrill, like those of a speared pig, so I guessed one had been stabbed by a soldier with the knife on his rifle on his way back here. The officer opened his eyes wide and pointed his pistol through the mist. The animal crashed through it. We were shocked to see it was not a pig. It was my mother. She stopped her shrieks and fell to her knees at our feet, then onto her left side in the mud.

She slept for the time it took the officer to smoke another cigarette as he stared along the route from which she fled the awful thing he did not yet know about. I knew it was Rand. Again the officer took from his shirt pocket something tiny and washed it down his throat with water from his metal bottle.

My mother's body was bare above the hips. The officer glared at her with disgust and continued to ignore me as I sat on the other end of his log, where the dog handler had been. It was a relief to see she was just muddy and not injured by Rand or the soldiers, or their devil-dog. Her red laplap was in no condition to please the officer.

When he finished his cigarette he became agitated and threw the butt beside my mother, who still slept. He took a few quick steps away from us, stood with his back to us and pissed for a long time as he glared at my mother over his shoulder. His eyes were now as wide open and alert as I had ever seen them. Now he seemed truly unafraid.

While he pissed my mother woke up and cried with a lot of noise but no tears. She stood, wrapped her muddied laplap under her arms and sat on the log where the officer had been. Her eyes were round and she did not blink. When the officer marched back to us he demanded to know what had happened to her. She did not answer. He swung his right arm behind his back until it could go no further, then released the arm with such force that when his open hand smacked against her cheek she choked and fell off the log. She tried to stand but could not do so. She rested her forehead on the log and went back to sleep. Her left cheek was bigger now. Her mouth twitched and seeped blood the colour of our laplaps.

The officer did not try to wake my mother and continued to ignore me, probably because I was black, perhaps because I was not beautiful. Did he have a pretty wife? Unlikely. The yellow skin of the Japanese makes them look ill so I could not imagine a yellow woman who looked ill and pretty. The Chinese women who live here are all ugly and yellow, a bit lighter than the Japanese soldiers. Their illness, whatever it may be, makes them nasty and dishonest. Black is better than yellow, worse than white. When I looked at the officer in disgust I thought about the beautiful cloud-white skin we get when we die and become ancestors among the other spirits. I tried to imagine my dead father, maybe now a sea creature with white skin or scales. Then I remembered Rand was white beneath the brown burnt onto him by the sun, so I stopped thinking about skin and beauty.

From the officer's face I could tell something bad was about to happen and started to sob. I screamed when the crow flew out of the mist past my mother's head and woke her, then flapped back into the canopy to hide. It squawked "Ya! Wah! Wah! Ya! Wahhh!" That was all. My mother lay on her back and wailed. Her wide right eye stared away to some other place. The left eye was swollen shut. The officer listened for something along the track. "Shut up!" he warned her. She still wailed. Without much anger he stomped his right heel on her stomach. His other boot squeaked as it took all of his weight. She belched, then lay there silent as her mouth bled into the mud. By now she had the left cheek of a puffer-fish. I felt sorry for her because she was my mother.

The officer almost shot Rand as two soldiers, not three, pushed him towards us out of the mist and light rain. We did not see them until they were five steps away. Rand was ugly, his face was swollen like my mother's. His left hand bled through a scrap of cloth wrapped around it. The injured hand was tied with a leather string to his healthy hand, in front of his belly. He wore his useless boots but no shirt or hat. I sniggered because his shorts were filthy and on backwards. Mud was all over him, apart from some streaks of white skin where sweat and raindrops dribbled down his chest.

One of the soldiers held his rifle and Rand's pistol. The other soldier had two rifles and the leather strap and collar that had been on the dog's neck. No dog. I hoped it was dead. What about the third soldier? Where was the long knife that had been on Rand's hip? How weak he was without his weapons, with his shorts on backwards. The soldiers let go of him and the officer hit him on the nose with his pistol. Rand sloshed into the mud like a rock. He stood up again, straight, and stared down at the officer, even shorter than Rand, who was not as tall as you, Masta Peter. The officer said nothing. He punched Rand in the stomach so hard that he fell and could not get up again, no matter how much he tried.

My mother looked at Rand with fear in her good eye, and then away from him through the mist, up towards the canopy she could not see. He tried to speak to her but no sound came from his mouth. She wailed and wailed and would not stop when I told her to. The officer, a dog about to bite, turned to her. I put my hand over her mouth to block her wails. She gasped with pain and made my palm messy with blood and spit. She stopped the racket and started to fall back into the mud. I let her drop. With a blank face and one eye she stared up at Rand. Her eye did not blink. It seemed to be awake but also asleep.

The officer yelled at the two soldiers and slapped the dog handler three times on the left cheek. I think he asked about the dog and the third soldier. The dog handler should have collapsed under the power of the attack but did not even totter. The soldiers bowed three times to the officer. "*Hai! Hai! Hai!*" They sounded a bit like the forest crow, with less confidence.

The officer calmed and they talked for a long time. He looked at the small clock on his wrist and shook his head. He turned to me and pointed down the track. He said he would walk fast back to the village with the white man and the soldiers. I could stay where I was with my mother for the night if she could not walk, or I could take her home at a slower pace if she could stagger. The soldiers laughed when he sneered at me and pretended to give me his pistol to protect us from pigs.

The soldiers dragged Rand to his feet and shoved him along the ill-defined track with the officer behind them. From the back Rand's shorts looked silly with the buttons down his arse. He stumbled but refused to fall. Although I knew he was brave because he slept alone on the mountain with the worst spirits and was defiant to the

Japanese, I hated him for the fear he caused me and my mother. Maybe I hated him because he rejected me, which should not have bothered me because I did not want him either.

After the men faded into the mist I could still hear the squeak of the pig-officer's boots. When I could no longer hear him I lifted my mother out of the mud and sat her on the log. She stopped staring into another place with her good eye and looked at me for the first time since the officer slapped the other one shut. I said "I found the crow." She gurgled a whisper through her mouth half full of blood: "So, you found the crow. I found something that scared me much more than the crow could ever do." Despite my persistence she would not tell me what she found and I still do not know what it was. Perhaps an evil ancestor, still black and wandering in the forest. A dancing pig? Jesus and Satan?

I asked if Rand had attacked her body or hurt her in some other way. She said no. I was not surprised as it made no sense for him to hurt her if he had no interest in playing with my much younger body. In that way he was harmless, which matched his girlish voice.

She could not walk well. She held my elbow with most of her weight as I wobbled her to the stream. The light was so dull that fireflies could not hide as they gathered to spy on us. They are beautiful and dangerous. If you watch them with too much interest they will draw you into the dark world of the dead on whom they feed. Some old people say they are spirits of the dead. Whatever they are, my mother was vulnerable, perhaps dying, so I warned her to ignore them.

As I was so close to her I soon accepted that some of the mud was not mud. That must have been why she disgusted the officer. I had smelled it before but ignored the reality of shit because she was my mother. She was too tired and upset to wash so I took off her laplap to do it for her. Where the officer had stomped on her stomach the skin and flesh were torn and red like a squashed crab. Her belly hair was still as black and thick and shiny as mine.

I lowered her into the stream, splashed water over her and rubbed at the mud and shit and blood with bunches of grass and leaves. Her bung eye flickered when the water went over it but the lids of the good one did not move, let alone close. When I asked if the eye and cheek hurt she said no. "So why do you gasp and shudder?" She replied, "Fear of a clear memory when I am old." As she scrubbed below her waist with a new bunch of grass she cried in a weird way that made me think she had learned to do it from the rare owl, the monstrous bird that all others fear, the one that hides high in the darkest part of the forest and howls louder and louder, sharper and sharper, like a female soul that wants to escape from some sort of agony into a painless realm. My warm tones calmed her only a little and I expected her to start howling again. She didn't.

My memory flapped its wings back to when my father tied my mother's dog to a post and thrashed it with a paddle after it ate one of his chickens. The dog screeched at first. It soon went silent even though my father still thrashed it. That chicken was his best layer. Eggs are still better than coins and almost as valuable as stick tobacco.

Long after my mother was clean and I had washed her laplap she refused to get out of the water. Four times I lifted her by the armpits but she squirmed out of my grasp, splashed back into the stream and searched around and around and up and down with her ears and good eye in fear of something she knew was with us, something beyond my senses. I could not grip her well because her skin was wet. Twice she kept her nose under water much too long and I had to jerk her head up by the hair so she could breathe again. Each time I saw her battered face I was tempted to let it drop back into the water and stay there, to let her escape, which the howling owl could never do.

If Missus Sharlet were here she would have one eye closed by now and the other would open and shut to squeeze out tears. I have talked too much, so I will pretend you need to blow out your lantern and drift together into your dreams. I have said too much to risk dreams, so all night I will listen to the sea and watch my lantern burn low. As usual, people here will see the glow during the night if they go out to piss, and will think, "She is even madder than her crazy dead uncle, the one who thought he was a great leader in the war because he had a hat captured from a white man." At first light I will go to my garden to sleep for a while.

Let us continue to pretend you are here instead of Tarawa. If you want to know more, sit on your step tomorrow night after the big-men have stopped pestering you with smoke and complaints about pigs, women and land, and have gone to their huts to suffer the snores and farts of the wives who called them home.

* * *

23 August 1971. Tonight the big-men left you later than usual. It does not matter because I will have less to say tonight than last time we met, a few days ago. Can you feel eyes watching us? I remember a day a few years ago when you held court and conducted the census here. Many of the women who sat under the meeting tree asked me what we three talked about the night before, when you asked me questions I would not answer then but can answer now in this long letter to you, even though I do not want to do so. Three men also wanted to know what we talked about. I said it was about trying to get children to go every day to the mission school, the one set up about three cigarettes away, long after the war. "*Giamin! Giamin!* You always lie to us," an old woman yelled. They often talk to me like that. When they do, I laugh to myself because they remind me of a joke my mother told me about children who lived a long way off in Kieta, before the Australians ran away, and went to school there. Then, there was no mission school nearby. I wanted to live in Kieta and go to that school. She said, "You are too old. Do you know how dogs are different from children in Kieta? No?

Sometimes the dogs go to school, sit near the door and learn how to read. The children sit at small tables and learn how to sing Jesus songs but not how to read."

All the women who questioned me after you held court here went to the Kieta school or the newer one nearby. Now they all sing well about Jesus in heaven. I do not go to the church, and the last time I sang was to my mother when I found her in the forest, long ago. Only three of the women can write the name of Jesus and Satan, and not much more. They are jealous of me. I never went to school. After the war I worked for the wives of missionaries and plantation managers near Kieta. They taught me to read and write well in Pidgin and read some English.

Missus Sharlet smiles. I will continue my story while she is happy. Sorry to say she will not stay that way. Please turn down your lantern to make it harder for the human watchers to watch.

When I lifted my mother out of the stream the afternoon was late and the forest dim, at the stage when birds sing less and flying fox colonies abandon their roost and rush to food trees, high on the mountain or closer to the coast. The spirits were still there, resting a little before their night-time carnage. They never sleep. It is easy for them to give us a bad dream and harm us while we try to sleep.

The wild pigs squealed and grunted and coughed as they shuffled closer. I could not see them through the mist or foliage. They stank more in the evening air, sharper than the village pigs, and I started to worry because they stink much the same as angry souls that escape with new energy at night from the earth and rocks and thorn trees, and search for someone to hurt, or a house to burn, or a canoe to set adrift and smash on the reef. In this forest of fear, that is why the flying foxes chatter in crowded anxiety towards evening and go to a safer place to eat. They eat at night.

There was still enough light to see my mother's fear of the Japanese and the forest and maybe something else. Extra fear, of the forest at night, might send her insane or kill her so I yelled at her in one ear then the other. "Get up from the water! The flying foxes will go soon!" She stood up straight. I wrapped her wet laplap around her body and pushed her in the back until we reached the track, then I pushed her along it. If she tried to stop I pushed her again and said we must reach the edge of the forest before dark to escape the mad souls. Once she replied, "The moon will be bright enough to force them back into their world", which was nonsense. I told her the moon was in the wrong phase to be bright and anyway the forest canopy was too dense for it to penetrate. That made her walk faster despite her pain and anguish.

She walked ahead of me, always fast despite her injuries, and did not complain or cry. As I tired and the light waned, the smell and feel of evil things came through my toes and the mist, which was more relaxed than before. It quietened as it settled closer to the ground for the night. I also heard distant cries, perhaps from the owl that sounded like my mother. My fear was so strong that I had to tell her to stop while I stepped off the track to shit.

While I squatted I looked over my shoulder for hungry pigs that eat shit, and for the large snakes that wake up late in the afternoon to roam like Satan and seize animals and birds, unwary as they mate or sing or search for food on the ground and in the trees. None of the snakes here are poisonous but still I fear them for their beautiful coldness and stealth. They are more than snakes.

I was even more afraid of sorcerers and invisible spirits, *maselais* that use your shit for *sanguma*, to cast spells on you and your family. I tried to shit as fast as a bird. Their shitting speed helps them live longer. This squat had none of the pleasure I felt when I shat with my mother or friends on the beach at night, or near our bush garden in daylight. Even now I cannot shit with pleasure and never do it in the bush near the garden unless I am too ill to wait for the beach at night. When I finished and stepped back onto the path my mother was gone. I had to run a long way in panic to catch up with her. She did not seem to know I had stopped or even if I was with her at all.

We could still see the track well enough by the time the gap in the forest wall glowed in the last light of the sunset and invited us out into a safer place. I coughed and snorted to get rid of the stink of pigs and poisonous souls. My mother did not bother. We sat on the ground to rest until we knew the sun had dipped into the sea, well beyond our sight, on the other side of the forest and over the mountains. The twilight showed us the permanent track past our garden back to the village, away from the worst spirits and other creatures.

When we came close to the village my attitude to it was the opposite of now. Then the place was a refuge. I sobbed with relief and imagined myself back in the safety of my mother's belly where there would be no knowledge of the future, just her heartbeat, the slosh of food and drink in her stomach, and the hiss of her blood and mine together. That was how I saw the village. The eyes of cooking fires welcomed us in the dusk. For the first time I enjoyed the yelps of the mongrels that smelled us long before they saw us.

Now the village is a prison, so many years later. People do not forget stories, only twist them and send them all over the island, so there is no place where people would be kind to me. Anyway, I do not belong anywhere else. My garden shelters me despite bad memories but I do not go beyond it through the wall of the forest, a world of evil that sucks in good people and makes them crazy, perhaps including Rand, whose spirit the old people say is in there with my mother's. Maybe the spirits stay there forever. We want them to turn white and escape to the happy place of other ancestors. Most people now say the happiest place is with white Jesus in paradise or heaven. We like to think the ancestor spirits find happiness there but maybe some of them prefer the forest. But remember, not all of the spirits in the forest are ancestors. Many are not from our families or clans. They are evil creatures who punish us if we do not perform correct ritual to control their malice. Maybe

Rand is there, turned as black as I am, and is still pleased to be evil.

I do not know what was in my mother's mind and soul as we got back to the village. When a few men came to see who we were, she ran to them much faster and steadier than I thought possible for anyone who had been kicked and slapped so hard. They saw it was her. One called her harsh names, slapped her on the top of her head and walked away as he hurled curses at both of us. Two others pushed her towards our house and one yelled at me to take her there and make sure she did not come out until the Japanese, who would come next morning, had left.

The young man Titus brought food to our house after dark. With his mouth close to my neck, he said the Japanese took the white man to their base camp. A small boy saw them put him on the boat that brought their supplies from Kieta. Soldiers would return next morning to take a few village men through the forest to get Rand's cargo and bring it down to the base camp. Titus did not say he was afraid but I could hear and smell fear in his voice.

* * *

26 August 1971. I should not pretend I put a true date every time I start to write. Sometimes I guess the date, start on that day and write all night and part of the next day, then add a bit the day after that, and maybe again a day or two later. So I will not put a date after today. Even so, I will still write every day when I feel like it until the story is complete, and will always pretend you are here to listen to my voice while you judge me.

I slept well that night, so I do not know if my mother stayed awake. I did not ask. Before I went to sleep she would not talk and ignored me in the morning when I asked if she felt better. Her left eye was still closed and her cheek swollen, blue-grey like a sailfish skin.

As the sun rose the Japanese officer returned with five soldiers, including the two from the previous day, and yelled for all the men to line up. They had no dog. My mother spoke to me for the second time since we met on the track where I waited with the officer. "The white man also made the men line up before he shot your father." That was all she said.

The soldiers went into every house to make sure all the men and adolescent boys came out. There were twenty-three altogether, all quiet and afraid, and some breathed so hard we could hear them from our house, ten steps away. Like my mother and me, the women and children watched from their houses. Many cried. One woman screamed in bursts a few seconds apart. The officer started to get annoyed, so her husband yelled from the line-up to tell her to shut up. A few children came out of their houses to tease puppies and throw scraps to chickens. A small boy chopped a house-post with a machete.

The officer strutted along the line four times, the biggest rooster on Bougainville. On his fifth pass he selected the strongest twelve men, who included Titus. The two soldiers from the previous day marched towards the garden track with the village men behind them in single file. The officer and three other soldiers followed. I noticed for the first time that his left boot squeaked louder than the right. As soon as they left, my mother went outside and lit our fire to boil water. Still she would not talk to me so I stayed inside to think and to listen to the village. Had the Japanese killed Rand? If so, how? Was he big-headed enough to defy them too much?

Through a gap in the wall I watched my mother's sister stand close to her and rant. "You and Bos helped the Japanese. You are worse than a yam thief. We can no longer talk to you. We cannot trust you. We do not know what you have told them and what you will tell them. The white man shot your husband but you should not try to avenge him. Why avenge him? Simeon used to beat you and fuck women in Kieta. The Japanese are small and ugly but they are smart in some ways and also vicious. They knew the white man had been here. Do you think they did not suspect our men carried his cargo through the forest, not men from other villages? Now they will know for sure. How many of us will not have husbands and sons by the end of the day? Answer me! Answer me!"

My mother did not reply. Her sister ranted on and on, and pushed my mother twice, almost hard enough to knock her down. The jolts made her grimace and bend over with the pain in her belly and face where the officer kicked and slapped her. Was my aunt stupid enough to think the Japanese would have hurt a friend as much as they hurt my mother? Maybe stupid with fear. Most of the other women watched from near their houses while their small children played. The older boys sat under the palms near the beach with the men, all waiting and hoping.

I went out to the top step of our house and could see the water pot steaming on our fire like the mist in the forest. I called out to my aunt, who loved me a lot, "If you push my mother again I will come down and pour hot water on your feet." She ignored me, spat on the ground near my mother and started to cry, then ran back to her children. They played with a puppy and tormented a baby bird on a string. From her house she called out that I was a toy for the Japanese. The liar. She knew I was a virgin.

My mother did not react to the taunt about me and I was surprised that I did not care about it. There was too much on my mind to take offence at an insult that might have led to my aunt's murder and my suicide in happier times. My mother squatted on her left heel and looked far out to sea with her good eye. The water boiled over but she did not hear the ashes spit or notice the cloud of steam until it scalded her left hand. She left it in the cloud for a long time. Even when she pulled the hand away the movement was slow and she did not move her gaze from the ocean beyond the reef. Her eye did not search. She stared at nothing.

The men sat near the beach all day and smoked, with an occasional murmur and nod of heads. Sometimes they stood to piss into the water or onto the sand. My mother and I stayed silent in the house. We were afraid to go out and risk verbal and physical abuse so we made a gap in the bamboo floor and pissed onto the ground, as we did on rainy nights. The village was quieter than ever before. The pigs and dogs dozed. Children played without much enthusiasm on the beach near the old men. A few planes flew over in the middle of the day, high in the clouds.

As my mother would not talk and did not want to move, or even breathe, I took her by her hands early in the afternoon and led her to her mat. I helped her lie down, then stroked her back until she dozed. So she could not dream, I sat beside her and poked her ribs whenever her face lost calmness.

The afternoon sea was placid because the day was calm and the tide was almost out. The loudest sound was the rustle of palm fronds in a breeze that cooled and calmed me so much I lay down near my mother and drifted into a world where the gardens produced twice as much as ours with less work and the fish jumped from the sea onto the beach. The pigs and dogs were pretty and smelled like flowers. The last crow died and the fearful owl flew into the clouds with all the *maselais* behind her like a long tail. Everyone smiled. There were no Japanese or white men, and the old men did not spit red betel juice or talk about the old days when their fathers stole girls from the mountains and the sunset coast, and played with them until they killed and ate them. Jesus and Satan had defeated one another and could no longer cooperate against us.

Five shots from the mountain wrecked my dream. Another three came after my mother's scream dragged me back into her life through a black cloud. The five shots in my dream were almost a single sound. There was a short space, and the other three shots close together. Women howled and threw metal pots against walls and floors. Children screamed and ran from their mothers in fear. Dogs yelped but the pigs the Japanese had not yet stolen stayed silent, perhaps hoping silence would protect them. Birds screeched in the scrub and from the sky above the beach as the shots interrupted their hunt for crabs and lazy fish. "Titus," I whispered so that only I could hear. "Titus, Titus, Titus."

A while later I counted eight more shots, not as loud or sharp as the first eight. They were spaced out more, over the time it would take me to stroll from my house to the beach. My mother sat on her heels and stared at the inside wall, an arm's length away, as if she could see through it to some hideous place. Women screamed abuse at us from inside their houses, then the village and scrub became quiet. For the rest of the afternoon the loudest noises were from waves on the reef and the chatter of palm leaves in the breeze. We also heard sobs. A baby cried twice. Three planes flew over, too high to care about us. I thought about the day I heard the shot that killed my father while I was at our garden, ignorant of his death.

We waited to find out if the Japanese would return alone. After the shots, for the time of about ten cigarettes everyone except the men stayed inside their houses unless they had to go to the beach or scrub to piss or shit. My mother and I drank water but did not eat. How pleasant it would be to take her to the stream near the village to bathe her and wash her worries into the sea for the tide to suck them over the reef, down through the green and deep blue, past the rainbow wall of coral.

Mid-afternoon she spoke to me for just the third time since we went into the forest to find the crow and found Rand as well. She did not look at me so perhaps she talked to herself. "Someone has to carry the cargo down through the forest from the mountain." That was all. She looked at the wall.

Soon after she spoke the dogs yelped and a bush rooster crowed twice from the direction of our garden. The pigs, safe now, complained about the racket. I looked through the doorway and saw the youngest four men who had left that morning. They staggered into the village with two of Rand's metal boxes hanging from bamboo poles. The soldiers strutted behind them, hit them with rifles and yelled at them not to stop, even though they were exhausted. My crazy uncle was with them. He wore a white hat like the ones we saw later in the war on the heads of Australian and American sea-captains. I guessed it was Rand's although I had not seen him wear it. My uncle waved his arms as if they were out of his control and gave orders to the carriers and the Japanese in his own private language, the one only he understood. Later he wore the hat at Rand's execution.

One of the carriers was Titus. As they went close by our house I stood on the top step, called his name and asked about the other men in our own language, which the Japanese could not understand. He glanced at me and shook his head. I asked, "Are they alive?" He shook his head again as he lurched on and gasped, "Burned!" He said it three times. No one else in the village was close enough to hear him. I was used to listening hard with my right ear when he whispered to me at night through the wall of our house while my parents slept. Even in the dark I would not turn my head to the side like my father. When I got older I did not try as hard, as it was too exhausting to always try not to do it. I am sure you saw me do it sometimes many years later but I do not think you knew about my deformity until you read this story.

The officer ran at Titus from behind and slapped him on the cheek, wet with tears and sweat. The officer looked at his hand and wiped it on the arse of his trousers. He charged towards me while he screeched in Pidgin that he would shove crushed peppers into me in two places if I spoke again. He turned and followed the others through the village and onto the track to the Japanese base. Why did he and Rand detest me so much?

Although I hated his words I was pleased he yelled them at me because the other villagers, even though most were idiots, would realise no one shoves crushed pepper into women who are their friends.

They were worse idiots than I expected. Two women picked

up sticks and ran to our house. One screamed, "Whore! Taught by your mother." The other yelled, "What did your lover say?" I feared for my mother so I pushed her back inside and looked down at the two women from the top step. Other women came out of their houses and men came from the beach to watch. The children stopped their torment of small creatures. An old woman from the nearest house rolled her eyes, pointed her machete up at me and twisted it in the air. A young woman swayed in slow rhythm from side to side and pretended to slice her throat, my throat, with a knife. An old man called out my mother's name and opened his mouth wide to show his black and yellow teeth, then chomped as he pointed at the face of his mournful wife, at a wide hole where her nose had been when she was young, before he bit it off to punish her for adultery reported to him by his sister because the wife had called her a yam thief, the worst of insults.

"You are dog-shit on the beach and between our toes! Where are the others? What about the shots? What did Titus say?" screamed the swayer with the knife. Red betel juice dripped onto her dugs. "He said the other men went with the rest of the cargo on another track to the Japanese base. The Japanese and a second white man, one we have not seen, fired shots as he ran away up the mountain where the Japanese do not go without dogs." Sometimes you have to lie.

Many people were now close to our house. The woman with the knife was close enough to spit betel juice on our bottom step. Those further away cheered and stomped. They hoped for murder. The woman with the machete surprised me when she sprang towards me on old legs and chopped the top step a toe's width from the outside edge of my left foot. I wanted to kick the ugly bulge that had been on her throat since her youth. Instead I looked at her and did not move. She chopped beside the other foot, then between my feet. I said nothing. Her husband pulled her away, slapped her hard on the back and pushed her towards their house. Sweat sprayed when he slapped her and its staleness drifted to me on the ocean breeze. Worse than a dead forest pig, which she might become soon if she pushed me too hard.

The man beckoned his ten-year-old grandson, the youngest brother of Titus, talked to him for a while, and pointed to the track taken by the four carriers, the Japanese soldiers and the lunatic with the white man's hat. The boy hesitated. When his grandfather raised his hand to strike him he wiped his eyes with both fists, ran to the track and vanished into the coconut grove beside the beach.

The boy returned two hours later in the darkness. He cried because he feared night-time *maselais* and because the Japanese put his brother and the other three men on a boat with the cargo and sailed southeast. He did not see the other eight men.

The villagers abused us from their houses for a long time, which frightened me because they might kill us without using what little brains they had to consider the retaliation of the Japanese, who these blind idiots said were our friends. Our friends? Couldn't they see my mother's injuries or remember the officer's threat to shove pepper into me?

Late at night my mother agreed that if we survived the night we should get up at dawn and walk towards our garden, then creep away from the track and through the scrub until we found a path to the Japanese base. We hated them and they might kill us but our murder was more likely if we stayed at home. As the village settled down to sleep we packed two pandanus-leaf bags, small ones so that no one would suspect us if they saw us leave.

When the village was asleep I felt brave enough to walk in the darkness to the beach, for the usual reasons. Two men grabbed me from behind and one put his hand over my mouth. They did not speak and I could not see them. I was too afraid to struggle. Like my mother and her sister, no doubt they assumed Rand and the Japanese officer had fucked me and I was therefore now available to other men, especially big-men. My father could no longer protect me.

I still do not know who they were. They were not young. Their skin was rough and they did not smell like anyone I knew. They were heavy and did not stink as much as spirits. Maybe they were spirits pretending to be real men. Whatever was the truth, the attack must have been punishment for some mistake I had made in the forest.

The one who blocked my mouth forced me to my knees and pushed my forehead into the sand. His hand smelled like fresh copra. The other man pulled off my old laplap and mounted me like a dog, his hands clasped on my belly to control me like a dog holds a bitch with his paws. Once when I was small I went to our garden when my mother did not expect me, and I hid and watched my father's brother doing the same thing to her with his laplap still on as he looked around for intruders. She planted three tomato vines while he mated with her.

It did not hurt me much, except when he gripped my belly hair. My main worry was lack of air. My nose was in the sand and a filthy hand was over my mouth. The first man soon spilled his water and growled like my father used to do at night after our bamboo house had trembled for a while when there was no earth tremor or storm. Then the second man took his hand from my mouth and they changed places, which gave me time to gulp air and blow sand and snot from my nostrils before the first man pushed my face down again. He did not cover my mouth, just pushed it into the sand. It was pointless to scream for help in that village. The second man soon fell overboard and they left me alone. They did not say a word to me or one another.

I cried for a few minutes as I washed them away in the sea and splashed my mouth and nose and eyes to get the sand out. I squatted on the beach for a while, then walked back to our house. A dog followed and whined. Maybe he thought I was his sister now, or it was his turn.

The second notebook is almost finished. I will start a new one tomorrow.

Notebook Three

31 August 1971. I have put a date. I said earlier that I would no longer do so. Does that make me a liar?

For the rest of the night I sat with my machete and thought about what had happened. I decided not to tell my mother as her mind was already delicate. I listened for people through the normal sounds of the sea and scrub as she slept, much better than ever. In case someone tried to stab us through the floor in the dark, I dragged her on her mat away from where she used to sleep and sat not far from the doorway, nowhere near my mat. I washed again with one of the dishes of water I kept to put out the fire if someone lit the house.

No one came for us in the night. They knew I listened for them and if necessary would attack like a barracuda to defend my mother. Well before dawn I woke her and we sneaked away with our pandanus bags. We left our sleeping mats. First she tied her dog to a pole under the house. I wanted to give him a final kick but thought he would yelp. We wore our best red laplaps. I threw the old one I wore the night before onto the coals of our cooking fire.

As the sun escaped the sea we smelled fresh shit so we knew we were near the Japanese base camp, a silent place apart from some coughs and spits. Quiet Japanese were the most dangerous. We hid in the scrub to watch them until we thought they would be in a good mood after breakfast, more alert and less likely to shoot us in panic or anger. I could not smell a tracker dog so I slept for a short time, with no dream. My mother woke me when the Japanese lined up. When I awoke I remembered that Rand shot one of their two dogs in the village and the other one was still up on the mountain, dead or alive. Dead and rotting, I hoped.

The Japanese sang a slow, sad song as they looked up at their red and white flag on a pole. They must line up, that's why they thought other people should do it too. The officer walked up and down as he gave a fierce speech. He hated his own soldiers. I heard his boots squeak but only in my mind as we were too far away for my good ear to hear it. Would his men laugh in their stomachs if they knew how small he was when I saw him wash in the stream? Maybe all Japanese had a baby sea-slug. I think he was a lot smaller than the first village man who attacked me and a bit smaller than the second, even though I could not see them. The officer did not attack me but I hated him more than them.

There were about twenty Japanese and no Bougainville people or Chinese. When the speech ended most of the soldiers marched away to do other things and the officer entered a small house with three other soldiers.

When my shadow shrank to twice my height I wrapped my laplap under my armpits, left my mother in the scrub, and stood on the path in clear view. I held my hands above my head and called out "Officer-*San*! Officer-*San*! Officer-*San*!" If they shot me she might escape. Some soldiers ran to the edge of the camp and lay on the ground with their rifles pointed at me. Others watched from behind buildings and trees. I waited for bullets to tear out my heart and belly. I would not let myself piss but could not stop a small puke.

The officer lurched towards me with his hand-gun pointed at my chest. When he saw it was me he slowed and I think he smiled for an instant. Maybe not. Then he became fierce and quick again. "What do you want?" He pointed the gun at my nose and told me to call my mother out of the scrub. How did he know she was there? In what other ways was he like Rand? I called her and she came, one hand on her head and our bags in the other. She said, "The people in the village want to kill us." The gun now pointed at my left eye.

"Why?" "They say we should have helped our men find the white coward to kill him and leave him in the forest for pigs to eat so he would not cause trouble for you, and so you would soon forget about him and not hurt anyone from our village." He said nothing. A short time later she added, "If we see white men we will tell you."

She had not said much to me or anyone else for a long time so I was surprised to hear so many words from her. No one had said those things, apart from the last bit. I said, "We want to thank you for saving us from the white pig, and want you to protect us." For a heartbeat, mine not his, his eyes became human, a bit more open than usual. Then he almost closed them, so I could not see them well. He watched my nose-tip and pointed the gun away from me, at my mother's forehead. She screamed and his finger twitched on the trigger. I told her to shut up. She did. I looked hard at his eyes and eyebrows, a few wisps of black fuzz that curved up and stayed high, a question without words. I understood it. He had changed his mind about me. I knew what he now wanted. I said, "Okay, I will" so that only he could hear me. His eyebrows went straight again. He looked up at a passing plane, put the gun into its leather bag and yelled at the soldiers who pointed rifles at us from the camp. Two of them ran to get us as he marched back to his house. My mother and I vomited after a few steps, then we were okay. Why she vomited I do not know. I did it because of my deal with the officer.

We stayed in a hut at the base camp for two nights. Twice each day a soldier gave us weak tea and tiny balls of cold rice that would not satisfy a chicken. He hated us and did not want to waste food on black animals. The soldiers ate fish and rice. The officer ignored us. We washed in their shower hut near his house with buckets of water a soldier brought from a stream. Whoever brought the water always squawked in Pidgin, "You stink. You wash!"

I dozed at the end of the first afternoon. My mother crept out and asked the Japanese officer what happened to the twelve carriers. She told him the boy saw four get on the boat for Kieta. He said the boy was wrong, that all twelve carriers put the cargo on the boat at the Japanese base and all walked towards Kieta with tobacco sticks as payment for their work, with promises of more work there. My mother had never heard him say so much, apart from when we heard him make the fierce speech to his soldiers in the morning.

As the officer did not send for me on the first night to complete our deal, and I was afraid to go to him, the next evening I went to wash as he sat on a stool at the front of his house. I knew he could see my skin shine in the last sunlight if I stood in the right place, just inside the entrance. I wanted him to know I would not cheat him, or he might kill us. He turned his head and saw me.

I knew from experience in the forest that it was a waste of effort to bend over for him to watch my arse, or to push out my breasts, so I faced him and washed between my legs for a long time. He stood up and beckoned me. I put on my red laplap and strolled to him as I shook water droplets from my hair. In the sunlight they flew and shone like spray from a wave when a canoe hits it.

When I reached him I smiled. He bashed me on the side of the head with a thick rattan stick, quicker than a snake snatching a bird off a branch, then kicked me on the hip with his squeakiest boot before I even hit the ground. He stood over me and did not speak.

My mother ran from our hut and dragged me back there as I scrambled on my knees and babbled in dizzy shame. She hugged me as we lay on our mats. "Fool, fool, fool," she sobbed. I told her I did not want him to fuck me anyway. He was a vile man, stuffed full of hatred. "Then why did you try?" she asked. I did not want her to feel guilty so I did not tell her about my deal with the officer to save her life. "I am old enough to stop being a virgin and I thought he wanted me. Then he would look after us." She stared at the ceiling and did not say anything for about ten breaths, then she said, "The white spy knows you are not a virgin." I wanted to say she had picked the lie but not the culprit. Instead I ignored her as she bathed the welt on my head.

Why did I excite only black men or spirits who pretended to be dogs? Why did Rand and the officer not want me? Maybe they knew I did not want them. I wondered if I hated Rand more for not wanting me than for the fear he caused me, and the officer for his rejection more than his violence. Was I so ugly? I am still not sure. Rand did not want anything I could give him. All the officer wanted from me was to be a target to bash, like my mother in the forest. Maybe he hit me because he did want me and was ashamed because I was black and probably a virgin that no one else wanted.

A soldier came and parrot-squawked at us in Pidgin to be ready at sunrise to walk back to our village with a patrol. When he went quiet and stared at me I tried to think he felt sorry for me because his boss had bashed me. The more likely truth was that he tried to decide whether I was more like a pig or a dog. His renewed squawks made my head ache more. If we were too scared to go back, his boss told him we could go on the dawn boat to Kieta to see the white spy get his head cut off. My mother said we would go to Kieta. He said, "Maybe you can wash our clothes or do other things for black men who work there without their wives." I hoped to find Titus.

We took our last chance to piss before we would reach Kieta and boarded the boat at dawn. We lay on our new mats near the bow, where a soldier told us to stay for the whole trip. It was good to go to Kieta to get away from the officer, and maybe get paid to work. We could not talk because the engine was too loud, so we ate our rice balls and went to sleep soon after the boat started to lift and fall as it danced with the smooth swells outside the reef. The movement and the sloshes of calm water made me dream I was a baby, safe in my mother's body as she swayed in slow rhythm to our garden.

When the sun was high and the steel deck too hot for sleep we sat up and looked along the boat. There were a few soldiers and crew, all Japanese. Most of them watched the sky. We were the only local people, so we were grateful to the Japanese for doing us a special favour, not a normal thing for them.

My mother dropped the coconut from which she drank and its milk spilled onto the deck. Her face went grey. Seasickness? I followed her gaze to the dirty glass window of the wheelhouse and saw the officer with the midget slug staring down at us. He drew his face back into the gloom. Even though I could not swim, my horror was worse than if we were in a storm and the boat was about to sink. I hoped for a storm to distract me, even destroy me. None came. Until we reached Kieta at sunset we watched the coconut roll back and forth with the swell. Our minds and bodies were numb.

We did not see the officer again on the boat, perhaps because we were too afraid to look for him or at him. A soldier shoved us down the gangway before anyone else disembarked. He took us to a small house in a row of ten, near the military base, and told us we could live there until the white spy was dead. The houses shared a hut to shit and another to wash. Children would bring food and water. We must not go near the soldiers' houses and must never approach the military commander. Some people said he was a policeman, not a real soldier.

The soldiers feared the senior man and bowed to him often, so we called him the commander anyway. He was stronger than most Japanese and stood up straighter. He looked kind enough when he walked his smooth walk past the houses to inspect us and the other people the next morning. My mistake. When he got to our house he screamed at us to bow like the others, so we did. Once we saw him give angry orders to the pig-officer from the base camp, in front of all the soldiers, after the sad morning song in front of the red and white flag. The base camp officer bowed many times to the commander, even to his back as he walked away. "*Hai! Hai! Hai!*"

We asked a few people if they knew about our four village men. No one had seen them arrive by boat or on foot. An old man said, "I think they finished their lives in the sea." One day we saw my uncle with Rand's white hat on his mad head. I do not know how he got to Kieta. He kept away from us but went to other houses in the row of ten to demand food. When the soldiers marched he followed and tried to copy them. They laughed and said "*Hai!*" when he gave them orders in his private language.

The native people went crazy the evening before the head-cutting. Many of us screamed when a monster, some sort of *maselais*, emerged from the sea behind the rising moon, moved across it like red bruise, and tried to pull it back into the deep. The moon escaped after a long battle. Now I know that a shadow attacked it. After the war I worked for the wife of a Seventh Day Adventist pastor. She said it was a shadow of our Earth on the moon, made by the sun, and sent by Jesus to show his power and warn us to join her church for safety. After a year of my hard work she sent me away because I still refused to join her church. The pastor wanted me to stay. He argued with her but she won.

Most of the Japanese soldiers ignored our racket. A few jeered or told us to shut up. Later, after the moon won the battle and grew smaller as it sailed higher, one of the Japanese played sad music inside his house. I did not know then who he was or how he played it. Later I found out it was the commander. Most of it sounded like the moans of sick pigeons, especially the low notes. Sometimes it sounded more beautiful, like our men blowing into the small pieces of bamboo they tie together to make music. That made me think about our garden.

As ordered by the Japanese, early on the morning of Rand's death the people from the ten houses, and many villagers from nearby, gathered in a half-circle behind the soldiers, on the edge of a sandy patch near the beach, not far from our house. My mother and I were the only women. There were no children. Before we arrived the soldiers had already lined up, sung the sad song to their flag, and marched there.

The commander did not give the morning speech. The vicious base-camp officer gave it that day. He had screeched louder than ever to the soldiers he hated. Now he stood with his back to them. His boots squeaked as he swayed his balance from foot to foot. I was close enough for my ear to tell me the left boot was definitely louder than the right, the one he stomped onto my mother's stomach in the forest. Beside him stood a soldier who held across his chest, in both hands, a long knife in a curved container, black and beautiful, with a small brass ring on one edge. A red cord and a brown one were attached to the handle, decorated with carved gold and a thin rope woven in a pretty pattern. The soldier was as stiff as a dead man, head up high, as the officer bowed low to him or the knife, took the container in both hands and hung it by the ring to a hook on the left side of his belt. He turned his back to us and waited almost motionless, with enough movement for his boots to complain a little. The commander stood to the left of the soldiers. Because he was a bit taller than they were I could see his head above them. There was no respect on his face as he looked at the pig-officer with the beautiful long knife. Now I know it is called a sword.

No dogs barked or whined. The Japanese shot them all before we got to Kieta. Pigs did not squeal and snort. The soldiers had eaten them. The only noises were calm splashes of waves, palm-frond whispers, and the rat-sound of two boots. No birds, a strange absence so close to the sea. The palm whispers made me think of Titus.

Two soldiers pushed and pulled Rand to the sandy patch and forced him to his knees. He looked more damaged than when we saw him last in the forest but today he stumbled less despite his injuries, perhaps because his feet were bare. Where were his awkward boots? The buttons of his filthy shorts were now at the front. He did not look at anyone and seemed to dream he was somewhere else, like Jesus in pain but without fear, looking past everyone to another place, just as he looked in a picture a Catholic priest gave to my aunt after the war. Rand stayed on his knees but soon sat back on his heels and rested his chin on his chest.

My brave or crazy mother went to the commander, then to the base camp officer and murmured to him as she waved her right hand from side to side, palm upwards. He glanced at her hand and nodded. She came back to me, seized me by the arm and pulled me until we stood right in front of Rand. He must have seen our feet because he lifted his head from his chest and searched up our legs and bodies until his eyes saw ours.

My mother slapped his left and right cheeks as hard as the officer slapped her when we were in the forest. Rand did not fall like she had. She put her head back, sniffed a long snort, and spat a glob that ran down his forehead and stuck to his right eyebrow like birdshit. She grabbed my hair so hard that I squealed. The soldiers laughed. She shoved my face down to his, so close that our noses almost touched and I could smell old blood in his mouth. His body stank worse than my mother's in the forest before I washed her in the stream. She held my hair up, twisted my head to show Rand my dead left ear, and sneered: "My daughter! She is Bos Simeon." She held out her open hand and showed him something she said she cut from a tree in our village. Later she showed it to me and said it was the bullet that killed my father. I still do not understand why she wanted to reveal another bodily fault, my bung ear, to add to the ones Rand disliked when he saw me in the village and the forest.

Rand coughed blood and replied to my mother, in his childish voice, "She is your friend Maria." That night she told me he said "*meri*", which you know is the Pidgin word for a black woman. "You are wrong," I told her. "He said 'Maria'. My one ear is better than your two." Since then I have learned that Maria is the mother of Jesus. She had Baby Jesus without fucking. When Jesus grew up he also had a companion called Maria but no one knows if he fucked her. Rand also mentioned a man called David but I did not know of him. Many years later I saw that name in the old part of the Christians' Bible.

Before my mother slapped Rand he said the name, David, and

asked her to bow close to him. When she did he whispered to her. I could not hear his words. After she slapped him and said I was her daughter Bos Simeon and he said no, I was her friend Maria, he again asked her to bend down and whispered something I could not hear. Later that day, when I asked her what he said, she would tell me only that his whispers before and after she slapped him made no sense unless he had fucked me. When I denied it her lips quivered. She sobbed but not for long.

I felt no sorrow for Rand when my mother hit him and spat on his face. After all, he hated me. Did he deserve the slaps and spit for making us fear him in the forest? Probably not. Maybe she did it because she thought he raped me the first time he took me into the forest, but that cannot be right because she seemed to think I had seduced him. I have never been sure and still wonder why she did those things to him when he was about to die. He had not really harmed her and had shot the one person who beat her, apart from the officer who was about to kill him. Was she a coward to slap him when his arms were tied and he was on his knees, almost dead? She should have left him to himself as he tried to deal with the greatest of all loneliness, with not one person there who loved him enough to try to ease it.

Even as he was about to lose his head, Rand tried to look as if he was in control. He was not in control of anything, but there was something strong and independent about him, like Jesus in the picture the Catholic missionary gave to my aunt. Rand was in pain, without fear, his head now raised, looking past everyone to another place and time where he would be less lonely. Jesus wore a hat made from twisted vines with sharp thorns, and held his head sideways as he looked up at the sky. Rand also held his head up but looked straight ahead, like my mother had looked through the mist in the forest and through the wall of our house.

I forgot to say that Rand seemed to wear a small hat when the soldiers brought him from his prison to the killing place. It was his yellow hair glued in a clump by thick blood.

We went back past the line of soldiers to our place in the audience behind them. Now a soldier put a rag across Rand's eyes and tied it at the back of his head with his finger-tips as he tried not to touch the blood-hat. What did those eyes see now?

The soldiers still grinned because I had squealed when my mother pulled my hair, and they stopped only when the pig-officer stomped over to Rand and drew the long sword from its container. The commander bowed a little and walked away to his office while Rand's head and body were still one.

The sword flashed in the sunlight when the officer pulled it from its beautiful container. He poured water on it even though it looked clean. Above the break of the waves, did Rand hear the officer pull it out? Did he hear the palms whisper last secrets to him, or did he not notice them because his mind had gone to his own place, maybe to his mother, or his wife if he had one? Did he hear the silence of birds that knew what would soon happen, just as they go silent when an earthquake is about to shake our world?

Rand twitched and farted when the officer with the sword squeaked to his side. The soldiers laughed. As I watched Rand's face go grey and his chin sank again onto his chest I thought about the horror of the day he killed my father. I was in the garden and did not see what happened but I know Rand strode into the village in the same way as you, Master Peter, and all the patrol officers who came before and after you. You were all confident that you were the boss, without any doubt that everyone would line up when you ordered it. We could not understand this because most of you were young and so many of the people you bossed were much older and therefore wiser. Did you have any respect for them?

My grandfather said the Germans were even more confident than Australians but less happy. The Japanese were more like Rand before his capture, always angry for no good reason. They stomped into the village and told us what to do, and hurt or killed anyone who did not do it right away. Unlike Germans and Australians, they always made their rules and demands clear, and we knew what to expect if we gave them trouble. They never wanted to mate with us. Women and girls had places to put pepper and nothing else, unless the Japanese wanted to punish us with rape, which did not happen very often.

Back to the killing of Rand. Pigs screech when someone is about to cut their throat with a knife or machete. We never shoot them because shotgun pellets spoil the meat, especially in the head, the best part. Unlike a doomed pig that knows what is about to happen, Rand stayed silent, but after the cut he bled like a pig, in a few spurts, a long one as he fell sideways, then weaker and weaker as he lay on the sand with his knees pulled up to his chest. His head did not fall straight onto the ground but first flipped away from his neck about half the length of my arm. Sometimes a coconut flips when it drops from a tree. His head did not have as far to fall and therefore did not have the speed to roll when it hit the loose sand. The jolt made the rag fly off his eyes. They were closed and he no longer looked like Jesus in the Catholic picture. His body did not move. My crazy uncle gibbered and jumped around in the sea-captain's hat. Everyone else whispered or was silent.

That was all. We went back to our house and ate rice and fish a child brought to us. We did not mention Rand and I do not know what happened to his body. Nor did we ever see the body of my mad uncle but we know he annoyed the Japanese as much as he annoyed us, enough for them to take him out to sea near our village a few weeks later and come back without him. Rand's spirit probably encouraged the Japanese to destroy my uncle because he stole and wore the sea-captain's hat.

* * *

We could not stay in that place. There was no work. The local people were not our people and the Japanese were too nasty for us to relax. We feared that Rand's spirit would wander to our hut at night in search of us, from wherever his body was buried or dumped, or from the place where his blood soaked into the sand. But no matter where we lived, he could harm us. Although we knew a sorcerer in our village who might be able to make Rand a bit less dangerous, we were afraid to go back there for reasons I have already told you. Then I had a good idea that I did not share with my mother before I acted on it.

On the evening of the day Rand died I bathed and went to the commander's house. I wore my red laplap, wrapped tight. That was when I realised the sad music I had heard the night before had come from this house. A soldier screeched at me to go away or he would beat me. I said, "I have important information for your commander. I can tell only him, not you." He raised his fist to hit me but changed his mind and went inside. The music of moaning pigeons stopped. He came back, told me to follow him in, bowed to the commander and went back out.

The commander sat at a desk and held a piece of old, yellow bamboo with a row of four holes along it. About as thick as a banana and as long as the distance between my armpit and my fingertips. To my surprise and his, I did not fear him. I pointed at the bamboo and asked, "Is that what makes the sad music? What is it called?" He put the bamboo on the desk near a bottle of drink with a picture on it of a woman, as shiny black as someone from Buka. He growled after a long wait, "It is called *shakuhachi*. Say it!" I did. He stared at me while he nodded, one slow movement. I got it right first try, which annoyed him.

"What do you want?" Quiet and angry. Dangerous. Now he could see I feared him a bit, so he relaxed a little. Maybe he was not as angry as he wanted me to think.

I already knew he spoke good Pidgin, not as well as the vicious officer. I said we wanted to go back home but were afraid our people would harm us for our friendship with the Japanese. He said nothing, just stared, a snake waiting for a bird to land too close. Then I complained about the missing carriers and told him what the pig-officer said about them at the base camp. I told him my friend Titus said eight men died on the mountain. The nasty officer was a liar because he said they were alive. Did another four die on the boat trip from the base camp to Kieta? He did not reply or move. I said, "He beat my mother in the forest, and bashed me at the base camp." No reply.

In case I had made a mistake and he liked the pig-officer, I was about to say how happy I was that the officer chopped off Rand's head, because Rand had killed my father, Simeon. I stopped in time to save a lot of lives and pepper torture among the villagers who had lied to the pig-officer about Simeon's disappearance at sea. I still wonder if he already knew the true story about my father's death, in which case I did not save anyone from anything.

As I stood in front of him, still not too afraid, he stared at my bare neck and shoulders in silence. My mother knew the power of a red laplap. He rested his elbows on his desk and clasped his hands under his chin like the German priest I once saw in a church before the war. After a few breaths, long and slow, the commander said he would arrange for two soldiers to go to the village next morning from the base camp. They would tell the villagers we were loyal to them and they must welcome us back in a few days or expect trouble. The Japanese would return to arrest anyone who hurt us. In return for protection, I must report any villager who said bad things about the Japanese, and tell them if white men came near the village.

He had said what I wanted him to say without my needing to ask him. I bowed and said, "*Hai!*" He did not move a body muscle as he stared hate at me for a few breaths and told me to get out and never come back.

When I told my mother what I did and how nasty the

commander had seemed, she said, "Our twelve men are all dead, including Titus. It is useless to ask about them or cry for them." A while later she said, "Sometimes a big-man hates you if he wants your body. You make him feel weaker than you." I replied, "If he really wanted me I would bow low and he could have my body if it would make him feel stronger than me." She sighed, put her hands over her eyes and looked at me for a long time through her fingers, then stared at the wall in keeping with her new habit.

The day before we left, a soldier told us a new officer would go to the base camp because a shark ate the other one. We said we were sorry and he bowed to us when we pretended to cry. He ordered us to be ready at dawn to get on the boat. Back inside our hut, my mother smiled, which she had not done for a long time.

When we returned to our village from Kieta our house and possessions were intact. My mother's dog dozed on the step with one open eye and did not care if we were back or not. He was as tubby as usual, so someone must have fed him. No one confronted us. Some people were kind and gave us yams because they thought we might know what happened to Titus and the other three men. We truly did not know. Even now no one knows for sure, only that we never saw them again, and that their fate was probably much the same as that of the eight men murdered on the mountain because they carried the cargo to get it and Rand away from the village out of Japanese sight, not because they supported him and Australia.

You still want to know what happened to my mother. A few nights ago I said I would tell you that same night about what happened to her. My timing was wrong and I told you about other things. Now I will return to that story.

Remember when I searched for my mother and the crow called me from the tall, beautiful tree where she hid when I met Rand in the forest for the second time? When he took me there alone the first time I did not go with him as far as that tree. Now when I searched for her the day after I told her I was pregnant and she got upset and went into the forest after some men pulled her out of the sea, I found her dog not far from that tree and ordered him to take me to her or I would do something bad to him.

The mist thinned but hummed louder and sharper all around me as the dog wiggled and whimpered his way to the tree. Such trees do not have low branches. When he looked up I followed his gaze and saw my mother high on a thick vine, where my ear could now locate most of the humming. It came from a swarm of blowflies. The vine, as thick as my neck, clung to the trunk and joined it to another tree ten steps away. Her machete was on the ground beneath her. She had chopped steps in the trunk so she could climb up the tree until she reached the vine, high, about three times my height above the ground. Then she went along the vine a little way.

One end of her best red laplap was tied to the vine and the other around her neck. She wore a white laplap tied in a knot above her breasts so that it would not slip down when her body jolted at the end of her jump. The laplap was not soiled much. She moved and I thought she was alive, but it was the vine that bobbed up and down as the spirits in the breeze and mist caught her body and twisted it one way, then the other. Her ankles were tied together with a strip of red cloth torn from her laplap.

I knew she was dead because her toes pointed to the ground. She held her arms a little way out from her sides in a way that made her hands look like the wingtips of a frightened bird about to fly away. Her spirit had gone but her body would not leave that perch until someone cut her down. Although she was high in the tree and there was some mist, I could see scratches on her face. Her tongue poked out to the left. One eye was closed and the other open wide as if some final thought had surprised her. Maybe she saw Satan. Then I saw she had only one eye. I vomited when I understood what happened to the other one. Above her, the crow sat contented on the vine and watched me. Her dog did not look up at her for long, just lay on the ground beneath her and chewed his balls like a normal dog on a normal day. The crow laughed and flapped off into the gloom.

I sang a sweet song up to her body on the vine for the time it takes to smoke one cigarette. I sang in rhythm with her bobbing and twisting in the breeze. Had her life moved into the trunk to consort with the tree's spirit? I stopped my song and lay my good ear hard against the trunk to listen for some sort of life, which I often heard in tree trunks as a noise like hands rubbed together. This time, silence.

I went to the other side of the tree to piss and saw that my mother or someone else had carved, on a buttress, the outline of a long head with big square ears. A cold and nasty face. Its eyes were sea-snail valves stuck in mud, which was also used to attach dead grass for hair and make a nose too narrow to breathe, and an open mouth without teeth, like the one I once saw on a dead man. I looked away and talked to the dog as I pissed, then I panicked when I looked again at the carving and saw patterns like the tattoos on my face.

My belly started to ache. Chased by the flap of wings and other evil sounds I left my mother and ran from this place, back through the forest to the garden track and on to the village. The dog did not follow me. I never saw him again, nor my mother.

I did not run without stopping. For a little while I had to lie down in the forest because the pain in my belly was too bad for me to run or even walk. I saw blood on my laplap and my feet. I was punished with rape on the beach for some mistake I had made, then with pregnancy, now with my baby's death because the pregnancy was against the rules of our society. Perhaps the father, whichever rapist he was, did not come from an approved clan and did not have the right totem.

The baby was a bit shorter than my thumb and had tiny arms, legs, toes and fingers. Eyes had started to grow on its swollen head. Also ears. The right one was no more use than my left one in such a young baby and might have stayed that way. I did not look at the left ear as I wanted to believe a hole was there already and I had not passed on my problem. I do not know if the baby was a boy or a girl. It was not beautiful and we are lucky our shape becomes less like a newborn pig by the time we leave our mother's body. That is, if we can stay in there long enough for our mothers to defeat the evil that tries to make pigs of us. My baby lost the battle. I also know that the mothers of many other girls, prettier than I am, fought the battle against ugliness better than my mother did.

I wrapped the baby in fragrant leaves to bury it. The earth was soft enough for me to dig a hole with my hands and a stick, and I hoped it was deep enough to confuse wild pigs for as long as it would take for the baby's spirit to rise from the earth, assuming the spirit was still in the tiny body that had left mine. No one knows for sure how long it takes for a spirit to leave a body, and how fiendish even a baby will be if we make ritual or other mistakes when it joins the other spirits and starts to wander among us. I put a heavy rock on the grave but took it away because it might get in the way of the rising spirit. I know a rock cannot stop the movement of a spirit. I am saying what I thought at the time, in my fear and distress.

When the pain was over I washed my body and laplap in a stream and sat on a rock for a short time as I suffered for my loss. I felt better when I realised there was no mist at that place and the only sound not made by me was the stream's babble. For the first time in the forest I was unafraid, for a short time.

When I got home I told my aunt about my mother but I did not tell her or anyone else about my baby.

Village men went to get my mother's body from the forest in the afternoon and soon found the tree with the steps cut into it. They also found her machete beside the dog, his throat cut. They threw sticks to frighten away a snake, as short as a paddle, which tried to swallow the dog's body from the rear but had too small a mouth. Snakes usually catch live animals and swallow them head first. They were a little frightened because they had never seen such a snake.

The red laplap was still tied to the vine. My mother was not attached to the other end and was nowhere in sight. The men told my aunt they left the strip there for fear of the tree spirit's anger if they climbed up and took it. They also left the machete. For no reason I asked if the loose end of the strip was cut or torn. No answer from them. They looked at me with anger and fear as if I had done something evil.

The men did not mention the face on the buttress and for some unclear reason I decided not to mention it. They must have seen it as they explored around the tree, but if they did not say so I sensed that I would be stupid to ask if they saw it. I would say nothing and let them assume I did not go to that side of the tree. Lucky for me the ground beneath the tree was firm, so I knew I left no footprints where I pissed, and the piss would have dried before the searchers got there.

My aunt said the men told her they chanted to foil *maselais* as they searched the forest for my mother's missing body until close to sunset. The next morning they went back, and the morning after that, but could not find her. My aunt told me pigs ate the dead dog that I used to beat. No one ever found her bones or her white laplap. There was no death ceremony for her and no one said they were sorry.

A week later an old man came naked to my house late at night and stood near the bottom step in the glow of my lamp. At first his face was in shade, but I could see his worn-out body and ropy arms shining with sweat, and in his right hand a machete pointed at the ground. He leaned forward so the light showed me his eyes, the white part stained yellow and the pupils tiny. He stared up at me in silence, with a cold expression. No hair. His few front teeth were black and broken and his cheeks sucked in because he had no teeth inside them. He stank like a rotten tree, dead and fallen in the forest. I had never seen him before.

After a while he asked in a voice like the hiss of wind if I saw the face on the buttress. He sounded further away than where he stood. I put my hands on my hips to pretend I was not afraid and said, "What face?" He put a foot on the bottom step and I expected him to leap at me like a younger man with a savage plan. Instead he took a long time in the dull light to shave a wart on his knee with the machete. I knew it was my mother's. He caught the tiny shavings in his spare hand so I could not use them for sorcery, then dissolved back into the darkness without another word or glance. For a long time I could smell him. In the morning there were no footprints near my house. I had swept the sandy earth around our house in the evening before he came, as we always do so that we can tell if anyone prowls at night while we sleep.

Two mornings later I found the machete on my doorstep. Again, no footprints. I still keep it near my pillow at night and grab it if I wake from a dream about the old man who stank, or the face on the tree, or my mother hanging from the vine in the breeze. Or my baby in the earth. In my dream the old man has a large penis and no navel.

Why did my mother hang herself? Was it because she thought Rand was the father of my baby? Was she jealous? Did she feel guilty for slapping him when he was about to die, even though he saved her from more attacks by my father? Surely not that guilty.

Whatever caused her to hang herself, I benefited because a few people felt sorry for me as an orphan and did not accuse me again of making trouble with the Japanese or anyone else. She was my mother, so maybe they assumed she was responsible for any problems caused by me. They could assume whatever they wanted. I did not ask and they did not tell me. Maybe they feared her spirit was still black and could inflict pain and destruction if they were unkind to me. I like to think she turned white and could not harm me, that she flew away to where the crow could not go, where the fearful owl wanted to fly to escape its agony. In case she still wanders with black skin, and consorts with the crow and pigs, I have never been deep into the forest again, even to the place where I buried my baby. I go often to the garden but always return to the village before the sun sinks behind the mountains.

The new Japanese officer from the base camp did not ask about my mother and we did not tell him about her disappearance. He was strict, not nasty. We were lucky a shark ate the pig-officer.

Near the end of the war the Japanese came more often to the village and our gardens to steal food until not much was left. If we tried to hide it they beat us. They took the last of our chickens and pigs and dogs, and pulled vegetables out of the ground too soon. We were always hungry and became skinny. We survived on coconuts, fish caught at night, and on scarce wild fruit from the forest. Sometimes we snared birds. The Japanese were not good fishermen and knew nothing of the forest. They soon shrank so much that some stayed always in the camp because they could not walk. Some who could still walk looked as if they had died already. Many did die. Some people said the Japanese ate their own dead, as we used to do before the Germans came. One day the white men came back to kill all of them, starving in burrows at their filthy camp along the coast towards Kieta. Some Japanese killed themselves with small bombs.

For about ten years after the war I worked on plantations and missions, and came and went from the village as I pleased. All the villagers except me are now Christians, or say they are. Some white missionaries from New Zealand and some black ones from Honiara in the Solomon Islands tried and failed to make me care about Jesus Christ because he wanted to save all of us from something, I am not sure what. He did not save my mother or my father, or Rand, or the officer eaten by the shark, or my crazy uncle. Jesus could not even save himself from layabouts and farmers and fishermen, let alone soldiers. The missionaries were fools to say he could have saved himself but instead decided to get speared and die for a few days, then recover his perfect body from the rot of death and disappear into the clouds, back to live with his father, who had never had a woman.

It is hard to write the truth, that the shock of my mother's hanging gave me another benefit besides people's reluctance to hurt me in words or actions. The shock meant I aborted and did not have to stop my aunt from making me drink hibiscus tea when she and others saw my belly grow. Therefore no one had another secret, this one true, to tell about me within or beyond the village. Only my mother and I knew I was pregnant. Even though I am thankful for other people's ignorance, I can never be ignorant. I wonder still if a spirit baby wanders free in the forest. Or is it confused by its dead left ear? Trapped like the owl? Has the baby's spirit met my mother's in the forest? Is Rand there with them?

I do not know why I have told only you and my mother about my pregnancy. Not to make you hang yourself.

So many years later, Rand continues to cause me much distress. Almost every day and night, bad memories go berserk in my mind like a school of fish when a man casts a net over them.

I have told you all I can. Perhaps my memories are incomplete or flawed. Too bad. I write only because telling you my story might silence you, and might help me cope with the terrible past that attacks me in the present, day after day, nightmare after nightmare. Sometimes constant pain is a bit easier to manage if you know others are aware of it, whether or not they care about you.

Most of my life I have struggled to push Rand away. He is a snake who never retreats far and always slithers back into my present, which includes the worst of my past. Long ago, in the Japanese time, my mother and I thought Rand's spirit would be contented and not harm us or anyone else, because the pig-officer who chopped off Rand's head was soon dead from a shark attack. You know that in our payback thinking one death is usually enough to retaliate for one killing. The spirit of the first victim is satisfied and goes off to a good place. He cannot ever give even minor trouble to the person who killed his attacker. People and spirits are probably like that everywhere.

There is no clear reason why Rand did not go away to a better place after the shark avenged him, back to his own country and spirits, to Jesus and Satan. He did not have to wait around and be a nuisance while he waited for someone to kill the pig-officer.

Perhaps Rand stayed to haunt me because my mother and I did not get someone to kill the commander who must have ordered the pig-officer to do the beheading. Rand might have thought himself important enough to demand two deaths, not one. Maybe it is simpler. Does he punish me because my mother spat on his face? It happened a long time ago, but time means nothing to vengeful spirits.

Sometimes when I think I have pushed Rand back a little way, you send me a letter with more questions, and so drag me closer to him when I try to sleep at night or wonder about my mother and my baby in the forest, and my father in the sea. If you are not heartless, some of the pressure of my endless past might disturb you and become your present too, not just mine. If so, I hope you can manage it better than I have done, and that someone helps you better than you have helped me.

* * *

18 September 1971. I will use a true date one last time because it is a day I have long awaited. I have kept these notebooks for two weeks after I finished them, in case I wanted to write more, or maybe decide not to send them, maybe burn them in the fire to boil water.

Do not send me another letter and do not come here. Keep my secrets and I will try to keep yours, if I hear of any. I will lie if anyone demands that I reveal them, as you have demanded of me and have therefore made me suffer in my mind and heart. Now I am going on a boat to Kieta to buy a big envelope and send these notebooks to you. As I travel I will whisper to my father if I see a stingray, his totem. Maybe he will follow the boat and watch me from the sea, and take me to live with him if I fall or jump overboard, which I might do on the way back. You will not know. Would you care? Rand might be there as a tiger shark or barracuda without a head. Some people, now dead, said the Japanese threw his head and body into the sea in two places far apart. They said no more before they died, so do not bother to ask me.

Ten white pages remain. I do not want to waste them but I cannot write more words to you. Maybe you can use the space to add stories you think I have forgotten or do not want to tell.

Goodbye. GOODBYE.

PART THREE

Gilbert and Ellice Islands Colony,
Western Pacific, 1971

The Millars in Paradise

Tuesday 5 October 1971. Tarawa, Gilbert Islands. Charlotte Millar itched for her husband to load the last straw onto her back. Peter Millar was custodian of a dwindling bale and would soon deposit the blade that would make her buckle; the last straw a log.

Their marriage started to flat-line as soon as they moved out of the Papua New Guinea Adventure Zone; she felt the wane but he did not. In Britain's Gilbert Islands Colony a few years later she realised she knew little more about him than when they married, and that she had lost interest in knowing.

Charlotte was at home alone with her teenage maid on the island of Tarawa, at Bairiki, the administrative capital of the Gilberts. Peter, a District Officer, magistrate and local government adviser contracted to the British Foreign and Commonwealth Office, had been away on duty to the outer islands for almost three weeks and would be away for another week, even longer if the tub they called a ship were to break down again, the only regular thing it ever did. She had sailed with him once in the previous three years and would never do it again. In calm seas, she suffered for ten days from the ship's bilious rise and twist and slide on the Western Pacific's rollercoaster swells. Diesel fumes spewed over her at sea and at anchor.

They met at Melbourne University at eighteen, in their first year of Arts. They married at twenty-two and went to Bougainville for him to work with the Australian Department of External Territories as a patrol officer, a generalist administrator with responsibility for policing, courts, elections, census, local government councils, and anything else his superiors told him to do. Charlotte spent much of the first year on a research project in Melanesian Pidgin to complete a postgraduate diploma in linguistics, started in Sydney while Peter did six months of training for the job.

Charlotte had delighted in the long foot patrols with Peter on Bougainville, two thousand kilometres to the southwest of Tarawa. He would lead and she would walk a few metres behind him, ahead of the carriers and police who strolled with a light touch, the former barefoot and the latter in black boots forced out of shape by feet tougher than the leather. She liked to watch Peter's tall frame and awkward gait, and would count his stumbles out loud. He would turn to her and grin each time he faltered. "Why do you do that?" he asked her at the end of the day on which he set a new record of 17 stumbles. In mock anger he dropped his boots onto the floor of the bamboo and thatch resthouse.

"To make the cops and carriers laugh, and because I want to see my master's pretty face and big blue eyes look back at me. You know I love your goat's hair, if not the red fluff on your chin. I wish the District Commissioner hadn't told you to try to grow a beard. You're still a boy."

"Charlotte, I love you to the moon and back but you can be such a smartarse, even an occasional bitch."

"I'll accept 'occasional'. Love you too."

After she adapted to the climate the hiking was almost always easy; the coastal tracks flat and shaded, one inland patrol route steep and tough. She liked the stealth of the rare Bougainville crow that followed them, which she never saw but sometimes heard laugh. Why did the local people never laugh with it, even when its laughter coincided with Peter's stumbles?

The villagers called her Missus Sharlet. The women, shy at first, cosseted her and contributed to her Sydney linguistics project without knowing it. She soon spoke Pidgin better than her husband.

Charlotte was never bored on patrol or at home in the town of Kieta. The wives of the other few patrol officers based there were contented, usually. Social life was busy and pleasant, at times marred by the devoted racism of a few plantation managers and their bitchy wives. Some of those wives lusted after young patrol officers, married or single. Peter seemed staunch.

Charlotte enjoyed the heavy rain and tolerated the heat, stickier than in Australian summers and always much hotter than any day she could remember from her childhood in south-eastern England before her family migrated to Melbourne.

At Bougainville she indulged Peter's obsession with the plight of Hugh Rand, a pre-war patrol officer beheaded by the Japanese at Kieta in 1943. A few years after the Bougainville sojourn she was bored and disgruntled in the Gilberts, in part because Peter could not leave his Rand mania in Bougainville. It had burgeoned.

After the lush, high island of Bougainville, Charlotte did not enjoy Tarawa atoll, a flat, 50 kilometre long, 300 metre wide string of islets of sand and crushed coral; the shape of a bent arm, a reversed capital L scribbled by a dyslexic child; no volcanic soil; infertile, parched; dominated by sea and sky and millions of coconut palms; a shallow lagoon to the west, within the reversed L; the deepest of deep open sea to the east; the highest point of land a little more than two metres above the sea at full tide.

Charlotte hated the oven of Tarawa, the glare that ricocheted off the lagoon and sand and sky, the rareness of rain, and the wind that loaded itself with salt and blew sticky all day and night from the open ocean, swinging northeast to southeast and back again across the year of relentless nothingness. Only salt and birds rode the wind over that sea from the Americas for 10,000 kilometres, too far for fragrance or dreams to fly. The clatter of palm fronds was not the rustle of Bougainville evenings that had romanticised her into serenity beyond time and place. No Adventure Zone here.

She despised Tarawa's expatriate social life, controlled by a clique of pretentious bitches with contrived accents of the English upper-middle class. To her, if not to Peter, their lives were a play; they acted out to one another their English poshness and veneer of self-control on a stage far from home. "Out here," they would say, as if they were on Mars, looking back to Tunbridge Wells.

She remembered enough from her childhood, and had learned enough as a qualified linguist, to pick the fakes. The more extravagant the act the more likely the actress's husband cultivated a smirk and a bored Eton-Oxbridge gaze directed over his interlocutor's shoulder. A few men and women would use the Royal impersonal pronoun 'one'; they might revert to 'you' after a few drinks. Charlotte called them 'monos'. The Scots and Welsh who kept the colony running, as they had done for most of the Empire, tended to be less pretentious than the English but most did affect an English accent, a little short of Received Pronunciation—the BBC standard taught to them at private schools such as Edinburgh's Fettes College.

Some of the women and their visiting daughters cultivated pretty English voices like Charlotte's, which was genuine. Several men practised laryngeal constriction that sounded to her like the product of tedium, constipation and insomnia, and in extreme cases the added misfortune of a bare-foot step in dog shit, or a fishbone caught in the throat. The performances a suit of armour that one should wear in the colonies if one were British, shouldn't one? Her father had played at being ultra-British until Australia slapped much of it out of him, so that he learned to speak well without lordliness.

The would-be aristocrats who most annoyed and amused Charlotte—she called them 'awistocwats'—were those who substituted a designer impediment just short of a clear 'w' for a voiced 'r' or 'l', like the patricians of Kent and some of the more absurd caricatures in Dickens. Two senior men would also convert an 's' to a lispish 'th'. "Oh, on Thunday you're going to Bwitten on weave? Any thpethific planth?"

As almost every woman listened more to herself than to others there was much clipped chatter but little conversation. Charlotte was not supposed to hear the only exchange that interested her during the previous two years, between two matrons who reminisced about a door-key party in Dar-Es-Salaam, long ago when they were still likely to get an invitation. Many women were fretful in mind and frail in liver by the age of forty. Some husbands of worn-out wives had a taste for the fattish local girls. Peter assured Charlotte they did not appeal to him and that they were robust, not fattish.

He chided her after almost two years of forbearance. "What the hell is wrong with you? You can't praise or even tolerate anyone, Brits or locals. Do you seriously object to clear, careful speech that screws up a bit after a few drinks? Yours does. The Brits don't fake their accents any more than you and I fake ours. We've converged a fair bit over the last few years, not because we're fakes but because we've lived in one another's pockets."

With a touch of sadness, much exaggeration but no guilt, she replied, "That's the most you've said to me in one hit for two years without mentioning Hugh fucking Rand."

"A lot of them also speak fluent Gilbertese and a few other languages. My Gilbertese is okay." Then the barb: "You're a professional linguist. How's yours? And do you see here the racism we saw in New Guinea from a few patrol officers and other suspects?" She conceded that she did not. Easy to explain, she said. No loggers or planters here. Admittedly more refined administrators, most of them with higher formal education than the patrol officers—the *kiaps*. She said her issue was with British conceits, not everything British.

To mollify Peter, she said more Australians and Americans should listen to themselves and adjust their speech. In unfamiliar territory, too many amplified their received intonation, accent and loudness with clownish effect, just as the British donned their linguistic suit of armour. Thank Christ for Peter's mother, who spoke well and passed the trait to him. He and Charlotte knew his accent annoyed some Britons because it did not match the Australian ocker stereotype they liked to mock.

A month after his rebuke she sabotaged a dinner party of seven guests and the host, Crispin Pike, a senior Treasury accountant; a bore, a bachelor whom in private she called 'Spwat' or 'the Grilled

Fish'. The dinner dragged out as Pike held the floor. She gagged on the last of her too many gins and giggled for much too long when he said, with the nasal resonance she abhorred in the most pretentious of the Britons, "The Pwime Minister bwought the Bwitish and Fwench together but Fiewd Marshaw Montgomewy awmost bwew the wewasonsip." In the post-giggle hush of stares she asked, "Cwispin, is it twue that he couldn't towewate De Gauwe?"

Ten mute seconds. The host snapped at her with dictionary perfect pronunciation and minimal resonance: "Mrs Millar, you are even more stupid than I thought you were when you arrived in Bairiki." He stared at the door until the Millars rose to leave. Four of his five other guests seized the moment and did the same.

She teased Peter as they ambled home in the moonlight: "Please do go on giving me the silent treatment. I love the way you sigh. A casuarina in the breeze."

"Plug it."

"Wewax, Darwing. Did one's wifey dwink too much? So sowwy. Weawy, I am. Pwease bewieve me."

"Hilarious, Charlotte. I have to work with Pike and the others while you hide at home. Too often you think something is funny but no one else does. Your mother and father warned me."

"Stop it, Peter. You know Pike is so far up himself his guts are on the outside. He pisses me off. He's a prat. You winced tonight when he said how wonderful it was to be in the front row a year ago at the Proms at Royal Albert Hall. I'll bet you were thinking what I was thinking."

"What was I thinking?"

"That he's the dickhead who leaps to his feet and yells 'Bravo! Bravo!' while the orchestra plays the last three notes."

"That would be 'Bwavo!' wouldn't it? You're inconsistent."

"Care to punish me when we get home? I've been getting away with far too much."

Through the darkness a cheerful male voice called from the

beach, thirty metres away. "Beautiful, Charlotte! Loved it. Truly. Peter, you're a lucky boy. Night!"

"Who was that?" she asked Peter.

"Aidan Conway. He was quiet tonight."

* * *

By 5pm on 5 October 1971, on the aforementioned day when she was at home alone with her teenage maid while Peter was on administrative tour to the outer islands, Charlotte's disposition was lethal. Her mind hunted for someone to ridicule. She might go to the Bairiki Club and seek a target. She needed another gin-tonic. No, not the club. She would have it at home rather than walk half a kilometre there, into the endless circular narrative about the impending disaster of Independence.

After some reflection she decided that the prospect of a local governance disaster was not the main worry of these loyal colonial administrators. A well-founded fear of identity loss caused the biting of nails. Whitehall would dump most of them back in Britain, foreign refugees with little money, no job, no servants, and not much hope of getting any of those things. They would have none of the political, administrative and social power they all had in the Gilberts and some had wielded in other colonies as far back as the Indian Raj, Ceylon, Malaya, Hong Kong, Rhodesia, and Nigeria; and in Kenya before the horror of Mau Mau. The most employable in other roles, including business and perhaps diplomacy, would be the smug few with experience in Hong Kong, the jewel that Britain would have to return to China before the turn of the century through diplomatic process. The British could not demur as mainland China controlled the water supply to the main island from the New Territories, for which the lease to Britain would expire in 1997. Too risky to cut a water deal with a sleeping dragon that might turn off the taps over some perceived slight. Despite the transfer of sovereignty, business deals in Hong Kong would flow and international companies would beg for Britons with experience there.

The End of Empire. The end of identity, without anyone using the word. On and on it went at Bairiki, evening after evening, as dusk and gloom settled on a relic of the Empire on which the sun was not supposed to set.

A few weeks after Charlotte and Peter arrived in Tarawa, and still bothered to go to the club, Harold Busch, one of the few Gilbertese members, a trader and rogue of part-German origin, interrupted the broken record with a heartfelt speech he had longed to make, as he wobbled to the door on his way home after too many drinks. "Chins up, my dear Britannic friends. Pretend you are merely going soon on a long holiday to Manchester or Glasgow or wherever. We'll stuff things up so badly here that we'll have to beg you to come back after six months. Tomorrow I'm off to visit my daughter at Cambridge. See you back here in a couple of weeks to report on the condition of Old Blighty." Harold paused to enjoy the silence. "I don't know if any of you have kids at Cambridge. If you do, let me know and I'll take them out for lunch. Nigel, old bean, I'm sorry but I can't make it to Bradford."

No, not the club tonight. Not without Peter. She did not think she could bite her tongue. She longed for a visit from her two Gilbertese friends, young female teachers. Peter had been unfair to accuse her of not liking local people. The pair always cheered her up, less with their infectious laughter than their languor of mind and body. They would sit cross-legged on the floor, contented and willing to chat at whatever pace and level suited Charlotte. She was sure Peter lusted after them, if only in his head. She became wary when he said, as he watched them saunter away from the house, "They walk as if they want someone to catch up with them." She replied, "Don't even move."

Maybe he had caught up with them. Where were they now? On tour with him? On that bloody tub? School was in recess for the end of term. She had not seen them for several weeks. Fucking hell.

Abstinence was on her mind. Her lust in Bougainville had given way to torpor due, in her mind, to Peter's habit of talking in bed about Hugh Rand. Why, then, had his interest also waned? Soon after they arrived in Tarawa the governor's wife warned her, during high tea, to be diligent. "The girls are flighty fowl, my dear, and your husband is a lovely rooster. They will entice him in order to get revenge on you and the rest of us because our men still hold power over theirs, if not for much longer."

She was sure Peter had not strayed at Bougainville or anywhere else, so why would he do it here? She was prettier than most Gilbertese women and had splendid legs, not their tree trunks; and a good figure, perhaps a little full in the chest but firm; about right in waist and hips and buttocks. Her feet pretty, not slabs with callused soles. She would have preferred symmetrical feet without the pigeon-toed turn of the left. Cute, Peter assured her. "Gives you an erotic twist. To men it looks guarded and enticing." He also said Michelangelo could not have sculpted a more sensual back and neck, or prettier ears.

She cropped her long hair soon after they arrived. Its blackness could compete with the colour and sheen of the local girls' hair but not the beauty of its flow to the waist. "I'm not too tall, or so short that I'm a bloody midget. A bit taller than their average. I've got less bulk and a higher centre of gravity. I don't have their tired elephant sway when I walk. All fine." Ubiquitous dark eyes, half shut and lazy, could not compete with hers—limpid emerald, wide open, alert. Delicate ears; studded with tiny pearls, a gift from Peter the day after they first coupled at university. Loved and always wore them. A few well-placed freckles on face and body.

Physical condition as-new, two months short of 28; local women much older by 20; often matronly at 28, with multiple fattish brats.

Peter would not stray. He had become a sexual sloth and she preferred frugality over the Bougainville feast of two or three years ago. She whispered to herself, "We're both much less greedy than we used to be. It's this bloody place. It reduces everyone to catalepsy. Boredom. Liver failure."

"Go home Ngauea," Charlotte called to the maid. "I'll cook my own dinner."

"Yes Missus Sarlot. See you tomorrow."

Charlotte would not eat. Instead she would have a second gin-tonic and perhaps a couple more after that. She would sit beneath the fan and watch the glare fade on the ceiling as the sun set and its rays no longer fired pain off the lagoon into her eyeballs through the mosquito-wired windows and French doors.

The second gin was half gone and the glare still harsh when Alastair Todd-Willox hailed her through the door screen. 'Al Todd' until three months earlier when he got promoted, and added a hyphen and his mother's maiden name.

"Come in Al," she called. "Feel free to bring your Astair suffix and your hyphenised Mum."

"Funny girl, aren't you Charlotte? Hilarious. I'll bring Aidan Conway as well if you can handle the Welsh. We're heading for the club and we've got mail for you. Well, we think it's for you and your apparent master, from someone who can't spell your name. A package."

"Bring him and it in. Any Welshman can take refuge here."

Alastair was Deputy Secretary to the Chief Minister, and responsible for broad administration of the whole colony apart from Tarawa. Peter's immediate superior. Aidan a former teacher at the local high school, five kilometres away; after an indiscretion, now an education bureaucrat based at government headquarters in Bairiki.

Gregarious Alastair, unfortunately faced; about forty; bald as glass. He would have parted his locks on the right, like all elite-school boys here, when he had some; lower British mortals in such areas as shipping and procurement parted on the left. Shortish, skinny, a non-smoker with a smoker's gasp; cyanotic road-map on a narrow nose, pointy and always catching a bad smell; lipless mouth cut with a broad axe; lizard eyes of grey with yellowish whites; koala ears without the fur.

Aidan also good-humoured but more reticent; about fifty; tallish, a little plump but not fat; short blonde hair, unparted; probably no grey camouflaged in it yet; wide eyes of brown below inquisitive brows; cupid-bow mouth under a straight, symmetrical nose; graceful ears, almost flat. Attractive, not handsome; fortunately faced.

Both men single, Alastair because three years earlier his wife over-dined on wine and barbiturates at the end of a holiday in England to mother their three children for a week at a hotel near their boarding school. Aidan single because a security guard asked Mrs Conway for a bribe after he spied her husband through a shutter-crack at night, tutoring a schoolgirl who lay beside her uniform on his office mat of fresh pandanus leaf.

Aidan left his shoes at the door, and Alastair his sandals, worn daily with long green socks and Bombay bloomers. Aidan always wore cotton trousers, khaki or white. At the beach she noticed he had better legs than most of the young foreign men, including Peter, who all wore variations on Alastair's unofficial uniform, with shoes not sandals, thank Christ. Alastair sometimes made himself look even sillier with a Gilbertese fisherman's hat, a squat cone of pandanus leaf stitched onto a palm-rib frame; shaped like a Chinese coolie's hat but less broad. On rare days when the wind was not too strong to displace it, Peter wore an expensive Panama, battered, with bits of broken straw glued back into place, more or less. Every time Charlotte saw and smelled the abomination, on or off his head, she also saw a camel's back.

"Gentlemen, there's ice, tonic and gin in the refrigerator. No Dom Perignon today. The village trade store is out of stock. Help yourselves. Sorry about the lime and lemon deficit. Market forces.

Peter took the Scotch with him, your official evening tipple. I know you are expected to prefer it after 4 pm but if you pretend you're at home alone and have a gin I won't tell anyone."

"Home is where the gin is," said Aidan en route to the kitchen to get the drinks. Alastair chose the planter's chair that would give him the best view of Mrs Millar's legs. He sat on its edge, leaned towards her and rocked a little from side to side as he handed over the package—a crammed C3 envelope, 32.4 x 45.8 cm; coffee-brown, tattered. Postmarked Kieta, Bougainville, Papua New Guinea, and addressed to DO Masta Peter Millar or Missus Sharlet, Chief Minister's Office, Bairiki, Tarawa. 'Gilbert Islands, Western Pacific' was added by another hand. On the back, 'From Bos Simeon'. It looked and felt as if it held a book or books, foolscap, hard cover.

Alastair said it didn't look official or he would have kept it at the office for Peter. "And I do suspect you are Missus Sharlet or thereabouts."

"I know who it's from," she said. "I'll open it after you go. Don't feel deprived. It's probably some boring historical research that Peter asked a friend in New Guinea to do for him." She told herself to burn it before Peter got home.

"Not the dreaded Hugh Rand fixation, I trust?"

"Afraid so." Charlotte flipped the package onto the floor and pushed it aside with her foot as Aidan returned with two drinks. When he saw her empty glass he gave her his drink, the other to Alastair, and went to make another for himself.

"Second World War stuff," said Alastair. "Look, Charlotte, between you and me, he more than pulls his weight with things that need to be done but he is a tad over-cooked about that period, you know. It was a long time ago. Coast watchers, head-lopping. That sort of tosh. He was into it from the time you came here, and he's not going to let up, my dear. A few days from now, starting on 9 October, he'll chaperone the first delegation of Japs coming to get war bones and other souvenirs from Betio, and to lament in private the inequity of their loss. He's an expert about that stuff but that doesn't help us knock this place into shape for the big exit. It's not far down the track."

"Al, don't I know what he's like? Don't I bloody well know it? It drives me mindless and legless."

"You are definitely not legless, my dear. Sorry, shouldn't have said that. By the end of the day one's executive function starts to pack up." She flicked away the flirtation and sipped her gin.

Alastair sucked his first drink since his two lunchtime gin-tonics and leaned back in the chair to savour the flow of Charlotte's legs from her bare toes to the hem of her dress, well up her thighs but held in modest place by her left fist.

Aidan returned with his drink, tasting it for muscle along the way. He sat on the less strategic of the two planter's chairs to contemplate Charlotte. "Look here, Charlotte. Peter's been away a long time and you sit here by yourself, day after day, night after night. You don't mix much with the memsahibs. We're off to the club for a couple of hours. Don't stay here alone. The place is tough enough without self-imposed loneliness. Peter will be having a great time at a village feast. Come with us. We'll shout you dinner of sorts and walk you back later, won't we Al? Alastair."

"We shall do that with much pleasure and minimal ado. Come on Charlotte, you know we all think you're a treat compared with the harridans that think they run the entire social life of this place."

"The worn-out bitches? Is that what you want to say?"

"That's not quite what Alastair means, Charlotte. Not quite. Is it Alastair?"

"Um, not quite. Not every last one of them."

"Thanks gentlemen," said Charlotte, with a mild grin, "but this is my third G-T for the evening and I plan and expect to collapse early."

"How about tomorrow, then?" said Alastair. "Can you make it Aidan, old fellow? No better-half now to chain you to the bed."

"Indeed I can. Come on Charlotte. Please. Yes for tomorrow. It will give you something to get excited about for the next twenty-four hours."

"Thanks gentlemen. The last bit convinced me. What shall I wear? Shall I get the village seamstress to tailor an evening gown? High heels? A fox fur?"

"Come as you are now," said Alastair. "That would be fine, very fine indeed."

"Time to go," said Aidan. "See you tomorrow at six, Charlotte. Thanks for the G-T."

Charlotte stayed where she was as they let themselves out. She gulped most of her drink and got up to close the door and the window shutters, despite the heat, to disappoint eyes that waited on the beach and in nearby houses for the lights to go on.

She turned on the lights and turned up the ceiling fan until it thumped out a gale and threatened to tear itself loose, to hack her and the furnishings into debris and offal. The racket stifled the roar of the sea on the southern reef, the barrier against rollers that hurtled across the Pacific from the northeast and then curled around the fulcrum of Tarawa's easternmost point—the atoll's elbow—before they charged towards her prison at Bairiki on the southern stretch of the island.

Charlotte picked up the envelope from Kieta and sat in the chair beneath the fan. Around the postage stamp she saw dried spittle infused with red betel chew. She had tried to be sociable to the men while part of her brooded on the address from the time Alastair gave her the package. "Missus Sharlet"?

Peter had written to Bos Simeon several times to ask questions about Hugh Rand that she and other villagers on Bougainville could not or would not answer while the Millars were there. He gave Charlotte his drafts to skim. They included inanities like "Charlotte sends her greetings and longs for the happy days she spent with you and your friends." It was bullshit but she let it pass. She never saw the final versions. Peter kept the copies at his office.

Bos Simeon was not stupid. Sharlet? Missus Sharlet? When they were in Bougainville there was no cause or opportunity for Bos to see 'Charlotte' in writing. Therefore Peter must have removed all reference to her, at least by name, from the despatched versions of his Tarawa letters. Why? She hissed, "Sharlet? Sharlet? What the fuck!" A whiff of straw twitched her nostrils.

Coconut oil, mould and cheap perfume clashed with straw when she ripped open the envelope. Inside were three cardboard-covered school notebooks, foolscap size, grubby, each about a centimetre thick. The covers titled 1, 2 and 3. Bos's Pidgin script, in sharp pencil on both sides of the page, was tiny and hard to read but its flow along the blue lines suggested consistent speed and rhythm. Almost no corrections. No paragraphs; full-stops the only punctuation.

Burn the notebooks? Yes. Easy enough to manage Peter's annoyance if Al or Aidan were to tell him about the package; easier than managing the heightened obsession with Rand that the content might trigger. But the notebooks might contain nothing significant and so dampen his obsession. And to burn them and be found out would surely obsess Peter more, and drive her to the wall as he fantasised about what might have been in them. To burn, or not to burn: that was the question. Read them, then decide.

Charlotte decided not to eat. She slurped the last of her gin-tonic and settled back to read the first notebook. A metre and a half above her the fan drummed at her ears and evaporated the sweat on her arms and legs and in her hair and dress. She cooled a little in mind and body; gripped the pages hard together to compose herself and prevent riffle by the fan.

After five pages her Pidgin returned to its Bougainville fluency. Well before she finished the notebook an hour and two gins later she could smell a stack of straw bales through the perfume, mould and coconut. She mixed another drink, turned down the fan and went outside; sat on the doorstep of coral block and listened to the menace of the fucking waves, all the way from Hawaii, trying to breach the southern reef. Tonight she could see no moon, but when it was bright she would often sit here to watch it rise smug above the battle between sea and reef from which it became ever more distant and safe. Not long ago she said to Peter, "Why doesn't the reef wear away, the way this bloody place wears at me?" He replied: "You know what, Charlotte? That sort of racket on the reef was probably the last thing Rand heard."

As Charlotte sat on the block she craved a benign obsession to draw her away from the boredom that nurtured too many emotions and other phenomena starting with 'dis'—disdain, disenchantment, disappointment, disgust, disaffection, disagreement, disadvantage, discord, distrust, disloyalty, dishonesty, disarray, disaster, distress, disrepair. Could she not surrender to the refuge of religion, even a faith as naïve as the syncretistic one the Gilbertese and Bougainvilleans now embraced in their flight to Christianity, away from the sinister forces that defined the tradition of their forebears? Life would be easier for her, less tense, less confused. Islam? No, too strict, too male-dominated. Buddhism? No, too static, too many flower children. Forget the idea.

She wanted to cry but refused because emotional upset might interfere with her search for the last straw, which she expected to find in the second or third notebook. She had already inferred the straw in part and created it in another part without concern for which part was which, like an academic who needs to find order in chaotic data and does not fret over the difference between extraction, massage and imposition.

She often sat on the coral step when she wanted her mind to wander or concentrate, depending on mood and purpose. The ritual began a year earlier on remote Abemama Island, the Land of Moonlight, where she stagnated for three weeks while Peter worked on local government and policing problems, some of his own making. On his way to Samoa in 1889, R. L. Stevenson stayed on Abemama in a house the villagers built for him from coconut and pandanus palms. Charlotte asked the English-speaking wife of a retired Gilbertese teacher to show her the site. Just the step was still there, covered with sand, chicken shit and rotting palm-fronds. The woman swept it with a broom made from a bundle of palm-leaf spines bound with coconut coir to a stick of driftwood. A surfeit of bloody self-sufficiency. No wonder they can't see past the beach.

For the next two weeks Charlotte sat every morning on Stevenson's step for at least two hours to read, agonise, and glance now and again at the village. The Abemama lifestyle was nonchalance to Peter, drudgery to her. The women brought her young coconuts from which to drink. She could speak no Gilbertese. There could be no conversation with anyone other than the teacher's wife; soon there was nothing to discuss and the woman left her to herself. After five days only children brought coconuts. She swore never to return to Abemama, even though travel here by light aircraft eliminated the seasickness she had suffered on her one other excursion with Peter into what she called the Wasteland.

Apart from a few hours on the step, she found nothing to do on this trip but swelter away the days on her bed in fitful naps until Peter got back to the resthouse each evening. Then she had to suffer his stories about wartime Abemama, which always led to Rand's fate at Kieta. Rand a dead man she had never met, about whom she knew too little to give him shape or character, of whom she had not seen a photograph. How could this nonentity imperil her marriage and annoy her so much on a godforsaken island thousands of kilometres from where he lost his head to a Japanese swordsman thirty years earlier?

Charlotte stayed celibate for the three weeks on Abemama because she was glum and Peter was too tired to seek what he called his 'nightcap'.

Early one afternoon a drawn out scream shattered her restless nap. She leapt from the bed, tripped as she tangled her bare feet in the mosquito net, and ran outside in terror. Fifteen metres away, at the top of the beach, two men held a trussed pig on a bed of pandanus leaves; held it there with their knees, hands and bodyweight. A third man of great bulk rammed a knife between the animal's ribs and eased the blade deeper as if he had the rest of the day to push the point to its destination, the heart. The pig screeched louder, like the dog Charlotte once heard flogged to tenderise it for a Korean barbeque. The pig's agony and fear died with a yelp when the butcher leaned hard on the hilt of the slow knife as it touched the heart.

The killer saw Charlotte. He left the knife in place and stood to wipe the crimson off his hands onto his shorts. He waved to her and called out in jovial English: "Pik for you and Komisina Peter eat tonight at big feast and dancing." He withdrew the knife, took a machete from another man and hacked off the pig's head. She heard the men laugh when she vomited on the beach and ran inside.

A beheading. Oh, Jesus Christ! The bloody Rand case stuck in her cranium. As she lay on the bed she held her temples and slammed the back of her head onto the pillow until her brain ached. "Rand. Rand. No, no, no. I'm so fucking sick of it." She dozed for an hour and was calm by the time Peter came to the resthouse. He already knew she had seen the slaughter. "This village always kills pigs in that place to ensure the meat is tender. Kill a pig anywhere else and it cooks like old leather. It's on the coals now. Can you smell it? You won't have to eat it if you don't want to."

At sunset they went to the village *maneaba*, the hub and symbol of all relationships, a meeting house about thirty metres long and twelve wide, with open sides and low eaves of pandanus leaf; the eaves designed to make adults stoop to enter in self-effacement. From the outside it looked all roof, majestic, pitched steep to a central ridge ten metres high, and thatched with coconut and pandanus leaf. The rafters, beams, battens, struts, joists and braces a skeletal puzzle of coconut and pandanus poles, large and small, long and short, held together with coir and wooden pegs. The frame rested on internal coconut piers, and one and a half metre columns of coral slab a few metres apart around the edges, just within the eaves.

One hundred people waited; silent, faces lit by hurricane lamps. They sat cross-legged on pandanus mats arranged on the pounded coral floor according to complex factors of rank: sex, age, genealogy, totem, wealth, fishing and sailing prowess, and historical affiliations, such as ancestors captured long ago on other islands and brought to Abemama as slaves. The previous day Peter warned her never to mention the last criterion. She said she had no interest in that or any other status criterion in this damned museum of tedium.

They bowed under the eaves to enter; the thatch brushed her hair. The leaf smelled of pandanus to him but wheat straw to her, a smell that would stay with her all evening despite the miasma of coconut oil, sweat, frangipani, cheap perfume, kerosene smoke, half-cooked pork, burnt fish, boiled rice, and sinewy chicken roasted in coconut cream with chunks of *babai*, the giant swamp taro, as tasty and digestible as wet chipboard.

An old man—an *unimane*—ushered them to their mats, laid on the lagoon side, the west, in the middle of a line of twelve senior men. Peter sat cross-legged with ease; Charlotte did so with pain and ignored the old man's whispered permission, translated by Peter, for her to break the rules of posture. She could wrap her sarong from hip to calf and sit on her haunches with her knees bent and feet pointed behind her, where no one sat to be offended by her soles.

She endured the pain as they heard a few speeches and used forks and spoons to eat the food served to them in china bowls by two semi-clad girls, who grinned at Peter but ignored her. One seemed to grin longer than the other. Like the old men, the visitors drank a choice of coconut toddy or warm South Pacific Lager. Charlotte asked Peter why there was pork in his bowl but not hers.

"Because word travels faster here than a pig-squeal."

No conversation between or after the speeches. People ate and drank, and drank again. After an hour of pain Charlotte uncrossed her legs and squatted as the old man had suggested. He nodded approval and grinned at her. Peter returned the nod and grin on her behalf. The women and girls giggled.

Three girls, crowned with flowers and dressed in pandanus leaf skirts slung low, thwarted her plan to feign migraine and go home. They lined up three metres away and started to dance as four men in the middle of the crowd crashed out a simple beat on metal cans. The girls ignored her and stared at her husband's groin as they shuffled forward with hip and leg and belly movements that left her in no doubt about the intended effect on him. As part of the game he had warned her about, he faked discomfort. The girls grinned and slapped one another as they danced. The crowd shook and slapped and bellowed laughter. She saw that the women were loudest, and all seemed to watch her. The dancers and the crowd made fun of her, not Peter.

The drummers stopped. Two of the girls shook their backsides at Peter and ran back into the crowd. The third leaned forward, her breasts a half-metre from his nose, and offered her hands to him. Charlotte could smell the girl's skin mingle with the straw whiff of her skirt. She was sure the girl wore no underwear. Peter took her hands as if he knew her well, and allowed her to pull him to his feet as the crowd clapped and cheered. The drummers resumed their drunken can-bashing, even more artless than before. The audience raucous, all their clamour directed at Charlotte. The arseholes.

The dance was lewd and her bastard of a husband had done it before with that little harlot. Charlotte was sure they had more than danced. The crowd knew it, and she could see they took pleasure in a secret they thought hidden from her.

As soon as Peter finished the beer handed to him after the dance ended and the girl giggled off into the hugs and slaps and squeals of her friends, Charlotte's migraine came on. After a men's dance that seemed to represent injured ostriches paddling a swamped canoe, she insisted Peter take her home, which he was happy to do because the traditional entertainment always gave way to an absurd adaptation of Chubby Checker's twist, shuffled to the banality of two or three mistuned ukuleles.

They strolled mute to their house and went to bed without a word or touch. An hour later, as Charlotte's mind whirled, Peter mumbled something about Abemama being the sole island in the Gilberts where women preferred oral to penile sex. "How do you know?" she asked. He sat up.

"The nurse who runs the aid post told me when I asked her why the population of Abemama was stable, whereas it was growing on all other islands if you adjusted for migration to Tarawa."

"Okay then. Listen to me. I think you've snuffled and fucked the girl you danced with tonight. Have you?"

"Nonsense. That tease is part of a game. We're written into it. On Abemama, more than other islands, I reckon it's to show colonials like us where the real power lay in the past and lies in the future. To bring us down a peg or two as we pass through. There's an unusual local monarchy in the background here, quite strong. Polynesian structure on Abemama, not Micronesian like most of the colony. The only way to temper the routine is to go along with the stage directions but play around a bit to show you understand the plot and won't let anyone embarrass or intimidate you. Are you listening? You don't look like it. If you don't play along you'll cop it harder. Laugh more, for Christ's sake. That's what they want and expect."

"Sounds like an interactive playbook. Nonsense."

"Nonsense? Don't you think you wrote yourself into the pig-kill this afternoon? For centuries they've killed pigs on that spot. You put yourself on that stage with your prima donna reaction. Vomiting on cue. You wrote yourself into their script, on their terms. Too late to edit that touch of creativity."

"Crap. Have you screwed her?"

"No. Go to sleep."

A minute later she said, "Admit you've been at her and I'll invite you to talk about Rand before you find a way to mention him anyway."

He was already asleep. An image of Rand, a nuisance of indistinct face, invaded her skull and stayed there all night. The image faded once to let her doze, then reasserted itself, now headless and with neck bleeding, to jolt her awake. She tried to focus on the roar of the surf on the reef on the other side of the island, and the slapping of the ebb tide on the lagoon beach a few metres from her bed. For the first time she wanted the sea to distract her, to be louder and more aggressive upon its normal loudness and aggression.

Even as the tide waned, here and at Tarawa, she could never hear it ebb and rest; only hear it bash the reef and slap the beach, louder than it was to anyone else. Were they all deaf? A week after they arrived at Bairiki she complained at low tide about the incessant racket from the lagoon and ocean beaches. Peter insisted she go with him to the lagoon to prove the sea on that side was calm and had retreated by more than a hundred metres across the sand.

From the house she had heard the lagoon and could hear it now; but she conceded that most of the sea noise at that time did come from the reef on the other side of the island, where she asserted the waves pounded no quieter than at high tide.

No doubt about it—constant noise from the lagoon. Her concern was not its measurable level on a particular day at a particular time. The sea at low or high tide, or anywhere between, always seemed to rally on both sides of the island for an attack on her mind. She ignored Peter when he said, "The waves on Bougainville didn't bother you. You said you enjoyed what you now call a racket, and you hear a racket on the lagoon side where everyone else hears nothing. Maybe you have tinnitus."

At Abemama, Charlotte's image of Rand dissolved when Peter stirred at dawn. To reorient her mind she nudged him: "Yesterday morning when I was sitting on Stevenson's step two women came up to me and started to sweep around me as if that's why they were there. But it wasn't, I could tell. They stopped and one of them asked me something like 'Missus Sarlot, *era ko nanokawaki?*' They didn't speak English, and they must have known I don't speak Gilbertese. Peter, are you listening to me? They whispered to one another, then the second woman grimaced and held her hand in front of her face. Then she took it away and I saw a smile. Then she raised her eyebrows a few times, the way they do to flag a question. What did she mean?"

"So, before the bloody roosters have crowed we're more talkative than ever, and interested in the local language at last, are we? You remembered what she said well enough. Roughly, 'Cheer up. Why are you so bloody miserable all the time?' You should have picked it from her gesture. Hope you smiled back."

"Of course I did." She had not.

He said it was a pity they had not come to Abemama during the school term as she could have read English stories to the students to cheer her up, to make her *kukurei*. She could offer to read anyway as a lot of children were around. No, she didn't feel like it. Anything medical she could do here? Peter said there was no call for the first aid she applied in Papua New Guinea. Unlike most Bougainville villages, this one had an aid-post and a barefoot nurse trained and supplied to do more than clean sores and apply bandages, the limits of Charlotte's medical skills.

As on Bougainville, the women and children were kind to her, other than at *maneaba* feasts; but here communication was limited because so few spoke any English. Peter spoke Gilbertese but she did not want to learn it, beyond a grasp of its structure, for fear the skill would lessen her resolve to get away from this hole which had none of the beauty, intrigue and cultural depth of Papua New

Guinea. The Gilberts a punishment; Bougainville an adventure, a prize. Bougainville further from the Gilberts than Heaven from Hell.

Peter worried about her disdain for the Gilberts and her consistent rejection of any attempt to soften her impressions. In bed at Abemama the night after the *maneaba* feast he said, "They're the toughest people I've ever met. To survive here you have to be tough. Australian desert Aborigines are tough too but they can wander off somewhere else when they need to. These people can't."

"Eureka! Their geography constricts their imagination. That's why there's bugger-all to the culture."

"Stop it, Charlotte. The Bougainvilleans are in the same situation. They're stuck where they live. What's the difference? And I think you meant 'affects', not 'constricts'. This culture is a lot richer than you want to think."

"The difference? Can't you see it? For a start, the dancing here doesn't connect to another dimension the way it does in Bougainville. Here it's mere entertainment. Peter, you are a bright boy in some ways but sometimes dim as a snuffed candle. And I meant constricts, as in boa constrictor. Go to sleep. If you mention Rand I'll constrict your neck."

"Have an intelligent look at the men's dancing next time. Think of frigatebirds, central to their culture. Don't dwell on the girls' tits and arses. Try to be a bit more of a local. Adjust to the geography, don't try to fight it. I preferred Bougainville too. Adapt to what you have. It won't change to suit you. And take the advice you're always giving me about Rand. Ignore him. He's my interest."

* * *

Stevenson had the sense to endure the Gilberts for only two months and move on to Samoa; Charlotte was still in Bairiki, where she sat dinnerless on a block of coral outside her house, late at night, full of gin but unaffected by it. Peter on tour.

When she could no longer bear the mosquitoes she went inside to the kitchen; drank two glasses of the boiled water she swore was tainted by the teaspoon of kerosene splashed into the house tank every month to stop mosquitoes from breeding there. No one else could taste it. Peter said the routine was mandatory but futile because most mosquitoes bred in the tiny pools where fronds joined the trunks of coconut palms. "Fascinating," she had replied.

Back in the living area she stood and stared at the notebooks on her chair for two minutes. To fill in time and practise her Pidgin, she would translate them into English. The fan had driven the torn envelope into a corner where she saw it flap; the wings of a beheaded chicken. "Oh, Christ! Beheading! What a bloody ridiculous association. If there's anyone up there, exorcise all memory of the Rand case from me and I'll become a nun. A Carmelite. I'm already back to virginity."

By 1am she had read all three notebooks. Bos Simeon had created in Charlotte's mind an individual to replace the nondescript image of Rand, who had been almost always headless, and with no clear features when he did have a head. From Bos's encounters with him and her description of the execution, including the dynamics of the severed head, Charlotte now discerned a shortish, awkward man with sandy hair; his distinctive clothing tattered and stained; awful injuries and much blood. No voice or face but aspects of his individuality rammed into her brain, where he registered pride, intelligence, fortitude, fearlessness; and the personality of a psychopath to rival the Japanese officer and his dogs. He stank.

She switched off the fan and lights and felt her way along the wall to her bedroom. Stripped to sleep naked on a sheet still pungent from her sweat of the night before. In the dark she switched on the ceiling fan and set the speed low to stir up enough breeze to buffet mosquitoes away from rips in the bed-net, a floor-length cube attached to wall-hooks by cords from its top corners.

Charlotte could not see Rand but knew he stood at the foot of the bed all night; sensed him through the net with minor fear and much annoyance. She did not want distraction while she considered the likelihood of her husband's infidelity with the mature Bos Simeon and the Abemama dancer. The sole discernible sound from Rand was a normal breathing pattern. She dozed for half an hour when he left her at about 4am.

She rose at dawn with her neighbours' roosters, the only time of day cool enough for prolonged sex if she and Peter could be bothered; not often. During the previous fitful night with Rand she decided Peter was getting it somewhere else and may have done the same in Bougainville, where the suspicion did not occur to her as the girls there did not seem to tempt him. Soon after they arrived at Kieta he said her allure made them gender-neutral to him, if not to his colleagues, plantation managers, a Catholic priest from Kentucky and the Seventh Day Adventist pastor from New Zealand.

Before the maid arrived at 7.30 Charlotte had typed a quarter of volume one of Bos's notebooks. As she translated from Pidgin to English she improved the flow, refined the punctuation and introduced paragraphing; otherwise tried to capture Bos's character and style.

Charlotte mulled over choice of words. 'The dog dribbled', 'slavered', 'drooled' or 'spat' as the best translation for *dok i spet tumas*, the dog spat a lot? Settled for 'drooled spit'; risked redundancy to enrich an image. 'Old man' or 'geriatric' for *lapun* in the context of near-death? Geriatric. Yes, geriatric; old man too general—Bos refers to an old man about to exhale his last. The first of the two men who rape her on the beach 'spills his water'—*kapsaitim wara*; the second 'capsizes his canoe'—*kapsaitim kanu*. Both mean ejaculate but that word detracts from the richness of Bos's metaphor, so Charlotte settles on 'spilled his water' for the first and 'fell overboard' for the second. Fake gentility must not veil mindset. Bougainvillean villagers do not 'defecate' or 'urinate' or 'relieve themselves'; therefore *pekpek* must translate as 'shit' and *pispis* as 'piss'. From discussion with Bougainville women, including Bos, she decided they do not 'make love' or 'have sex'—*puspus* best translates as 'fuck'.

Peter's oral Pidgin was fluent but long written tracts bored him. He would skip detail, which gave her credible reason to prepare an English version for him to allay her *taedium vitae* at Bairiki. He would not ask for a reason, just glance over the original notebooks, pass them from hand to hand a few times and smell them with nostalgia for a more beguiling place to live and work.

He would read only her translation. She would retype an early page to exclude Bos's accusation that Charlotte had betrayed woman-to-woman confidence when she told him Bos had known and feared Rand, who still marred her life; that the betrayal begot Peter's harassment of Bos in person at Bougainville and by letter from Tarawa. Charlotte was not about to accept any responsibility for Peter's Rand mania. Peter had never reminded her how he heard about Rand's connection with Bos; Charlotte would bank on his having forgotten the source.

Charlotte finished typing the first notebook mid-afternoon; napped for an hour under a fan to help her endure an evening at the Bairiki Club with Al and Aidan. She showered and put on a knee-length dress of Indonesian linen, strapless, sleeveless, white and loose, with a built-in brassiere of soft cotton. Put on flat sandals, then sat outside on the step to await her escorts.

She looked up at low billows of maroon and dark blue cloud, an unusual formation for this often cloudless desert in the ocean. The sun shone through a break on the western horizon. She wanted the cloud cover to grow into a starless bank and pour rain upon the night. It would rain; she would come to wish it had not.

The men crunched along the path of coral pebbles at 6pm when the sun was on the wane and yellowing rich off the clouds. She held her head back and pretended not to hear them. From three metres away, Aidan made his fingertips brush her flawless skin, from the top of her dress along the flow of her neck to the tip of her raised chin. Sculpted with Bernini's touch and lustred coffee-cream by the brush of Ingres. Aidan's fingers imagined their way along each side of her jaw to velvet earlobes pierced with tiny studs of pearl. He wanted to rush to her, lean over and sniff her hair.

Alastair torpedoed the spell. "Petite ear-rings shine in the golden sunset! One doesn't see them often here, does one? Lovely, Charlotte." Aidan nodded and grinned at her while he tried to retain the image of her head tilted back.

She tried not to baulk at Al's impersonal pronoun, affected twice in a short sentence. He had never used it before he created his hyphen and retrieved the lost 'Astair' his parents gave him at birth. "Mono-man", thought Charlotte. He did not yet have the Kentish 'almost-w' or lisp but she expected him to phase them in. He helped her get up from the step.

She wanted to stroll to the club but gave up trying to control the pace when the men strode ahead as if they had not had a drink for days, as fast as they would bolt to a London pub after work. They were at their fastest when a drink awaited them. At any other time it was de rigueur for those who had attended a private school and Oxbridge, or wanted you to think they had done so, to be laconic and so demonstrate the ease with which people of their breeding could manage the Empire. At Melbourne University she had seen the trait among students from elite schools based on English models. They swotted hard late into the night for good results but pretended their life was all play and no work, that their grades had a genetic origin. In Tarawa, Peter's hyperactivity made him an impostor.

Aidan grabbed Alastair's elbow to slow him down. Charlotte had stopped. Aidan turned and saw her looking up at the last glow of what was now an unbroken sheet of rolling cloud, as restless as she seemed to be. That neck and jawline. The breasts that held up the white dress.

"Sorry Charlotte," said Aidan. "We shouldn't gallop like this.

All day we stay calm to show we're still in charge of the bloody colony. The self-control absolutely buggers and parches us. Can't control ourselves after we leave the Secretariat."

"Spot on," said Alastair. "We go the last two hours without water or tea to ensure we're primed for our tipple. Sorry Charlotte. It's middling silly but one has done it for so damned long one can't reform, even in the company of a ravishing woman such as thyself, can one? In we go. Athenaeum here we come." Oh, Jesus. Three 'one's' in a single sentence. That's five in ten minutes. If there had been no cloud she would have stayed alone outside for a few minutes to watch the brightest stars arrive, to transport herself as far from Bairiki and its tedium as her senses would allow. She planned to eat her fish, then swoon and have to go home. It was always fish, almost always trevally; not always fresh but not often toxic.

Charlotte was the sole woman at the club apart from the barman's assistant, a Tarawa girl with a simple role—to be watched by fifteen white men of diverse age and rank, and to collect and wash empty glasses. Shapely to them, plump to Charlotte.

None of the drinkers greeted Charlotte with more than a nod. She assumed they thought her at least a fool and perhaps a class traitor, a well-bred English girl married to an overzealous colonial; the man a peasant coddled under the wing of His Excellency the Governor, a career administrator of mediocre breeding, still not knighted. H.E. had promoted Peter Millar above most of them despite his youth and Australian origins; the letter of promotion signed in the red ink reserved for British governors. Millar was a damned impostor and second-rater without an Oxbridge degree, which several of them had with high honours; and others let you think they had unless you asked them the unforgivable question, which Charlotte had asked too often.

She knew the facts of Peter's recruitment. So did most of his critics. He was telephoned on leave in Australia by the British High Commissioner, whom he had met when the diplomat visited Papua

New Guinea. Peter was soon appointed by the British Foreign and Commonwealth Office because his Bougainville experience and record fitted him to help decentralise the Gilbert Islands administration as a prelude to Independence. No suitable Briton was available to strengthen district administration in the outer islands. Peter agreed to spend half his time there, to live hard while most of his British colleagues preferred the comfort of Tarawa and daily visits to their dedicated stools at the club, where they could avoid their wives, watch the plump or shapely girl and lament the brass handshake they would get from the British Government at Independence. He put too much enthusiasm into his work; annoyed his colleagues because he earned too many accolades from His Excellency.

The more encouragement Peter got from the governor, the more time he spent away from Charlotte. She lost interest in travelling with him because he would leave her to days of relentless boredom in a village or resthouse and have little to say to her at night, unless he tried to interest her in new speculation about Rand that had weaselled into his brain during the day while he trained local government clerks, inspected a fishery or held court.

Under the revised arrangement, with Charlotte in Tarawa and Peter away, she could evict Rand from her presence for a while but could not block his return. She expected Peter to talk about him the night he returned home and every subsequent day and night, at least once. On the rare days he did not mention Rand, the headless man still intruded on her after Peter went to sleep. As soon as they went to bed, she would expect something between a Rand mention and a lecture through the din of the sea and the clatter-clack of palm fronds in the wind. If Rand did not intrude she was relieved; not for long because she was too aware of why she felt relieved.

As Charlotte entered the club with Alastair and Aidan, Rand tagged along. In Bos Simeon's notebooks Charlotte discovered she was not the sole victim of Peter's fixation and now Rand's personal attention. For both women Rand was a lodger they could not evict. A migraine; a tumour. Malignant because Peter made him so. The tumour grew because he would not drop Rand's case as she and Bos wanted. Against himself, Peter created an unintended alliance between the two women, which Charlotte alone recognised. She expected to dwell on it all evening at the club while Rand looked on.

They sat at a small bamboo table in a corner away from the bar. Aidan said, "No Scotch this evening. Not even a G-T, Charlotte. We have a special tipple for you, and we'll have a drop ourselves. I'll get it and order our fish while I'm at it. And the gourmet rice. Weevil garnish for everyone?"

Alastair put his hands on Charlotte's. "You'll like this bottle, young Charlotte. Aidan's successor at the school got it for him yesterday in Noumea and brought it this morning on Air Pacific. Aidan drove to the school to take delivery and rushed it straight here to put in the fridge for you. Lovely. Here he is." Not even one Royal 'one'. Aidan held three champagne flutes and a flower pot with ice packed around a bottle of Bollinger. She would swoon a little later than planned.

"The glasses are mine," said Aidan. "They've been in the fridge for five hours with the bottle." When Aidan popped the cork the barman clapped and the bar guardians swivelled towards the corner table. The cork bounced off the fan and struck the glass collector on the shoulder. She did not seem to notice. The guardians swivelled back to lean on the bar.

The first frosty glass frothed too much as Aidan poured. He pulled the bottle away but the froth continued to rise. Charlotte leaned forward to suck in the bubbles before they spilled over the rim. She giggled for the first time since her faux pas at Crispin Pike's dinner. While the first glass settled she wiped the other two with the hem of her dress to remove the last of the frost, which the heat had almost cleared. "It's clean, gentleman. Spotless. Picked it up from the city laundry at 4.30 this afternoon. Not much sweat in it."

Alastair said he would take the risk.

They clinked glasses and sipped in silence. Rand withdrew. Alastair thought of Hong Kong, where his brother held exclusive distribution rights for Dom Perignon. Aidan wished he had imported champagne for his ex-wife. Charlotte drew the nuttiness deep into her lungs and savoured the fizz-dance on her tongue. The last time she and Peter drank champagne was in their hotel room after their Melbourne wedding, six years earlier.

To hell with sips and decorum. She took a swill and held it in puffed cheeks; in mock ecstasy, pouted her lips and rolled her eyes at the men. They joined in. She let the gold roll down her throat before the fizzle died. Aidan half-filled the glasses and they repeated the game until the bottle was empty. They tilted their heads back to relish the last drops just as the glass collector delivered a large burnt fish and three rice dollops to the table. "Lovely trevally. Rare species. Haven't had one since yesterday," said Alastair. "Don't take away the glasses, my little South Seas beauty. They're ours."

"South Seas?" said Aidan. "We're about 150 km north of the bloody equator."

"There's that damned geographer in you," said Alastair.

* * *

While Charlotte swilled champagne in Tarawa with two wifeless men, her husband sat alone in the dark at the remote island of Kuria with half a bottle of Scotch, on a director's chair at the bow of the government ship, a converted trawler. Unlike most of the Gilberts this island had no navigable lagoon. The ship was anchored on a shelf in quiet water 25 metres deep beside the western reef, far enough from the beach to ensure the mosquitoes stayed ashore to torment villagers who dozed on pandanus mats in houses sharp with smoke. The throb of the ship's generator was dullest at the bow. The German captain and most of the crew slept.

Peter had no more work to do here and not enough to justify the stopover at all. As a favour he called in late that afternoon to pick up two of Charlotte's Gilbertese friends, dropped here two weeks earlier on the voyage south, now asleep in steerage. The ship would weigh anchor at 1am on the high tide and head southwest to the safety of open water, then turn north-northwest for Maiana, 100 kilometres away. The captain would pace the ship to arrive on the midday peak so the water would be deep enough for Peter to go ashore in the ship's lighter. The lagoon navigable if you could get into it; this captain new and under orders to anchor outside.

They would stay one night, and part of the next day while the ship loaded copra. Peter would disembark as soon as the ship anchored and would hold court to sentence islanders to trivial penalties for trite offences. He would sleep ashore in the government resthouse, where villagers could call on him until late to talk about suspected murder, sorcery or nothing much, as in New Guinea. On the second day he would hold a meeting with island leaders to try to convince them it was time for villagers to give free labour to construct an airstrip for light planes. When the strip was built he could fly to Maiana, as he already could to some islands, and spend less time away from Charlotte.

He liked the Gilbertese for the toughness that caused them to find, settle and survive on mid-ocean semi-deserts, reminders of outback Australia; dry, featureless, almost infertile. But the people bored him, as did much of his work; but he would not tell Charlotte. His few enthusiasms had little to do with his job description, apart from the 'miscellaneous other duties' category, namely disposal of Second World War ordnance, preservation of war relics, including human remains, and ornithological research conducted for two scholars who came from the University of Hawaii to train him. He had mapped a lot of ordnance for disposal by British demolition experts and would soon meet his first Japanese delegation to collect soldiers' remains from the battle of Betio, defended by the Japanese against the first amphibious landing of Allied forces on an atoll, a misguided campaign of slaughter for meagre purpose other than logistic and tactical experiment.

The ornithology gave him occasional opportunity to sail by 5-metre outrigger canoe across the Nonouti Island lagoon at 15 knots for two hours to an uninhabited islet, Numatong, the vulnerable tip of a mountain far from Tarawa and its social absurdities, remote from other main islands, themselves precarious collars of growing, dying and smashed coral on the peaks of submerged mountains.

The sailors, surely the world's most intrepid, would take the canoe back to the main island and leave him alone for a few days to identify, observe, photograph and count the thousands of birds that rested here on migration routes between North America, northern Asia and Australasia. When the canoe left he would remove his watch and strip naked; would wear just a fisherman's hat in the daytime and wrap himself in a sarong at night. When he saw the triangle of sail on the horizon a few days later, an hour before the pick-up, society and time would resume as he put on his shorts, shirt and wrist-watch.

At night his only light, apart from the moon and stars, was a waterproof torch and a fire. At home he read every night for at least two hours, usually anthropology, war history and classical novels; but the one book he ever took to Numatong was a bird manual supplied by the University of Hawaii. Why distract himself from Numatong, itself the ultimate distraction?

When he studied birds in the daylight and darkness he carried a camera and binoculars on straps around his neck. His favourite species among forty-eight he identified was the white tern, *gygis alba candida*; pure white feathers, black eyes, and a blue-black beak with a needle point. One of several species of tern on the island, it did not pass through like the migratory birds he was there to record. In contrast with the Bougainville crow it was delicate in form and behaviour. He did not have to stalk it and unlike the crow it never caught him by surprise. Almost always alone, it came chirping to him and hovered two metres above him in a blur of angel wings, diaphanous; the bird's location as fixed as that of a hawk riveted on a mouse in a field of grain.

He had never seen this bird at Bougainville but knew that, if he had, it would have made him wonder if Rand was still there; some sort of spiritual presence. From the little information about Rand that anyone could give him, Peter guessed that both the man and the tern wanted solitude. Solitude and loneliness were different. Did the bird and Rand die in contented solitude? Or lonely, with other lives all around them?

It never rained while he was at Numatong. There were no mosquitoes on this dry islet, far from the breeding sites in wells, palm forests and mangrove swamps on the main island to the east. Why didn't mosquitoes and other insects migrate on the easterly wind? Maybe they did but could not evade the hunger of waiting birds on this confined and isolated death-trap. Did any of these seabirds eat mosquitoes?

The nights were as clear as in the dry deserts of central Australia. He would lie back on the sand in the breeze with a bottle of Scotch and long for Charlotte as he studied the stars, moon and planets through binoculars; not as external observer, as with the birds, but from within the spectacle, himself an element of the universe. Eight kilometres to his north at the tip of Nonouti the open ocean was a remote rumble on the skirting reef, much further away from him than Charlotte would be from the illusory bombardment that distressed her as she lay in their house at Bairiki.

Charlotte and the universe would always give way to rehashed thoughts about Rand. Could he see the stars on the night before he died? Did his cell have a window? How might Peter's chosen solitude relate to the loneliness that Rand must have felt with people all around him as he approached death, the most secret and mysterious of all life's experiences? Did he hear the surf roar to protest his fate? Perhaps the sea's power reassured him that even though his turn was now, everyone and everything would crumble and re-blend with the void.

Peter caught fish with ease from the steep beach with a short, tough rod of fibreglass and a bait-caster reel filled with 20-pound line; baited the hooks with hermit crabs, which fought as he skewered them with clinical care to cause a few minutes of death-wriggle that would attract prey. He grilled his catch on the coals of a perpetual fire, garnished them with canned beans, and washed his feast down with water, or with coconut milk when his water supply was low, near the end of his visit.

Sometimes, before he could land a fish, a shark would tear it from the hook close to the beach in a flurry of guts, blood, and spray laced with blue and silver scales. Only once was there no flurry. On his first visit he waded a few metres into the water at sunset, up to his hips, to get a longer cast seaward than he could get from the beach. He hooked a hefty fish which raced behind him and forced him to play it over his shoulder. As he struggled to hold his balance, the victim became much heavier, then much lighter than when he hooked it. The surface did not break. No fight for freedom.

Peter backed up to the beach and dragged his catch onto the sand. All he had was a trevally head, separated from the missing body by a 30-centimetre arc, perfect in broad view, ragged in detail. One mindless bite and rip. Peter squatted above the shallow wash to shit. When he finished he threw the fish-head as far out to sea as he could manage.

He sat on the sand to contemplate his luck. His mind soon wandered to Rand. If the Japanese dumped his body at sea, did sharks or barracuda tear him apart and turn him into nutritious shit for other sea creatures that ended up in the bellies of Bougainvilleans, who in turn fertilised the soil through shit and their own deaths? At the end of the chain, how much of Rand was left? Mere reverie; but one thing was certain to Peter—no one who knew Rand could have guessed that thirty years later, at one of the most remote places on Earth, he would be on the mind of a lucky fisherman not yet conceived when the coast watcher died.

Peter would raise such thoughts in bed with Charlotte each time he got back home, after the lights were out. He would ask her if she thought it strange that when he was at Numatong he always speculated about Rand's possible state of mind. "Yes," she would say. "Yes, Peter. As I've said many times. Yes." Once she added, "He plagues us both, thanks to you." The arrow did not strike even the outer ring of the target. To stop him she pretended to snore.

On the ship's deck at Kuria his mind wandered back from islet and Rand and the Japanese delegation to refocus on Charlotte. He loved her incidental sharp humour but worried about her ennui and bitchiness. She despaired at the monotony of Tarawa and the outer islands. She now drank too much; the increase coincided with her libido's ebb and her greater disdain for expatriate social life. She would not learn Gilbertese, let alone research it as a linguist to feed her intellect. Her closest friends, the two teachers on leave that he dropped and picked up at Kuria, told him on the outward voyage that they loved her but did not think she wanted them to visit her so often, and perhaps not at all.

As the two girls leaned on one another and swayed with the ship, Teata said to him, "Does she think you like us too much?" Safaila pinched her on the hip and whispered to her in Gilbertese; told her not to embarrass Peter or insult Charlotte. She was prettier than they were. Then in English, "Teata is sorry. Her mind is lying to her. We like you and we know you like us but you are Charlotte's husband and so we are loyal to her. Teata is sorry too for the time at your house when she showed you more than a man with a wife should see, when she stood up and wrapped her loose sarong while Charlotte was in the kitchen. We are going now."

Teata said, "We will not talk to you again until we come to see Charlotte in Bairiki. We are ashamed." He did not reply. They walked away faster than he had ever seen them move. They did not want him to follow.

What were those girls on about? He remembered the jolt of Teata's fleeting display of nudity from hip to knee at home in Bairiki but thought it accidental and pretended not to notice. Deliberate? No matter. He did not want Gilbertese girls to seduce him even though Charlotte's libido had waned. "Petered out," she said. He decided his monasticism was paltry compared with the loneliness and sexless hell that Rand must have suffered in the mountains of Bougainville and in the Japanese prison at Kieta.

Charlotte did not seem to trust him with British women or her Gilbertese friends. As her libido withered she drank more and more. Tried to drown the distrust with gin? Christ. Twenty minutes before the voyage began, Safaila and Teata had hailed him from the jetty and asked if he could drop them at Kuria. He told them to pay a bribe to the first mate and find a spot in steerage. If Charlotte found out he took them aboard, where would her fancy drag her? Oh shit.

On Tarawa and the outer islands several girls had signalled their availability and would do it again the next day at Maiana. He had no interest in them, nor in several British women who chatted too close to him at the club or at dinner parties when their husbands were away. The Governor's teenage daughter displayed fondness when she visited from England at the end of every school term. His sole interest was Charlotte. How could someone with her intelligence think otherwise? He would sort out this nonsense as soon as he got home.

For relief he returned to his fixation, the execution of Hugh Rand. Charlotte once called it his fetish. When he objected she said, "Okay, your fixation. Or your fix, your opium substitute." The death intrigued him from the day he heard about it, a week after he and Charlotte arrived in Bougainville. As the wind and current rocked the anchored ship at Kuria, he drank Scotch to help him reconstruct the detail of his search so far. He brooded over

Charlotte's continual analysis, always dismissive, of what he said he had learned and she said he had concocted without evidence or good sense.

He first heard Rand's name when a Burns Philp plantation manager near Kieta told him about the execution but knew no detail. Nothing was on file in the district records at Kieta, apart from a single sentence that identified Rand as a pre-war patrol officer in New Ireland, commissioned as a coast watcher, who lost his head to the Japanese at Kieta. A friend in New Ireland said the district archives there listed him as a pre-war patrol officer but gave no further detail; the Japanese had destroyed most personnel and other records. Nothing significant about Rand at head office in Port Moresby.

None of the Christian missions had any record of Rand, either in their Papua New Guinea archives or overseas. By the time he arrived on Bougainville almost all foreign missionaries had evacuated or were in Japanese prisons elsewhere. Local men left in their place had not left records and could not be located by the time Peter Millar started his research, 30 years later. The same applied to a German cleric who may have stayed at his post for the entire Japanese occupation.

Peter's work contacts in Melbourne and Canberra found no detail of Rand's service in the archives of the Department of External Territories, responsible for Papua New Guinea administration. The only leads were his appointment date and last known Australian addresses, in Brisbane and at Nyngan in the central west of New South Wales.

On leave from Tarawa in 1970, Peter flew alone from Melbourne to Brisbane. Rand's last known residence in that city was now a brothel and had been a medical clinic for 24 years before that. Estate agent and State government archives showed Rand's mother as the vendor to the medical practice but included no subsequent address for her.

Millar went back to Melbourne and convinced Charlotte to drive northwest with him to Nyngan. The postmaster there did not know of Hugh Rand. He directed them to an isolated wheat farm where he said an ancient Mr Rand lived with a sister who moved in after his wife died in 1960.

To Charlotte, Nyngan was desolate. The farm—flat, vast and dry—took deadness and desolation to a nadir that rivalled Tarawa and made Bougainville a paradise. "Even the bloody crows way out there above the wheat stubble are pissing me off, a lot more than the one that hung around Bos Simeon's village. At least it was happy and used to laugh. These bastards whine non-stop to remind us we're all about to drop off our perch."

The visit fruitless and dull, apart from the spectacle of two pungent ferrets at war in a cage beside the house as Peter knocked on the door and waited; to Charlotte, the battle vicious, bloody, and chilling; inconsequential to Dave Rand's sister, who answered the knock. A minute after the battle started, one ferret dead and the other dying.

Dave Rand, Hugh's father, sullen and demented; his sister, well into her 80s, much the same. She knew nothing of Hugh apart from the fact of his death in New Guinea, could not remember him and had no photographs, other records or anecdotes. "No brothers or sisters or cousins or other family except me. You're leavin' all this a bit late." All Dave could or would say was "I told him to watch out for the Japs' cutlery. Wrecked his Mum. Yeah."

"Yeah, it did," said the sister. "Gutted her a bit more every day for fifteen years 'til she topped herself in the dunny. Rusty First War bayonet. Throat job. Yep."

The Returned and Services League club had no detailed record of Rand, according to the manager-barman; just his name on the honour roll. Two veterans at the almost deserted bar knew of him but had never met him. One said, "He left here and went to Brisbane with his Mum when he was a kid, about ten. Came back to see his old man for a couple of days during the war. She came back here after the war. All on her lonesome. Well, Hughie was too dead to come with her, wasn't he? His name's on record here at the club and on the town memorial because he was born here. Don't try to talk to Dave Rand. His brain went for a holiday a long time ago and didn't come back. Or his bloody sister. Thick as two short planks. After he was about sixty Dave went more cuckoo every time there was a thunderstorm. Slow process out here. We don't get many. Reckoned the Huns were trying to blow him out of his trench. Mad as a meat-axe."

The other man, mulling until now, turned on his barstool: "All I know is Hugh Rand wasn't really one of us. Didn't enlist here or anywhere else as far as I know, but still got a navy rank. Probably got a white feather to stir him up to be a spy or whatever he was, thinking he'd be safer." His voluble companion took over: "Yeah, right on. If he had proper soldier's training he mightn't have lost his noggin at Kokoda or wherever it was, up north in the islands. Stan and me weren't in New Guinea, were we mate? Don't know of anyone around here now who was. A few were but they've left town, apart from a couple boxed up in the cemetery. Ray Stocker drank himself to death right here, at this bar. When we saw where he was headed we used to call his stool the box seat. Tried to get him on the wagon for a rest but he'd seen too much. Japs tortured him."

Stan cut in: "Ray was with us two in Singapore when the Poms and our officers chickened out and gave us to the Japs. Could've wiped out the little yellow bastards. Ended up in Changi and Siam. But we don't talk about it, mate, so don't ask. Nah."

Peter was allowed to buy them and himself a drink because he was a former New Guinea Patrol Officer and therefore an honoured guest at any RSL club. "You do the same job now with the Poms, eh? Near enough," said the barman. "Where's Colbert Island?"

As they left after 15 minutes discussing the weather and the sale price of sheep, Charlotte said, "Not one of those old pricks even looked at me. And you bought me a drink as an afterthought."

"Not so old," he said, "still in their 50s. You might look older than 28 if you spent a couple of years as a guest of the Japanese in Changi and Thailand."

"Why don't they get over it and move on?"

"What about someone who has a car accident that kills his mates and smashes hell out of him? The accident took a few seconds, didn't it? Just get over it, you reckon?"

The next morning they left for Melbourne after a sexless, overpriced night in a motel that smelled of public urinal disinfectant, like most motels in rural Australia. "Sorry I went straight to sleep last night." she said. "A year of maidenhood wouldn't parch me enough to break the drought in a public toilet."

"Fine. But don't flash your delicious arse in front of me. My older mates warned me to keep you single for a few more years to delay the marital drought. I should have listened. Joke only." No answer. "No clever riposte?" he said. She feigned a yawn.

On the way through town they stopped at the Nyngan and District War Memorial in front of the Bogan Shire offices. A five-block sandstone obelisk about six metres high, diminishing from a one and a half metre base block to a half-metre flat top, sat on a bronze cube which recorded the names of several hundred servicemen from both world wars and more minor conflicts. A laurel wreath in bronze decorated the lowest and largest block of sandstone. Unlike many—probably most—Australian memorials, this one named survivors and the dead, not just the latter. On each side of the memorial, right above the names, "LEST WE FORGET" was set in metal letters. The dead might be dead but this mausoleum was intended to house them forever in spirit, no matter where their bodies rotted into oblivion. However and wherever they died, they were heroes.

Rand was there, rankless; no tiny cross to say he died in action.

"There he is," said Peter. "To anyone who sees this and doesn't know his story, he could be living in the next town."

"Is he telling you any secrets?" asked Charlotte. "No? What a shock! Let's go then. Ignore the 'lest' bit. I wish you would bloody forget. You've been obsessed with this nonentity for years and still know bugger-all about him. Nothing from Bougainville. Nothing from anywhere or anyone in Australia, including his old man and his auntie, in his home town. Lest we forget? Forget, for fuck's sake and mine. Forget!"

"Obsessed? 'Interested' might be more accurate and a bit fairer. Have you thought about finding your own obsession instead of worrying about mine? Even a minor interest would help. You've got a diploma in linguistics but you still speak less Gilbertese than I do after two years with nothing else to do, which you whinge about."

"Please fuck off," she said.

"Hang on, Charlotte. Live the moment. This memorial was constructed after the First World War. Hasn't it occurred to you that as a little kid Rand might have read the names on it, obviously not realising his would be there one day?"

"And idolised all the heroes before he was old enough to think? Isn't this where the bloody ridiculous Coo-ee March started in 1915? If it didn't, it came through here on its way to Sydney, didn't it?"

"No, and no."

"Heroes on horseback, publicly intimidating men and boys into getting their heads shot off for the faraway rulers of the Empire. Maybe the ones with the guts to defy the pressure were the bravest."

"You don't know what you are talking about."

"Is that so? How would you feel if you were called a coward by your sister or your girlfriend or your wife, or the local kids? Because you didn't believe in the cause and rejected the coercion from blue-bloods and their lackeys on high horses? What if you had an Irish background and your family had been treated like shit by the Brits at home? What if your recent ancestor was shipped to Australia as a convict because his family was starving in London and he nicked an apple for one of his kids or his pregnant wife?"

"That was the Great War, and it's your personal view of history. It's got nothing to do with Rand between the wars. Stick to linguistics."

"Great War? Great? Are you serious? And it has nothing to do with Rand? Two minutes ago you created my vision of a manipulated little boy adoring the Gallipoli and Somme heroes with names chiselled on this bloody lump of rock. Don't you remember what your new best mate in the bar said about the white feather? He was talking about the Second World War. The bloody Coo-ee mindlessness lived on and people like you make it keep on living. Rand gives me the shits, but if the poor little bastard believed all that crap and that's what got his head chopped of on Bougainville, I feel sorry for what fake history did to him. And bloody sorrier for what you are still making his fantasy and yours do to us."

"All done, Charlotte? Have you considered a lecturing career in linguistics? Military history? You'd get to talk at students for an hour at a time without interruption."

"Lecturing? That reminds me. You were a uni student when your birthdate missed the conscription ballot for the Vietnam nonsense that won't end any time soon. If your date had been drawn, would you have asked for a deferral? Or would you have applied for exemption as a convenient conscientious objector, like so many privileged little fakes have done? I know you disagree with Australian involvement in Vietnam, but would you have accepted conscription so your friends and family, maybe me, wouldn't give you a white feather? Then hoped you didn't get sent to Vietnam?"

"Where in hell is all this coming from?"

"They call it National Service so that semi-educated people accept it rather than get stigmatised as unpatriotic as well as gutless. Two hundred dead Nashos so far. How many do you think are middle-class kids or higher?"

"There are at least couple of officers. I don't really know and nor do you."

"A couple? That's one per cent. Out of proportion, don't you think? Ninety-nine per cent of dead Nashos are working-class, I bet. Ninety-nine per cent of Australians aren't working-class. See what I mean now about the Coo-ee heroes high up on their chargers?"

"Not really."

"What about the permanently stoned American guys and their imported Thai tarts that we met in Kathmandu a few years ago? All rich, smug, noisy brats in the bloody useless Peace Corps; all loaded with cash, in the PC to get a US draft exemption while their pleb compatriots got blown away. Name one of the Peace Corps wankers who wasn't Ivy League."

"You're exaggerating again, Charlotte. I can't remember names but not many were what you say. I didn't know you were a class warrior. Rand's background wasn't affluent. That's obvious from what we saw today. Doesn't that mean he could be a hero to you from those origins, but not if his parents were patrician? And he did get to be an officer, a lieutenant."

"You once told me it was a token rank intended to make the Japanese adhere to the Geneva Convention. Not the usual officer rank derived from socioeconomic status."

"Enough, Charlotte. You don't know what in hell you're talking about. You've spent ten minutes disrespecting extremely courageous men. And women. Nurses, mainly."

"Oh fuck. I didn't mention nurses. You don't get it. Let's clear out of this bloody wasteland. Look, if you're going to carry on with this Rand crap while we're on leave, do what I suggested before we came here. Park your arse at your Mum's place. Ring every Rand in the phonebook while Mummy massages your feet and I have a good time with friends I haven't seen for years."

For a day in the Victorian State Library he searched the nation's telephone directories and wrote down the address and number of every Rand on record, a total of forty-seven. The next day he spent several hours calling them from his mother's without a strike. Towards midday, after he had tried nineteen numbers and left messages on three answering machines, an old man called. "I'm not a Rand but I heard on the grapevine that you're interested in Hugh. I never met him and don't know anything about him. Nothing more I can do or say but I know of someone who might help." He declined to give his own name but referred Peter to Walter Brooksbank, the wartime Civil Assistant to the Director of Naval Intelligence, now living in Melbourne. "Got a pencil and paper? Here's his number."

From Peter's study of Eric Feldt's 1946 book *The Coast Watchers* he remembered that Brooksbank did all the detailed work of building up the wartime coastwatching service. Thought he was dead by now. The book mentioned Rand only in the appendix that listed those who served: Lieut. H. Rand, Bougainville, Feb. 43, Killed.

Brooksbank hesitated when Peter called and asked to talk about Rand. "The gentleman who gave you my number and suggested you call me should not have done so." Silence for ten seconds. "Alas, the deed is done. Can you meet me for lunch tomorrow at the Queen's Club in the city? Ask for me at reception. I will tell you what I can, which will not be much. Midday?"

Peter called the other twenty-eight numbers without a strike.

At the Queen's Club, Brooksbank—ancient, sharp-eyed and dapper—said he remembered Rand fairly well before deployment but knew little of him after that; almost nothing about his death. "It was all a long time ago. He was a little eccentric. Let's see what I can recall." A steady and clear voice for his age, probably well over 80.

During induction, such as it was, he said Rand was sharp of mind and perhaps the most skilful of all coast watchers in close combat, for which anything that might be called training was brief and incidental. Strong Pidgin speaker. A quick learner with a first-rate memory. A strong arts degree, excellent English expression, both oral and written. Didn't talk much, for most of the time, but gave a little speech now and again if he got stirred up. Impressive with numbers in ways that went well beyond arithmetic.

"Entertained us with mental calculations. He had some strange ideas about the nature of courage. Didn't really believe in associated concepts like heroism, which suited us because we wanted him to stay in place for at least a year and not take risks that might get him killed and render him zero in usefulness."

"His name is now on the cenotaph at Nyngan. Do you think he would have approved?"

"Probably not. Two of his fellow trainees in Townsville complained because he said cenotaphs were fraudulent. They taught vulnerable kids that every corpse was a hero who wasn't really dead; would live forever inside a chunk of rock with his name on it. He said some of the heroes must have died cowards. Shot in the arse while they were running away. Others blasted while they cowered in a trench with their trousers full of faeces, crying out for their mothers."

Brooksbank sipped his wine three times and rested for two minutes in some faraway time and place. "I was there and did see such things, but I told him I also saw a lot of brave men give their lives to save others, in an immediate sense, and more broadly for their country, family, and so on. He replied, 'And for politicians and rich aristocrats at home and abroad, a lot more in that war than this one. Brave men or not, my old man would say most of those lives were taken for dubious reasons, not given.' I let that comment pass. If he hadn't differentiated between the two wars I might have had him removed from the Ferdinand Group. You know that's what we called the coast watchers? After Disney's pacifist bull, which would rather sniff flowers than brawl. Gather intelligence, avoid direct combat.

"Rand objected to calling dead soldiers 'the fallen', as if they were ballet dancers who had an elegant little trip-over. He said it was a lie, not just a euphemism, and we should call them 'the blown apart'. He said no dead or dying soldiers were much like Bernini's ecstatic St Theresa, contrary to the way they were depicted fully intact in lots of statuary and paintings around Australia and Europe. Not much like the paintings of St Sebastian getting an erotic buzz from the arrows stuck into him like a precursor to shrapnel.

"Rand mentioned St Sebastian a few times to me and a couple of other blokes over a beer. He said El Greco did two versions, and Rubens and a couple of other painters did one each. Mantegna? I'm not sure. Few of us knew what he was talking about. I knew a couple of those works and thought he had a point, so to speak. I didn't say so. He knew a lot about art, especially Gauguin.

"Anyway, he claimed everyone ignored the chunk of rock for most of the year; then adults made kids worship it on Anzac Day and 11 November, Armistice Day. His interpretations seemed to have something to do with his father's experience on the Somme. I can't remember any more detail."

"Mr Brooksbank, did Rand know you won a Military Medal at Ypres?"

"Been to the State Library this morning, Peter? Call me Walter, please. I didn't mention it to him but someone else might have done. Ah, yes. An MM for some spur of the moment mortar work that I didn't have to do, in the sense that no one ordered me to do it."

"In that case, why did you do it?"

"I'm not sure. Rand might have been right. With hindsight, I probably did it because the Germans would overrun us and shoot me in the backside if someone didn't take it to them. I didn't want to be overrun or shot in the arse so I thought it would be a good idea to jump them before they moved. It took me about five seconds to decide what to do. The major-general's recommendation made me look far less hasty and much more intelligent."

"Can you remember what he wrote?"

"No. Let me rephrase that. I see you are equipped with antennae that can pick a liar. The recommendation is seared on my brain like one of those corpse-names carved on the cenotaphs that Rand disdained. 'For conspicuous gallantry and devotion to duty during the attack east of Ypres on 20th September, 1917. He brought up his mortars to forward positions under very heavy enemy fire and kept up ammunition supply under very difficult conditions. The excellent service done by these mortars assisted very greatly in making complete the reduction of enemy strong points and the breaking up of his counter attacks.' I believe I included every 'very'."

"Are you sure Rand didn't know about the MM?"

"Well, I didn't tell him and he didn't mention it. But, to move our chat along, his comments about soldiers who had been through the mill did get up my nostrils. I let it pass. He was provocative but I sensed he was not completely without compassion or respect. Maybe he wanted us to think he was the ultimate realist. Who knows? Not me. I often think about him, still. More than about most other coast watchers, really. Muse rather than think. Most of the others were easier to understand. I admired them all, which is why I came up with the proposal for a lighthouse memorial, built at Madang in 1959, to commemorate 28 dead coast watchers and locals. He wasn't around to object, so his name is on it. I do wonder if he philosophised about variations on courage when the Japs were on his tail and after they got him, especially when his head was about to roll."

"Did you get anything of value from him in the short time he was on Bougainville?"

"Nothing. We put him in place for nothing and as far as we know he died for nothing. We don't know if he was a hero—perhaps a reluctant one, given his disdain for heroism. Nor do we know if he gave away any information that might have cost lives. I think not. I live in hope that he saved some. The Japanese tortured him. This we managed to squeeze from unenthusiastic, amnesiac witnesses who lived near the barracks and saw his condition when the Japanese dragged him out for execution."

"Amnesiac witnesses?"

"After the war, the locals all reckoned they helped Rand and other coast watchers but couldn't remember anything specific, apart from the execution. The fact is that the locals dobbed, and not just because the Japanese approach was 'dob them or die'. That's why we had to get Jack Read and others out not long after Rand's demise. Post-war, no one was going to talk too much for fear of being identified as a dobber to the Japanese. Even now, as I suspect you have discovered, they probably claim to know nothing."

"Correct. If the locals were less secretive I probably wouldn't be all that interested in the case. My wife says it's an obsession, but she exaggerates."

"I've guessed you do like a challenge. Don't over challenge yourself. Along with the Japanese, that might be what caught up with Hugh Rand. So far, so good, Peter?"

"Indeed, Walter. You talk, I'll listen."

"Fine. Stop me if I become tedious. There were no detailed Japanese records—unusual for them—and our meagre official record made six months after the war said the officer who interrogated and executed him was taken by a shark a day or two later, according to a girl who said a Japanese soldier told her so. The place wasn't a mine of information. We couldn't even find out the soldier's name or his commander's. The latter left Bougainville a few weeks after the execution and no one tried to trace him or his successor after the war. Too many clearer cases and bigger fish. He couldn't have been classified as a war criminal anyway, because we didn't know enough about him or his subordinate, the interrogator-cum-executioner who ended up as shark fodder.

"We didn't have the supply of willing witnesses you got for crimes in POW camps, for instance. And we didn't have the resources to trace any Japanese troops who were in Bougainville at the time. They wouldn't have talked anyway. A lot of them would have been transferred at least once by the end of the war. If they didn't get away before the Bougainville carnage they probably died in it. Big Japanese losses there from late 1943. Anyone who saw the Rand incident and stayed on Bougainville to the end would have been too dead or shattered or disinclined to remember anything. It would have been a dead end, so to speak.

"Despite the naval cover, we also knew Rand's status was in doubt, legally. A high chance that the war crimes tribunal would decide he was a spy and got what captured spies tend to get in wartime, under the accepted rules.

"So, we are in the dark about Rand. He didn't make friends with the other trainees so the few who are still around couldn't tell you much about him. He was polite and good-humoured to my female support staff. I don't think they got up to anything after hours, even though a couple seemed to lust after him. Most kept their distance."

"Walter, do you think he would have been another Jack Read or Paul Mason if the Japanese hadn't caught him so soon?"

"My guess is that he would have handled himself well if he had survived long enough to settle into the role. A loner, socially erratic and sometimes difficult, but probably forthright under pressure. Jack Read was a bit like that but not as extreme. Have you talked to Jack? Les Williams? Paul Mason?"

"I didn't get a chance to talk to Les. He was District Commissioner in New Ireland when I was on Bougainville. I had a chat with Mason when he visited Kieta a few years ago. He said he left Bougainville before Rand arrived, but someone else told him he heard Rand trying to make radio contact a couple of times. Couldn't risk a reply. My chat with Mason came to an abrupt halt when I asked him if there was any truth in the story that he shot at least one villager who dobbed him to the Japanese. It was a dumb question, and he took offence. I didn't get a chance to say I could understand why he might have needed to do that. He clammed up on me and left without finishing his beer. I know he was damned heroic. No doubt about that. But I got the feeling he saw himself as a celebrity who should do the talking and not be questioned."

Brooksbank stared in silence over Peter Millar's right shoulder for ten seconds, then looked down and occupied his mouth with rare steak for two minutes. He mopped his lips with a crisp napkin and watched Peter's nose. "Well, I can't comment on Mason, other than to say he did a mighty job for us, as you know from Eric Feldt's book. Have you talked to Jack Read? He's still Lands Titles Commissioner up there in the Territory, based in Moresby. I suppose you know that already. Did you get a chance to meet him before you went to Tarawa?"

"I went on patrol with him for a few days on Bougainville to help him work on land disputes. He was circumspect at first. The District Commissioner had warned me not to mention the war and certainly not to ask about Jack's role in it. And told me not to offer him alcohol. After a day or so he opened up about the war without any prompting from me. I asked him a few questions about Rand. He didn't know much."

No reaction from Brooksbank. Peter went on: "He said much the same as Mason. He knew Rand was in place near Cape Nehuss, to the southeast of Jack's territory, and that he had radio trouble. He said the Japs were onto Rand like lightning. They got him within a couple of weeks. Probably because the locals betrayed him. Jack knew Rand was beheaded in Kieta and dumped at sea but that was about all. That's what he told me; and a few other things about his own experience that I already knew from Feldt's book."

"Peter, did you ask him about Mason's management of difficult villagers?"

"With discretion. I asked how difficult it was for people like him and Mason to handle the issue of locals being caught between a rock and a hard place when they had to decide if they would protect

Australian coast watchers or dob them to the Japanese. After a lot of thought Jack said, 'Things were done under pressure that maybe shouldn't have been done, maybe didn't need to be done. I'll leave it at that. You'll have to make of that what you will.' He said he had work to do, and I didn't get another opportunity to delve. Do you know how Mason handled the problem I asked him about?"

Brooksbank studied his wine, then Millar's forehead, as he prepared another pellucid exposition, perfect in grammar and flow; this one would be personal, almost intimate in content but distant in style and terminal in purpose. He took a last sip of wine, the glass still almost full, clasped his hands on the table and leaned back.

"Mr Millar, allow me to become a trite formal. I would like to say more about many things, but please understand I am still morally bound by certain regulations and confidences. That's why, from where you sit, I might seem to have retained too much of my wartime demeanour. Let me finish with the point that Hugh Rand might have been too impetuous for the job we expected him to do. Despite the mythology, a diligent patrol officer did not always make a good coast watcher.

"Another thing. I suggested he concern himself less with monuments and dead heroes or he might lead himself to dwell on the possibility that every second out there, by himself most of the time, might be his last. Do that too much, I said, and soon your internal headwork might overshadow your need to concentrate on who's out there trying to get you, and turn the last-second hypothesis into a prediction. As usual, Mr Rand had a quick riposte: 'If I don't dwell on the possibility I might let my guard down and turn the odds against myself.' He always had to feel he was in control."

Over the next minute, Brooksbank stared at his empty glass and moved his lips twice, preparing to speak but deciding otherwise. Then: "Back to Mason. In March 1943, he wrote a long letter to Commander Feldt at Townsville HQ in which he outlined events leading up to the full scale Japanese invasion of Bougainville a year earlier. On the second page he said something like this: 'We gave the stick to some natives who told the Nips about us.' I didn't read too much into that at the time, and perhaps we should not do so now. Even so, before we part, one more comment for you to consider. Read, Mason, and the other New Guinea coast watchers, including Hugh Rand, were at war. They had to play a harsh game of hide and seek that sometimes required them to kill or be killed. There was room for error, but they did not have a week or three and the help of a committee to consider their options. I must go. My train awaits me."

They walked to Flinders Street Station; spoke little, none of it about Rand or the war until they shook hands to part. "Peter, I think I mentioned that even though Rand lectured us now and again he clearly did not *like* to talk at length. I might add that he seemed not to want to hear his own voice, a sort of early teenage falsetto.

"Oh, another thing—he often referred to life as a 'script' that we could all write and rewrite for ourselves and others as circumstances changed for better or worse. All we had to do was stay alert to opportunity. A sort of anti-determinist approach to life. A philosophy of unfettered free will to manipulate, to always get your own way if you were savvy enough. Obviously he couldn't get the Japanese to buy his script. Damn it. Missed my train. Fifteen minutes to the next one. Shall we sit and wait? In silence if you wish."

Peter's train would leave in 20 minutes so he opted to sit on a platform bench and wait with Brooksbank. They watched the crowd pass.

"Look at them, Peter, all living in one-off worlds unknown in any depth to anyone but themselves. They're like us, are they not? And like Hugh Rand? You know, there may have been another dimension to Rand's world that we did not broach today. A very private dimension. You will recall my saying the locals were reticent right after the war, and they have retained that reticence, in your experience. It's not on the written record, meagre as it is; but one amnesiac witness to the beheading said Rand may have got mixed up with the wrong woman, perhaps the girl who claimed the Japanese soldier told her the executioner died in a shark attack. Apparently the girl denied the liaison story to the army officer who asked. She said she had never even met Rand and did not even know his name. The bloke let it go and that was that. But even a mere rumour that he was fiddling with their women would have encouraged the locals to dob him. Have you heard that rumour in recent times?"

Peter Millar said he had never heard the rumour and did not think it credible. To himself: "Bos Simeon? Doubt it." They agreed that Rand would have been under such pressure before his capture that he could not have had the time, inclination or opportunity for a liaison, fleeting or otherwise. If the locals betrayed him they did so because he was a former colonial administrator, not a philanderer.

Trains arrived; the men parted, with no offer of further contact from Brooksbank, his parting handshake and glance definitive; then off into his own history, unknown in any depth to anyone but himself.

* * *

In bed that night Peter told Charlotte about his lunch with Brooksbank; laboured over Rand's plausible idea that life was a script you could follow if it suited you, or rewrite if it didn't. She did not react well; ridiculed the idea of life as so malleable that anyone could manipulate it at will to any significant extent; scoffed at Rand's idea that determinism and destiny were complete delusions.

"Here we go again, Peter. You want to turn Rand and now Brooksbank into a mysterious figure, an enigma, as if you're the one who's making up a play or a novel as you go, like your bloody hero Rand. But there's not a shred of evidence for anything hidden or mysterious about those guys. Things are not mysterious just because you and Brooksbank want them to be. And I don't want to hear any more of this 'script' and 'play' shit. You broached it at Abemama and gave me the shits. Now you know Rand was into it too you'll never let it go. Oh Jesus!"

At a deeper, more honest level Rand's philosophy appealed to her. Must resist it. Why? Don't try to think it through. Powerful in concept, limited in application; a functional fantasy sure to frustrate her if she did not quash its appeal. Appealed to her because her life seemed beyond her control? Most lives probably like that. Emotional reaction. Resist, resist, for Christ's sake. Don't let a fantasy net you.

Peter asked her, "If there's nothing hidden or mysterious about Rand, why won't Bos Simeon and her mates and his family tell me anything about him? No Japanese or Australian military records? Bullshit. And Brooksbank knows more than he's prepared to tell me."

"They don't have anything to fucking tell. Rand didn't leave letters or a diary. His family was small. His mother topped herself. His old man's demented from shell-shock and thunder. His aunt's a nutcase. He didn't have friends in Australia or anywhere else. Other coast watchers told you they knew bugger-all about him. They have no reason to lie. To them he's a bloke who was silly or unlucky enough to get his head lopped almost as soon as he landed in Japanese territory. As for Walter Brooksbank, he deployed Rand for no productive result and doesn't want to admit he recruited the wrong man."

"Brooksbank did seem to have doubts, with hindsight. Anyway, why did everyone on Bougainville clam up whenever I asked about Rand? They knew more than they let on."

"Maybe. Consider the possibility of a parallel between Melbourne and Bougainville. Brooksbank says he knows nothing significant about the circumstances of Rand's death and that's probably the truth, but he can't resist turning it into a top secret his-eyes-only thriller to suit his self-image. The war was probably the highlight of his life and he goes on living it in the here and now because the rest of his life has been a great bore. He says he's still duty-bound not to talk too much. Bullshit. About what, for Christ's sake?"

"How does that relate to tight mouths in Bougainville?"

"No mystery. As Brooksbank suggested and we already guessed, most of the locals collaborated with the Japanese and were responsible for a lot of Allied deaths. Maybe Rand's. It's a mere twenty-five years since the war ended and a lot of them must have come close to a lead injection or the end of a rope for their trouble. The old men are wise enough not to talk even though we know from experience with other subjects that they'd rather make up a story to keep you happy than plead ignorance. Ask any honest anthropologist, if you can find one."

"What about the younger villagers?"

"They won't disclose any snippet they've heard about the demise of Rand and other outsiders because the old blokes have told them not to. Brooksbank suggests he can't say everything he would like to say, because once a spook always a spook. He's sworn to secrecy as part of his act, even though he's probably got nothing of interest to hide. The Bougainvilleans also probably know nothing much but wouldn't even broach the subject because they were too scared you'd find out stuff that would come back to bite them. Minor indiscretions they'd forgotten long ago. Their secrecy has different origins to his. No matter. There's still a sort of parallel that probably doesn't have much to do with what anyone really knows."

"I don't get your clever meaning about things being parallel. Anyway, several old men told me about his execution in much the same detail. Explain that if you can."

"They told you the Japanese forced them to attend the performance. Nothing there to hide. No collaboration in that. I'll bet they said how sorry they were. And they'd sound idiotic if they said no one witnessed the killing, or the Japs forced them to watch but no one could remember it. Am I right so far?"

"I'm sure Bos Simeon knew plenty, much more than she saw from the sidelines on the day. Why wouldn't she talk?"

"For the same reason as the others. You're wrong. Nothing significant to tell."

"We'll see. I'll write to Bos as many times as necessary to get her story."

"If she wouldn't talk, she won't write. Maybe she can't write."

* * *

At this point of historical reconstruction in the darkness, wind and engine-throb at Kuria Island, Peter Millar tongued the last drops of Scotch from the bottle. He pitched it overboard and chided Bos Simeon for not answering his letters from Tarawa. He would not try again to quiz her from a distance. One day, maybe during his next leave, he would turn up at her village on Bougainville. Catch her by surprise. Yes, next leave. Charlotte could stay in Melbourne.

When the rain started to sprinkle at 8.45pm he pissed over the gunwale a few degrees too close to windward, and swayed cursing to his cabin.

In the darkness he lay in his shorts, damp from piss, rain and salt-spray, and continued to reconstruct his investigation of the Rand case. Charlotte did not react well last time he raised it as she tried to sleep. She fought her way through the mosquito net, got out of bed and switched on the light. The memory blasted at him through the throb of the engine. With hands on hips she yelled, "What fucking story do you think Bos Simeon or anyone else can tell? Leave it alone. Bloody leave it alone! There is no fucking story."

"Quiet! We have neighbours. You know damned well there's something. I told you how Bos baulked the first time I did the census and saw in the bloody census book that her father and mother were dead, and I asked her what happened to them. She said she didn't know because she was a kid when they died. Well, she was fifteen. As if she didn't know what happened to them. Later I asked a couple of old blokes and they said her father drowned early in the war when he went fishing, and her mother disappeared in the forest not long after and was never found. Probably killed by pigs or the Japanese, or savages from the mountains. Pretty straightforward. Why didn't Bos say so?"

"Oh, Jesus," said Charlotte. "Probably erased the horror of the loss from her memory. Afraid to talk of the dead because a lot of them are still around. You know they think like that. Or maybe she simply thought it was none of your business. Lots of possibilities. It's all pretty banal, so quit trying to turn it into an epic mystery. Go to bloody sleep. Have a nightmare instead of giving me one every fucking night."

PART FOUR

Gilbert and Ellice Islands Colony,
Western Pacific, 1971

Peter Millar's Enlightenment

Thursday 7 October 1971. Kuria, Gilbert Islands. At 12.30am the screech of the winch and rattle of the chain woke Peter Millar as the ship weighed anchor at Kuria in the steadiest rain he had seen since Bougainville. At dinner the captain had told him the unusual cloud formation at sunset meant heavy rain from about 9pm. The bureau of meteorology in Fiji told him it would pass by sunrise and the sea would stay calm.

The rain sprayed Peter through an open porthole. He half-closed it and turned on the small fan attached to the bulkhead; lay on his back in the breeze from the porthole and fan and willed the ship to rock him back to sleep.

In Bairiki at 12.30am, the rain hammered on the corrugated iron roof and babbled along the guttering into the tank near Charlotte Millar's bedroom window, open to the breeze. Ten minutes later she unclasped her legs and arms from Aidan Conway and let him roll off her for the third time in two hours. They lay on their backs in the darkness until their breathing and heart-rate eased back to normal. The ceiling fan and window breeze dried their sweat and cooled them to a delicious temperature in this most comfortable of nights. If there had been a top sheet, never before needed in Tarawa, she would have pulled it over them. No mosquitoes on rainy nights, so Aidan had unhooked two corners of the net and tucked it behind the bedhead to exploit the breeze on their skin.

The rain had started at about 9pm, long after the three finished their champagne and fish at the club. They drank beer and chatted for an hour after the champagne ran out. To prime them for their dash home through the downpour, which the experts at the bar proclaimed a night-long deluge, Alastair bought three double Scotches, Johnnie Walker Red on the rocks with a splash of soda. She would have preferred gin-tonic but did not get a chance to ask.

As they sipped they spoke little. They could not hear one another through the rain that belted on the iron roof of the club like nuts and bolts dumped from a bomber.

Little to say anyway. They knew how the next day would punish them. With or without continuous rain, and whether or not the cloud dispersed to let the sun shine, the temperature would rise and the coolish damp would turn to steam. Everyone would start to yawn before 10am. No matter when the rain did stop and the sun shone, lethargy would become exhaustion by mid-afternoon. Lungs and livers would suffer. A few Gilbertese ancients and babies would die. Expatriate wives would drink even more than usual to lift their plummeting morale. Magazines, yellowed novels and British newspapers would lose any vestige of crispness they might have, depending on how old they were and how often their owners basked them in strong sunlight.

Alastair beckoned the other two heads to come close to his so they could hear him. "It seems to have eased a bit. Let's get you home, Charlotte. Lovely to spend time with you. Lucky the club had fish for a change. One is a comedian, isn't one? Sorry one didn't think to bring an umbrella when one saw the clouds gather. This illustrious institution doesn't provide any, unlike the Oxford and Cambridge Club in the wilds of Pall Mall, so one and all must swim through the new Bairiki River to get home. Now, Aidan, it's bloody dark out there. No stars to guide us tonight. Got that dinky torch you usually have to prevent you from breaking your ankles when you're pissed and on the way home?" Aidan took it from his shirt pocket and switched it on and off: "New batteries this evening."

"Good lad. Let's swim Princess Charlotte through the moat to her palace, then I'll prevail on you to light the way to my ark, if it hasn't bobbed away, before you seek refuge in yours. Leave the bloody glasses here until tomorrow or you'll drop them in the flood and never find them."

Drenched ten seconds beyond the club door. Away from the

barrage on the roof, they could hear well enough. "Hang on to us, Charlotte, and don't hurry or you'll fall and skin your knees," said Alastair. "Watch the torch-beam, in close. Usually people wander all over the place at night. One won't bump into anyone tonight in this torrent. Most of the white lords and ladies are at home pissed. The locals in their houses minding their own business for a change. Maybe reading if they know how and they've got a good enough light."

With a man on each side, she walked towards the spot of torchlight that bobbed two metres ahead of them. The raindrops splattered in the light; bullets from a Gatling gun. To her left she held Alastair's upper arm; her right forearm rested on the small of Aidan's back and her hand cupped his right hip. She worried at her comfort in its movement. Aidan transferred the torch from his right hand to his left so he could hold his arm forward to avoid more of the accidental contact of her right thigh with the back of his hand, and her breast with his elbow.

For Charlotte, the rain that spattered on the thatched roofs of local people's houses loaded the unusually light breeze with the nostalgia of wet Australian hay. Hay? Bloody straw. The aroma diminished when they reached the rows of foreigners' houses, fenced and set further apart on each side of the road. The rain now attacked corrugated iron.

When they neared her door a little after 10pm she patted Aidan's hip three times with a light touch, as she might pat a horse after a smooth trot. Brushed her fingers across his back as she drew her hand away to take the house key from her dress pocket. It took much more effort to unwedge her other hand from the vice of Alastair's upper arm and body.

They stood under the eaves as she unlocked the door in the torchlight. "We won't come in, my dear," said Alastair, "or we'll flood your living room. Take Aidan's torch and get a towel to dry your feet and hands before you turn on the light. The electrical work in these houses is dodgy. Can't have you ending up like that grilled trevally." She did as he said and a minute later returned the torch to Aidan.

They kissed her damp cheek, then followed their spot of light along the path and back onto the road. After a few drinks in the company of an attractive woman, Alastair could never control his habit of saying too much of what he thought. "Exquisite in that soaked dress after she switched on the light. Indeed exquisite. Clung to her vital bits like the skin she was born with. And her hair. Her bloody wet hair. Not at all an average pooch after a swim. And not a whiff of the old coconut oil. Aidan, old man, don't tell me the smell didn't shiver your loins when you snuffled her cheek. I drank the drops off it. Even better than your champers. Peter the Oz should never go away without that beauty."

The more Aidan drank, the less inclined he was to talk, especially about women and sexuality. "Yes, Al. She is exquisite. Now watch your step or you'll fall over and drown." He wanted to trip Alastair face-down into a deep hole, put a foot on his back, and listen to his lungs suck water.

Aidan showed Alastair to his house and waited while he completed the same safety routine as Charlotte. He went to his own house but could not go inside despite his conviction that he ought to do so. Switched off the torch, went purblind through his yard to the beach and stood in the downpour for fifteen minutes. The waves lapped at his ruined shoes. No stink of shit tonight. The rain and tide had washed away the twilight deposits made at the water's edge. With the torch still off, he walked along the beach until he reached the Millar house, located between the beach and the road. The lights off. He made a hole in the thatch fence, crawled through it, replaced the thatch, and felt his way along the house wall to the corner near the front door.

"How did you manage that journey in the dark and deluge? I hope you didn't use the torch," said Charlotte, from her seat on the step of coral block. Almost invisible apart from her dress.

He leaned over her and spoke just loud enough to be heard above the rain's assault on the roof and palm fronds. "Quieter voice Charlotte. Please. Might be big ears nearby. No torch. Too many eyes that might not be shut."

She replied in a raucous whisper. "Did you hitch a ride with Noah?"

"I did but the other animals petitioned him to throw me overboard because I was too much of an animal. Look, Charlotte, I'm embarrassed that I thought you wanted me to come back."

"Nothing deliberate. I wondered if you would but I really tried not to pass that on."

"So why are you sitting here in the bloody rain?"

"Who knows? If I'm alone and it rains at night the house is a worse prison than usual. I sit out here if my head can't turn the prison into a water-tight refuge from my vigilant neighbours. Sit on the step with me. Not much rain is getting to me here. We can chat a bit, then you can go home if you want. Was anyone on the road or on the beach?"

He sat beside her. "No one."

She put her head on his shoulder. "Do you want to smell my hair again? I noticed you and Al catching your breath and sipping my raindrops."

He turned his head away. "I'm red-faced even though you can't tell. Contrary to popular mythology, I haven't been near a woman or girl since Enid went back to her old flame in Cardiff. She was waiting for an idiot-proof reason to do it, you know."

"And you gave her one."

"I did. But back to the catching-of-breath. I don't think you led me on, but your Braille practice on my back and the soaked hair got together and did me in. The wet dress didn't help when you switched the light on."

"Does the dress bother you?" She laughed and stood up. The night as dark as any night had ever been. He could make out the dress as a vague patch of whiteness; no clear outline of her body. The patch moved like a wraith as she took it off, wrung it out under the eaves and tossed it through the open door.

"You remind me of the Invisible Man taking off his bandages," he said. "Now I can barely see you. Apart from your white knickers, vaguely." She took them off and threw them towards the dress, then stood in front of him as he sat on the wet step. She took him by the wrists and put his hands on her buttocks; clasped the back of his head with both hands and pressed her belly against his forehead.

She spoke down to his crown: "Feel free to take your time. Don't try to answer."

Two minutes later the rain thrashed harder and noisier, and the eaves gave them less protection. Rather than raise her voice she pulled away from him and leaned forward to murmur in his ear. "Better postpone that adventure and come inside. Chuck off your gear first and wring it out. Put it inside where you can find it if you have to leave in a hurry."

As they coupled they bantered, their voices loud enough to hear above the rain, quiet enough not to escape through the open window shutters. Soon after 1am they dozed off.

At about 3am he woke and patted her hip. "Time for me to withdraw, so to speak, while the rain's still heavy and all eyes and ears are in their own houses."

"Why do the locals detest heavy rain? Fear of making themselves vulnerable to TB or some other deadly affliction. Pneumonia?"

"I'm an ex-teacher of geography, not a doctor or mortician."

"A research geographer as well as teacher. Intrepid enthusiasm for new terrain. Explored all my contours. How do the findings compare with what you found a while ago in more virginal country at the school?"

"The first bits were funny, Charlotte, but not the last bit. Anyway, virginal? Her sister's husband had well and truly explored her. Convenient cultural thing, while big sister was pregnant. The families will still require a virginal marriage. Her grandma will fix that with the help of a substitute marriage mat, a knife and a chicken that thought it was onto a good thing when it got a temporary reprieve from the wedding feast. Next day her brother-in-law will be the first one to race up and down on his motorbike while he waves a red flag. The mat's the proof."

"Peter told me about that and I didn't believe him. Sorry I brought up your mat-laying. Indiscreet of me. Now, hear this. You are more than a geographer. I proclaim you Dr Aidan Conway, psychiatrist, on the grounds that I feel a lot better than I did yesterday and the day before that."

"You forgot about Conway the mortician."

"You're no mortician. They confirm deadness. You resuscitated a faded linguist and invented a new discipline along the way. Linguistic Geography."

"I studied linguistics for a term at Oxford. Hang on, Charlotte. I think I get you. Slow of me. I'm tired."

"That doesn't surprise me. The tiredness. I'm surprised you can talk. You slaved enough for an honorary PhD in phonetics. I can hear the Chancellor now: 'Awarded for persistent improvisation beyond the international phonetic system'. "

"Thank you, Charlotte. Could be a journal article for you in the fine detail of all that research. Creative fricatives, and so on."

"Good idea, Dr Conway. Might start a new journal and call it Exploratory and Experimental Linguistics. Now, I have a question for you. What's the difference between a Gilbertese girl and me, apart from about 12 years in your tutoring case?"

"Ummmm. Both bellies are smooth but yours wobbles a bit less. Same goes for your rear."

"My puppy fat melted long ago. Anything else?"

"You talk to me while we're at it."

"Do you get a better reaction from me when you tickle my feet?"

"Clever, Charlotte, and true. The local girls' soles are leather. What else can I say? You stay awake and don't even yawn. And you squirm around quite a lot."

"Don't talk so loudly. That will do. No, give me one last comparison. Serious praise, if you please."

"Righto. You have more intrinsic value. A bottle of Bollinger, a few beers, a Scotch and a grilled fish cost a lot more than a can of Coke and a Tasmanian apple."

She giggled, so he kissed her to quell her noise, as he had done several times for fear it might carry to nearby houses through the racket of the rain. She straddled him and held his elbows against the mattress. "This is for you. Mainly. And a little bit for me." She stayed there for the six minutes it took to complete her offering, as mobile and carnal as before, when Aidan had worked harder to please her than himself.

She stayed in place until he calmed, then rolled onto her back and lay to his right with her head close to his. She stared at the black ceiling and forced herself to think only of her body and mind, relaxed and gratified. Aidan turned on his side and put his lips against her left ear. He whispered, "That was to die for. Expert execution."

"Oh Jesus, Aidan! Did you have to say 'execution'?"

"Sorry. I don't read you."

"Don't try. It's my problem not yours. It's been a sublime night. Haven't had a man of your age and expertise since high school, on Mum's favourite mat. A merino sheepskin. You'd better go while it's still black outside and the rain's heavy. Before the streets drain and the city comes back to life."

"Right, I'll dissolve into the night. May I see you again?"

He knew she sat up; her voice was above him. "Look, Aidan. That was a great meeting of minds but it has to be a one-off that didn't happen. I won't tell Peter, you don't tell anyone, ever. Agreed?"

"Agreed, of course. I'll have forgotten by the time I get home. Like hell. But you misread my 'see you'. I meant 'look at you.' I want to switch on the bedside lamp for an overview, all at once, raw as the day you were honeymooned. The torch was fine for mapping local detail but I want to assess the large-scale terrain. Need to know how well my head put it all together."

Even the occasional flash of the torch had been risky during the night with the shutters open. "Okay. Let's hope you're not disappointed. Close the shutters first. No guarantee they're crackless. Spies out there. Sorry. Your schoolgirl shag again. Half a minute max. I'll control the switch."

He closed the shutters and stood beside the bed. She relaxed on her back with hands behind head and elbows on the pillow. She switched on the bedside lamp. He studied her without a blink for fifteen seconds, much to her amusement. "Charlotte, your landscape was sculpted and cultivated by a deity, definitely not a committee. You are no camel." As she turned over with loose legs she reached for the light and waited ten seconds to switch it off. She said, "Did your terrain synthesiser work okay?"

"Indeed it did. I'll vamoose with my cerebral photographs."

"Open the shutters, then check the terrain again to make sure you don't lose your feel for it."

A minute after they reconnected she giggled, relaxed her arms a little, but not her legs, and asked him if he wanted to hear something funny. "I'm sure I do," he said. "Can't you tell I'm bored and looking for something funny to occupy me?" He loosened the grip of his fingers on her backside.

"It is funny," she said. "I thought of something Al said to you tonight that he might say to me now if he were watching."

"Umm. Got me there. Awful thought. Carry on."

"He'd say 'There's that damned geographer in you'." He laughed as she gripped him again and stared over his shoulder into the darkness. The joke was an attempt to erase the image of a little boy of indistinct face, never seen before; the demeanour of a boy entranced, in a way he would come to deride in adulthood, by a column of rock at the council chambers in a town of Anzac Day patriots. The faceless boy whispering to the obelisk, like a visitor to a cemetery who ignores the horror of the coffin down below and whispers to the tombstone or plaque as if it houses an immortal loved one. Neither laughter nor lust could rid her of Rand the boy, whose image soon transformed into that of Rand the man. Seemed more than an image; more like an external entity she could see, independent of her.

"Back to the brutish bum-grip, Aidan. Hard as you can." Twenty minutes later he ran his tongue-tip along her neck from collarbone to chin and back again, then rose to leave. "Aidan, please don't forget about tonight. It's too good to forget. But don't talk about it."

"Done. My synthesiser says you are divine. Further to that religious note, thank God it rained. "

"Done? I sure feel like it. By a champion therapist. And not a bad comedian. I'd become used to the idea that fucking is staid and brief. No second serves. Usually a routine designed by missionaries and invaded by an image of a headless big boy. Tonight a little boy first, right after you said 'execution', who became the big boy. He seemed more real than usual. Not to worry. I handled him well enough, thanks to you."

"Pardon?"

"Don't ask. Off you go. He left a couple of minutes ago."

"Indeed. Ummm, well. Off I go, back to the charm of celibacy."

"If you want advice on how to deal with celibacy, swap notes with Peter."

"You said you were on the pill."

"That's to keep me regular so I don't lose track of time in this timeless wonderland for more than four weeks in a row. Before you go, I've got a geography question for you. Why doesn't the reef wear away, the way this bloody place wears at me? I asked Peter and he managed to bring his Hugh Rand fetish into his non-answer."

"The reef wears away. You know that. Into sand. For every pulverised polyp another grows to replace it. We wear away a bit, then we grow back a lot of what we've lost."

"So you're a philosopher too. Right then. By your logic I'll wear away and renew forever if I stay here. Off you go. Thanks for the shag and banter. Sounds like an Irish pub. Look, I shouldn't say this but what the hell. The last time Peter spoke to me while he was shagging me, and wasn't talking about Hugh Rand, he said, 'I've calculated that even though Abemama is only a few hundred metres wide and 25 kilometres long, there are about five million coconut palms'."

"That would be about right. I'll check and we can talk about it next time we get caught in the rain. Off I go while I can still walk. You don't want to tell me about the little boy who grew up tonight in a flash?"

"Not tonight, Dr Conway." He squeezed her feet and left.

In a reddish glow through fingers held over the torch to stifle its beam, he found his way to the living room. Located his wet clothes and ruined shoes. Charlotte's clothes were further away from the door, behind a planter's chair. He dressed and followed the glow to the door; switched off the torch, opened the door, pressed the lock button on the inside knob and shut the door without a sound that could penetrate the tumult of the rain. He retraced his route along the wall and through the fence, realigned the thatch and walked back home along the beach without switching on the torch. Wonderful not to have to worry about stepping in shit. The rain teemed and the night was as cool as lovers had ever savoured in this place.

Charlotte drifted towards Randless sleep as soon as Aidan left. She drifted back out of it when she could not repel her irritation at Rand's invasion of her mind and her room when the tryst was almost over; when Aidan alluded by chance to the beheading. Rand himself dormant now, but he would be back soon with more intensity than ever, mainly because she would be so aware for several days that he had not been there for most of the coupling. A paradox; absurd but no less real for that.

In the last of the darkness she felt her way outside and showered Aidan away in the rain; towelled off and wrapped herself in a sarong, switched on the living room light and went to her typing chair. By sunrise at 6.30 she had translated and typed five pages of Bos Simeon's second notebook.

The rain had stopped at about 5.00am as the reinvigorated wind drove the cloud away; as the sun rose the air began to steam. Ngauea the housemaid arrived at 7am. She greeted Charlotte and went to the bedroom to strip the sheet for the wash. When she emerged with it bundled against her chest she stood in the hallway and stared at Charlotte, who caught her eye and looked back to her typewriter. "I'm washing this sheet now. And your clothes from yesterday. I pick up and wash the clothes behind your chair? Okay Missus Sarlot?"

Oh, fuck! "Yes, Ngauea. Do that. I'll work here for a while."

Ngauea picked up the damp dress and underwear with no interest in why they were there. As she walked across the room and back down the hallway her feet slapped on the tiled floor, as always. In the slapping Charlotte heard an echo of the final bout of the night just gone. Her skin cringed, much as Aidan made it tingle with pleasure; but this was fear.

She knows. She almost smirked at me. Deliberate foot-slaps, like damp bellies. The little bitch knows. She knew before she even got to the sheet. Oh shit. To her it's a marriage mat. 'The sheet's the proof.' And I forgot about the bloody giveaway dress and knickers. Charlotte, you are a fuckwit. Jesus Christ. Why did it have to piss down so hard while Peter was away?

Ngauea hung out the clothes and slap-padded up to Charlotte as she worked on Bos Simeon's journal. "Missus Sarlot, when I am hanging the clothes a message boy came from Mister Peter's office to say he will come back on the ship tomorrow night. He says I will not cook. He will bring fish. I will get the table ready."

"Thanks, Ngauea."

The maid listened to the typewriter and admired the speed of Charlotte's fingers. "Missus Sarlot, it's good because your friends will also come back on the ship, and they can visit you again when they have a day not teaching."

The rat-tat of the typewriter stopped, a machine-gun out of bullets. Charlotte turned to stare at Ngauea. "Teata and Safaila?"

"Yes. They went on Mister Peter's ship for their holiday."

After she heard Ngauea's broom scratch at the kitchen floor, Charlotte returned to her typing and built its speed to a frenzy for two minutes, without loss of accuracy. She slowed and stopped; sobbed into her hands for a few seconds; stopped for fear of the girl's vigilance. Peter, the bastard, had laid one or both of the teachers, her friends. Also Ngauea? She was less dumpy than most Gilbertese girls.

In retrospect her night with Aidan Conway was defensible. Their tryst achieved balance; restored the dignity eroded by Peter's infidelity with her friends and probably her maid, and the dancing little bitch at Abemama. And Peter was infatuated with Rand, the loser whose case and image her own husband had embedded in her mind and raised so often at night that he expunged their bed-life. What was it with Peter and Rand? Subliminal homosexual adultery? Without Peter's obsession, would Rand have now become more than an image?

Bos Simeon? What of her? Her tattoos and body intrigued Peter. Once on patrol he exalted her skin as it gleamed bare and blue-black when she passed two metres from their guesthouse in the evening on her way to wash in the stream. "Charlotte, did you see that back." Her young woman's breasts, never sucked flat by a baby, were half-concealed with a towel that hung from her neck. A constellation of four prominent moles on her right shoulder-blade.

Bos was much older than Peter, but attractive, and he did spend a lot of time with her on Bougainville when they were on patrol. Merely interested in what she knew about Rand, was he? What about the two patrols when he convinced Charlotte to stay at home in Kieta to study?

Until she read the journal Charlotte did not know Bos had a deaf ear, and assumed her occasional fleeting turn of the head was a mannerism to make her look attentive. A couple of times Charlotte watched her and Peter from a distance and thought the head-turn was a touch coquettish. Peter had never said Bos was deaf in one ear. On the other hand, if he had told Charlotte about a bung ear under that long hair, she would have asked him how he got close enough to find out. Another straw that might drop when the ship comes in. See if he knew about the ear.

Charlotte worked on the notebooks all day and well into the night, and again the next morning after three hours of sleep. She drank only water and told Ngauea not to prepare lunch. "Are you sick, Missus Sarlot?"

"Yes. I sure am."

Four hours before Peter returned she had translated and typed all three of Bos Simeon's notebooks. She could find no mention of sex with Peter but did find innuendo, including a reference to a comment by Peter about Bos's back when Charlotte was not on patrol with him.

Late the previous night, halfway through the second notebook, she had read two long sentences that would seem innocuous to anyone else but reeked of the straw-bale to her. She pondered them for ten minutes, then interpolated nine words between them. If the words were accurate they would trap him; if they were not, and he checked the original and picked her interpolation, she could dismiss them as the joke of a chattel left in a cocoon for weeks while the chattel's owner cruised the Pacific.

She might soak the handwritten notebooks in water until they became *papier mâché*, beyond page-turning and readability, in case he did decide to check her interpolated and censored version against Bos Simeon's original. "I left them on the step when I sat there to do a final check of my translation two afternoons ago and forgot to go and get them when the rain started. By morning they were mulch. I tried to dry them out in the oven." No need. She would watch him as he read the typed version. If he had strayed with Bos, his immediate reaction to the interpolation would tell much more than the tell of a weak poker player.

Charlotte sent Ngauea home and waited for Peter. She would cook his fish if he wanted any after she had dealt with him. Straw-stink wafted as she reclined in the planter's chair with a gin-tonic and listened, eyes shut, to the pulse of the ceiling fan. Peter would never suspect her of infidelity with Aidan or anyone else. Probably. But what if he were to discern even mild guilt and ask her about it? Where might his conspiratorial bent take the discussion? She must evade even a smidgeon of guilt, which she should be able to achieve on the grounds that Peter's dabbling had caused her infidelity with Aidan. Even if he could prove he had not dabbled with Bos Simeon or anyone else, he was at fault because his lack of sexual interest in her had hatched suspicion since they arrived in Tarawa.

Surely Aidan would not betray her to Peter or anyone else and would have the sense not to try to couple with her again. No complication of love between them; just compatibility, delicious and carnal. Here in the Gilberts she had loved Peter in undulations but had never loved or liked him as much as on Bougainville, where love and liking and compatibility were elevated and steady despite the burgeoning intrusion of the Rand factor.

She liked Aidan a lot, but no—she did not love him at all. Their tryst was intense in its pleasure, an almost Randless feast of lust peppered by mirth and the thrill of secrecy. It was never to be divulged and would be as impossible to repeat as loss of virginity for anyone other than a Gilbertese bride with a grandmother who had a new mat, a chicken and a sharp knife.

Charlotte opened her eyes to watch the fan whirl, and listen to it thump at her brain. Relentless, like her doubts about her marriage, and like the recurring script from which she could not excise the destructive, invasive character of Rand; for years he had come back again and again as a mental image; and two nights ago as an independent presence. A good play ruined by a long-dead misfit. Might be something in Rand's idea of life as a script but the malleability of the script was dubious.

Aidan would escape on annual leave the next Monday. As he put his files in order at his desk in the Secretariat a few hundred metres away from Charlotte, he reached the same resolve as her from another angle, a symbolic rather than literal one. There would be no re-run over Charlotte's terrain before he left or after his return. A friend, exhausted and baffled on his second ascent of Mount Everest, complained to fellow climbers, an hour before he slipped on ice and squealed into space, that he should have tried a new mountain.

* * *

"So I finally squeezed the story out of her?" said Peter after they kissed and she told him about Bos's notebooks and the typed translation. She gave him the typed version, the originals and a gin-tonic as they stood in the living room, two metres apart after the kiss, a distance she maintained when he tried to sidle closer. "Okay," he said. "I'll take it easy. Anything significant about Rand or is it all about what she doesn't know?"

"There's a lot about Rand and a fair bit about you."

"Good, good. Look, I'll finish my drink while I grill the fish and fry some spud slices. Fillets of mahi-mahi, golden dolphin. Not the crap trevally they cremate at the club. The crew caught it an hour from home, as they always do. I'll read Bos's story after we eat. If I start to read it now I'll want to keep at it until I finish. You look scrumptious. I've really missed you a lot, thought about you all the time."

"Same here. While you were out there on the high seas, all alone like me, I realised we needed to talk about a few things."

"We do. Nothing dramatic. Did you get out at all while I was away?"

"Al and Aidan took me to the club for cremated fish on the night of the deluge. Did you get that too? The deluge, I mean."

"Sure did. It started as I drained the last of my Scotch. Then I committed an unforgivable sin. You might forgive me for it but I don't think so."

A straw, so soon? "Did you now? What sin was that?"

"I pitched the bottle overboard into the pristine Pacific."

He returned the typed pages to the table, put the original notebooks back on top of them so the fan would not hurl them around the room, and went to the kitchen. She sat and stared at her drink for a few minutes, then flicked through the stack of pages until she came to her interpolation. She took out the page, read it, and wavered; reinserted it.

The fish was superb; she surprised herself by eating more than her share as they chatted about trivia. She would have to provoke him soon as he was too pleased to see her and she did not mind his company. "When I told you about Bos's notebooks you said in triumph that you finally squeezed the story out of her."

"No triumph. A simple observation. What's up?"

"You squeezed 'the' story out of her? It might be 'a' story."

"I'll read it and decide what story she's given me. I'll clean up here and read it right away. Are you okay? You seem a bit jumpy. A bit distant."

"I'm fine but I know Bos is not. You harassed her like a colonial upstart. 'Tell me your life story or I won't give you a shilling and a stick of tobacco'. Well, it's her bloody story, whatever she wants it to be, not yours. She owned it, whatever it was, until you gave her such hell that she saw you as a louse and she had to tell you something, anything, to get you out of her hair. Your Rand mania drove her even more nuts than it's driven me."

"Here we go again. Unknot your knickers. Look, Charlotte, I'm too pleased to be home to get into an argument. I'll start reading while you have another drink."

"Home? Sure. This is Tarawa. So you think I drink too much, do you?"

"No, probably not enough. Go for it. I'll have another one too if you don't mind. Lovely fish, wasn't it?"

When she returned with the drinks he was sniffing the cover of the first original notebook. "Smells a bit like pandanus leaf garnished with mould and sprinkled with cheap perfume."

"Some of the content stinks too. You read on. I'll read a novel."

As she expected, within a minute he tired of the original, long before he reached Bos's charge that Charlotte had betrayed woman-to-woman confidence; the rebuke that did not make the final typed translation. "My Pidgin's gone flat and her handwriting's a bit small for tired eyes. She's never heard of punctuation or paragraphs. I'll go with your version to save time and pain. Thanks for doing it for me." How predictable. If she were right about his attitude to the original, she must be right about a lot more.

He read and she pretended to read for half an hour without a word to one another. She could tell he was enthralled. No emotion or other giveaway. When he reached the folded blank page that denoted the end of the first notebook she asked him for his thoughts on what he had read.

"Some interesting anthropological stuff. No specific thoughts about her angle on one thing or another. I'm not really digesting it yet. The poor bloody woman. Bos's mother, I mean. The Japs were real bastards."

"What about Rand?"

"Not enough to go on yet. We've got only Bos's view of her father's death. It might be a fabrication. Same goes for other things she claims. We have to read it as one of several possible stories."

"Thanks. That's what I suggested earlier. Do you think there's much to read between the lines?"

"Probably not. I'll take another hour or two to skim the rest of it, then I'll let it cook before I read it all again in a couple of days. Then we can analyse it together. Let's have another drink while I go on with it. I'm skimming to rush it through so I can concentrate on you. As you mentioned Rand, don't object when I tell you I'm feeling randy."

"Oh, shit. Hilarious pun. Fucking hilarious. Don't get too turned on unless you've brought a condom home. I forgot to take my pill while you were away. Take your time with the reading."

He stared at the page in his hand without seeing words. "Unless I've brought a condom home? Thanks for that. You get us a drink. I'll read. You read. Then we sleep. Tomorrow we talk. Agreed?"

"Okay. As I said, take your time with the reading. Let it all soak in."

He read with care to keep his mind off the next day's discussion, but every few minutes the prospect emerged from the core of his mind, and he pushed it away again, always aware of Charlotte's gaze from the corner of her eye as she pretended to read her novel without a single turn of a page. She's waiting for something in the story.

A few pages into the second notebook he reached a page with a folded corner. He glanced at Charlotte and saw she now stared straight at him. He read the page and put it on the stack, then started the next page. His expression did not change.

"What do you think of the page you just read?"

"Nothing much. I presume you knew which page I'd reached, given the folded corner and your patient observation for the past half hour." He unfolded the corner. "It really pisses me off when people do that with library books."

"It's not a library book. What about the content? Read the page again."

"No need. Some of my colleagues made fools of themselves. You know them. Are you surprised?"

"No. Read out the whole paragraph that starts with 'You, Masta Peter.' "

"As you require, Missus. Here goes. 'You, Masta Peter, made me feel a little better about white men until you started to throw questions at me like rocks at a dog. When you came here without Missus Sharlet and we searched for birds and animals in the forest, you were interested in my tattoos. When I walked ahead you said you admired my bare back and strong legs. Later you came close enough to smell my hair. But when we got back to the village you were not stupid enough, like some other kiaps, especially the old one, to invite me to come to your bunk while the village slept.' There we go. How was my diction? Do you want to congratulate me on my fidelity?"

She had seen no poker-style tell when he read her interpolation: 'Later you came close enough to smell my hair.' She quoted it back to him and asked him to explain it. He asked her what Bos wrote in Pidgin. She lied: "*Bihain yu kam klostu long me na pulim win long gras bilong het.*" She knew he would not check the original.

"Now I get you. Here's the truth, inspired by gin-tonic. Mine, not yours. Bos stopped suddenly and I bumped my nose against the back of her head. The whiff of coconut and hibiscus made me randy—Get it?—so I decided to jump her from behind. She wasn't wearing a bodice so I ripped off her laplap instead. I told her to stand still on her Hollywood legs and bend over as if she were planting potatoes. That made her stick out her glorious bare arse. Then I heavy-breathed on her neck while I latched onto her perfect knockers and gave her a good one from behind. She moaned like a cow in need of a dairy. It's a wonder you didn't hear her in Kieta. I had nothing left after two hours, so we staggered back to the village and had dinner with coconut wine. Excellent vintage. I was too buggered to invite her to my bunk so I squeezed her tits for a few minutes, gave her a coffee and a cigarette, and then rang for a taxi to take her home. Does that suit your purpose, whatever it might be? Bunk's the word, Charlotte. Bunkum, Dearest. You won't come with me, and when you're here by yourself you don't keep your brain occupied. You let it wander off to strange places."

She had never known him to be so clever or earnest at dissimulation, at diversion. Too calm. Straw stink riper than ever. Peter must have needed sex with Bos to bring him closer to Rand, as if to be him, on the probably wrong assumption that Rand had fucked her; to recreate that part of the coast watcher's demise as the peak of Peter's obsession with the lunatic. "Speech over?" she asked. "Mock me all you want. It won't work."

"Not a speech, Charlotte. I'm trying to get you to see your suspicions are ridiculous. Get yourself an obsession to match the one you say I've got with Rand. It keeps me busy and reduces paranoia. Have I accused you of sleeping around while I've been on tour? It wouldn't occur to me. I've nothing more to say. Let me read on."

She would not let him fool her. "Did you have a good time with Teata and Sufaila?"

"Oh Jesus. Yes, I fucked them both, alone and together, lots of times, in every way you want to imagine. They're probably pregnant now because I ran out of condoms, which is why I couldn't bring one home to use on you. Oh, and I did have the dancer on Abemama, 16 times to match her age. I'm trying to read. For Christ's sake do the same. Study some Gilbertese grammar."

"What about Ngauea?"

"Twice a week minimum since we've been here. Ask her and see what she says. Cut it out, Charlotte. Maybe you're drinking too much. It happens to a lot of European women here. The liver acts up first, then the brain addles."

He protested too much. Clumsy attempts to belittle her, make light of her suspicions. Weak camouflage.

She asked him if he had mentioned her by name in the final versions of the letters he wrote to Bos Simeon, as he had done in the drafts he gave Charlotte to check his Pidgin. He said he had done so. "Why then," she asked, "did she spell my name on the envelope as S-h-a-r-l-e-t instead of C-h-a-r-l-o-t-t-e?"

"Nonsense. It was always the correct spelling. Charlotte in the drafts and the final versions. Who knows why Bos Pidginised you? I'll bring the originals home tomorrow. I saved them in case you needed to check my credibility."

"Don't bother. You'll do substitutes. I'm not an idiot. Why didn't you Pidginise Peter to P-e-t-a or P-i-t-a? In the notebooks she uses the English version, so that's what you must have used."

"Oh, Jesus. I confess. I confess to everything you think I should confess to. Now let me read."

Too smooth, Peter Millar, too calm, too condescending. The fan scattered the smell of a just-broken bale of hay.

Charlotte said she was going to bed. He asked her to wait for an hour or until he finished the notebooks. "I know how you've made yourself feel. Okay, no pill, no condom, no sex. But I want to watch you strip. I've missed that. No matter what you think of yourself these days, you're still a stunner in the buff."

Without logic, she thought it would look suspicious not to wait. "That's a bit teenage," she said. "As you wish, Mr Hefner. Have you worn out your Playboy library?"

She watched him for the hour and ten minutes it took him to finish. "Well?" she asked. "Did Bos unveil the enigmatic Mr Rand for you, Sherlock?"

"Made it all deeper. I'll take a few days to digest it. The main issue is Rand's alleged killing of Simeon. I reckon Walter Brooksbank knew about it but wasn't going to mention it unless he thought I knew, and he correctly concluded that I didn't. Hence my feeling that he was holding back. It's the sort of record that might disappear, even if the killing was justified, which it would have been in the context of war. Kill or be killed, and so on. Don't roll your eyes. I'll contact Brooksbank for another chat next time we're in Melbourne."

"Great. I do look forward to our chat in bed at the end of that day. Any other brilliant insights into the enigmatic, kindly Mr Rand?"

"Not yet. Other interesting revelations, which have nothing to do with him, include her pregnancy from the beach rape and her deafness in one ear. So, that's why she wore her hair long and sometimes twisted her head briefly to one side to listen. And why we thought she sometimes ignored us. We must have been on her bung side. You didn't pick it either or you would have told me."

Peter decided to reserve judgement on Bos's notebooks. Were there significant twists and omissions? A few minor ones were obvious. For example, he had never told Charlotte why Bos left her job at the Seventh day Adventist Mission. The departure had nothing to do with Bos's claim that the pastor's wife fired her for not becoming an SDA. A plantation manager told Peter the wife of the pastor twice saw him caress Bos's back and shoulders in a way that suggested familiarity with the rest of her body. Perhaps Bos's penile experience post-war was less limited than she wanted him and Charlotte to think. So what? Every magistrate knew some people distorted trivia to give themselves a sense of power in otherwise subjugated lives.

As a magistrate in Bougainville and the Gilberts, he saw how witnesses to a common event were often at odds about what they saw and how they interpreted it. He had also seen minor truth massaged and elevated as camouflage for weightier aberration that the witness or perpetrator did not want the court to detect. With Bos, what was true, from her point of view? What did she omit or distort or lie about? Did she hide or massage significant information about Rand and the context of his downfall? Had he fathered her baby? When honest, how accurate and complete was she, and how mistaken? How had time moulded her memory?

Charlotte asked him if he thought Bos's story of double rape on the beach was a cloak for Rand's paternity of her aborted baby. He shrugged. She said, "You don't want to consider that he might be a rapist, do you?"

"Do you want him to be? She didn't say he was the father, and says they did not have sex. How can you surmise rape from that? Have you heard of Occam's Razor? The best explanation tends to rely on the least speculation. She knew we were smart enough to see the father was one of the men on the beach. No need for her to explain."

"It's obvious her mother killed herself over the pregnancy. Would her mother have been that horrified if the father was a local? Titus, maybe? Even one of the rapists? The Japanese didn't want her, which pissed her off. She doesn't say whether or not she told her mother who the father was. I think it was Rand."

"Maybe, Charlotte. You want him to be the father, and a rapist. I don't think so. The journal says Bos's mother thought he fucked her little girl but Bos denies it. Anyway, why should rape and paternity by Rand rather than a local be more likely to make the mother top herself?"

"Okay, maybe he didn't rape her. Maybe it was consensual. Does that feel better? Is he still your hero? Rape or no rape, consider this. If I were Bos's mother I might hang myself if my daughter told me she was having a kid and I thought it was fathered by the man who just murdered its grandfather. She suspected Bos and Rand had it off. Maybe Bos told her so but won't tell you. Her mother could cope until she heard about the pregnancy. Before that, she could live with the murder of Simeon and the screwing of Bos, because she had revenge. She put the Japanese onto Rand and had the pleasure of making sure your hero lost his head. But the murder-pregnancy combination was too much for her."

"How rational you are, clever Charlotte. Enlighten me a little more. After Bos's mother led the Japs to Rand, which she clearly did, she bolted back in terror to where Bos and the officer were waiting, and was catatonic when Rand turned up a bit later with the soldiers. Why?"

"Simple enough, Sherlock. She was not in her right mind and couldn't think the whole matter through. Let me speculate a bit." Peter said she had been doing that since he came home. Charlotte ignored him. "The woman started to wonder if she had betrayed a decent man who killed her thug of a husband, and gave her daughter the sex she needed to convince herself she was attractive, with or without a buggered ear. And by the time Rand arrived with the soldiers the officer had given her a personal demo of what Rand was in for. His condition horrified her and she knew it wouldn't improve. Over the next few days she reconsidered it all and went into reverse. Saw him as a murdering bastard again, which was probably the right call. So, she changed her mind about him before the execution, after she had time to think it all through. Get my drift?"

"Not sure I follow you, Charlotte. For instance, if the Japanese tortured Simeon but he didn't give Rand away, how could Simeon's wife, even in a temporarily confused state, not have a permanent impulse to get revenge against Rand?"

"To her, Simeon was a thug but for a little while she decided Rand wasn't. Simeon's thuggery was enough for her to conclude, at least until she got her head back together, that Simeon was such a gutless bastard he deserved to be done over by the Japanese as well as Rand."

"Still don't follow you too well, Charlotte. You want to believe Rand was a bastard because you've been pissed off for a long time about my interest in him. It's the witching hour. Don't take that personally. Bed?"

"Sure. One more question before we hit the hay." She wanted to annoy him, to reinforce his assurance that he would not try to couple with her. "At the beginning of the first notebook, why did Bos wonder if Missus Sharlet was still your wife?"

"Isn't it obvious? She thought I was too vigorous and insatiable to screw any woman long-term without causing her mortal injury. Look, Charlotte, don't read so much into trivia. Get back to linguistics. Learn Gilbertese. Occupy your head before you lose it."

"Oh, Christ. Another beheading. Did you do that to piss me off? How in hell could you miss that one? Maybe your tongue's too fast for your brain. Association of words and ideas often passes you by." She pointed to the bedroom and walked away.

He called after her, "Word associations? Back towards linguistics at last." She replied, "You miss a lot, including Bos's last sentences about leaving blank pages for you 'to add stories you think I have forgotten or do not want to tell'. Do you still want the teenage strip-show?"

"You bet." He yawned, closed the living room shutters, switched off the lights and fan, and followed her.

She closed the bedroom shutters and sat on her side of the bed while Peter went to the bathroom. For the first time in three weeks, he showered in fresh rainwater instead of brine from a village well or rusty water from the ship's tank. He knew the house-tank was full so showered longer than usual.

Charlotte thought too much while she waited for him. She did not want to do this, not for fear it would lead to sex, which he would not seek; but because she could not subdue her memory of the lust with which she displayed herself to Aidan in the lamp-light at the end of their night together. To cheat in mind and body while her husband was hundreds of kilometres away was one thing. To cheat in front of him now, if only in fantasy, would be crass.

With little insight and no success, she tried to control her memory by scripting herself in a re-enactment of Bos Simeon's sexless strip to wash in front of the Japanese officer in the forest stream. The spurious connection was hostile to her purpose. She jumped to a replay of the officer's ensuing onslaught on Bos's mother, which invoked his violence against Rand; thuggery against him in the forest and his execution on the sand. She might as well have invited him into the bedroom to distress her.

When Peter returned naked she stood up and moved aside for him to unfurl the mosquito net; he let its weighted lower edges drop to the floor, then lifted an edge and eased under it to lie on the bed. Held up the edge just enough to get a clear view of her from knees to neck.

A relief not to see his face as that meant he could not see hers. "Are you ready for the show, Mr Hefner? Camera ready for the test-shots?"

He liked her red skirt and black t-shirt but would have preferred to watch her take off the white linen dress he bought for her in Yogyakarta. "Go for it, Gypsy Rose. I've got a photographic memory."

She wanted to get it over with; faced him and removed her clothes as if they were soaked in boiling water. Stood up straight to throw off her shirt and brassiere, and shove her skirt down to her ankles so she could kick it away. To remove her knickers she had to bend forward; as she did so she glanced through the gap in the net and saw not Peter but the horror of the adult Rand; a faceless, independent being. She leapt up in fear and tried in vain to replace him with Aidan.

"*Sublime frontage, Charlotte*," said Rand, in the girlish pitch described by Bos. "*Now show me your arse.*"

She turned around. On her otherwise flawless left buttock, out of her view without a large mirror, which they did not own, were four small bruises in a fifteen centimetre arc. The right buttock in shadow.

Peter's voice now: "Stunning. Back up to the lamp so I can get a better look." When she did, he saw another four bruises on the right, in symmetry with the pattern on the left. Ardent fingertips. Did they grip her in this bed or someone else's?

"There you go," she said. "Am I Playboy material?"

"Perfect, Babe," said Peter. "All done. Time to sleep."

Rand: "*You get next month's centrefold spot.*"

By the time she got back from vomiting and showering in the bathroom, her toxic memories and associations had retreated; so too her sense of deception. Rand had gone and Peter appeared to be asleep on his back. The ordeal over. She switched off the lamp, kissed him on the cheek and turned her back to him; slumbered from the moment her head hit the pillow. He got out of bed to open the shutters.

Peter had lies to tell her; the chances high that she would believe them because most European women in colonial situations, the Adventure Zone, eventually became paranoid about their husband's actual or presumed infidelity. She would want to believe him anyway. The marriage over for her, and her resolve ineluctable. To create guilt or beg her to reconsider would add to her distress and his. Pointless. Lie to her. Confess to crimes you have not committed. Do what you have to do, now.

At 3am he nudged her out of a dreamless sleep. "Charlotte, I have to level with you."

"Level away. I was only sleeping."

"You're right to feel the way you do. I've done bloody awful things with women, after that married woman I told you about. Well, she was before you anyway. I mean more recent stuff." Silence from her. He went on: "I tried last night to steer you away from the facts but I know it didn't work. Bos Simeon. I knew about her ear, and a lot more of her. And the dancer at Abemama, on the trip before the one with you."

She sat up in the darkness. "Only two? I did exaggerate, didn't I?"

"A girl at Maiana a couple of days ago. I can't even remember her name. But not your friends. Not Teata or Sufaila. I guess I've groomed Teata. Not Ngauea. I told the Governor's daughter we might get together on her next visit from the UK."

Got him. His serial infidelity dwarfed her single, unplanned tryst. Therefore she need not tell him about Aidan. The definitive straw had landed; it was supposed to create unbearable weight on her shoulders but somehow it lightened the load. She baulked for a few seconds at the stink of rotten silage that should have been the scent of fresh-mown hay.

She said nothing for half a minute; then, "Go to sleep. You've got the Japanese delegation coming in tomorrow morning. When you go to meet them, book me a one-way ticket to Fiji and Melbourne on the afternoon turnaround flight. It never has a full load." He could not reply, could not bring himself to retract despite an urge to rescind his absurd confession; to try to convince her he had lied about his deceit. She wanted to leave him, with or without evidence of his infidelity, and he should not get in her way. His future without her would be hell, but she would feel better about herself for the rest of her life only if she were sure he had strayed too far for any wife to forgive. Let her become carefree.

She resumed her slumber; he grieved sleepless as the surf-artillery crashed through his brain the way it used to crash through hers at night.

At dawn he left her asleep, wrote a note to say he would pick her up for the airport at 1pm, and walked to his office in leaden shoes. Saturday; no one would disturb him until his driver arrived at 10.30 to take him to the airport for the inward flight. While he waited he drank tea and read the Japanese War Remains file that he already knew in fine detail. It was too lean. It included photocopied extracts from Robert Sherrod's 1944 classic 'Tarawa: The Story of a Battle' and more recent official histories that brushed over the incompetence and stupidity that killed Americans who should not have died. A delicate file with no room for evidence or opinion that any American soldier was less than heroic; or that many Japanese soldiers may have died after they surrendered.

A year earlier Peter added a note, since expurgated by his senior, Al Todd-Willox, that wondered if some Japanese dead were victims of American murder rather than casualties of battle. "We can chat informally about such matters, young Peter, but don't file them. Too touchy. Might cause someone to say the right thing in the wrong place and give the UK Foreign Minister a bit of work to do with his US counterpart, Rogers. And bloody Kissinger. Might upset the Japan-US lovefest."

On Abemama a retired school teacher from the Ellice Islands, Iosefa Lameko, told Peter he was on the main island of Tarawa the day after the nearby battle of Betio islet in November 1943. In 76 hours it killed 1696 Americans, 3490 Japanese soldiers, and 1200 Koreans who laboured for the Japanese. The official history said the Japanese fought to the death; 17 survivors. The Americans had recruited the teacher, who spoke good English, to supervise local men as they helped bury the dead. He told Peter a remarkable number of the Japanese who were said to have fought to the death rather than surrender had bullet-holes in the middle of the forehead and large chunks missing from the back of the skull. Some lay in orderly groups where they seemed to have died systematic deaths.

The story may have been apocryphal but Peter knew several local men who believed it, perhaps to win a point against white colonials. Any whites would do. Whatever the truth might be, he would not broach the tale with the Japanese delegation; nor would he mention the decapitation of 17 New Zealand coast watchers at Betio on 15 October 1942. To avenge Rand in some obscure way, to be loyal to him, to give him some sort of minor victory by proxy, Peter would take the delegates to the spot under a pretext and make them stand there in ignorance; not tell them what had happened where they stood.

With little interest, he glanced over the three delegates' curricula vitae. Two spoke good English. The leader was a war veteran, aged 57, now an academic based in Japan. From 1938 to 1945, served mainly in Manchuria; brief stints in Indochina, the Philippines and Japan, but not the Pacific Islands. Marginal note in red by the governor: "A good diplomatic move by FCO and Japan not to send a Pacific veteran here." The other two younger; one, the non-English speaker, a 42 year old civil servant responsible for veterans' affairs; the other a restaurateur of 46 who represented families of soldiers missing at Tarawa.

Millar retched as he drove past his house on the way to the airport. Ngauea would be helping Charlotte pack for a sudden holiday in Australia. He wanted to be alone with the birds and fish and stars and crescent moon at Numatong. A kilometre down the road, away from houses and people, he told the driver to stop; lurched a few steps on earthquake legs to spew and piss on the lagoon beach.

Nine spare seats on the outward flight. While he waited for the plane he booked Charlotte's ticket to liberty and new fantasies, perhaps to recovery of lost happiness.

He took the Japanese to the simple, single-story Otintai, the one hotel on Tarawa, and stayed with them for a pot of tea served with aplomb by the gnomish Cockney manager. Much nodding and fleeting eye contact; minimal talk, most of it a slow monologue by the robust veteran about his old camera, a pre-war British Contax II, still with its original leather cover and neck-strap. He bought it in New York from a seller who claimed it had belonged to Robert Capa, who might have taken his famous D-Day shots with it.

"Mr Millar, this model was prized by Japanese war

photographers but hard to get. Sometimes they found one in battle. They were supposed to use the Hansa Canon, developed in Japan in the 1930s to improve on the German Leica III. But, Mr Millar, quality is quality."

"You have it with you, so I assume it still works well."

"This one is still perfect. I prefer it to modern cameras. And this one has history. Feel it. Be Capa for a moment." Peter weighed it from hand to hand. Its custodian wanted a photograph of the group at their table. "I will send you a copy from Japan." The hotel manager took the shot after meticulous instruction. *Hai!* Three bows from the delegates.

Peter rose to leave at midday; reminded them that the Governor's driver would pick them up at 6pm for drinks and dinner at the Bairiki Residency. On Sunday His Excellency and his wife would take them sailing on the lagoon in a Gilbertese canoe. They would have a picnic lunch on Bikeman, an uninhabited islet. On Monday morning Peter would pick them up at the Otintai Hotel and take them to Betio on the ferry to examine remains stored in a government warehouse. "*Hai. Hai. Hai.*"

At 12.45 he told the driver to wait and went into his house. Two suitcases just inside the door. Charlotte with a gin-tonic, under the fan in her favourite chair. She wore the white Indonesian dress that she knew was his favourite. He worried she would be cold on arrival in Melbourne. Maybe she could change into warmer clothes on the plane from Fiji.

"They're in my cabin bag. I've eaten," she said. "Ngauea saved some for you. Ngauea!" The girl brought him a bowl of rice and fish. He sat at the table to eat; to force himself to be seen to eat. No one spoke until he finished.

After Ngauea took the empty plate and gin-tonic glass back to the kitchen, Charlotte said, "Do me the courtesy of staying off her until I've reached Melbourne, if you don't mind. Then tell her I won't be back and do what you want to her. She thinks I'm going on a holiday."

He could only whisper a feeble retort. "I'll try to give it a week." He pointed to Bos Simeon's notebooks and the typescript on the side table, his voice now stronger. "Do you want to take them with you? To remind you of a better time and place? Better company?"

"Burn them. Keep the transcript."

"Let's go. We'll pick up your ticket at the airport."

"You're shaking. Stay here. It's better for both of us if I go alone."

She called Ngauea and told her to put the suitcases in the car. "Peter, you've done what you've done. That's it. It would have been wonderful for us to last forever. We haven't. You made sure of that. Right?"

"I feel as if I'm dying."

"Suicide is never fun. Stay here. I'll take Ngauea with me to the airport. You'll recover before she gets back. Go to the club for a drink. Give me your hand." He reached towards her with both hands; she took the right and shook it. "I'm off. Don't come out. I'll call your family in a week or so and tell them what's going on."

"What about, what about ... arrangements?" he whispered.

She did not hesitate. "No legal stuff yet. We can do that when your contract runs out in April and you have the sense not to renew it. When you pack up the house, put my stuff in separate boxes. Meet me in Melbourne to sort things out. Send me a few bucks over the next month or two, so that I don't starve. Okay? *Ating bai mi lukim yu narapela taim, Kiap Peter.*" New Guinea Pidgin with a Bougainville woman's accent. Intended to rub in a point that seemed to pass him by. Maybe I'll see you again one day, Patrol Officer Peter.

He whispered a nonsensical reply in Gilbertese. It hurt both of them; him because he hurt her and her because he took his last chance to ridicule her almost total ignorance of the language: "*E koriri ai rake. Tai kakiroa taningam.*" A strong current flows east.

Don't fall asleep. She picked up her shoulder-bag, opened the door and took long steps over the coral block onto the path.

He stood on the block and watched her until she reached the gate. The unique scent of her sweat. The tiny golden hairs on her neck. The tiny pearls in her ears. The face he had read and misread for so long. Intelligent eyes that had misread him and Bos's notebooks, and had vented woe for more than a year. Her eyes the green of a deep pool on the reef at low tide on a calm morning. The perfection of her figure and the lightness of her walk. The pigeon-toed turn of the left foot. That dress and the bruises hidden under it, secret from her. His sole deceit, apart from his self-demolition, was not to tell her he saw them.

She half-turned to him and called out over her shoulder. "Peter, don't mention Rand to the Japanese, for fuck's sake! Or anyone else, ever again, for everyone's sake." Slammed the gate.

He went inside and cried into his palms for half an hour, then sat outside on the doorstep until he heard, above the surf din, the far-off whine of her plane.

He put on sunglasses to hide his grief from Ngauea. His upper lip was stiff by the time she got back to the house with a bottle of Johnnie Walker that Charlotte bought for him from the Air Pacific pilot. Peter spoke to her in Gilbertese, which they used when Charlotte was not at home. "Ngauea, Charlotte will not come back for a few weeks. I will be away a lot on the outer islands. Take a long holiday, like her. I'll get in touch with you when she is on her way back."

"She told me she will not return for a long time. She gave me a lot of money." He gave her a wad of soggy cash and thanked her for everything. She stared at his mouth and asked if he needed anything else, anything at all, now or some other time.

"No. I'll call you when I hear Charlotte is coming back. I won't need a maid before then."

In the dusk he walked to the club; gagged on burnt fish, and contested drinks with Alastair. "Conway and I had a lovely evening here with Charlotte while you were away." Peter watched Alastair for any clue that he had participated in the tryst or otherwise knew about it. An aristocratic pretender, easy to read. Nothing written there. "Bugger of a night though, by the time we escorted her home. Absolute bloody deluge. All of us soaked by the time we returned her to the mansion. Then one had to swim home right away before the flood got deeper." 'One' would be right. The other, Aidan for sure, would have sheltered a while, or come back after Alastair was out of the way. Peter would not pursue the matter with either man.

"Thanks for looking after her. She said she had a great time."

"She didn't complain about the champers Aidan got from somewhere. He was here a while ago for an early piscatorial pyre. Your maid told mine that Charlotte caught the outward flight today. All okay?"

"Sure. Family business. Anyway, she needs a break, like the rest of us."

"Aidan's on leave for a month from Monday. Why didn't you take a couple of weeks with Charlotte? You must have leave owing."

Good. Aidan and he would not cross paths. "I have. I wanted to go, but the bloody Japanese corpse collectors arrived today, and I'm their tour guide."

"Ah, yes. Do tell them one laments the Allied murder of misunderstood Japanese altruists who wanted the East Asia Co-prosperity Sphere to free natives from the imperial yoke. Won't hurt to help them rewrite history a little more. They're already good at it, mind you. We play along for the sake of commerce and because Japan is some sort of buffer against Red China. That's the theory."

Peter went home and tried to listen to the BBC. The latest news of the Vietnam War did not interest him, nor the idiocy of British politics. The announcers' accents grated for the first time. He switched off the radio, grabbed an audio tape at random from a shelf of classics and jammed it into the player. Faure's Requiem, for fuck's sake. He kicked the tape deck onto the floor and went outside with a large Scotch to sit on the step and listen to the surf thrash the reef, and to the wind-worried clatter of palm fronds in his yard. A mosquito squadron attacked his head and hands.

Early to bed to savour the last of Charlotte's scent on sheet and pillows. The bed had been stripped and remade, and the pillows and mattress sprayed with deodoriser. Most of her clothes and all of her shoes gone. He settled into a night of agony, during which he tried with some success to distract himself from Charlotte's bruises and enter the mind of Rand on his last night, when his destiny was certain and surely clearer than Peter's.

He rose early on Sunday and stumbled out to the reef to fish the open ocean without bait or lures until midday. Charlotte was always at one shoulder or the other despite his resolve to ignore her.

He walked back to the beach and along the road to the house of a junior colleague, a single man of 24 doing his stint 'out there' before postgraduate study in a field unrelated to colonial administration; exercising his right to bed brown girls, far away from his well-bred parents. Along the road Peter did not notice greetings from Gilbertese on their way home from church.

"Sorry if you had to dismount from your maid or whoever, Marcus, but it's payback time for all the feeds you've cadged at our place. Charlotte's away and Ngauea's on leave, and I'm stuffed if I'm getting my own lunch or going to the club for a mouldy sandwich or another incinerated fish. Relied on your method. Walked along the road at mealtime and went into the place that had the best food aroma. What's cooking?"

"Drop your fishing gear and come in. The maid's gone home for a rest. She put a stringy chicken in the oven before she left. Want the feathers to make lures? Peter, you're agitated. What's up? My maid said that your maid said Charlotte's on holiday without you."

"Family business. All fine. I'm pissed off that I have to pander to the Japanese carcass detectives for the next week or so. I want to tell them a bit of history from here and New Guinea that they wouldn't want to know about, but I've been gagged."

"Wear the gag. Then write and publish what you want when your contract's over. If you say anything contentious now the heavies will get wind of it and jump on you."

After a lunch of boiled rice and leathered chicken washed down with three beers, Peter again ignored local people as he ambled a hundred metres across the island to the lagoon beach, dotted with turds dropped in the early morning, too far from the water to catch the ebb. Walked another hundred metres across the tidal sandflat to the water's edge. Fished baitless for three hours. Two men fished nearby but he did not know or care if they caught anything. No one came near him, unusual in this place with no concept of privacy, and with a vexing need to know if fish were on the bite and what successful or failed bait was on the hook.

As the tide rose he reversed back to the beach, inch by inch. For the first time he gagged at the shit and rotten garbage that swirled around his feet in the rising tide. Charlotte was right. He thought about the beach-as-sewer at Bos Simeon's village, the beach where Rand landed from a submarine in 1943. Shit on the beach at Bougainville had not disgusted him or Charlotte.

He sat on the beach above the sewerage line until sunset. At home he drank four straight gins to finish off Charlotte's supply, kissed the bottle she had held, and took two throws to shatter it in the garbage can at the back door. He resolved never to drink another gin. Ate a cold can of baked beans, showered and went to bed for another night of distress. At dawn on Monday he saw himself at one with Rand, in a comparison he knew was absurd, about to deal with Japanese because he had no choice.

He did not want to travel on the road towards the airport, so told his driver to pick up the Japanese at the Otintai Hotel and bring them to the house gate.

All three Japanese sat in the back seat. Peter greeted them as he got in the front, and told the driver to go to the Betio ferry wharf. On the way he stopped at his office to collect a compass and maps of the tiny islet that showed where, since the war, Japanese and American remains had risen to the surface or washed out of the beachhead in storms. The Japanese had maps based on American sources. None of the 17 Japanese survivors of the battle had reliable information about graves, and nobody bothered to ask Gilbertese people, or the few Korean labourers who survived, or Ellice Islanders such as Peter's informant on Abemama.

Sandwiched in a crowd of heedless Gilbertese, they stood on the deck of the old landing-craft, steel still hot from the sun of the previous day and countless days before that. Peter wore his casual work clothes and battered Panama. The Japanese were triplets in lightweight black suits, black shoes, and white shirts without ties; and broad-brimmed straw hats with chin-straps, as worn by Japanese fishermen and farmers. The younger two wore glasses. The restaurateur carried a small suitcase that held whatever they would need to cremate bones. The leader wore his treasured camera on a strap around his neck.

The diesel engine clanked and stank. The four were too tense to talk for the twenty-minute trip on a flat sea. All dwelled in private on the American landing of 20 November 1943. Peter saw himself as an American marine, a turkey about to die in a landing craft stuck on the reef because the US Navy ignored the tidal advice of the former harbourmaster, a New Zealander who had lived at Betio for twenty years before the British evacuation. The other three men imagined themselves ashore in concrete bunkers still intact after bombardment from air and sea.

Only the leader had the experience to imagine himself a shattered lunatic, doomed to cremation by flamethrower or disintegration by grenade or shell. An Emperor's servant caked in concrete dust, shit, sand, piss; and his comrades' brain tissue, guts and blood.

The ramp dropped with a rattle-roar of chains, a shriek of

metal on metal and a crash of steel onto concrete. The four stood still and watched the Gilbertese passengers stroll off around them when it seemed more fitting for everyone to run. The leader's face expressionless, controlled, but Peter could sense he was upset within.

A senior colleague, Alan McDermott, waited for them with another car but no driver, the car too small for six people to ride in comfort. They drove to the warehouse of bones, personal possessions, rusted weapons, helmets, buckles, and other nondescript relics that might have been military. Any name-tags or other relics that could identify a dead man had already been sent to Japan. The party left their hats and maps and a briefcase in the car. The veteran carried his camera.

The morning's work had started well for Peter despite Charlotte's weight on him, but he expected it to deteriorate.

The delegates bowed and murmured to a shelf of loose bones they saw in the gloom as they entered the warehouse. The veteran said that on the last day of their visit the delegates would cremate the bones at a suitable site, yet to be selected, along with any others they might find on Betio over the next four days. Millar confirmed that the British Government would ship the ashes back to Japan for interment at Chidorigafuchi National Cemetery.

No window, and meagre light from the open door. The delegation stood and gazed around in the glow of an erratic fluorescent tube. The veteran noticed nine rusted helmets on a shelf at the other end of the decrepit shed that did his dead compatriots no honour. He marched seven slow steps to the shelf and picked up a helmet with a bullet-hole at front-centre, where the star symbol used to be; a bulge at the back of the helmet. He put his finger in the hole and turned to quiz the other delegates with a raised eyebrow and prolonged glance; wordless. They nodded in unison. He rummaged among the other eight helmets and found one with identical damage; held one in each hand and turned around.

"Mr Millar. Mr McDermott. I think we can see how some

soldiers became bones." A pause. "Maybe not the bones in this warehouse, but some bones, found or not yet found." Another pause, longer. "Nine random helmets. Two with questionable damage. A high proportion?"

"Perhaps, Professor," said Peter. "Many stories about men's behaviour in the war are yet to be told."

"Here, you mean, Mr Millar? At Tarawa?"

"Here and elsewhere. China. The Philippines. Singapore. The truth should be told everywhere, about everywhere."

The veteran spoke in calm monotone. "We are here now. Other stories are for other places and times. Do you realise what I am thinking, about how these helmets acquired their condition? I do not mean the rust."

"I have heard a story that might align with your thinking."

Alan McDermott intervened. "Professor, let's tour Betio now, before the day gets too hot. We'll come back here after lunch and leave you to examine the collection, alone with your team. You can decide what you want to take with you when you leave and what you want us to ship to Japan for you."

"Thank you, Mr McDermott. May I first hear Mr Millar's story?" The other two delegates nodded when the veteran spoke to them in Japanese. Alan McDermott spoke one Gilbertese word to Peter: "*Karaua*." Be careful. McDermott stared at the ceiling. The veteran wanted to ask for a translation but did not do so.

Peter took half a minute to tell Iosefa Lameko's tale that suggested some Japanese who died at Betio might not have fought to the death. The restaurateur summarised the tale for the civil servant who spoke no English. The veteran walked towards the door. Peter stayed where he was and asked him if he had a story to tell from his wartime observation of Japanese troops in the Philippines or Manchuria. McDermott whispered "*karaua*" from behind Peter. The veteran walked out and his companions followed.

As they sat in the car the veteran said to Peter, in the front passenger seat, "I have no story to match yours, Mr Millar. Another time, perhaps, if we meet in Japan. This is not the time or place. Our visit is about Tarawa, Betio in particular. We know too little about this place to have a local story. We now have the one you just gave us, and we thank you for it."

McDermott drove for a few hundred metres as the Japanese studied their map. Peter tried not to think of Charlotte in Melbourne, which made him think more about her. What was she doing now? His mind moved her aside as Melbourne led him to his lunch with Walter Brooksbank, and from there to Rand's death. "Stop about 50 metres ahead, please Alan, near that stand of three palms close together, near the beach. There's something I want to show our visitors."

"Whatever it is, Peter, *karaua*, bloody *karaua*." The absurdity of a Scot with a cultivated British accent trying to speak Gilbertese. Alan did not know about this spot even though he lived on Betio, only 381 acres.

The delegates got out and put on their hats. Peter showed them where they were on the map, at a nameless spot with no building or people nearby, on an otherwise crowded islet. They stood on the shelf of the beach in the shade of palms. The veteran asked, "What is the significance of this nameless place, Mr Millar?"

"On the other side of the road, Professor, where there is nothing now, there used to be an asylum for lunatics. It was destroyed in the bombardment before the American landing and never rebuilt."

"Forgive me, Mr Millar, Mr McDermott, for pondering aloud the insanity of an asylum for lunatics being destroyed by other lunatics."

Rand heavy on Peter's shoulders. "Professor, there is another story, specific to Betio, that might interest you. It's probably better than my other story. Shall I tell it?"

The restaurateur interpreted for his colleague while the veteran waited. McDermott stared above Peter's head at a coconut, willing it to fall. The veteran said, "Please tell the story, Mr Millar."

"It will be better if we stand on the beach," said Peter. "The tide's a fair way out, so we won't ruin our shoes in saltwater." The party followed him onto the sand. "*Karaua*, Peter," said McDermott.

"Ignore the weak bastard," said Peter to himself. "That's what Rand would say."

"Gentlemen," said Peter Millar, "it's hot in the sun, so I'll be brief. Your forces captured 17 New Zealand coast watchers throughout the Gilberts around the middle of 1942. They brought them to Betio and tied them up to coconut palms for three days in front of the commandant's house, which was about 200 metres from here, near that *nakatari*, in English a tidal shithouse built over the water." He stopped for the restaurateur to interpret but the veteran shook his head. "Then they put them in the asylum. On 15 October the Americans bombed and shelled this area. One of the prisoners escaped and ran onto the beach to wave to the American planes. The Japanese caught him and killed him, I'm not sure how."

The restaurateur summarised to the civil servant: "An American spy who tried to kill our soldiers was tried and executed on Betio." The veteran nodded.

McDermott intervened. "The horrors of war, Mr Millar. It's hot as hell. Let's go, gentlemen."

Stuff this gibbering Scot with his gob full of haggis. Finish the story. They don't like it so far but they're hooked. They'll remember it even if they don't discuss it among themselves or tell anyone at home.

McDermott started to walk away; no one else moved. The veteran stared at the tip of Peter's nose. "Go on, please, Mr Millar."

"That afternoon the Sons of Nippon brought the other prisoners to the beach, right here where we are standing. They made them kneel to make it easier to cut off their heads. You could say there are heads in the sand around here. End of story." The restaurateur did not interpret.

The veteran thanked Peter for "a sad story" and asked McDermott to take them back to the warehouse to spend an hour before lunching at his house. They stopped halfway to drink from coconuts Peter bought from an old woman who would not allow herself to look at the Japanese after a first glance. She chopped each nut and gave it to Peter to give to them. She gave McDermott his. While they drank, her eyes admonished the two Europeans as if to say, "Why are these bastards here with you? I'm not too old or young to remember them."

Peter went to McDermott's house to rest in the sitting room before lunch while the delegates rummaged alone through the relics at the warehouse. He heard McDermott make a long telephone call in another room but could not catch the detail. When he returned he told Peter the Chief Secretary, a step above Alastair, his immediate boss, wanted to see him at Bairiki right away. McDermott would manage the rest of the Japanese visit for today. "The Secretary's office has radioed the ferry captain to hold the boat for you. It's due to leave. I'll drop you now. Let's go. Sorry about lunch."

"You're a weak bastard, McDermott. These fuckers think all dead Japanese are victims. If Iosefa Lameko was right, some are, but the overall ratio of Japanese victims to perpetrators doesn't make them look all that merciful, compared with the Allies."

"How many times did I warn you to be diplomatic? Christ, Peter. We know they're bloody hypocrites who detest us because we know their war history much better than the population of Japan knows it. You might as well have handed that fucking smug academic a sword and asked him to trim your ears with it."

At the ferry Peter got out of the car and held open the door to tell McDermott, "Go on. Pander to their victimhood a bit more. When they finish rummaging through the junk, and photographing helmets with suspicious holes, take them into the big bunker in the middle of the island and show them the body shapes stencilled into the concrete walls by Yank flamethrowers. Great photographic possibilities there. Real works of art to perpetuate the victimhood project."

"Peter, only you can see those shapes."

"Ask them which was worse. The flamethrowers, or what they did to disarmed and tortured coast watchers, here and in other places, including Bougainville? I'm a bit sensitive about it. They murdered someone of personal interest there. The boffin will take photos of the scorches and helmets but he didn't want to take any on the beach."

"Personal interest? Rand? Yes, we've all heard about this fellow. Didn't know he was close enough to make you risk a diplomatic rift. You know the standard list of perceived offences. Cross-cultural insensitivity, racism, victors writing the history, colonial attitudes. Now I've got to clean up for you in a single lunchtime, before that bloody professor can get on a phone to Tokyo." Peter slammed the door and squeezed into the crowd of passengers who watched and waited for him on the ferry.

The Chief Secretary was in a meeting with the Chief Minister and Alastair. A clerk waited. He gave Peter some files, a radio valve and a handwritten note from the Secretary: "I can't see you today or tonight. McDermott will manage the Japanese delegates until they leave on 17 October. The chief magistrate is ill. Please get on the plane to Butaritari Island tomorrow morning. I want you to hear the five cases in the files my clerk will give you. Show the new District Officer up there how to do it, as he's too green to do it himself. He might not agree. Put him in his place if necessary. He will not be expecting you as the radio up there broke down when we tried to make contact this morning. Sounded like a valve failure. Install the new one my clerk gives you. If the radio still doesn't work, bring it back with you. Please do not return to Tarawa until 18th at earliest, and do not go to the Otintai Hotel tonight."

The clerk offered to book the ticket. Peter said he would do it himself as he had to see the Air Pacific agent about another matter.

The agent, a pretty girl with a Gilbertese mother and long-absconded Polish father, booked Peter's return ticket south to Nonouti Island, in the opposite direction to Butaritari. "Charge to the Chief Minister's Office, Mr Millar?" she asked.

"No, Tema. I'll pay cash and claim later. Keep the destination a secret between you and me. Any other *imatangs* or local admin people on the flight?"

"No Europeans, no civil servants. All passengers local. Your seat is the last." She was alone in her office; smiled at him and looked at his mouth. "Your wife has gone to Australia on a one-way ticket, the one you bought at the airport from my brother. You didn't wave her goodbye. She is on a very long holiday, says Ngauea. True, Peter Millar?"

"Yes, Tema. Family business. I must go now. See you at the airport tomorrow."

"Not me tomorrow. My brother. You want to talk with me tonight?"

What would Charlotte advise? "Do what you've been doing anyway. Fuck her."

Peter said, "Thank you Tema. You are always happy and kind. Let's talk when I get back."

"Okay, Peter. I'll bring work papers to your house at lunchtime the day after you get back." She thought lunchtime would look innocent to neighbours. Ngauea would be on leave; just Tema and him. He nodded.

At home he put the radio valve and court files in a cupboard. Drank two Scotches and saved the rest for his trip. Packed the bottle, a few clothes, a hand-towel, his fishing reel, hooks, sinkers, swivels, his camera and binoculars, a spare film, a torch and batteries, waterproof matches, two cans of baked beans, a fork, two bottles of boiled water, toiletries, and an old Japanese bayonet to cut fish and open young coconuts for their milk, sterile as a saline drip. He added Charlotte's transcript of Bos Simeon's notebooks, then zipped the bag and lay his two-piece fishing rod across it.

He took Bos's notebook originals to the lagoon beach and burned them as the sun set. Back at the house he sat on the step in the darkness for an hour to contemplate the din of the reef; let the mosquitoes attack him in a sortie of stings on last night's stings. Went to bed early without dinner and all night suffered the spectacle of fingers digging into Charlotte's rump, his agony mitigated for a few seconds at a time by a drowsy need to scratch his mosquito bites until they bled.

He sat in the co-pilot's seat on the 70-minute flight to Nonouti in the Britten-Norman Trislander, flown by a Fijian prattler with early beer on his breath. Through headphones Peter heard him waffle about fishing, the disposition of phosphate royalties from Ocean Island, the athletic sexuality of Fijian women, and the deterioration of beer in unrefrigerated ships that carried it into the tropics from Australia's temperate zone.

The plane tracked Charlotte's escape route south-southeast towards Fiji for 40 minutes. At 2500 metres altitude the plane levelled, almost above Maiana Island, the last place Peter had spent a painless night, sure of his marriage, with no more sense of the precarious than the islanders down there had of life on a flat chunk of coral and sand, perched a metre above deep blue nothingness on the peak of a swamped mountain. Not solid and sure and ancient like Bougainville, Charlotte had said. There, less chance of a tectonic slide and plunge into blue-black oblivion.

A few kilometres west of the Abemama lagoon, the pilot peeled Peter away from the pursuit of his wife. The plane turned a little further to the southeast towards Nonouti, still unseen but given away by the reef's red-green shimmer on the base of a cumulonimbus monolith, a boiler that threatened daily carnage it could not deliver. How can that cloud develop here in eternal wind? Ah, the base is well above the island. Calm up here, windy down there, so the base can seldom form at sea level. On the other side of the monster, on rare days when the base touches the sea, a waterspout might wait in ambush to savage the plane; the torment of pilots, the passengers' nightmare.

Don't fly into that cloud. Don't land at Nonouti. Keep going, on to Melbourne.

Thirteen minutes later they shuddered from the cloud and bumped down a cushion of hot air above the lagoon towards the strip of crushed coral; the pilot tight-gripped, the passengers stolid in the Gilbertese way, Peter a tense child with heels about to strike earth at the bottom of a playground slide. He watched Numatong Islet quiver through salt-mist far to the west, until the horizon rose too far and sank his favourite refuge.

At Nonouti Peter told the council president and sleepy clerk that ornithologists at the University of Hawaii had asked him to make a sudden trip to Numatong to look for a rare bird. They nodded. No question from them about the particular bird. No interference with us here on the main island if he's going to Numatong.

He hired his usual canoe and crew of old captain and three fit men, much younger. All roasted deep tan, the captain squint-eyed from decades of marine glare; each wore only a tired sarong and a fisherman's hat chin-cinched with coir.

The sea calm, the weather and wind perfect for a fast trip. Two crewmen managed the sail; the other two shuffled back and forth along the struts of the outrigger log to keep it balanced a metre above the water, as if weighing and reweighing themselves.

On one voyage he had asked them to sail a few kilometres past Numatong, out of the lagoon into the open ocean. In the transitional zone the crewmen yelled "*Takua! Takua! Takua!*" Dolphin. A pair darted to them from the open sea, turned at the bow and led them through a safe channel over the submerged reef. Out in the deep, the sailors' feet read the canoe's balance and worked the struts for an hour as the hull dashed up the mirror walls of waveless swells and skated down into cobalt blue troughs from ridges as high as the mast was long. The dolphins capered with them and later guided the canoe back into the lagoon. For the entire romp, Peter had held Charlotte and Rand out of sight and immersed himself in raw pleasure at the interplay between the sailors and their particular part of the natural world, a virtuoso's realm much different from his own stage.

Today, as they neared Numatong, the captain asked to do it again in the perfect conditions. "Sorry, I can't," said Peter. "The afternoon is half gone and I have much work to do before dark. Drop me ashore and then go out there by yourselves. I'll pay the canoe owner for the extra time."

He told them to pick him up early on 18th in time to get back to the airstrip for the flight to Tarawa. For thirty minutes he watched them continue the voyage west of Numatong, across the last stretch of the lagoon and over the submerged reef into the ocean swell. Through his birder binoculars he watched the canoe frolic, visible and then lost to him as it scaled ridges and dropped into valleys. Too far away to see much detail, but dolphins would be there.

He did not do his usual strip. After 15 minutes he sat on the shoulder of the beach and started to re-read Charlotte's transcript of Bos Simeon's notebooks. An hour and a half after the sailors dropped him he had read much of it and skimmed the rest. Bos's depiction of Rand, endorsed by Charlotte on impulse, looked even more spiteful and counterfeit than it did at home on the first reading. Charlotte's claim of sexual innuendo was still bizarre.

What a fucking farce. Talk to Charlotte again? He might call the sailors back to him as they sailed close to Numatong on their way home. He could return to Tarawa on tomorrow's flight, telephone her, and tell her he lied about his infidelity because he knew she wanted to split and he wanted her to have a happy future without any sense of guilt. Salvage his reputation if not his marriage.

As he took a shit while considering his future, the sailors waved and whooped on their zigzag sprint for home across the easterly, two men perched on the raised outrigger, with mast and sail tilted towards tragedy as the canoe sped past Numatong. Missed his chance; put his shorts back on.

When the canoe was a kilometre away towards Nonouti, he turned away and built a fire on the beach with palm leaves and twigs of driftwood. He read no more; burned the transcript two pages at a time until the accidental conspiracy of Charlotte and Bos was reduced to ashes that would flush with his shit on the next tide.

Two angelic white terns—black of eye, blue of beak and leg—hovered, fluttered, chirped and beckoned two metres above his head. He took his camera and followed them, or they followed him, 100 metres to the pandemonium of birds at roost, boasting their survival of another day in fifty languages and dialects. No song-birds on these atolls, just a Babel of screechers and chirpers at one pitch or another. Thousands of birds arranged and rearranged themselves before sunset on sandbanks, coconut palms, pandanus, and a few scrubby trees that might have grown taller with a better-balanced diet than the guano replenished daily on a dry, flattish dune of sand and broken coral. No soil. Nothing but birdshit and yourself to make you dirty; glare and salt-laden wind to mummify skin and burn eyes. Like any desert, beautiful to visit, hell to endure for more than a few days.

He photographed a bristle-thighed curlew that glided onshore after a landless marathon, smooth until its feet touched sand and its legs collapsed. *Numenius tahitiensis*. From where? Alaska, via Hawaii? No, a long way out of season. A recalcitrant. Confused straggler? Who cares? Another shot of it, on its side, baffled, defeated, head propped up by a long beak curved into the sand. Not enough energy to cry out in protest or fear. Five minutes later a shot of its triumphant stand, pushed up by wing-tips and beak, on the fifth try after four mid-rise crumples of geriatric legs. Two upper register whistles of victory, *pee-weet*, *pee-weet*, pierced through the Babel of other birds; too exhausted for the usual five or eight calls, but too tough to wilt. Peter Miller wished he had been born the bird. Hatched.

Ten more random shots through the 105mm lens, long enough for unskittish birds with no fear of humans. Seventeen shots total; that would be enough.

The sun waned behind him as he searched the shallows for bait. Hermit crabs retreated into the safety of their cone-shell squats when they saw his feet. He selected a shell about five centimetres long and held it close to the high-pitched kisses he made with tight lips to entice the squatter out to die on a hook for its curiosity.

After three casts he hooked a two kilogram trevally, all jerks and twists and flips; flashes of blue, silver and gold in its last light. He hauled the unwilling fish into shallow water; a metre from the tail, a shark rammed its belly onto the sandy bottom and rolled off course in a splatter of foam and terrified minnows.

Peter pitched the trevally over the shelf of the beach onto sand beside his bag near the shelter he built on his first visit. He photographed the fish as it flipped in fury and tried to gulp life from waterless air.

He refurbished the roof with fallen palm fronds and put his bag, camera and other gear inside. As he worked he watched the fish go grey and die on a patch of tiny silver scales torn off in the clash with sand; the sand as ignorant of the fish as the rest of the universe was ignorant of this meteoroid's human occupants; trapped, and deluded about their significance.

A can of baked beans, bayonetted open, sat on the coals until the label burned off and the contents bubbled. By the time the beans were hot a quarter of the Scotch was gone. Peter took a long time to eat them with the fork, without hunger, with unaccustomed daintiness. Dusk settled upon him and he stared at the moon's last quarter, eclipsed from time to time by remnants of the cloud mountain that earlier bullied Nonouti proper. The crushed can cracked and scorched black on the coals. Scotch and baked beans, a little short of gourmet fusion.

The Gilbertese weather almost always comes from the east. The current close to the beach at Numatong is always strong but waves pound the sand only in a rare and dangerous westerly, heralded from the open ocean by clouds of deep indigo terror. In today's evening-calm breeze, wavelets lapped the sand, playful slaps on Charlotte's bare skin.

Far from Numatong the ocean breakers hammered the reef on the north and east of Nonouti. From here the sound should have been what it was earlier in the day, the moan of smooth traffic flow on a distant motorway. Yet parallel to that sound, punctuated by the trevally's death-slaps, was a new, unfamiliar intrusion, a steady raucous hiss, like the one that woke him and Charlotte at night in Bairiki if they forgot to switch off the bedroom radio and the BBC signal transferred to another frequency. A crescendo of cicadas became an unbroken hiss of leaking gas. No cicadas here. No snakes, except in the sea. No gas bottle. No kettle to hiss and whistle at the boil. No burning stick or coals doused with water. No one pissing on the campfire. The bird cacophony, no hiss anyway, long silent.

Five times he rotated clockwise and anticlockwise to locate the source of the annoyance. Relentless, maddening, always in stereo at the centre of the circle, within his head. Tinnitus. Bloody tinnitus. His mother's legacy. Thank you Mum, always ready to help. The onset confirmed his future.

By 9.30pm, a smooth ebb current from the lagoon streamed past Numatong to the open ocean. Peter Millar held his torch in his mouth and cut the trevally into small pieces. He took off his shirt and smeared fish blood and guts onto his head, chest and legs, then jammed chunks of fillet into the patch pockets of his shorts. He wrapped the head, skeleton and tail in the shirt and threw the bundle into the tidal current; waded in.

No moon now; only brilliant starshine candling the water a few metres down to sand. Peter Millar floated on his back so the stars and planets could draw his eyes and mind while his body coasted into deep water. Saw them as a snowstorm absconded from its climatic zone.

A dead Viking? No. No pyre-boat or flaming arrows, just a shooting star—a snowflake trying to evade tropical air; no mourners to see him off, no heroic legacy.

The seawater a smell and taste of salted fish. A turtle rose and gasped beside him. The revitalised curlew warned him with five policeman's whistles, shrill and robust. What was that? A taunt? He heard the scornful quin-call of the Bougainville crow. No crows here.

The curlew back to silent crabbing, the crow off to mock another misfit. Peter redefined his tinnitus as the eternal drone of the universe into which his wretchedness would soon dissolve like the snowflake star. Listen to the stars and planets. Stare into them; no, that's delusional, for stars anyway; rather, stare into recent reflection of light off planets, and into the hurtle of sparks fired at Numatong by stars a billion years perished. God's another delusion. Our Father who aren't in heaven. The Planets. Love Holst. How long will it take the bagged camera to rust in salt air?

Whispered calm love to Charlotte, fondled his wedding ring. Within the universal drone, her reply rose to him, a sigh through the wordless female chorus of Holst's 'Neptune, the Mystic', pianissimo. "*E koriri ai rake, Peter. Tai kakiroa taningam.*" A strong current flows east, Peter. Don't fall asleep.

Twenty metres away an anxious shadow picked up the berley trail.

Two passings occupied the last few seconds of Peter Millar's mind: one his own demise now in physical solitude; the other long ago and far away on Bougainville in front of a crowd; both passings lonely, remote. Death, the most secluded act of life; private, secret, even with an audience like the one for Rand that Bos Simeon described.

*   *   *

On a sticky bed at the Otintai Hotel the leader of the Japanese delegation lay naked on his belly in darkness under a fan of erratic pace and token churn. It wobbled, bumped and squeaked—beat aerial mice to death. The airflow too feeble to push back the shit and garbage stink that seeped into the room from the beach on a cat's-paw breeze. Too sultry to close the glass louvres; even more stink and too many mosquitoes if he were to open the door.

His dinner of charred fish and rice-glue reasserted itself. The best duty-free Suntory whisky could not cut into it. Millar, the upstart British official, was hostile and smart and therefore best out of the way. Australian. Misunderstands war as a chivalrous duel that can and should be fair, honest, civilised. North to Butaritari for him, said McDermott, until we've left for Japan.

In the dark slumber of a village house in Bairiki, Tema the Air Pacific agent lay on her back with eyes and mouth wide open, enveloped in the biscuit perfume of a new pandanus mat, too close to her parents and younger sister to risk more than the slow roll of a finger-tip under her night sarong. Peter Millar would soon return but not his woman. He would make her toes curl even tighter than now. Ambushed by an unbridled sigh, she converted it into a cough.

Alastair Todd-Willox pranced home alone in darkness from the Bairiki Club, smacking mosquitoes on his face and arms. Millar will have been in court all afternoon at Butaritari. Still no radio contact so the valve's not the problem. One must pull him into line after his episode with the Japs. How to get the idea of an official warning past His Excellency the Governor? The Secretary entitled to do it without consulting him. No, not wise.

At breakfast in a London flat, a girlfriend of His Excellency's teenage daughter served bacon and eggs to Aidan Conway.

On their freehold stools at the Nyngan RSL Club, two nostalgic warriors toasted and re-toasted Dave Rand, a Great War wreck, two days dead by his own hand. Toe, really—he used a shotgun with a long barrel. A wonder he lasted that long, with that bitch of a sister. Yeah, and his kid long gone by a Jap sword and his missus by Dave's old bayonet. Right. And his head fucked up by thunder, lightning and whatever. Right.

Bos Simeon sat on her house step, chin in agitated hands. Would not try to sleep tonight. In a recurring nightmare that started after she sent her notebooks to Peter Millar, Rand might again invade her dreams to make her watch him perform the impossible horror of hanging her mother in the forest. Impossible because he was dead when she hanged. But who knows what the forest and its inhabitants can do? She stretched an arm over her shoulder to scratch a mole in the star cluster on her back; the top star had started to swell and ooze about a moon ago; maybe a moon and a half.

Walter Brooksbank, at home alone in Melbourne, looked past the television news he always saw at this time of night. He again thought about his lunch a few months earlier at the Queens Club with Peter Millar in person and Hugh Rand in tow as insistent history. Should have gone to see to see his parents in 1943 straight after I got the navy to send the telegram. Wrote to them. Asked them to pass on the news to any girlfriend he might have had. No answer. Didn't have a phone in those days. Called the local police and asked them to get Dave to agree to my visit. He told them no. Not too late now, so bloody long after it all, if he's still kicking, or she is. Mother called me from the post office in 1947. Made no sense. Didn't want to meet me. I gave up. Anyway, no talk so no chance of a security breach.

Four kilometres from Walter Brooksbank, Charlotte Millar drank another Riesling and chatted with her parents after a long dinner led by lamb roast. They and her husband's parents and sister still thought she was on holiday from Tarawa while Peter did his duty in the field. In a couple of weeks she would come clean. They were too happy to see her, too eager for intrepid stories of Peter; cruel to break the spell too soon, to divulge the split, so she wrote them a benign script and would stick to it for a while. This script thing handy at times.

No matter what tale she told, with merriment or gravity, a corner of her mind watched her husband and Hugh Rand take turns to hump the mature Bos Simeon; two lechers, less dignified than wanton dogs, slaver-tongued, bitchless for a year.

She hated Rand the spoiler, the unwitting first cause of her marital ruin. If his fate had not obsessed Peter, and the obsession had not burgeoned after they moved from Bougainville, and Peter had not badgered the notebooks out of Bos Simeon, Charlotte would not have despaired; would not have been inspired by Bos's story to expose her husband's infidelities in Tarawa, and would not have been driven to the solace of Aidan Conway.

Bos Simeon must also carry blame that preceded her writing of the notebooks. Her refusal to talk about Rand to Peter on Bougainville created a stronger presence of the dead loser in Peter's mind and therefore Charlotte's life. Rand at first an annoying but controllable mental image; later, thousands of kilometres from the site of the beheading, the mere image had been superseded during sex with Aidan by the advent of Rand as an active external entity.

Yes, that's about the gist of it. Mum and Dad gone to bed. A few more sips, then bed for me too. Minimal intrusion at night by Rand since the return to Melbourne. Nothing of him during the day. In Tarawa it's now two hours later than here. Peter up late with the Japanese group? Probably excused himself right after dinner at the Otintai and at home bonking Ngauea right now. Or bloody Teata. Both?

PART FIVE

Kyoto, Japan, 1982

The First Gallery of Professor Hiroyuki Ayanokoji

Wednesday 15 December 1982. Kyoto. Dear Jesus, haul me out of this bog. Dr Charlotte Fonseka, lecturer in linguistic theory at Sydney University, could not fathom the dreary presenter at the conference in the Clock Tower building at Kyoto University. For fuck's sake, man, choke so someone will call an ambulance. Might wake us up, create some interest.

Although she had not missed a session, two days of the three-day linguistics conference had passed her by. On the first day, she presented her paper to little acclaim despite her well-massaged statistics and praise for prior work by the linguistics royalty in attendance. She detected more male and female interest in her body, legs and good looks than her mind. Now, on the morning of the third day, her 39th birthday, she could bear no more of the pretentiousness, the unintelligible waffle about simple things, or the sometimes intelligible waffle about simple or complex things that were not worth the funding, the writing, the delivery, the presenter's salary, or Charlotte's attention. Her paper, like most papers at most academic conferences, was tedious and unoriginal; crafted with cowardice and care to ensure she would not disjoint any luminary's nose if his or her worn-out theory and boring research were not cited and lauded as the inspiration for her mini-advance in their field. Her PhD supervisor had called it strategic incrementalism.

She rasped a drawn-out cough to give herself an excuse to shoulder her bag and leave the auditorium in deference to the speaker and listeners; there may have been ten of the latter in a kipping, hungover audience of 125. She went down the stairs of the Clock Tower building, the hub of the main campus, out into the cool air, and flipped her bundle of conference papers into a garbage bin. Five students dashed for the prize. She did not stop to see who won it.

Charlotte celibate in Kyoto and a little tense; close to the end of her six-year marriage to Professor Gamini Fonseka of the University of New South Wales, a Sri Lankan national and expert on post-colonial civil wars, one of which simmered in his country of origin, a pressure cooker about to explode. He had long been a pain in her arse. To him all problems in Sri Lanka and other former colonies, especially those of the British Empire, were the colonists' fault. For example, the rancour between the minority Tamils and majority Sinhalese Buddhists was a colonial legacy. Never mind that the two ethno-religious groups had spatted on and off since they invaded the island from India at about the same time, well over 2000 years earlier. The Hindu Tamils came from the south; the Aryan Brahmins came to the island from the north along India's Ganges Valley, and a few centuries later adopted the belief system of Buddhist immigrants to the island from Orissa and Bengal in the Indian northeast.

Charlotte was weary of Gamini's allusions to her former husband as a colonial exploiter, abetted by her; even wearier of his racism and his default perspective on colonialism and its legacy. She called it the toe-stub model. If a Sri Lankan drunkard were to stub his toe in a pothole as he staggered home along a road in the dark, his injury would be the fault of the British because they built the road. Any Caucasian who disagreed with Gamini was a white supremacist, a racist with no brain; anyone else a white sympathiser, also brainless. His racism went from silly to rabid after he missed out on a Rhodes Scholarship funded by the African profits of that benign investor, Sir Cecil. He redefined a friend who had won a Rhodes two years earlier as a lickspittle and lapdog to white colonisers, and therefore an enemy.

Eager in private, reluctant in public, Gamini succumbed to family pressure to attend Oxford at parental expense. He saw no moral or other contradiction in going there, and later to an academic career in Australia. He explained to Charlotte that he had felt obliged to master British educational weaponry, then use it for intellectual guerrilla attacks on the enemy's home ground, which included Australia.

Oh, Jesus. How could he be so intelligent in some ways and so idiotic in others, especially his assumption that everyone else was stupid enough to swallow the Teachings of Gamini Fonseka? On her single visit to Sri Lanka a few people's tacit reactions to him— blank stares, head wobbles—suggested they shared her diagnosis. But there were too few doubters to ever draw her back there. In Colombo she dismissed Hugh Rand's mockery: *What would Peter say? Be the way you were in Bougainville. Go deeper, Charlotte, in exile and with aliens at home. Is Gamini the problem? Sri Lankans? Are you sure? You, perhaps? Have you tried hard enough?* Fuck off, Rand. Please. *Don't forget you chose theoretical linguistics to reduce your chances of having to do research outside the West.*

Gamini cherished his BBC accent and Oxford PhD, the Rolls Royce of badges for a child of Sinhalese Buddhist aristocrats in a class-ridden country with a socialist political bent, and a Sinhalese caste system at odds with Buddhism. In Gamini's company only foolhardy foreigners broached such incongruities but anyone could deplore Hindu caste and other Tamil flaws at will.

In the colonial sewer of Sydney, Gamini's castigation of the British earned him social and promotional points in academia, and generous funding for research into European oppression in Southeast Asia; pre-war, so that he did not have to mention the Japanese Greater East Asia Co-Prosperity Sphere. He did the entire project without leaving Sydney, except to deliver conference papers in Europe and the United States.

Gamini avoided Aborigines but knew a lot about them and the theft of their land. A Canadian student ended up at another university after he asked Professor Fonseka, in an open forum attended by Charlotte, if any Sinhalese now occupied land acquired long ago from Sri Lanka's original inhabitants, the Vedda; and if so, what had been the method of acquisition; and where were the Vedda now. From his professorial high horse, Gamini shrilled objection to the implications of the question, without saying what they were. "That said, empirical research leaves no doubt about voluntary integration into Sinhalese society." The boy asked for a peer-reviewed reference. Gamini said the request was insolent. "Next question? One would prefer it from someone else." The bloody Royal impersonal pronoun, affected after their marriage. She would not have married him if he already had it.

A pretty girl, whom Gamini greeted with a micro-nod, stood up and shook her beaded plaits, new from Bali. Almost in tears, all chest-wobble, cheesecloth and stale incense, she asked him to describe the racism he must have suffered at Oxford. Charlotte crept away from her seat at the back of the lecture theatre. Oh, fuck. One of his conquests.

Professor Fonseka agreed to couple with his wife at bedtime about once a month if she asked, and if no student had been available to worship him that day. With Charlotte he could not avoid direct or implied reference to his superiority; nor did he try to disguise the smug triumph of access to a white woman, not quite a starlet but of passable English breeding.

Did he love her? Probably never. Did she love him? Not for long. A little, in their first year of marriage. Neither wanted children with the other. Why did she marry him? Loneliness, after three celibate years while she struggled to rewrite her role in the script about her first husband's end, and researched and wrote her PhD thesis in Melbourne; and two years of serial relationships with boys and men who serviced her lust while she relieved theirs, with Aidan Conway on her mind; but as with him she did not want to love them, whether or not they loved her. Orgasmic success was itself and nothing more. She favoured teenage boys; with her figure and eyes, easy to entice them with dignity in coffee shops and libraries; balls on the boil, breast-gluttons not yet weaned, eager for scent and feel of woman, vigorous, trainable within an hour; raw fornicators too young to have a wife to betray as Peter Millar and Gamini Fonseka had done.

Charlotte would cope with a split. She had done so 11 years earlier in more traumatic circumstances. Peter's body was never found. She sobbed when the British High Commissioner in Melbourne called her twelve days after her arrival in Melbourne from Tarawa. Her parents were out. Husband missing, presumed drowned; items left at Numatong gave no persuasive clue to the disappearance. An empty Scotch bottle and an ocean of fast currents told of an impetuous swim, but no one knew if he swilled the bottle in one lethal binge or tippled over several days. "Mrs Millar, one simply cannot know, can one?" Hesitation. "Forgive me, but the coroner at Bairiki must examine the case and has asked me to put to you a delicate question. Purely procedural, of course. As far as you know, would Mr Millar have had any reason or ex tempore impulse, that makes sense in hindsight, to take his own life?" Not a chance. No chance at all. No, no erratic behaviour. No, she could not help explain why he went south to Nonouti and Numatong when he was supposed to go north to Butaritari. "Yes, quite so, Mrs Millar. The Air Pacific agent and pilot, and Mr Millar's canoe crew at Nonouti said he seemed normal."

No chance of suicide, she and the High Commissioner agreed when he called a month later to tell her the open finding of the coronial investigation. He said Peter took 18 photographs of birds and fish, to what purpose if he planned to die? In a rethatched shelter he spread his sleeping mat and put his bag on it; the bag, with camera inside, zippered to keep out salt spray and sand. He cooked and ate canned food, and perhaps a fish. He used his rod and reel. Why bother with all that if one intended to kill oneself?

The High Commissioner would call her if new information became available. None ever did.

A simple drowning suited Charlotte. Neither her family nor Peter's nor anyone else need know of the split in Tarawa that preceded the loss of a fisherman, reckless on Scotch, who took one intrepid step too far into a riptide. With genuine horror she told her parents he was gone but could not tell Peter's; her father carried the burden to their house and came home a much older man.

Five weeks after Peter vanished, Aidan Conway sent a registered letter of shock and sorrow. He assured Charlotte that Peter could not have known of their tryst unless she told him. Aidan would never tell anyone. She replied, also by registered mail, to thank him for his condolences and for his friendship with her and Peter in Tarawa, and to tell him Peter was delighted that Alastair and Aidan had hosted her at the Bairiki Club on the night of the deluge.

This would be her last contact with Aidan, and he would know it. She wanted to thank him for the pleasure he gave her mind and body, and assure him Peter knew nothing, but she could not write such things—even registered mail sometimes went astray in Tarawa. Aidan would read between her lines.

What about her one-way ticket? That smart-arse little tart and her brother at Air Pacific might already have scandal-mongered that bit of serendipity. No matter. Aidan would not question Charlotte's claim that on the day the high commissioner called to tell her the news she had already booked a flight back to Tarawa. She had planned to stay in Australia for ten weeks but decided to return much sooner.

His Excellency the Governor sent a letter in praise of Peter; Alastair sent a bereavement card—Aidan must have brought it back from leave—signed by 19 of Peter's British and Gilbertese colleagues, and three English women. The girl from Air Pacific sent a note on pink paper, scented with a dab of cheap aftershave, to lament the passing of her favourite client. Slut. No doubt he had been on her too. And the English women?

She assumed no one in Tarawa knew of the split. Peter would have kept it to himself. If Aidan wondered about a split he would have said so; only he would have cause to wonder, and if he did not do so, no one else would.

There was no clue to suicide in the two crates of personal effects that came four months later to her parents' home. She had told the High Commissioner to donate their 50 or so books and tape-deck to the high school but to send her their audiotapes, as well as his camera and clothes. Clothes that she left in Bairiki were also there; whoever packed up the house would have spread the word about her clothes and so reduced the chances of a rumoured split that might have had something to do with Peter's disappearance.

The crates did not include Bos Simeon's original notebooks or Charlotte's edited translation. Peter would have destroyed them. Even if they were on the coroner's file in Tarawa there was nothing in them to hurt her or suggest Peter's suicide.

Her distress was deep for three days after she distributed his clothes to family and the St Vincent de Paul Society. She gave his empty camera, two lenses and 14 boxes of slides to his father without going through them. She kept a box of 18 slides, 17 of birds and one of a fish dying—not dead, because it had rich colour and a bright eye, and a tail blurred mid-flip. The detail on the Kodak label showed they were developed in Australia and returned to the coroner at Tarawa after Peter embraced Charybdis, spirit of whirlpools and tides; female, of course. The shots would have been taken at Numatong, and the film removed from his camera in Bairiki and sent to Australia for development to see if it held any clue to his demise. None that she or the coroner could see.

Charlotte wailed for an hour in her room after she fired up the backyard barbeque pit to burn her precious Indonesian dress and Peter's personal file on the Rand case. She did not read the contents; spat on the folder and threw it into the backyard crematorium. She decided that Hugh Rand, an exorcised *maselais*, had coiled out of her life in white and grey wisps from the pyre.

For five years, while she studied and taught at university, she thought little about Rand and he did not bother her, except as an occasional memory. Then he started to accost her at night with gratuitous advice, infrequent and only when she was alone. At first his whispers seemed to come from within her; soon from outside, like the faceless Rand's taunts in her Tarawa bedroom the night before the split with Peter.

Over the next few years Rand, usually disembodied, always faceless, became a regular but still infrequent nuisance at any time of day and night, now when she was either alone or in company. Gamini advised her to see a psychiatrist to probe the occasional solo chats that she refused to discuss with him. She said he needed a psychiatrist more than she did. He could cope with the soliloquies at home but had been embarrassed a couple of times by colleagues, his and hers, who asked if she was well. None of her colleagues felt a need to mention their more or less weekly observations to her, on the grounds that eccentricity was an academic privilege, and her quirk did not interfere with her work or social interaction.

She tended to dismiss Rand most of the time, or ignore him until he went away. A few weeks before the Kyoto conference his intrusions became much more frequent and prolonged, and his style so insistent that to snub him was infeasible.

* * *

Dr Charlotte Fonseka strolled around the Kyoto campus, a muddle of modern architecture, most of it functional and dull; with a couple of exceptions it represented the worst of the 20th century. In Europe, she had never been east of Berlin.

A Randless day so far. Green space minimal here compared with most Australian universities. In the cool sunshine of early winter a few reddish leaves, wizened and stubborn, clung to branches in the aftermath of autumn and a recent storm. She imagined the intense colour and the mood of imminent loss that might have perturbed her three weeks earlier when she had come to accept the end of her second marriage. It had waned rather than collapsed. She would tell Gamini on her return. He would not demur, and was a fool if, like Peter, he did not already know her mind.

Like the main streets of Kyoto, the campus bustled but was uncrowded by Asian standards. Hundreds of identical bicycles, of a design ridden in Australia by girls, were racked with military perfection between a building and a pathway. Students in twos and threes smiled and stopped walking or got off their bicycles to practise their English on her, which surprised her with its weakness in a country where most students study English right through school from elementary level.

Her vain search for coffee, along a route guaranteed by a student wearing a surgical mask, took her to a small gallery. On the top step, a neat sign on a sandwich-board. The top half in Japanese and below it she assumed an exact English translation: 'Travel Photography by Hiroyuki Ayanokoji PhD, Professor Emeritus, Faculty of Liberal Arts, Kyoto University. Please Enter. Free.' From an amplifier somewhere in the gallery, slow *koto* strings and a constricted voice, perhaps male, enticed her through the doorway. No shoes outside so she kept hers on. No one else there.

From the door she counted 25 monochrome photographs, all about 40cm by 30cm, seven in portrait format and the others landscape, all with off-white framing mats in identical frames of narrow black wood. Metal? A title card with tiny print on the wall to the left of each shot.

A few metres to her left an ink-blue ceramic pot of yellow chrysanthemums, Emblems of the Emperor, squatted on a low table. On the wall behind the flowers she guessed she saw the photographer's biography, half a metre wide and almost a metre long; in English, she presumed—no discernible Japanese characters. She could not read it from here but could see it was headed by a portrait, probably of him, and closed by another photograph, more complex, a little larger but too distant to guess its subject.

An English sign in block letters on the wall above the biography instructed visitors to start there, which prompted her to do the opposite; to turn around and begin with the intended last photograph and go counter-clockwise back to the biography. She usually scanned magazines from back to front before choosing an article to read. Her reaction to the sign was not defiance of an instruction. On her first circuit of a solo exhibition she always went counter-clockwise to ensure she did not read the analytical spiel within most biographies; it would meddle with her perception of the exhibits. Later she would read the spiel, digest it, and go clockwise around the walls to reassess what she had already seen. She would ignore each title until she had digested the picture.

The 25th photograph, her first, was a back-lit head and neck portrait, an Asian girl of about ten facing left in close profile. The girl watched someone or something out of frame, with shyness. Then Charlotte saw fear and doubt in an upper lip that seemed to tremble, and in a drop of sweat about to run down the girl's forehead into her left eye. A tendril of coarse hair flowed downward in a black dance with her profile. To Charlotte's eyes and ears, the visual flow clashed with the girl's mood and the gallery's background music, arrhythmic and melancholic. On the wall she read 'Philippines, Child #2, 1975'.

The girl's skin did not have the glow of privileged Filipinas Charlotte had heard about, polished daily by a nanny and kept in shade. Where was the nameless girl now, seven years later? In Ermita, Manila's hub of whores, pimps, pot and cocaine? Had she returned pregnant or diseased, or both, from there to her village? Did she have a baby girl who would repeat the cycle to fund the extended family, and so keep other girls at school and perhaps break the cycle for them? Had Child #2 migrated to the West as the bride of a customer? Not to Japan, probably the home of most customers. Did she still live?

In unconscious and awkward time with the instruments and

throttled voice, Charlotte side-stepped to a portrait of a boy of two or three. Despite her perhaps faulty interpretation of what Ayanokoji saw and captured, a possibility that did not occur to her, the shot confirmed her impression that he knew how to express his mind's eye with a camera. This shot resembled the one of the girl insofar as they were profiles, watching left. The latter solid and detailed at first glance, this one spectral and almost all black; about ten per cent lit, on a grey-white spectrum. Charlotte created a boy from wisps of light reflected off his nose-tip, left eye, left cheek, thick bottom lip, and beautiful curve of forehead. Could she have deciphered a face if the photograph were presented sideways or upside down? No, she decided. Ayanokoji must have taken the shot after much planning; or he had manipulated the print in his darkroom to create an insinuation of a solid, wistful boy who could not be mistaken for any other despite the meagre detail. 'Philippines, Child #1, 1975'. She made a brother and sister of the pair.

She was right about the family link between the subjects and what the photographer thought he had achieved, more or less; but not about his means. Ayanokoji saw the boy through the unglazed window of a village house in northern Luzon, and took the shot on impulse as he readied the sister for Child #2. He did not tinker with the negative or the print.

After two photographs Charlotte knew Ayanokoji was a master of light, observation, timing, composition and darkroom alchemy. She also thought him foolhardy. In 1975, the Filipino people still hated the Japanese for their wartime savagery but tolerated their hordes in Manila for their outlay on Air Philippines charters, food, alcohol, artefacts, tailored suits, strip-shows, whores, bribes and five-star hotel rooms. Ayanokoji would have been in danger if he had wandered alone in any other part of the country. He must have taken a bodyguard on his photographic odyssey. She was right on all points.

The *koto* and strangled dirge gave way to *shakuhachi*—bamboo flute—that lured Charlotte from intellectual analysis towards reverie. She stepped left. The girl in Child #2 held Child #1 as they looked up at her in natural, even light. Ayanokoji must have stood on a chair and looked down on them; in truth, on the top step of their house.

How could this girl who beamed delight and confidence be the one Charlotte saw and understood a few minutes earlier? It was that child, no doubt. Ayanokoji must have taken this shot first, then upset the girl in some way before he took the solo portrait. The brother she nursed with pride held a fistful of her hair. His dark skin and now clear features explained the tone of his solo portrait. A black father, probably an American serviceman on rest and recreation leave from Vietnam. Who was he? Charlotte resisted four winsome eyes that tried to entice her into other lives. 'Philippines, Sister and Brother, 1975'.

The girl seemed to invite her to look at the three photographs in the intended order; maybe change her mind about some things. *Go on, Dr Fonseka*, said Rand, who now accosted her often and had become an intruder in her life, almost daily; nightly. She withstood the challenge by the girl and Rand, and escaped with two side-steps to the 22nd photograph, a hip to shoulder nude taken from behind, in close. Like the shot of the boy, light from left of frame recorded minimal detail but prompted Charlotte to give the subject shape, mass and life. The only detail she did not need to create was a cluster of goose-bumps on a patch of light reflected off the black girl's hip. A cold studio. Hotel room? 'Young Woman #2, New York, USA, 1954'.

Still alone in this room in a city of 1.2 million people. The *shakuhachi* and the nude relaxed her so much she wanted to sit for a few minutes on one of the five low stools of heavy wood provided for visitors. No. She would sit when she could get coffee, which was not here. Look at two more photographs, leave for coffee and lunch, and return to see the rest.

Two steps left to confront what she expected to be 'Young Woman #1', the other side of the American woman's torso, with pubic mop in shade so as not to offend visitors. Instead, a sharp head and shoulders portrait of an ancient man. A man? No, a woman; she faced half-left to gaze over Charlotte's shoulder, and chewed a rough cigar in the delicate hold of left thumb and first two fingers; the other two fingers raised as a British lady raises them to drink tea from a bone china cup. No, more like a flautist holds her instrument.

Above high cheek-bones the bright left eye reflected the camera; the right eye dull, perhaps blind. Glaucoma? From the left corner of her mouth she puffed smoke past the cigar down to the right corner of the frame. Grey hair, thick, coarse, wet or oiled, combed back from her forehead over her crown, and above her ears from the temples. Right ear out of sight. A time-gnarled nose, aquiline, swollen. A vein bulged from her left eyebrow and wobbled up through her forehead creases into her hairline. Her good eye said she knew secrets and would keep them. Charlotte found her impenetrable and therefore vexing, unlike the children.

In this shot Ayanokoji revealed himself, as Charlotte now saw in the other three photographs, as a master of energy around the Golden Mean, where he had fixed the woman's left eye, eagle alert. Charlotte saw a contradiction. Soon to die and well aware of it, the woman was calm; but every other element of the photograph ran the watcher to and from that golden eye on a sprint of light and shade, shape and line, balance and instability.

Charlotte flinched when her gaze jumped over the frame to the title card. The woman would be Javanese or Balinese; the card said 'Old Woman, Gilbert Islands (Kiribati), 1971'. What? 1971? She backed up to a stool and sat. She said aloud to no listener, "I was there." She stood and went up to the next photograph and glanced at the two after it, all portraits of Japanese women. She span on clumsy feet to scan all three walls, portraits all around, and could see no other shot with a likely Gilbertese subject. This was Japan, the seat of order in all things public, and the photographs were ordered by country; there would be no other Gilbertese shot.

Charlotte returned to the stool. She would contemplate this waning woman for another minute from three metres, then continue her counter-clockwise tour for a few minutes before an intermission for lunch and coffee. After 30 confused seconds she chose to break her habit and go to the start of the exhibition. Gilbert Islands? She must read the biography; stood with more of an abrupt leap than a stand, so that her leather bag slipped off her shoulder and smacked onto the hardwood floor.

She grabbed the bag and clomped to Ayanokoji's biography. A much-enlarged passport photograph; a crude portrait, blurred, out of place in this gallery of aesthetic and technical talent. The facial features in the shot drew out a memory of its opposite in slickness, Otto Karsh's 1969 portrait of Yasunari Kawabata, the 1968 winner of the Nobel Prize for Literature, self-assassinated in 1972, the year she cried over a copy of the portrait in an Australian magazine.

Peter Millar had read all of Kawabata's translated works. In Tarawa, and now as Ayanokoji stared, she listened to Peter read a sentence from the Nobel acceptance speech in a British newspaper, six months old: "Among those who give thought to things, is there one who does not think of suicide?" Kawabata quoted an ancient whom she could not now name. Until the day she heard Peter had gone to the sea at Numatong, she did not know she had even stored the Kawabata comment that came back to her then, and again returned when she saw the Kawabata portrait in Melbourne; and again today when Ayanokoji's portrait reminded her of Karsh's Kawabata. To parry her horror at what Peter may have done, and why, she had tried in vain to erase the quote immediately after it surfaced at news of his disappearance.

Ignore the second photograph; descend to it through the biography. Born Kyoto 1918. Studied at Kyoto University 1935-

40. Army in several Asian countries during war. Commercial photographer until 1946-50, Tokyo. Studied 1951-57 at Columbia University, undergraduate through to PhD in sociology. Taught 1958-70 at Columbia and Princeton; then Kyoto, now Professor Emeritus. Travel photography USA, Australia, Europe, Cambodia, Philippines, Thailand, Marshall Islands, Gilbert Islands (now Kiribati). Married. Nameless wife. No children? Makes own prints. Travel photography more about people than places. Mainly portraits. Some landscapes, figure studies. Intrigued by individuals. Gets to human universals by neutralising place. Blah.

She drifted past the rest of his philosophy, down to the second photograph, sharp, twice the size of a postcard. Again her bag smacked to the floor. She choked and collapsed to her knees, then onto her haunches, hands over open mouth, scream smothered. Three Japanese men, including Ayanokoji, sat with Peter Millar behind bottles and glasses of beer on a table. Her husband smiled at her. Her left shoe skidded across the floor as she tried to rise to look again at the photograph, hidden now behind the chrysanthemums. Skirt too tight so she leaned forward with trembling hands to part the arrangement. In small print, a caption below the photograph: 'Delegation with British Official, Hotel Otintai (pron. O-shin-tai), Tarawa, Gilbert Islands, 1971.' The last photograph of Peter, unless Ayanokoji had more.

To shield herself from Peter's smile, Charlotte released the flowers to fall back more or less into place. The music stopped. A tiny, elderly woman in kimono and toed white socks, shoeless, arranged the flowers back to perfection; then held out her hands to Charlotte and helped her raise her haunches to a stool. The woman stared through round wire-rimmed spectacles from dark eyes, limpid and beautiful for her age; no plan to die soon in those eyes with minimal epicanthic fold. Surgery? Absurd to wonder about that. Every few seconds the woman wrung her hands and bowed, fretful. Whispers of concern in Japanese made no sense to Charlotte;

armpits and groin sogged with sweat; dumbstruck but wanting to reply in English, which would make no sense to this woman.

Charlotte begged herself not to piss where she sat; could not hold back if she were to take on Peter's dare to look at him again. Unambiguous hand signals had the woman retrieve the shoe, help Charlotte put it on, and lead her to a toilet near the gallery door. When she came out, the minder, the hand-wringer, nodded towards an alcove with chairs at a table. As Charlotte sat down she knocked over an adjacent chair. The woman calmed her hands, put the chair back in place, and placed a brilliant glass in front of her guest; with clinical control, poured the right amount of iced water from a glass jug, also brilliant.

As if trying to settle an edgy dog, the woman motioned with hands palms-down for Charlotte to stay put, then shuffled to a telephone on the alcove wall. Made a brief call, calm and formal on the surface, urgent and strained a little deeper; bowed several times to someone she could not see and could not see her. "*Hai. Hai.*"

She stood sentry near Charlotte, now calm enough to echo the nod when their eyes met. Japanese echopraxia? I must be settling in. Charlotte, too exhausted to sit straight, moved the water-glass aside and pillowed her head on her bag.

Professor Ayanokoji arrived seven minutes later, beckoned the woman out of the alcove and spoke with her for half a minute. Charlotte raised her head from the bag when she heard them. Still anxious, the woman bowed to her from a few metres away and went back into the gallery.

Ayanokoji bowed to Charlotte; minimal body movement, more polite nod than bow. Taller than her and most Japanese. He sat opposite with elbows on table and palms against cheeks; bemused and serene like Kawabata in the Karsh portrait, but nowhere near as fragile. Silence for almost a minute. He did resemble Kawabata despite more potent eyes and a much more muscular face to match a robust body; his hair much like Kawabata's and the old Gilbertese woman's, but a little thinner. All three had similar ears, large and winglike. Charlotte saw the absence of Kawabata's ancient heart-faced figurine; the one the Melbourne magazine said was a *dogu*—the author always had it on his desk to speak to him, to inspire him as he fought blank paper. Miserable, unlike its owner. With the insight of 12,000 years of misery, had it counselled him to suicide? Was Rand Peter Millar's modern *dogu*? Focus, fool. Rand whispered: *All okay, Charlotte? Always here to help you stay in control, to define and redefine things the way you want them to be. Yell if you need me.*

With a touch of American Ivy League accent, Ayanokoji murmured, "Are you unwell, madam? Shall I call a doctor? Many are based nearby, in the medical school." She raised her head to look at him, into eyes that had looked into Peter's since she last did so in the flesh, at Bairiki. Even so, today in the photograph Peter had looked at her as if alive, long after his pupils had dilated for the last time and the sea and its snapping, shitting creatures had reduced him to molecules trapped in currents of cobalt soup that would sometimes wash him onto reefs and beaches, then suck him back into the eternal flow. *Settle down, Charlotte*, whispered Rand.

Ayanokoji uncupped his cheeks, clasped his hands; a reserved smile. He took a small packet of tissues from the inside pocket of his suit jacket and gave her a few to mop her brow. He nodded. "Thank you, Professor. I'm fine now."

"My wife said my photography upset you. Although I doubt it is my fault in any culpable sense, I do apologise for any unpleasant effect."

"Thank you, Professor. Your photography is not the culprit. I'm to blame. I didn't have time to eat breakfast and I sometimes feel faint if I get up late and miss it."

He grinned. "Slept too long to eat? Yet you have survived the day fairly well. Americans tell me breakfast is the most important meal of the day, and should be substantial, as should all the other snacks and meals that take up so much of the American day. Which, of course, is why so many Americans are much more substantial than I am, or you. They would do well to do as you have done and sometimes sleep past mealtime. Rice, fish, seaweed and *sake* for me. No hamburgers, fries or gallons of insipid beer. But you are Australian?"

She tried to grin back at him. "Your photographs are beautiful. And powerful, subtle. I haven't seen all of them but I'll come back after lunch. Please thank your wife for her kindness. Will she be here when I get back? I wanted to explain my problem to her before you arrived but I knew she wouldn't understand me."

Ayanokoji returned his hands to the Kawabata position, closed his eyes, chuckled. "She speaks excellent English and assumed you didn't because you didn't answer her. We were together in the US for many years. That's where she learned it. Mine was already good as my parents insisted I learn it in the 1930s. To prepare me long in advance for overseas study, they paid a lot of money to personal tutors, British and American. Then the war got in the way, but I worked on the language at my various postings and later refined it to a much higher level in the USA. My wife soon became fluent there, after she joined me."

"Oh, no. Please apologise for me if I don't see her again. I'm embarrassed."

"I shall do so, Ms...?"

"Charlotte Fonseka." She took a business card from her bag and gave it to him with both hands and a slight bow. He echoed her gesture as he took the card.

"Ah, Dr Fonseka. A specialist in linguistic theory. I take it you also have an interest in fine arts, photography at least. You are here for the linguistics conference at the Clock Tower building?"

"Yes. And I do love photography. A watcher, not a shutterbug."

He chuckled again. "But you are not at the conference. It must have bored you, as conferences have always done to me. My motto is 'give your paper early, and go somewhere interesting.' My less than humble assumption is that the gallery is more interesting than the conference."

Charlotte warmed to him. "Please allow me to take you to lunch, Professor Ayanokoji. And your wife, if she can join us. I must refuel so I don't faint again."

"Hiroyuki, please. I shall call you Charlotte. I'm a fan of aspects of Western informality. Thank you for the invitation. Unfortunately my wife has gone out for a while and I must lock the gallery and go back to my office. She will return here but I cannot say when. A postgraduate student awaits me. I'm retired but still supervise two PhD candidates. You will find good restaurants on Imadegawa Street. When you leave the gallery, go back to the Clock Tower building, exit the main gate and walk right on Higashioji Street until you get to Imadegawa. Beware of bicycles on the footpath. The riders coming from behind assume you are like Japanese and will walk a straight line. We are a bit like that. My apologies for not offering you my card. I rushed from my office when my wife called and didn't bring my card folder. I do hope you will come back to see the rest of the exhibits."

"Thank you, Hiroyuki. I will come back." Damn. Should be 'shall'. He bloody noticed.

"My wife will be here. Where will you resume? She said you started counter-clockwise, then dashed across to everyone else's starting point, where you collapsed."

"I'll break my lifelong habit and begin at the beginning this time to honour your intention, and your kindness." She could not return. Ayanokoji knew it. He led her out of the building and pointed towards the main gate. "The restaurants are in that direction. All Japanese. If Italian pasta is good for athletes, noodles will be good for you today. A quick carbohydrate fix for a starveling, the first I have met to be starved by sleep. I must rush. It has been my honour to meet you."

Ayanokoji dawdled back to his office. She lied. Why?

Charlotte ordered blind; a small serve of the waiter's suggestion, *oyako domburi*, which turned out to be chicken and eggs with rice, no noodles. They did not serve coffee; the waitress agonised for ten seconds, and went out to get a mug from somewhere else.

Charlotte nibbled as she strained to erase the photograph of Peter; each time it started to fade it came back with his face a little larger and sharper, his grin wider, and the other faces smaller and less distinct. The final return distressed her. The faces all reverted to the original; but there was an extra person. Hugh Rand, most of him hidden, at Peter's shoulder. Faceless, as in their bed at Bairiki when he took Peter's place; him, no doubt about it.

Always here for you, Charlotte. Enjoy your cross-cultural lunch. Ignore him.

She wondered, as she had done a few times, if Rand was her creation or independent of her. He had no clear face when she saw him replace Peter in her bed in Tarawa, nor in this photograph. Now, if she turned to look at him when he whispered in her ear, his face would be vague at best, if he allowed her to see him at all. No matter how hard she tried to see his facial features or imagine them, he did not have any. If Rand the pest was her creation, surely her imagination would have given him a face by now; would have given him one at the outset.

No, Rand was real in one potent sense or another; more than a figment, despite an uncomfortably precise accord between her attitude to life and his anti-determinism—including his idea of a malleable script—as reported to Peter by Walter Brooksbank in 1971 and relayed to her that night in Melbourne. Mere coincidence. No significance in that, when it came to deciding whether or not he was her figment. Irrelevant.

Figment or not, Rand was real enough to identify and feed her resolve to control her life and steer the lives of others as necessary. Over the past few years he had reminded her several times, without going into detail, of his anti-determinism and the notion of a potent life, scripted and rescripted as required. She considered her position to be much more refined and potent than his. Now, in a restaurant in Kyoto, she scoffed at the quality of his script-writing and direction, at his grasp and application of his own philosophy. If he was a master puppeteer, how come he lost his head?

The waitress ignored Charlotte's whispers: "Great to have you here to watch me eat, Rand. Listen to me for a change. Trap shut. I've got a few things to tell you. I'm all for high contextual intelligence, which you clearly do not have, based on some of the gratuitous advice you give me. Unlike me, I doubt you can tell the difference between the influence of a sparrow-fart and something that really matters. You have to identify the significant factors as they happen—and keep on happening—and tweak the future by your reactions to them. Ignore the trivia. True, a touch and go process to some extent. Maybe they're accurate identifications and favourable reactions, maybe not always. Anyway, it never ends. I doubt that you realise it. New influences always kicking in, old ones changing or fading to nothing. So you rewrite the script as best you can, non-stop. Perpetual rewrite, not the occasional edits that you seem to think are enough. Get it, Rand? I doubt it. That's why you lost your head."

Maybe, Dr Fonseka. Your 'as best you can' wasn't too impressive today in the gallery. Perpetual rewrite? Sounds like trying to fix your mistakes all the time. Too much academic blather in the speech you just gave me. Trying for perfect control of yourself and the rest of the world. Found your obsession at last? Not too obsessive, Charlotte? Delusional? Won't send you nuts? No, no, no and no. Anyway, Rand, my contextual management has done more for me than your fake anti-determinism ever did for you. *So far, maybe. But your view of it all smells like an ivory tower attempt to show yourself how clever you are, and it has the opposite effect. You seem to have turned a simple idea, a rough guideline to living,* into a weird, block-headed mania. *I might have started all this, but aren't you a bigger control freak than I've ever been?* Fuck off. You don't get it. I have to go.

She gulped the coffee, paid the bill, left Rand in the restaurant. A figment evicted from her head by insults? Maybe. Whatever the case, whatever he was, however he was created, whoever created him, he would be back to exert his influence, to taunt her, to give her hell. That was real.

She would walk two kilometres to her hotel on Karasuma Street, beyond the Imperial Palace. Until well away from the campus she strode long and fast, almost trotted, to deter inquisitive students. Feet stirred autumn leaves on the path; a few spiralled down in the breeze as she passed the trees that gave birth to them. To occupy her head, to keep Rand at bay, she recited aloud her favourite poem, taught to her by Peter when they were student lovers—'Spring and Fall, To a Young Child', by Gerard Manley Hopkins:

Margaret, are you grieving
Over Goldengrove unleaving?
Leaves, like the things of man, you
With your fresh thoughts care for, can you?
Ah! As the heart grows older
It will come to such sights colder
By and by, nor spare a sigh
Though worlds of wanwood leafmeal lie:
And yet you will weep and know why.
Now no matter, child, the name:
Sorrows springs are the same.
Nor mouth had, no nor mind, expressed
What heart heard of, ghost guessed:
It is the blight man was born for,
It is Margaret you mourn for.

She adjusted her pace to the poetic metre and tried to translate the poem into Pidgin. The effect ridiculous, the task futile. At the fifth repetition in English, Rand changed the last line: *Is it Charlotte you mourn for? Are you just another leaf?* At the hotel she slept deep, dreamless, Randless, until the telephone woke her at 6pm.

When Hiroyuki Ayanokoji arrived home at 5.30pm, early for professors, emeritus and otherwise, he told his wife she might or might not have misread Charlotte's swoon. The patient said it was generated by hunger, not his photography. Hitomi Ayanokoji said Charlotte collapsed in front of the biography, not one of his photographs. She could not stand up but was so desperate to see his biography again that she wrecked the chrysanthemum display to get a line of sight from where she squatted. Hunger? Was she someone with whom he had an affair on an overseas jaunt? No.

He brooded in his American easychair with a glass of straight bourbon. She sat with poise on a mat and watched him sip, both mute. He swilled the second half of the bourbon as he used to do in New York bars. Why did this woman rush from near the end of his the exhibition to the start, and collapse when she read his credentials? Why did she give him a silly explanation? Why did he sense she could not return to the gallery after lunch? Why did she unsettle him? Her face, body and legs were attractive but that was not the cause.

Maybe there was no problem to solve. Why should there be? Not all human behaviour was rational. She said she missed breakfast and so she fainted. Perhaps neither silly nor dishonest. Perhaps.

Ayanokoji telephoned a friend in university administration and asked him to find out Dr Charlotte Fonseka's hotel. He sat and held the glass toward his wife to refill with bourbon. He received the return call within ten minutes, wrote down the details, and asked Hitomi to call Charlotte. "Invite her to visit us tomorrow evening. Tell her I cannot talk to her now as I am in my darkroom. Say we know she admires good photography, and thought she might like to see the many photos on our walls. Perhaps go through a couple of albums over a drink. Say it doesn't matter that she could not return to the gallery today as the albums include exact copies. If she reacts well, ask her to stay for a modest dinner."

"*Hai.*"

Charlotte thanked Mrs Ayanokoji for her kindness that morning and said she would be delighted to visit. She accepted the dinner invitation to replace a booking with three colleagues who, like her, would take leave in Japan for a week after the conference. Mrs Ayanokoji would call the hotel reception next day and ask them to arrange a taxi for Charlotte. "Their English might not be strong enough if I leave it to you to tell them exactly where you want to go. The driver may have no English, so we must eliminate the possibility of even minor misapprehension. By the way, do you eat fish? Hiroyuki does a perfect grill. I think you call it a barbeque. He supervises, I grill."

I get the bloody point. You can speak English. "Grilled fish is a favourite dish, Mrs Ayanokoji. I haven't had it recently. I look forward to it, and to the photographs."

"Please call me Hitomi. Please come at 5.15. Your hotel will arrange the taxi for 4.50. Goodbye, Dr Fonseka."

Charlotte guzzled a gin-tonic, stared at the wall; thought about champagne and cremated fish at the Bairiki Club. Aidan Conway. Needed a second drink to deal with the memory, always poignant with complex associations whenever it came to her, most often on rainy nights.

She showered; watched herself in the long mirror as she slow-dressed. In the foyer she met 20 other conference participants; walked with them 200 metres to the post-conference dinner. The Japanese food superb, but the speeches and table conversation even more boring than her own conference paper, than her profession; than her lifestyle. After the ordeal she refused an invitation to go to a club with a handsome German student, at 24 almost too old for her, who seemed to mistake her stress for libido. She walked back to her hotel to doze alone, fitful, after a nightcap.

In bed her cares buzzed in a two-hour assault by hornets within her skull. Why did she not tell Ayanokoji why she collapsed? Why not tell him Peter was her husband? That she lived with him on Tarawa? That she left the day Ayanokoji and his colleagues arrived there? Why did she not ask him about his time with Peter? How was Peter's mood? His demeanour? What did they do together? What did they discuss? Did Peter mention her? Did he know Peter died? Why not say the photograph of the ancient Gilbertese woman surprised her and prompted her to scramble to Ayanokoji's biography and succumb to the shock of her husband's smile?

Did Ayanokoji know she lied? Should she confess at dinner the next evening? Apologise? Back to "Why the fuck didn't I tell him today why I collapsed?" She could not answer her questions, each with its own sting; only hear and feel them as hornets.

At 1am she switched on the bed-lamp and went to the toilet. On the way back she detoured to mix a gin-tonic, turned off the light and opened the curtain to look down on the city, still alive but almost silent from within her cocoon. The hornets retreated one at a time as she stood and sipped her drink for 15 minutes. When they were gone like Abemama mosquitoes at dawn, and she was too sleepy to think anything, she closed the curtain; with tiny steps probed her dark way back to bed.

A hornet returned to buzz a final sortie. She lay on her back and sobbed for the Bougainville days with Peter. Hugh Rand taunted from the pillow beside her: *It is the blight you were born for, it is Charlotte you mourn for, not for Peter Millar*. Fuck off! He obeyed. Usually a lot harder to get rid of him. Used to bugger off if ever I asked why he shot Bos Simeon's father. Never answered. Would go away for a day or two; but if I try it now he becomes a worse gadfly than usual. Not worth it. She sank into blankness for six hours, from which she awoke refreshed, with no hint of a hangover. Arose for a day of leisure.

She returned to the hotel at 3pm after a guided tour of Kyoto with the three colleagues who would not dine with her that night. Five hours of temple visits, laughter, and expensive food. The receptionist bowed twice as he both-handed her the room key: "Your taxi will be ready at 4.50pm, Madam Fonseka." Well, it would be pm, wouldn't it? The doorman had already told her. In the corridor to her room a chambermaid bowed thrice and told her again in broken English. Lucky no tipping in Japan.

In the room a telephone light flashed message red: "Madam Fonseka, your taxi will be ready at 4.50 pm. Thank you." Bet he was bowing. She slammed down the phone and stared at the ceiling. Please God, if you exist and can hear my plea ahead of today's millions of supplicants, please bloody free me from people who wear belts and braces at the same time. Amen.

For an hour she lay on her bed in her underwear and tried to relax while she fought her greed for gin. She distracted herself with incongruities experienced already in Japan. The first, about the conference, had nothing to do with Japan in particular. Most delegates were fairly intelligent people but they focused their lives on too much esoteric inconsequence, too many cabalistic banalities, in order to display their genius to other bores, and confirm it to themselves.

Away from the conference, she found other incongruities. Kyoto, the seat of Japanese cultural, religious, architectural and aesthetic refinement, was also a modern mishap devoid of planning; a more random mess of bland buildings and tangled overhead wires than she had seen anywhere else, maybe apart from Bombay. On her tour that day her map of Kyoto gave insight into Japanese thinking, or not thinking, about reality. Surely the many temples and gardens and palaces and castles, icons of ancient culture, could comfort only if you were to ignore their stranding, most of them, like islands in an ocean of metropolitan wreckage. They were beautiful; serene if you toured like an idiot with your fingers in your ears to muffle traffic, trains and amplified announcements. *Back off and have a fresh look, Charlotte*. Fuck off. How many times did she have to tell him? Must be 5000 times by now. More.

The Japanese seemed to fixate on an image of personal and social control that verged on national obsessive-compulsive disorder: doing things the proper way; being orderly and predictable, perhaps to cope with fear of a world teetering on a razor-edge. Something to do with the daily earth tremors? Conformist, no doubt, but not mindless minnows in a synchronised school of millions. Much more to it, much deeper. Baffling. The image of control no more than a mask?

As for masks, why did so many people, she estimated one in fifteen, wear surgical masks in public? No epidemic she knew about. No one coughing up chunks of lung. No corpses in the gutter. No serious air pollution. Maybe the masks allowed wearers to withdraw into the dubious safety of themselves.

When she watched Japanese visitors to temples and gardens she saw shared refinement and pride; but why did the demeanour of so many people, masked and unmasked on crowded trains and in the street, suggest isolation and stoic resolve? Some trying to will away an itch they dared not scratch? Others trying to cope with bowel cramp that deterred any interest beyond the inner self? Maybe not exclusive to Japan. Similar self-absorption and isolation in the monomorphs, pallid, homeward bound in John Brack's painting 'Collins Street at 5pm' in Melbourne's National Gallery of Victoria? Maybe. Brack may have exaggerated what his mind saw; she did not think she did so in Kyoto, where social and personal restraint seemed dormant volcanic. Volcanic bowels? Quite unlike the deadness in Brack's herd of automatons, all dressed alike, and all headed in the same direction, expressionless. No volcanic anything, let alone bowels. Seriously represents Australians? No.

The British in Tarawa. The Japanese veneer and theirs have

armour and role-play in common. Similar armour, different acts—British self-assurance, Japanese restraint. Constraint? Both nationalities anal retentive. *Stop it, Dr Fonseka. As Peter advised you, stick to linguistics.*

Reception rang at 4.20pm to say her taxi would be ready at 4.50 to take her to Professor Ayanokoji's house in Nanzenji.

"Where?"

"Nanzenji, madam. That is where the professor lives. The night will not rain, madam, but cold. Do not worry. The house will have warming."

"Do you have that arrangement here too?"

"Madam?"

She put on stockings, a dress of medium weight and a gabardine overcoat. Taxied mindless until she saw a convenience store and asked the driver to stop; returned with a box of Belgian chocolates.

"Nanzenji coming now, madam." They left the main road and rolled along a carless narrow street; lights in perfect place to shape designer trees and give pastel colour to unshed leaves that still fought early winter. Almost no leaves on path or road. How come? A rugged-up woman with cart and straw broom. Ah yes. Fallen leaves are messy. Heard of Sisyphus? Must control the natural mess of Goldengrove unleaving. *Memento mori.*

Charlotte could read no house numbers in the gloom. The driver knew where to stop. "Ayanokoji house, madam." When she read the meter and leaned forward from the back seat to pay the driver he would not take the cash from her. He nodded at a black plastic tray built into the console between the two front seats. She put two new notes on it; he took them and arranged her coin-change by denominational rank on the tray. The driver blank, looking elsewhere, nowhere, until she picked up the change. No tips here. "*Arigato*, madam." She tried to open the door. "No, no, no, please madam. Still sit. Driver will do it." From his seat he released the lock with a lever or button, then came around to her door. Impeccable in chauffeur's black cap, white gloves, black suit, white shirt, and black tie knotted perfectly; in the dull light, black shoes glossy, heels together. He bowed low as he opened the door and she got out.

"*Arigato*, driver-san."

"*Arigato*, Doctor Fonseka. Thank you. Please push button on gate." He waited until she pushed it.

Hitomi Ayanokoji's welcome burbled from another world through an unseen speaker. Sounded like the BBC broadcast quavering into and out of earshot at Bairiki. "Push the gate, Dr Fonseka. I am waiting at the door. Take a left at the T-intersection five metres in front of you. Fourteen stepping-stones will deliver you to me eight metres later. See you soon." Hear my English today? Smartarse. *Wrong mood, Charlotte*, said Rand.

Hitomi stood at the open door. "Lucky you didn't go right instead of left, Dr Fonseka. One of Hiroyuki's most brilliant students, a foreigner, misunderstood my directions. We had to fish her out of the pond in the dark. A doctoral candidate, no less. Please let me take your coat. It's warm inside."

"Please call me Charlotte." No music, thank Christ. She presented the chocolates, removed her coat and handed it over; took off her shoes, did not kick them off as at home; twinned them in the space left by her house slippers, corrugated maroon felt, less than elegant, the same as the hostess's; and the host's as she saw when Ayanokoji shuffled into the hallway to greet her.

"Welcome Charlotte. You will forgive us for our casual Western attire instead of the exotica you might have expected. We want you to feel at home with the Ayanokojis. Ah! Belgian chocolates. My wife and I are addicted to them."

"Excellent. Me too. That means we already have at least three things in common."

"Let me guess the other two. Disdain for scholarly conferences and a love of photography?"

"Indeed, Hiroyuki. And a fourth. A taste for grilled fish. I can smell the charcoal heating up." Hitomi said it would be ready for the fish in 27 minutes; she would try not to let the fish imitate the charcoal. She hoped Charlotte had had breakfast and lunch and did not need to eat immediately. Clever bitch. Not now the volcanic-bowel-cramped woman she met in the gallery. In control of whatever happens here, but not so confident elsewhere if a spanner falls into the works. Hitomi would drink with them and withdraw to the kitchen in about half an hour.

"No cook today, but not a problem for my husband and I." Not 'I', Mrs Fluency; 'me'.

Chilled *sake* for three. The professor poured into matching shot-cups from a small porcelain decanter, lustred with melded blues. The two scholars sat in American armchairs too large for the room; Charlotte more on the edge of hers rather than in it. In front of them, Hitomi lounged with grace on a Persian mat; smiled to herself for a few seconds after she settled on her left hip with legs tucked to one side and feet pointed away from the audience. I get you, Mrs Poise. You are the swan to my hippopotamus, flopped on its arse in the gallery. I sat like that at Abemama but you wouldn't have done it because the floor would have been too septic.

Hitomi said, "You are our first foreign guest not to remark after their first sip that our house is so Japanese in construction, so traditional on the outside, but more or less Western on the inside." She smiled at Charlotte, then at her husband. Charlotte smiled back. Why do I need to dislike this woman? *You don't need to dislike her*, said Hugh Rand.

Charlotte recalled a story heard long ago. "Isn't spontaneous memory astounding? The unexpected jogging of it."

"I'm not sure what prompted that observation," said Hitomi. "But I agree. Unanticipated recognition astounds me more than recall. Although the former does segue into the latter, does it not?" The bitch. She knows why I freaked out at the gallery. No she doesn't. How could she?

"Quite so, Hitomi. Your comment about Japanese exterior and Western interior prompted my memory of a Japanese story my former husband read to me many years ago. Well, re-prompted it. It first recurred at your gallery when you so kindly came to my assistance, calm but worried." She paused to sip. *Why is my speech so formal? Why lie about remembering the story at the gallery? Why do I sit upright on the edge of this bloody chair?*

"A story?" asked Hitomi.

"Fiction?" asked the professor.

"Yes, Japanese fiction, a short story, written many years pre-war. It features simultaneous Japanese-European clash and synthesis. Social relations, public face versus private pain; culture, philosophy, theatre, even furniture. I can't remember the author or title. You probably know it. Do I ring a bell?"

Hitomi shook her head. "Not a tinkle, Dr Fonseka." The professor said the story was perhaps 'The Handkerchief' by Ryunosuke Akutagawa. Original published in Japanese in 1916; an English translation in The Asia Magazine during the war. Charlotte nodded, unsurprised, and asked Hitomi if she knew of it. She said she did not recall it; Charlotte caught the fleeting doubt in the professor's eyes. *Got you, Mrs Ayanokoji. Lying. Why?*

"Let me tell you what I can remember of it, Hitomi. My former husband said the author committed suicide in 1927, aged 35. Seems to happen a lot with Japanese authors. Hiroyuki can correct me if I get the story wrong. It's been a long time so I can't remember much about it, certainly none of the finer points." *Like hell I can't.* "Roughly, it goes like this. A Japanese law professor with an American wife, a Japanophile like him, has long experience in the USA and Europe. They are drawn to things Western and Japanese, and furnish their house accordingly, like many professional Japanese of the time who consider themselves progressive. Like his American wife, the professor prefers Japanese dress, especially at home. He reads Western philosophers. So far, so good, Hiroyuki?"

"Indeed so. I might add that he wonders where Japan is headed. He sees moral and spiritual decline since the Meiji Restoration in the 1860s and wonders if the best recovery is offered by a resurgence of *bushido*. We now know the answer. Anyway, he is torn between Japanese restraint and the freedom of progressive thinking and behaviour. Please continue while I top up our *sake*. You like it? Gekkeikan, from Kyoto. Not too expensive, but excellent."

"Delicious," said Charlotte. "While he ponders a European author, on acting.... Help me, Hiroyuki."

"The professor's name is Hasegawa Kinzo. He is reading Strindberg's 'Dramaturgy'." Damn him. She saw Hitomi's blankness not quite conceal a smirk. Damn her too.

"That's it", said Charlotte. "Influenced by Strindberg, he wonders about actors' excessive reliance on signature devices learned to express emotion and attitudes."

Hitomi said, "Mannerism? I have heard of it. From the French *manier*? On the stage, a formulaic way of handling a situation, expressing its essence. Too predictable?" Oh, you fucker. *Don't let her get at you*, whispered Rand, girlish, into her left ear.

"Good guess, Hitomi", said Charlotte. "Anyway, something makes him wonder about mannerism in Japanese daily life." The volcanic bowel came to mind. "The mother of one of his students turns up to say her son has died. She puts on a composed face, all control and restraint, little smiles, no tears, as they discuss at arm's length the boy's death. He worries about this woman who cannot weep for her son, even though emotional abandon seen in Westerners during his travels has distressed him more."

Hitomi nodded. "It would have been at odds with his belief in the stoicism of *bushido*. Please excuse my interjection. Please continue, Charlotte." A fishbone at dinner might adjust Hitomi's style.

"Anyway, he drops something as they sit at opposite sides of a table. I can't remember what he dropped." Of course she could.

"Hiroyuki. Can you please help me?"

"A fan. A Korean fan."

"Yes, that's it, Hiroyuki. As he picks it up he looks at her under the table and sees her hands tremble in her lap as she twists a handkerchief. Almost rips it. Before this, he has noticed only her face, its occasional subdued smile, and her composure. Her *manier* conveys what she wants him to see and think, that she epitomises Japanese restraint, or constraint, whatever you want to call it. He is shocked to realise his focus on her face has distracted him from her weeping body. That's about it. How did your furniture lead to this full stop?" They laughed together and sipped.

The professor spoke: "A deep story, indeed. May I add a little? The lady leaves and Professor Hasegawa has a bath, then dinner with his wife, then relaxes in his chair near an open door to catch the light of the summer evening."

"Pardon me, husband. Is the chair rattan, and does he munch on cherries?" Oh, Jesus. I hope I get a chance to shove the whole fucking fish skeleton down her gullet.

"Correct." The professor went on. "During dinner he has told his wife, an excellent listener, that he admires the *bushido* spirit of the woman, whose name escapes me."

"Pardon me, Hiroyuki and Charlotte. Is she Madame Nishiyama Atsuko?" The fucking *sake* decanter might find its way into your gullet before the fish skeleton.

Charlotte smiled. "I'm not sure, Hitomi. But if you say so I'm sure you are right. Hiroyuki?"

"I believe so. I shall proceed. It is clear that Akutagawa got the handkerchief idea from Strindberg, who writes with disdain of a German actress who would often rip a handkerchief as a mannerism. Akutagawa makes Hasegawa read the relevant Strindberg quote as he settles back in his rattan chair. A bit too contrived in itself, don't you think? Authorial licence can be overwrought." So clever. Shall proceed, not the bloody 'will' that I would have used.

"Indeed." Charlotte paused to sip *sake*; smiled at Hitomi. "Anything we've missed?"

"Perhaps. I'll leave it to Hiroyuki. Unless you have more, Charlotte." Fuck you, lady.

"No, I'm all done. Hiroyuki?"

"A little more. The professor's complacency wanes as a likeness dawns on him between the banality of the actress's mannerism and that of *bushido*. To allay his disquiet, to put his armour back on, he looks up to concentrate on his prized symbol of Japanese tradition, a Gifu lantern which flames above his chair. But the story ends there and we do not know if he retrieves his complacency." Half a minute of sips and knowing nods.

Hitomi said Akutagawa used the handkerchief as more than a mere device to bring out the mannerist parallel with *bushido*. She did not elaborate. Charlotte would not ask her to do so. Hiroyuki said he thought he knew what she meant but was unsure. Perhaps she would elaborate, in brief, as the grill awaited the fish. Charlotte tonged a few chunks of white-hot charcoal down Hitomi's gullet. "Please enlighten us, Hitomi."

"I'll be brief. Handkerchiefs, *hankechi*, were unknown in Japan before the onset of European influence after the Meiji restoration. They became de rigeur for progressives." You upstart. Drop in a French cliché, ever so casually. "The author presents the twisting of the *hankechi* by the traditional woman as a cultural conflict analogy. Societal disruption." That was all.

Hankechi. Sounds like Pidgin. Charlotte congratulated her for remembering the story so well; for her segue from recognition to recall. Hiroyuki said, "Quite so. Quite so. Hitomi, the fish calls, or whatever fish do to attract attention." She smiled at Charlotte and raised herself from the Persian mat with extreme elegance. Well done, Mrs Literature. Remind me I'm a hippo.

"Can I help in the kitchen, Hitomi?" Hitomi said she would be fine.

The academic pair sat silent for half a minute. Hiroyuki refilled her cup. She scanned the walls. Hugh Rand put his hands on her shoulders from behind and congratulated her on remembering the story Peter had told her so long ago. *You sound confident and look calm. So why do you sit on the edge of your chair, wringing your handkerchief? Why smile while you struggle to be civil to Mrs Professor? Have you added yourself to Akutagawa's story?* She willed him to fuck off. *Ask the professor what he thinks about the brave Knights of Bushido at Bougainville and Nanjing. Ask him if it's possible to be mannerist heroic and genuine heroic at the same time.*

Hiroyuki saw her purse her lips for a few seconds. "Charlotte, are we all like the grieving mother to some extent?" She agreed that what we show the world is often a sham, a persona at odds with what goes on inside us. Why did I say that? Fucking banal.

"Indeed, Charlotte. We all twist a handkerchief under the table from time to time, under pressure of some sort. Shock, for instance." He's turned from me to study the *sake* decanter. How mannerist. He alludes to my gallery freak-out.

Rand whispered to her, *Call him out now. Ask him about the Knights of Bushido. He was one. You read it in his biography at the gallery. Has he ever twisted his handkerchief about that part of his life? Go on, ask him.* Fuck off. *Okay, for a while. Wouldn't you love to work out how to move me on for good?* She asked the host to direct her to the toilet.

When she returned there was no sense of Rand. She sat well back in the chair. Must not sit on its edge. Hiroyuki raised his eyebrows—the right much higher than the left—and smiled. Smooth forehead rutted now. "I could see the story struck home for some reason that you need not explain. It's good to see you sit in the chair, not on its edge as you sat before."

"To return to Hitomi's comment about East-West fusion, I guess your house reflects your cross-cultural experience, its creation of some sort of third culture in you and Hitomi, an amalgam. Maybe I'm like my house. Inside it's a quarter English-Australian and a quarter Sri Lankan. My husband is Sri Lankan." Hitomi had returned but did not sit.

Hitomi asked, "And the other half?"

"Indeterminate. Fluid. Loose. Maybe vulnerable. Always open to the influence of new experience." The professor said a bit of Kyoto might find its way into the flexible half. They all grinned and nodded. Hitomi excused herself. Dinner in 22 minutes. After she was well gone, Hiroyuki leaned towards Charlotte and again raised his eyebrows to create a chain effect, a concertina of forehead ruts. He murmured: "I have noticed that your mind and eyes are inquisitive, perhaps addicted to research. You have scanned the room and family photographs on the walls around us again and again. You must truly love photography. Do you search for technique or content? Perhaps both."

Brows still raised. Look over his shoulder, not at his eyes. Moved her rump forward to the chair-edge and stammered, "I am searching for my husband."

"Mmmm. Is he not in Sydney? Or do you think he is hiding in my house?" Kawabata smile, fleeting. Silence for 15 seconds. This man is cool. "Please relax, Charlotte. You are again sitting on the edge of your chair and your grip threatens to crush my great-grandfather's *sake* cup. What bothers you? Please tell me before Hitomi returns."

Sotto voce, she told him why she collapsed at the gallery. When she revealed Peter's death, a micro-second of bewilderment widened Ayanokoji's eyes and furrowed his brow; then back to normal. Why didn't he look less cool for a few seconds longer? Is he wringing a handkerchief or doesn't he own the prop he sees in others? How could he return so fast to a poker face if he did not know of Peter's death until she told him?

"I am shocked and sorry, Charlotte. I met Peter Millar when he picked up my delegation at the airport. We had drinks at the Otintai Hotel, as you saw in the photograph."

"How many people were at the table in the photograph? I can't quite remember."

"Four. Your husband, my two colleagues and me."

"No other foreigner in the bar? A European?"

"One. The little Cockney manager who took the photograph. Homosexual, I think. After dinner I shall show you the camera. I still treasure it." The lens through which Peter looked at her. "Two days later we worked with him for half a day. He took us to the war remains warehouse at Betio and showed us relevant locations around the island. Such a tiny area for the degree of horror that troubled all of us. But to our regret Peter was recalled to Bairiki around midday to prepare for an urgent, unforeseen assignment the next day. Butaritari, I seem to recall."

"Did you see him at your hotel or anywhere else that evening?"

"We had no further contact. That was disappointing as I had hoped to find out more about his life and work at Tarawa, and any work he might have done before that in other places. We of international bent do like to share our experiences, do we not? From what you have told me, by the time we left Tarawa for Japan he was not thought to be missing. I wrote to him, a letter marked personal, a few weeks later. As promised to him, it included a copy of the photograph you saw today. He did not reply. Now, of course, I know why. Such a tragedy." Liar. A letter marked personal would have come to me. *Maybe lost or stolen at the Tarawa Post Office,* said Rand, now in girlish full voice, not a whisper. Unusual. To whisper was normal unless she was alone. The professor must have heard him; pretends he didn't.

"I understand, Hiroyuki. It took his headquarters a week to realise there was a problem, and a bit longer to notify me in Melbourne, on holiday. No trace of him was ever found. No cause of death established. Much speculation, of course."

"Your gut-feeling? If it's not too hard to tell me."

"Peter liked Scotch, he fished in a frenzy, he sought solitude, and he didn't fear the sea or anything in it."

"Indeed a dangerous set of predilections, especially when alone in a remote spot. Numatong, you said? Near Nonouti. So, he did not go to Butaritari. I wonder why. He did not mention fishing to me. I do not fish. But we had other interests in common. Cameras. The savagery of warfare. Military history. Not Scotch. I prefer bourbon. Do you like it? If so we shall have a night-cap after dinner while we await your taxi." Jesus! What a smooth transition from fish, death and savagery to booze.

"Yes, I'll need it. Thank you for your compassion." None at all.

"I do understand and regret the shock my photograph gave you. *Mea culpa*. Let's lighten the conversation before my wife calls us to dinner. But tell me, did you have breakfast yesterday morning?" That right eyebrow again, a question-mark dotted with an eye.

She grinned. "*Mea maxima culpa* for the lie. It's the first one I have ever told to anyone other than myself. Oh dear, that was the second. And that was the third. And so on."

He laughed at her wit and told her his mother had warned him, when he was about 15, not to open too many Chinese boxes. Her lie was impulsive and therefore not dishonest. "A jolt to you. Shock generates impulse, embarrassment, a need to shield ourselves. Please don't worry about it. Guilt is as pointless as slicing off our noses. I'm the nominal victim of your lie but I don't feel like one."

"Thank you. And I appreciate your wife's concern for me at the gallery." A hankie twister back then, if not tonight in her East-West Castle.

"That's Hitomi's style. Under all the various circumstances, shall we agree not to adore the camera or look at photographs tonight?"

"A good idea. But I would love to see them. Perhaps on my next visit to Kyoto. Before we move on to other things, may I ask if you have any other photograph of my husband."

"No. Just that one. Shall I make a copy for you?"

"Thank you, Hiroyuki. Not yet. I'll think about it and let you know."

"Perhaps we could arrange for you to view my photographs another day if you feel up to it, before you return to Sydney. Apart from the family shots in this room, there are several albums and a gallery in a separate building in our garden. Thirty-one shots out there. What do you think?"

"Perhaps, Hiroyuki. Could I let you know tomorrow? Let me see how I wake up."

"Certainly." He leaned towards her: "Leave me to tell Hitomi your story after you go tonight. She is quite emotive by Japanese standards, despite her confident demeanour. We should not disconcert her, considering her obvious wish for a cheerful dinner after her fastidious preparation. *Sake*?" Constructs sentences like a robot. Grog as another full stop.

Hitomi presented dinner as a work of art; Japanese crockery in rustic style; utensils, napkins and food all synchronised with the fish as centrepiece. Charlotte said the arrangement was too beautiful to disturb. Hitomi bowed and replied, "So kind of you to say so. Dinner is not a Western element of our lifestyle here, as you can see."

"Apart from the table and chairs," said the guest. Hitomi bowed again; smiled, wordless. So sincere, Madame Michelin.

Hitomi said the French valued complex food with austere presentation, pretty much the opposite to the Japanese preference for more natural food with aesthetic presentation. Americans and Germans did neither; their meals vulgar stomach refills, great quantity, meagre quality, served in functional containers; utensils as tools. "How about Australians, Dr Fonseka?"

"Please call me Charlotte. Australian cuisine? Simple and wholesome to encourage congenial discussion, occasional laughter.

Food is for having a good time together. Maybe Italian and Irish influence. A catalyst, far from a thing of beauty created as an end in itself. No sense that it should be admired but not disturbed." Cop that. "In Australia, with food and many other things, what you see is what you get." Digest that, Princess Gastronome.

"Ah," said Hitomi, "I see. Down Under, is there no wringing of *hankechi*?" Coprolite. Charlotte laughed and the hosts laughed with her. She said the tablecloth was superb. From where in Japan? Kyoto? Blank-faced, Hitomi ignored her; the professor said, "It is Plauen lace."

"Plauen? Where is that?" She knew. Oh serendipity, I love you. Genuine blank this time, Hitomi.

"Germany," said Hiroyuki. "Saxony, about 75 kilometres from Leipzig." Five seconds hesitation. "I suspect you would like to know where we bought it. Manhattan, not Plauen or Leipzig, I confess." Charlotte nodded approval as she ran her fingertips across the lace pattern. Hitomi had no fucking idea. *Such pleasure in petty victory, Charlotte*, said Rand. Fuck off, I've told you. *By the way, Serendip is the ancient name of your favourite place, Sri Lanka, long before it was Ceylon.* I knew that. Disappear. He faded. She must find a way to make it permanent.

"Please start, Dr Fonseka," said Hitomi. Hiroyuki poured more *sake* into the same cups from another decanter, this one asymmetric but much the same size as the first; glazed rougher, in motley avocado green and charcoal. All three toasted the chef, a touch sullen now. Not cool to toast yourself, Madame Three-Star. A bit touchy, *n'est-ce pas*? Default to silence, petulance, if things don't go your way. Passive aggression. Does the professor cop this all the time? All Japanese women, or Hitomi alone? She's never been wrong about anything in her life. Are Japanese the French of Asia? Not quite. Similar attitude, different delivery. French expect you to lift your game under their influence; Japanese taciturn, disengaged, as if it's a waste of time trying to get through alien skulls. *Here we go again, Charlotte. How long have you been in Japan? Hasty judgement. Wouldn't want you on my jury.*

A brief dinner, about 45 minutes; the discussion desultory at first. Charlotte welcomed the early reticence and hoped she would be able to leave within an hour. For the first fifteen minutes Professor Ayanokoji pretended to concentrate on the food and *sake*. Watched Charlotte for a few seconds at a time from eye-corners. He sensed and believed he understood much of the internal struggle that belied her calm demeanour. No doubt a handkerchief twisted in her gut. He noted that neither Charlotte nor Hitomi, unlike him, had touched their table napkins, let alone put them out of sight on their laps. Charlotte twice caught his eye. He knows I'm struggling. Cannot know what the charcoal and fish did to my memory. *Sake* tasted like champagne. The scent and blind touch of Aidan Conway tightened her pelvic muscles. Thank Christ no sign of Rand.

The food gone, the discussion picked up; at first against her will—she wanted to go. They chatted mainly about the rustic beauty of crockery in the *raku* and related styles, and the paradox of its use in the refined tea ceremony; also its elegant placement on dinner tables. When the lull came, Hitomi summarised: "So, Dr Fonseka, the rusticity is deliberate and honest, and difficult to achieve with aesthetic success. Without experience in such matters you might see *raku* as faulty work. What you will see is not what you get." Touché, Madam Céramique, you smartarse. Hitomi said a fault and a flaw were different concepts in Japanese aesthetics. A fault was due to incompetence. Flaws from age and normal usage, or included with skill, were in keeping with *wabi-sabi*, derived from the Buddhist philosophy of impermanence, suffering, worldly imperfection, modesty, and so on. "Am I boring you, Charlotte?"

"Not at all, Hitomi. It's intriguing." True. Hate to admit it.

"Thank you so much. A bit more to finish off. We see beauty in imperfection, impermanence, incompleteness. Excellent artists and artisans build clever flaws into their works. A paradox. For some people it's a game to search for them. The artist will not say what and where they are." Lovely English, Lady Fowler. Hiroyuki silent, awaiting Charlotte's reaction.

After a fifteen second stare at the wall, Charlotte said there might be another paradox, a contradiction in logic and attitude. "If they deliberately include a flaw, doesn't that leave them open to a charge of arrogance?" She waited.

Hiroyuki prompted Hitomi. What did she think of Charlotte's proposition? Blinkless, Hitomi eyeballed him for five seconds, then raised the corners of her mouth to Charlotte; a slight bow, no genuine deference. "Please elaborate, Dr Fonseka. In what sense arrogant? I am no philosopher. My apologies."

Rand: *I can see where you are trying to take her, Charlotte. So subtle, as usual. Deluxe social finesse from a model guest.*

Charlotte told herself to smile a little; look a little unsure of herself. "Arrogance is inconsistent with Buddhist philosophy, is it not? It seems that way to me. Of course, as a callow outsider." No sign of life. Right through one ear and out the other. When she chooses, deafer in each ear than Bos Simeon in one. "I'll go on and you can tell me if I make sense. An expert potter—a technical and aesthetic expert—is likely to assume he can make a flawless pot, otherwise the idea of building a flaw into a pot would not make sense. Isn't it arrogant, and inconsistent with *wabi-sabi*, to assume, consciously or otherwise, that the pot will be flawed only if he chooses to make it so? And is it bogus *wabi-sabi* for us to believe an expert's pot is flawed, immediately or over time, by his choice? Do you get me?" She could but doesn't. Won't admit I'm right. She's never wrong. Anyway, not when she's dealing with an alien. He gets it and agrees with me. Won't say so in front of her.

Hitomi micro-nodded towards her husband. He said, "Charlotte, your argument seems plausible to me tonight, after much *sake*. It's deep and original. Let me think on it. We can write about it to one another. Maybe co-author a conference paper." Uniform laughter. So much fun. A concession from him? Hitomi's not happy. Maybe my view of the Japanese as patronising, uncompromising, applies more to women than men, especially to her. *Maybe to no one, Charlotte. You might be completely wrong. About the French and Gilbertese, too. And your beloved Bougainvilleans. How about that?* Fuck off.

At 9.20 she pleaded exhaustion and declined the nightcap, a superior Kentucky bourbon. Could Hitomi please call a taxi? Hitomi said, "He's waiting outside. The same one who brought you here."

"Oh, thank you. You pre-booked him? He didn't tell me."

"Hiroyuki told me you love to walk. We didn't want to risk your deciding to walk part-way in the mist before hailing a cab." Had to demonstrate your expertise with the gerund, didn't you? "The forecast is for the mist to become light drizzle. Also, you might not get an English-speaker. Perhaps end up in Osaka."

"Thanks for your concern, Hitomi. After a few more trips to Japan I might even be able to order my own taxi." Grins all round. "Thanks so much to you and Hiroyuki for the delicious dinner and fine company. I really enjoyed our chat about the Akutagawa story." Pity a fishbone didn't hear my plea.

"Goodnight, Charlotte. You are welcome anytime. Here's your coat. Don't forget your shoes. The slippers wouldn't be much of a swap for them. Hiroyuki will show you to the taxi." The crackpot would rather I went alone and fell into the pond.

On the path to the taxi in the fog-breath cold of a misty night, Hiroyuki said he hoped for her call to his office next morning to say whether or not she would return to view his photographs. "Hotel reception will connect you to the number written on the back of this card. It's my direct line. Thank you for coming, and again I must say I'm sorry about your shock at the gallery, and the death of your husband. He and I got on well. Please come back here but if you cannot I do understand."

"Goodnight, Hiroyuki. Maybe on my next visit to Japan. I'll call you tomorrow anyway." Like hell I will. Shall.

Charlotte gone, Ayanokoji gazed skyward for a minute then went inside to sit eyes-closed in his armchair with a double bourbon, no ice. He was troubled for no clear reason, other than the mutual dislike—mild enough—of his wife and Dr Fonseka, disguised less than well by the latter, even less well by Hitomi. Let it lie. They were unlikely to meet again. A commonplace fact of life, one that crosses cultural boundaries; a mere spat between two attractive women, both articulate, intelligent, and in this case one much younger than the other; the latter ready to exploit her home-ground advantage to compensate for loss of youth. Like teenage girls circling one another as they lust after the same boy. Hitomi's direct style sometimes too direct, almost American or German; not classic Japanese, that's certain. To be expected of her. He had exposed her to the freedom of the West. Sometimes she did not get the balance right.

Ayanokoji listened to Hitomi hum as she cleared the table and stacked crockery in the kitchen to wash next morning. Why not wash them now? The maid away tomorrow.

Hitomi went to her husband, his eyes still closed, and sat at his feet. "Hitomi, I have a story to tell you, with Dr Fonseka's permission. By the way, she might return to view our home gallery." He told the story as Charlotte had told it to him. When he finished, Hitomi said she remembered his comment, long ago, about a difficult British official, not much more than a boy, whose passive hostility and his anecdote about executed spies at Tarawa had caused him to be replaced as Ayanokoji's guide. "You laughed because your hurt facial expression, after the boy told the story, must have been enough to have his older colleague report him to their boss. You called it your *kabuki* face. Remember? Was he that bad? Did you know he died?"

"I didn't know until she told me tonight. Not an unpleasant young man. Unwise to make an old soldier lose face, to feel shame, because of dead spies. To me, they were agents of death; innocents to him. Naïve. Too naïve to see and accept the realities of war." One of three comments ever made to her about the war. Hitomi stroked his knees and shins; he thanked her for the fine dinner. They went to their *futon* bed. As he drifted towards slumber she said, "Her husband must have discussed such matters with her before she left and you arrived. The things he told you about." He reopened his eyes to the darkness but did not reply.

For much of the night he lay on his back and stared at nothingness. What did Charlotte Fonseka know? What had her husband known that he did not divulge? Millar did suggest he knew more than he said, unlike so many Westerners who say more than they know. Passive hostility. Perhaps no more than anti-Japanese bias instilled in youngsters by fathers and uncles who felt the bite of Nippon in battle. Would have been smarter not to do the *kabuki* act? Better to tolerate Peter Millar, draw out all he knew; wear out his hostility, manoeuvre him to relaxation, or at least détente. Almost 40 years now since the war ended. Still with us. Merely a few years of our lives. Why dwell on it now? Get on with life. Not feasible. Nothing to do with time as duration. Intensity matters. Strange woman, Charlotte. Sometimes looks as if she listens to someone when everyone is silent. Whispers an answer. Schizophrenia? Unlikely. No other apparent symptoms. Roll over. Sleep. Stop wringing the *hankechi*.

While Professor Ayanokoji ruminated at home, engulfed in his wife's snores and purrs, Charlotte stood near the window in her dark room. She looked out through the drizzle at the lights of Kyoto, her hair still damp from the walk she took after she stopped the taxi 500 metres before the hotel. The driver protested; she insisted. After she paid and he let her out, he drove on fast to the original destination. On her arrival the receptionist said he was about to send a bellboy with an umbrella to keep the drizzle at bay.

Rand had not harassed her after she left the Ayanokoji house, yet she could not scrub the evening's intrusions from her memory. He might as well be in her room now. For a few years after Peter died, Rand had bothered her little. For no reason she knew, his trespass had become frequent over the past year as her marriage to Gamini decayed.

Where was Gamini now? Doing what? 'Doing whom' would be more like it. Most likely on a student in Charlotte's bed, claiming his aristocratic birthright, using the girl to take revenge on white colonialism, even if her parents were Swiss or Lithuanian. Who cares? *You do.* Oh, Christ. *Relax. I'm off now, through that window.*

She drank a quick gin-tonic and went to bed. As she dozed the Ayanokojis came to her dressed as emperor and empress; did not speak; bowed with mock respect that said she was an alien and therefore could not hope to understand why it was the apex of human existence to be Japanese; to be born omniscient, superior, and clever enough to let you know it without a word. Again, a style contrast with the French, who send a similar message with unequivocal, dismissive words and demeanour. The Japanese, more self-controlled and aloof, send the message the way a cat lets you know your place. That's it—haughty French poodle to Japanese cat. The French, though, readier to assume you are smart enough to understand their superiority, maybe to learn their native language to a basic level of function. Whereas it was a Japanese duty to tolerate your inability to understand their superiority—beyond having a general sense of it—or to learn more of their language than a Japanese toddler. In the abstract, the Japanese a bit like Gamini-the-Superior and a few other professorial deities she knew in Australia: the role of lesser beings was to concede superiority, and not try to understand it—perhaps a logical impossibility anyway.

I'm back, Charlotte. Cut it out. It's nonsense. Peter warned you to question your cynical view of the Gilbertese. Told you to dwell less on shallow negatives, on stereotypes that don't exist in individuals. He said you could not and need not get a complete grasp of the familiar, let alone the unfamiliar. Negatives are easiest to spot. Stop looking for them or you'll never be as happy as you were at Bougainville. Did he say those things, Charlotte? No, she said. Your girly voice gives me the shits. *He bloody did. You're doing the same thing now in Japan. How about Sri Lanka? With Gamini? Why didn't you do it in Paradise Bougainville?* She said aloud that she was fine there until Rand himself started to get at Peter and ruin her life through his obsession with a dill who didn't take his father's advice to watch out for the Japanese cutlery. Anyway, why in hell was Rand now a defender of the Japanese? No answer. Go to hell. Exhaustion numbed her limbs and sedated her mind until sleep absorbed her, claimed her from Rand and the Ayanokojis.

At 7am she made coffee and called one of her three close colleagues. Something had come up which might lead to a job; she could not go with them to Nara for the day, as planned. Yes, she would check out of the hotel with them next morning and take the *Shinkansen*—the bullet train—to Hiroshima.

After breakfast in the hotel restaurant she returned to her room and at 9.15 telephoned Ayanokoji on his direct line. As she started to hang up, relieved that he was not there and had no answering machine, he picked up the phone. He said two students were with him. Could she come to his office in an hour? They could chat, have lunch, and go to view his home gallery if she still wanted to do so. He had a key to the exhibition at the university gallery, closed today, but he preferred not to go there for fear of upsetting her. His wife was at home and would be delighted to see her again.

"Agreed, Hiroyuki. Thanks for your concern. I'll see you soon. I look forward to seeing Hitomi but I'm a little reluctant to intrude on her so soon." *More reluctant if I didn't think another visit would give me the opportunity to piss her off again.* Hitomi would be pleased, he assured Charlotte.

No students were with Professor Ayanokoji. He did not know why he said two were there. He expected one in three hours and another mid-afternoon. The departmental secretary would put them off until the next day. He called Hitomi to tell her the plan. No answer. His message asked her to call back.

He locked his office door and sat on the sofa to brood about this woman. Unlike almost every Westerner he knew—many—she always seemed to behave in a way that others did rarely. That is, think one thing and say another. Relaxed on the outside, perturbed inside. Exudes high intelligence, by Caucasian standards, and generous sexuality without classical beauty of face. Shapely body and legs. Beautiful feet; slight pigeon toes, natural, unlike the cutesy pose of Japanese girls. Neck the lustre of pale marble, craved by most Japanese women. Last night and the day before, cool emerald eyes seemed to soften in lighter moments to the shamrock hue he had seen on flags, jackets and hats in New York on St Patrick's day. The emeralds challenged him to enter her mind. Conscious challenge? Probably not. Straight nose; slight nostril flair. Dark hair short enough to display pretty earlobes, pearl-studded.

Difficult to analyse and judge her with confidence. Take care. Not a teenage American student of the 1950s with a need to atone for Hiroshima by fucking him. So many penitents before he married Hitomi and took her back to the USA. Since then, several more on exchange to Kyoto. Don't try it with this woman. Open sexuality but older and much more difficult to seduce than an American teenager, or a married Japanese woman with all her bottled-up emotions and fantasies, secretly eager for someone to pull the cork.

* * *

A dawn shower had yielded to sunshine, so Charlotte walked to the university despite fatigue she could not shake off, even though she slept deeply after Rand left her. Was Kyoto the sole city in Asia where taxi drivers did not kerb-crawl her and beg for sex?

Most of the stalwart autumn leaves of two days earlier had

surrendered to the night wind and rain. Swept up; mulched by now. Must not let such garbage defile the footpath. No idea why I'm not on my way to Nara instead of Ayanokoji's office. Don't give a stuff about his photographs. His contact with Peter? That's it. Makes him a magnet of some sort. Does he know more about Peter? Probably not.

After five trees, against her will she again walked in time with the metre of Gerard Manley Hopkins: "Margaret are you grieving over Goldengrove unleaving?" On the third recital another voice pitched in, a ball-less falsetto: "*Charlotte are you....*" Oh, fuck! Didn't you jump from the hotel window last night? No more from him.

At the university entrance she realised she did not know how to get to Ayanokoji's office. A young woman eager to practise English approached her; Charlotte got in first. "I'll teach you a few English phrases for free if you tell me where to find Professor Hiroyuki Ayanokoji's office. Deal?"

No bow. Quick talker. American Ivy League accent. "You mean Ayanokoji Hiroyuki? Yes, I know where to go. My English is tolerable, thanks a lot. You looked lost."

"Sorry."

"All fine. You're Australian with a touch of Brit. Melodious combination. I'll take you to the Prof's building. I wouldn't mind a practice chat along the way." Wide grin and exaggerated bow. "I'm a bit smartarse. My apologies. I haven't had a significant English conversation since I got back here a year ago from nine years at Duke, in North Carolina. This way. Let's go. It's close."

I bloody know where Duke is. Grin a bit. "I wondered about your rich American accent. What did you study at Duke?"

"Medical degree, then postgraduate radiology. World's best place for that." What? Not in Japan?

"What are you doing here now? More study? Teaching? Research?"

"I've come to see my father. He's a Professor of Medicine. He stepped down as Dean two years ago to prepare for retirement. Retires next week."

"You know Professor Ayanokoji?"

"He's an old friend of my father. They studied medicine here together in the 1930s and have been buddies ever since."

"Professor Ayanokoji studied medicine? I thought he was a sociologist."

The woman hesitates. "He is. Here we are. Must rush. Go through that doorway and the receptionist will show you where to go. Speak slowly and give her a little bow." Smartarse grin.

"Thanks so much."

"Bye. Have a nice day." Are all Japanese women smartarses or just the ones who have lived in the USA?

The smartarse walks a few metres; bites her bottom lip for thinking too little before saying too much, a habit learned at Duke; stops, turns, calls out to Charlotte to wait awhile, goes back to her. "I suggest you not raise Professor Ayanokoji's former calling, with him or anyone else in Kyoto. Jumping professions is not regarded with favour here, for reasons I don't have time to explain at length. It's about the shame of assumed failure. A sociocultural thing. Best not to delve."

So, Dr Duke plays the cross-cultural insensitivity card; Ace of Clubs. Tell her to relax; as a Westerner I'm always penitent, clad in sackcloth and ashes.

"Thanks for the advice. I wouldn't want to offend through cross-cultural ignorance, would I? Never fear. All I care about is what he does now. So long."

Medicine. How did he end up in the humanities? Don't really care.

She asked for Professor Hiroyuki Ayanokoji. The receptionist bowed and replied "Professor Ayanokoji Hiroyuki. You are Dr Fonseka?"

Charlotte smiled and bowed. "Okay, you win. Next time I'll get the order right. Yes, I'm Dr Fonseka. Did you expect another foreign female this morning?" The woman seemed not to hear; bowed again.

"*Hai*. Room 15, madam. That way please. He waits for you."

"Have his students gone?"

"No students in the morning on this day of the week, madam. Only the afternoon, but cancelled for today."

Charlotte squinted. "No students at all today?"

The woman nodded: "No students, madam." He had lied on the telephone.

She dawdled along the corridor the way she used to walk to primary school, the destination uninviting but inevitable. Stopped halfway for a minute; did not want to meet Ayanokoji again. Why come then? Perhaps she needed to see the camera Peter had stared into, at the Otintai Hotel.

A few metres away, beyond a grey plastered wall, Professor Ayanokoji sat in his office chair and studied cracks in the ceiling. No budget for repairs. Reluctant to see Charlotte again; compelled to see her for no clear reason. Artistic vanity? He did want to gauge her reaction to his photographs at home but would not insist she go there to see them.

Hitomi would be indifferent to either a visit or no visit. She had not told him she disliked Charlotte; yet he knew she did dislike her, perhaps because Charlotte understood the Akutagawa *hankechi* too well in the grip of Japanese women. Women everywhere tended to distrust other women who understood masking. Hitomi had once told him that men were less inclined to question the female veneer. To him, men ignored the absurdity of women's need to compete with other women, especially in male company. Women seemed to want men to judge them superior specimens while they tried to play the role of congenial female so well that no hint of envy or rivalry broke their surface with even a rippled warning of what swam below. Did they see or sense Darwinian advantage if they played the role better than other women? Those who could better maintain their act and sabotage the acts of other woman might marry and breed at a higher level. Crazy thought-stream. Two knocks on his door; the first gentle, the second firm.

"Charlotte. Welcome. Do come in. Leave your shoes on. My last student for the day has left, so we are free to chat." Right.

"I'm sorry I missed her."

"Him."

They sat a metre apart, well back on a hard sofa of leather in burnished bottle green. The receptionist brought percolated coffee in *raku* mugs, twisted as if from the Hiroshima or Nagasaki blast; milk, demerara sugar, and four tiny rice-cakes. Small talk about leaves dead and dying in the sunshine, hard-to-get coffee beans, expensive sugar, the manufacture of rice-cakes, and ceiling cracks ignored by the university budget masters. Sorry he did not play musical tapes at dinner. Intended to play some from their collection of *koto*, *shamisen* and *shakuhachi* but thought better of it after she said why she collapsed; did not want to trigger anxiety by association with the music in the gallery. She thanked him for his thoughtfulness. Or did he forget to put the tape on? No students this morning. Her father had warned her. If you lie little lies at first, then a few more times, and tell a few bigger ones, they will all become a clogged stew that might make you vomit, perhaps in public. In Japan, spew into your *hankechi*? Ayanokoji a candidate for a stew yawn.

In a lull, Charlotte said the daughter of his friend, a Professor of Medicine, had guided her to his office. Ayanokoji impassive on the surface; a bit deeper he wanted to smash something. They turned to look at one another. She saw his pupils dilate for a second and shrink back to normal as he tried to probe through the emeralds to the back of her brain.

"Indeed. An old friend. Old in at least two senses. Shall we indulge in our coffee and cakes?" She sipped her coffee twice and put the mug down on the table.

"The girl said you and her father studied medicine together before the war. I missed that in your biographical notes at the gallery. Maybe I read it and didn't remember. If the girl had not mentioned it I probably wouldn't have remembered anyway, all things considered."

Ayanokoji leaned back and looked again at the ceiling cracks. "Your memory is fine. It's not in the biography. As Americans say, shall we cut to the chase? You wonder why I did not practise medicine after the war. Am I right?" He turned to her, his question-mark eyebrow held high to compel a reply. She said she wondered but did not want to intrude; people sometimes change professions and other jobs for personal reasons. Ayanokoji dropped his eyebrow back into place, and his forehead creases vanished into smooth skin.

He's edgy behind that poker face. Wringing the *hankechi*. Take it easy. *No*, whispered Rand. *Don't let up. Make him tangle it in knots.* Horse crap. Piss off. *Okay. I'll wait in the wings for you to call me onstage when you can't proceed without me.*

Ayanokoji palmed hands on knees and nodded with a movement so slight her blink might have missed it. He said it was natural, as an outsider, for her to wonder about his career change. No one had ever asked him but he had always expected the question, one day, somewhere other than Japan. He did not have to explain; even so, he would try. They would attend to her question through their mutual interest in photography. He raised his right hand from his knee and waved at the single photograph on the office wall behind his desk. "A 16 inch by 12 inch monochrome of no aesthetic value. Agreed?"

"It does show your expertise in development and printing." Feed his ego a bit; cheer him up.

"Yes, it's one of mine, and I thank you for the unwarranted compliment. Tell me what you see. Content, not technique. Please summarise it in a few words. One clue. I took it two years ago in Phnom Penh, Cambodia. A diplomatic contact got me into the country." I know where Phnom Penh is, Professor.

Where is he trying to take me? *Somewhere he doesn't really want to go*, Rand told her. *Not too far for comfort though*. Charlotte stood and walked around the desk to the photograph. "Please excuse my back, Hiroyuki. Hmmm. Cambodia in 1980. A year or so after the Vietnamese ousted the Khmer Rouge. You took the shot close in, over a soldier's shoulder. He's probably Vietnamese, given the year. On his desk are one, two, three... Nine photographs arranged in three rows, a neat rectangle. Each shot about seven inches by five inches. Men, women, boys and girls. Three men and one woman with serious facial injuries. A woman with a clear face holds a baby. A girl? Apart from the baby and one boy, they have a number on a card attached to their shirt or dress with a safety pin. One man has a 3 and a 7 pinned side by side to make 37. Mug-shots of prisoners and their children? They all look wretched, resigned. Ah, yes. The story is now emerging in the Australian press. These poor people are murder victims of the Khmer Rouge, are they not? Photographed like the Nazis photographed Jews for the slaughter. Am I right, Hiroyuki? My God. The baby and the other children, a few years older. The women." Her hands now want to clamp over her mouth in horror; instead she clasps them at her navel.

"You are right, Charlotte, up to a point. A point a little short of something about them that history may tell us eventually, if it is honest enough. Something that did not occur to you, nor to me as I took the shot. Probably could not have occurred to us, with reportage so limited, so controlled. The soldier, indeed Vietnamese, enlightened me through a military interpreter with good English."

What could she have missed? She asked him to elaborate. They returned to the sofa, this time sat on its edge. After a minute of contemplation, he said the soldier's job was to prepare photographs for display, inside the former Tuol Sleng prison, to visiting UN and other officials. At Tuol Sleng, once a school, thousands of Cambodians and a few foreigners were tortured to death, or almost. In most cases they were tortured at Tuol Sleng and taken into the countryside; bashed to death with farm tools. Small children were held by the ankles and whacked against a tree trunk. The bodies were dumped en masse into muddy holes. "But none of that is what we missed."

"Hiroyuki, what did I … we … miss?"

"You have a tear in your eye. Understandable. Now, as you deduced, this soldier is looking at photographs of people marked for death. But." He hesitated. "But, experience tells him some of the condemned, including the older children, are themselves likely to be murderers, about to take their turn as victims because they or their relatives fell out with the Khmer Rouge. They broke rules, or a malicious person lied about them. Whatever the case may be, the perpetrator is now the victim. Who could have guessed? Not me, not you."

"Which ones in this case?"

"Perhaps none. The soldier did not know. Research incomplete."

Charlotte lay her hands palms-up on her knees. "I'm not sure where we are going with this."

"On a journey with a map that we create or modify as we go. Let's see where we end up. Meanwhile, consider this. As perpetrators—if any of those people are such—are they also victims of murder in the same way as others who did not kill? Do they deserve their imminent finale under a totalitarian system that has created them and their behaviour?" Finale. Someone else is into scripts.

"Not the baby or the older children. I'm not sure about the adults. Probably not."

"Nor have I made up my mind. On the surface, I think 'No'. Deeper within, I still wonder. Let's continue the journey. Before, you seemed to exonerate women and children but not men. Women bashed their compatriots to death. Under the Khmer Rouge, children bashed in the skulls of adults and other children. At what age and under what circumstances are they guilty? Which ones were coerced? Which not? Some more than others? Under a totalitarian system, something much bigger than individuals coerces everyone, including Big Brother and his inner circle. Fear of annihilation makes perpetrators of potential victims, so that everyone—as a potential victim—becomes an actual or potential perpetrator, an active element of the system, in an often vain attempt to survive. In such circumstances, who is blameworthy? Everyone? No one? Not even the tyrant at the top of the pile?"

Hugh Rand told Charlotte to get rid of the tear, now on a slow meander down her left cheek. She burst the droplet with a fingertip. *Stay with the professor. Don't wilt.* She nodded, told Ayanokoji she could see his purpose; that the photograph's ambiguity and historical context, as explained by him, had negated her initial interpretation.

"I think you mean your original perceptions may have stopped short through lack of information. Like those of the professor in Akutagawa's story, the Strindberg devotee, until he looked under the table when he bent down to pick up the Korean fan he had dropped unintentionally."

"Yes, Hiroyuki, I accept my wrong assumptions in this case. We are too ready to form impressions, opinions, based on binary exclusions. I saw innocence and excluded the possibility of its opposite in the same people. Then again, not necessarily guilty if they were coerced, brainwashed. Simplistic impulses cloud our perception." *Too ready to form impressions, and so on? No, Charlotte. Surely that doesn't include you! That's everyone else. You've never jumped to rigid conclusions about anything, have you, Dr Einstein? Peter knew that, didn't he?*

Ayanokoji sees her listening, again, to another voice, one he cannot hear. "Quite so, Charlotte, even if it sounds obvious, even banal. Life is not so simple that it splits into good or bad, black or white, guilty or innocent; benign or evil; visible or non-existent; remorse or indifference. We all make the same mistake as we try to impose manageable order on chaotic minds and perceptions and emotions; on our lives. Some of us question ourselves as we go along, at least to keep life interesting. Others are less inclined to do so, especially in warfare and its aftermath." He leaned forward to look straight into her eyes. "Charlotte, would you classify marriage and break-up as forms of warfare?"

The raised eyebrow again demanded a response. She held his stare until the eyebrow relaxed. What does this clever bastard know about me? What did Peter tell him? Rand told her to grin, a little. *Relax. He probably knows bugger-all. Merely a misguided joke.*

"Charlotte, you are wistful. I'm sorry. An insensitive joke, a weak one at that." She grinned as Rand had directed, and told Ayanokoji the joke was surely out of character for him and therefore did not matter. He thanked her, said he hoped she was right.

"Now, Charlotte, let's revisit my purpose in analysing the photograph with you." Not *with* me at all, Professor. Made me a marionette. Pulled my strings. Wrote and rewrote my script as I rolled over like a dog afraid of a kick in the guts.

He went on. "I wanted us to open a few Chinese boxes, no more than we would need. We should not paralyse ourselves like the conference delegates holed up in the Clock Tower building, opening boxes ad infinitum. Let's move on. Chat for a while and go to lunch." Tyranny, torture, child murder and murderers, and an easy transition to his lunch, while my guts and head still churn.

"Yes, Hiroyuki. A droll allusion to academia. Timely."

Ayanokoji knows this woman twists the handkerchief. She cannot hide it well today.

"Indeed, Charlotte. Now, you will want to know what all this has to do with why I did not practise medicine after the war. Correct?" She nodded. *Here we go. Act Two.* Fuck off. Go find your head.

Ayanokoji knows he does not have to explain to anyone, let alone her, why he changed careers, and how the change relates to his war service. Why do it then? Has long wanted to tell someone. Wants to do it now, chooses to do it. Will do it. How to rationalise his decision?

Ayanokoji said he felt compelled to explain, as she had asked and would be suspicious if he were to demur. She would talk to others in Australia and perhaps together they would draw impetuous conclusions as part of a normal human need to impose order on uncertainty, then move on to another hatchet job. "You see, Charlotte, you have entrapped me, without intending to do so, with a question that no Japanese would ask me, and I must explain to protect myself against ignorant and judgmental others, especially outside my own country. No one has ever asked me that question but I knew it would come one day from an inquisitive outsider. I fear the reputational effects of not answering it." *Poor Charlotte. He's sending you on a guilt trip. He has a map after all. And a clever script.*

Ayanokoji said his difficulty now was that he must explain something she might believe, but if she were to relay his story in the West to, say, a war historian or an Asia-Pacific War veteran, as she was entitled to do, that person might reinterpret and perhaps misinterpret his story in bizarre and unfair ways. "In our natural need to create intelligible order, especially strong in academics, you and I at first imposed a suspect interpretation—which I was in a position to correct—on the evidence before us in the photograph. Did we not, Charlotte?" *He means I did.*

"We did, Hiroyuki. You are saying you might tell me something about you in all honesty that I might misinterpret and pass on for more misinterpretation that does you no justice?"

"Not necessarily. You might interpret as I consider correct. You pass it all on to someone who misinterprets, or overinterprets— which is likely if that person is an academic. You know what we scholars are like. We need to modify and complicate what other people say, to prove our brain is better than theirs. How often have you heard an academic say 'I agree' or 'I don't know' and leave it at that? Never? You nod. Now, Charlotte, let's look at another possibility. You might misinterpret what I say but the person you tell reinterprets in a way that I consider accurate. What then? There are other angles on the matter but that's enough Chinese boxes for one day. I feel comfortable with you, and so I shall tell you my story with all the honesty I can muster. You can judge me if you wish, as you wish. Conditions acceptable? That is, no conditions apart from your agreement not to forget my Tuol Sleng photograph." Please construct a faulty sentence, Professor. Insert a deliberate flaw.

For a long time, dear Professor, you have feared you would need to do this one day; to explain whatever it is you plan to explain, from your point of view. She asked him to confirm that no one else had ever pressed him to explain his career change. "No, as I have told you already. Before you ask, not even my wife. And I have no children to ask me. The few Japanese who know do not raise the matter with me or anyone else. I honour them for it."

Charlotte agreed to keep the Tuol Sleng photograph in mind. They sat well back on the sofa. He crossed his legs, locked his hands behind his head and stared at the ceiling; she folded her hands in her lap and stared at the wall below the photograph. The two would hold their pose for most of the next two hours—two statues—as he told his tale, unflagging, slow, clear.

"Charlotte, I assume Unit 731 of the Japanese Imperial Army means nothing to you. If it does, please tell me now." She shook her head. He waited a few seconds. "I infer that you have not heard of Unit 731, not that you do know about it but will not tell me. You will hear a lot about it over the next few years. Until recent times it has been an embarrassment, off limits to the few Japanese who know about it, and to the post-war government of the USA. Also academia. I shall outline the unit and tell you how it concerns me."

He said Unit 731 was a "secret research facility" set up at Harbin, Manchuria, by the Kempeitai, Japan's military police, during the occupation of the part of China the Japanese called Manchukuo; their puppet state, rich in natural resources coveted by Japan. Construction of Unit 731 began in 1934 and finished in 1939. In English, its original name was the Epidemic Prevention and Water Purification Department of the Kwantung Army. By 1941, the year of Ayanokoji's posting there, it was known as Unit 731, and still commanded by its founder, Surgeon General Shiro Ishii, doctor and microbiologist, acquainted with Ayanokoji's father; both were graduates of Kyoto Imperial University Medical School. Japan located Unit 731 in China to exploit the ready availability of men, women and children for surgical, biological and chemical research. Seventy per cent of "participants" were Chinese; some Russian; a couple of Americans, maybe; others Southeast Asian; a few Pacific Islanders. The Kempeitai and the army kept up the supply.

Participants? Charlotte bit her bottom lip. Oh Jesus. Was she with some non-human creature even more base than the worst of men? *Hear him out*, said Hugh Rand. *As Peter said, you jump too fast to interpretations that you refuse to question. Look at the photograph while he talks. Give him a chance to be what you don't expect. Remember Tuol Sleng.* She obeyed and released her lip to quiver at will.

Ayanokoji continued, detached from her and perhaps himself, devoid of emotion. Unit 731 was just some place that existed, happened, independent of him even as he described his "association" with it.

He joined the army after graduation and a year of surgical training, and was assigned to Harbin through paternal influence. His father and the officer who advised him of the appointment gave him no detail about the unit but assured him the opportunity would be excellent for career development. The most senior people, including his father's acquaintance at the top, were aristocratic professors and graduates from the Kyoto Medical School. He must consider their post-war value to his career. On appointment he was ordered not to reveal the unit's existence to any outsider in Japan or China, unless he found himself constrained to confirm Unit 731 as a field hospital for Japanese servicemen.

As his staff-car approached Unit 731 at Harbin in late afternoon drizzle, he saw a much bigger complex than imagined. The largest building was a square fortress of dull brick and concrete; several other buildings, large and small, most with barred windows; the administrative centre a two-storey block of fawn bricks and stucco, well-proportioned in functional Bavarian style, with a roof of red tiles. A boiler house with three chimneys exhaled lazy steam towards low cloud. Created the cloud?

He expected to find an army hospital with a research wing devoted to better Chinese health and longevity. Inside the administrative building and its courtyard he saw no soldiers other than guards, and nothing he recognised as a hospital even though he met several men introduced as doctors. He asked to see the wards; the most senior of his new colleagues told him he would see them next day. Today he should settle into his living quarters and rest.

That night he dined with four doctors, all army officers from Kyoto, two of whom had taught him there. What were the unit's primary activities, apart from the repair of damaged servicemen? His expected role? Silence, blank glances, wry grins, fleeting. The senior officer said his questions would get answers next day. Right now he should dine, chat and drink *sake* with them. Dr Ayanokoji brushed off his colleagues' reticence as a symptom of fatigue after a hard day of work. He slept well.

The next morning his immediate superior took him to the commanding officer, Surgeon General Ishii, and left them alone. Ayanokoji stood before his father's demi-god and saluted. In silence, the general looked up at him through round glasses for half a minute without a blink. In his late 40s, maybe older; undemonstrative, no hint of a smile; greyer and sparser in hair, and more worn in skin, than in a portrait Ayanokoji saw in Kyoto. Jug ears. Near his left nostril a large mole and a larger one halfway between nostril and flabby earlobe. A moustache in British Royal style and a scraggled beard, both in need of scissors and razor. Simple uniform.

Charlotte wondered why Ayanokoji gave her so much detail, as if he were an artist sizing up Ishii for a portrait in oils. *The eloquent professor procrastinates, that's why*, said Rand.

Ishii spoke in gentle monotone, with a five second pause after each sentence; all brevity and precision. He had heard encouraging things from Ayanokoji's father and the head of Kyoto Medical School. Ayanokoji's participation in the Emperor's project would do his father proud. Exponential learning curve and promotion. He must not breach confidentiality about Unit 731 in China, Japan or anywhere else he might be posted over his entire career within or outside the military.

"Dr Ayanokoji, you must accept what everyone here knows. We must do unpleasant things from time to time that will bring well-being to the Chinese peasants and humankind, as well as our troops. As doctors and scientists, our minds must control our emotions. Always remember that most of the patients are criminals, Communists and spies who have harmed innocent people, including our soldiers. Also remember that the Chinese have harmed more of their people than we have done or shall ever do. Take the Taiping Rebellion from 1850 to 1864. They killed 20 million of their own people in order to regress to a feudal system dressed up as progress. Any occasional, accidental mortality at Harbin and elsewhere has a higher purpose, but is nonetheless regretted." Ten second pause. "Any questions, Dr Ayanokoji?"

"Sir! How many servicemen are patients here? Sir!"

"Not many." Eyes of gun-metal black dared Ayanokoji to ask another question.

Ayanokoji told Charlotte the General puzzled him. "I decided to hold firm. Before I could request an explanation he grinned, out of character, and slapped his palms on his desk to signify the end of our chat. The last thing he said shocked me, a man who does not shock easily. 'Unit 731 is known to be a lumber mill. We call the patients *maruta*.' That is, logs. I had no choice but to salute, bow and leave the room." *He had no choice? Bullshit*, said Rand. The meeting lasted thirteen minutes.

Charlotte and Ayanokoji still sat like statues. He spoke again after a minute, hands clenched behind his head, voice normal, as he watched the ceiling. He warned her to be ready for his description of what he saw that day, and the next, and the next.

His immediate superior led him first in a stroll through a museum of specimens: dead babies and body parts of adults marinated in glass jars of formaldehyde, labelled by nationality, mostly Chinese; also a few Americans, English and French. A monstrous jar held the pickled body of a Russian man, split in almost perfect symmetry from crown to groin; a tailor would have said he was hung left. "By the time we quit that display I believed myself immune to anything that might follow in the wards. Anatomical specimens, apart from the whole Russian man—well, not quite whole—were not new to me." How very amusing, Professor.

His next experience troubled him much more than the first, especially when he saw the implications for warfare. They approached a door with a small glass window, such as you see in hospitals, designed to avoid catastrophe if someone is on the other side with a tray of instruments or a trolley of bedpans. Or a patient on crutches. How very amusing, Professor.

"The little window at the lumber mill had a different purpose. The door was locked for staff safety. Through the glass I saw an old man, naked, putrid; dotted all over with red spots like rubies or tiny red blossoms. I did not recognise the disease and did not ask what it was. He lay strapped to a bed. Another putrid man, young and without spots, lay strapped to another bed a metre way. Both thin, starving. My escort said these *maruta* participated in an experiment to find out how long it took a diseased criminal to infect a healthy one, both giving up food to see if fasting influenced the speed and severity of infection, compared with a control pair given plenty to eat and drink in another room. Researchers experimented for many diseases. They used vaccination to infect the *maruta* who would transmit the disease."

Ayanokoji asked if the research related to biological warfare. "Yes," snapped the escort. "Germ-assisted defence. The Geneva Convention of 1925 banned it, so General Ishii realised it must therefore be an effective weapon available to enemies of Emperor Hirohito, and so we should develop it through experiments with criminals." Such experiments assisted medical science to create treatments for illness and injury suffered by the heroic defence forces of Emperor Hirohito, whose son visited Harbin from time to time to vet progress. The criminals atoned for their crimes by saving the lives of the Knights of Bushido. *'Vet' sounds about right*, Rand whispered to Charlotte, stoic on the outside, frail in the gut. She nodded.

"Charlotte, stop me if my story is too much to bear. I do not have to tell it. I tell it for you, not me."

"Go on, Hiroyuki. I haven't lived my life in a cocoon." How can he narrate such horror in his normal voice? No emotion. Why? Because it did not bother him as much as he wants me to think? Or to cope with the horror?

"Quite so, Charlotte. Please forgive me for the inadvertent slight." He went on. After the two doctors studied the criminals through the window for a few minutes in silence, the senior officer looked at his watch. "Lunchtime." With Ayanokoji in shock, the doctors scrubbed away their morning's work with hot towels, and ate sushi at the officers' canteen. In keeping with the rule at Unit 731, they discussed matters other than work. The tour resumed after lunch.

"Charlotte, I shall not disturb us with more fine detail." Us? He hasn't disturbed himself yet. No sign of the *hankechi*. Bloody 'shall'.

He proceeded to contradict himself with fine detail that tried to pump her rice-cakes and coffee back up her gullet and onto the floor.

"I spent that afternoon, and another two days, observing surgical experiments, dreading the inevitable order to participate. I waited, like a man condemned but not told his date of execution. I saw vivisection, without anaesthetic, of men, women and children who shrieked until they fainted or died, or their larynx lay in a dish. Foetuses near full-term cried themselves to death inside or beside their mothers.

"Surgical science was the source of the stink I had smelt and the racket I had heard echo along corridors on the first morning while I toured silent exhibits of people in jars, and inspected logs transmitting and catching diseases. On that first tour I had also observed participants locked in an airtight, soundproof chamber to help scientists discover the effects of lethal gases pumped into it at different rates and quantities. Also, what pressures would suck or push eyes from their sockets, and damage other organs?

"I heard about but did not witness field tests on trussed Chinese criminals with gases developed at Unit 731. Grenades exploded at different distances to explore the spectrum of effect on people tied to poles. Troops infected Communist village wells with typhoid the unit supplied in test tubes, and in sweets for children." No wonder you sanitise your history books, Professor.

Charlotte wanted to stand but realised that if she did so her options would be to flop back onto the sofa or crash to the floor. Gut churned. No more would she tell anyone of her childhood agony when a dentist filled three molars without anaesthetic.

"Back to the vivisections, Charlotte." He paused, still in the same pose, hands behind head. "Some looked more like practice for civilian surgeons than military research. Visitors from medical schools and private clinics in Japan. At my first observation, my escort anticipated a question. He said anaesthesia would devalue the research because body organs and other parts under study might be affected and therefore not in their normal condition."

Vivisection. Charlotte again remembered Dave Rand's rant at Nyngan about warning his son to beware of the Japs' cutlery. Now, as she sat on Ayanokoji's sofa, she felt hands of ice grip her shoulders from behind. *Toughen up, Princess.* She jerked forward to escape Rand's hold; it moved with her. Ayanokoji hesitated. "I shall stop if you wish." She told him to continue; said she had visited a slaughterhouse as a teenager.

"Ah," he said, "I say 'abattoir', a pretty French word, like your name. Hitomi tells me it is derived from Charles, and is more or less its opposite in meaning. 'Manly' becomes 'feminine and petite'; 'petite' in the sense of delicate. You are indeed feminine in the extreme, but not delicate in body or mind. Regardless, your name suits you."

She did not reply. Yes, Hitomi, you arsehole. So clever to link tough Charles with delicate Charlotte. Dear husband, Dr Fonseka is strong in body but delicate in constitution. Faints in photography exhibitions. That's me, you *hankechi*-wringing bitch.

"Thank you, Hiroyuki. I do like my name."

Rand shook her shoulders and leaned forward to whisper stern advice in her left ear. *Keep your eyes and mind on the Tuol Sleng photograph.* If she were Bos Simeon, she thought, she would not have heard his whisper on that side and might not have returned her gaze to the photograph, and her mind to its warning not to cloud her perception with premature conclusions.

Ayanokoji released his hands from the back of his head and put the right one on her left shoulder to replace Rand's grip on that side. Warmer hand. Rand's left hand moved to chill her nape. Ayanokoji told her to look at him. *Don't obey; keep your focus on Tuol Sleng.* She stared at the photograph.

"Charlotte, perhaps contrary to your first impressions, this was a nightmare for me, first as a doctor, foremost as a human being. You might now begin to understand why I escaped Unit 731, left medicine. Not after the war, during the war." Some cadence now in his speech. Turn to him. His calm eyes seek a reaction. Raised eyebrow; corrugated forehead.

"Much more of a nightmare for your research participants, don't you think, Hiroyuki? The *maruta*?" He nodded, and jerked his hand from her shoulder, the first rapid movement she had seen him make. Rand's hand replaced Ayanokoji's. *Charlotte, consider what his soothing hand might have done at Unit 731.*

She wanted Ayanokoji to get to the point, to quit the procrastination flagged earlier by Rand. "Why did you leave medicine? Something to do with the Hippocratic Oath, I hope. But why during the war? And how, in those years, when no one could question their superiors? Why not a transfer to a different medical unit?" No reply. She went on: "How did you manage to escape from Harbin and still be available to tell me about it 40 years later?"

"The process was simple, as were the consequences. I could not do this research on even Japan's most savage enemies, or the lowest form of human life, as we saw the Chinese. After I had observed my colleagues at work for a few days, my superior scheduled me to assist a surgeon to excise a third of a girl's liver the next morning, to investigate the effect on her kidneys and the rest of the liver. I would remove and dissect the organs a week later if she still lived, sooner if she died." Ten second hiatus. "Our findings might help save the lives of wounded soldiers. Given the right treatment and its timing, how much liver could a man lose and live to fight again?" Silence for fifteen seconds. "Late in the afternoon I was told to observe her. My superior said 'She is alone in what she thinks is a staging room, and expects to be released tomorrow. Showered, a clean smock, excellent food from the staff canteen. To keep her calm, to prevent her from self-harm.'

"She smiled as I entered her room. A pretty girl, aged about 16. Treated well for several weeks to prepare her for the operation, which had to be done on a healthy person, fit as a well-fed soldier." Ten seconds. "We had no common language. Even so, I came to understand she thought she was to be released because she had ... gratified ... the head surgeon several times over previous months. No prophylactic. Her smiles compounded my shock. She expected me to copulate with her. I bowed and left in such disgust that I almost vomited. I believe she was scheduled a little early because was pregnant and we needed her participation in the liver experiment before she swelled too much. Enough about her."

Charlotte did not speak; nor Rand. Ayanokoji stood and walked around his desk to sit in his work chair. He adopted the Kawabata pose; they stared at one another's nose-tip. Rand still gripped her; one icicled paw on her neck, the other on her right shoulder. She did not try to pull away; the grip and the cold sharpened her mind.

Dr Ayanokoji lowered his gaze to Charlotte's waist and resumed his tale. The evening before his scheduled surgery on the girl he complained of nausea and excused himself from the daily bathhouse chat, drinks and dinner. As he lay on his bed with eyes shut he pondered an anti-malarial research project, described on his first day at Unit 731. Logs were fed super-doses of mepacrine to lower blood pressure to lethal levels; researchers studied the effects on soon-to-be-dissected hearts. The logs developed severe hypotension, ventricular flutter, and nausea; some died of heart attack as blood-flow ebbed near zero.

Ayanokoji would get mepacrine from the research stores, to which he had approved access, and overdose enough to lower his blood pressure; to induce mild arrhythmia, but not cause a heart attack; enough to warrant discharge from Unit 731 and probably exempt him from further military service overseas.

He went to the pharmacy storehouse, still open but apparently unstaffed. Found the mepacrine stock, took one pill from each of eight small jars, put the pills in his trouser pocket, and shouted for any storeman who might be there. He needed a witness. A drowsy attendant came to the service bench and gave Dr Ayanokoji the three anti-nausea pills he requested.

Ayanokoji returned to his quarters, washed two anti-nausea pills down a basin and put the third in his shirt pocket; took six of the eight mepacrine pills—three times the weekly dose as an antimalarial—and put the other two under his pillow. He lay on his bed. At 10pm a colleague found him awake; convulsing, soaked in sweat. Ayanokoji refused to go to the infirmary, the closest thing to a ward in the complex; he said he felt sleepy but well. "You don't look well, Hiroyuki. I've drunk a bit too much. I'll get sober help."

Two doctors brought a blood pressure device; it read the equivalent of a modern 78 systolic over 46 diastolic, in the danger zone. Heart rate 172 per minute. Arrhythmic beat. Had he taken medication for the nausea he complained about earlier?

"Yes. Two of three pills from the pharmacy. Dimenhydrinate. The third is in my shirt pocket." He gave the pill to a doctor, who examined it and dismissed it as a cause of these symptoms. The other doctor injected something into his upper left arm. Fifteen minutes later Ayanokoji's blood pressure read 118/68, his heart rate 64; steady beat. The nausea, convulsions and high temperature had also passed. An hour later he was alert and his vital signs normal. A doctor would return at 7am.

Ayanokoji slept until 6am. At 6.30 he took the seventh and eighth mepacrine pills. At 7.10 he read 84/50; heart rate 142, unsteady beat; copious sweat. There could be no repeat of the injection for fear of heart failure. At 7.30 the signs were better but not normal. The doctor told him to stay in bed, to eat rice and fruit for breakfast; no coffee or tea.

At 9.30am General Ishii came to his room. He said Ayanokoji might recover fully and might not suffer another episode of this aberration. Nonetheless, even a tiny risk was too great. Consider the danger to colleagues if he were involved in research with chemicals or germs and had a relapse. Impaired control and judgement might put colleagues in jeopardy. Many researchers and guards had died when experiments went wrong in the best of hands. Dr Ayanokoji would go now to another hospital for observation. There he would be told his next posting, if fit for one. "I am in sorrow at your plight, Dr Ayanokoji. I shall write to your father to explain."

"*Hai! Hai! Ryokai shimashita.*" Yes, yes, I understand.

That was all. The Surgeon General bowed and left. "His compassion for me—my health and diminished career prospects— was genuine," Ayonokoji told Charlotte. Within an hour two soldiers loaded him into a field ambulance. A truckload of *maruta* arrived as he left Unit 731. *By now someone else would have been slicing up the Chinese girl, maybe a real screamer. Right Charlotte? Has that occurred to the professor? He hasn't said so, but it's obvious. Didn't object, let alone try to stop it. Did you pick up on that? I doubt it. Have another look at the Tuol Sleng photograph to recharge your analytical brain.* She looked, and did not tell Rand to fuck off or take his icicle hands off her.

The two scholars sat in silence. He watched her lizard-like for approval; she watched him owl-like for hesitation or a flinch. Neither saw the thing they watched for.

"Where did you end up, Hiroyuki?" Discharged from the military hospital with an order to fly to Tokyo and report to the head of army medicine, who told him he was unfit for immediate posting as a doctor but could be recommended for an army medical role if he were to have no relapse of his undiagnosed condition during the month's leave he must now take. If he did not wish to continue in military service he could take up private medical practice.

"After some manoeuvring by my father, through Surgeon General Ishii, I took leave, then spent three months in medical emergency training at Hiroshima. Owing to my full recovery, my high level of education, my performance in the course, and my father's connections, I became a major and was posted to a field hospital in the Philippines. I stayed there for nine months, then went to Singapore. That answers your previous question about a transfer to another medical unit."

"Fine. Back to my original interest and your offer to explain. Why didn't you take up medical practice after the war? Surely, with your father's connections...."

"I saw too much horror at Unit 731 in the name of medicine. Too much blood and cruelty after that as a junior medico in the Philippines and elsewhere. My resolve never to return to medicine became fixed when the Americans and their allies agreed to overlook the existence of Unit 731, and the role of Ishii and his staff, in exchange for the unit's research data, which had generated over 100 scientific papers published during the war about experiments on 'monkeys'. The Americans offered immunity from war crimes prosecution, and promised generous living allowances to these sadists, the same sadists who killed 400 *maruta* after Japan's surrender. General Ishii handed over the data that he had buried in the garden of his luxury villa near Tokyo. He and his scientists cooperated for years with American colleagues, as friends. He retired in government-funded comfort and lived until 1959. Soon after the war his colleagues assumed control of Japanese medicine as professors, practitioners and health administrators. One became President of the Japan Medical Association. Another the Governor of Tokyo. Another the Chairman of Japan's Olympic Committee. All but one of several post-war directors of the Japan National Institute of Health have been members of Unit 731 or an affiliate. A senior officer founded Green Cross, Japan's dominant pharmaceutical company, and employed many colleagues. Over the past 40 years I have declined regular invitations to join the *Seikonkai*, the association of Unit 731 scientists, Japan's most active society of veterans. The name means 'Refined Spirits'."

"What about your friend, whose daughter I met today?" Never

at Unit 731; spent the war at military hospitals in Tokyo; nothing for the Americans to overlook. *Bullshit, Dr Fonseka*. She nodded to Rand. Ayanokoji read the nod as acceptance of his reply to her question.

"Or for the Japanese to overlook," she added. No reaction. What will move this robot? She asked if his friend's career might have been even more illustrious if he had been at Unit 731.

"Not all of us were savages, Charlotte. Even the worst sometimes showed a humanitarian touch. You know of Prime Minister Hidaki Tojo?"

"Yes. Hanged after the war. He should have studied medicine." Ayanokoji ignored her sarcasm. *Brilliant, Charlotte*, said Rand, his hands on her again. Oh, shit. *See his studied non-reaction. That one got to him.*

"Tojo stepped down as our PM but still had great influence. He blocked a plan by the most senior generals to use biological weapons against the USA, at home and abroad." Rand told her to ask him why.

"Why did he block it?"

"Conscience, probably." *Go get him, Charlotte. Give him a Tuol Sleng moment.*

"No longer PM, therefore late in the war? About 1944? 1945?"

Ayanokoji maintained the Kawabata pose, already held more than long enough for an artist to sketch him. "I see where you want to go, Charlotte. 1944. Unverified history, by the victors, claims Tojo knew Japan would lose and that war crimes trials would follow. Most Japanese believe he feared for his own people. The Americans might retaliate with their own chemicals and germs. Well, they went further than that at Hiroshima and Nagasaki, without justification. Of course, a moot point."

"Would the Japanese have dropped such a bomb on Pearl Harbour or Los Angeles if they had one?" *Nice, nice one, Charlotte. That'll make him twist his* hankechi.

"Probably not, for fear that the Russians might make one, or soon take one from Germany, and drop it on us. The word was out that Russia was working on both possibilities. We suspected the Americans were well ahead but didn't think their people would condone its use. Well, we got Hiroshima, confirmed by Nagasaki. Tokyo next?"

Back to Tojo. She said his belated concern for his own people after sacrificing so many of them hardly made him humanitarian. "And why just his own people? In the preferred history, does he mention non-Japanese?" No reaction. "But I agree with you about the Hiroshima and Nagasaki bombs. Any justification is moot." Anytime, anywhere, she decried incineration, dismemberment and radiation for soldiers, let alone civilians. Children.

"Yet, Hiroyuki, the matter is indeed moot. Was incineration deserved justice for any Japanese savages on leave from Unit 731 in those two cities at the time? Or officers from the Thai-Burma railway camps? Pilots who sank refugee and hospital ships? Liberators of Nanjing? Officers who beheaded coast watchers in the Pacific Islands." *Thanks for thinking of me*, said Rand. Aloud, she replied, "I wish I couldn't."

Ayanokoji's eyes quizzed her. Again this woman seems to address an invisible companion. She told him to ignore the last utterance; a personal matter.

"Of course, Charlotte. Back to your questions. My photograph of Tuol Sleng continues to interest you; for its ambiguity, no doubt. Good. Now, if killing perpetrators in Cambodia was justified, which we would agree is questionable, what about Japanese perpetrators of questionable acts in various places who happened to be in Hiroshima and Nagasaki at the wrong time, on leave with families who had done no wrong? Maybe we should focus on the latter, and other clear innocents. To temper your thoughts on the morality of the Hiroshima bomb for perpetrators, and the horror they suffered, I suggest you read John Hersey's 1946 article in the New Yorker. He does not mention perpetrators as victims, deserving or otherwise, but his article is relevant to our discussion.

"I admit that the label 'perpetrator' is too complex for me to grasp in all its nuances, if not for you. Were the Enola Gay crewmen perpetrators, or are the connotations of that label too harsh for any men conditioned to perform their duty? Soldiers? Doctors? Researchers? Kempeitai?"

Here we go, Charlotte. The Knights of Bushido as victims of the Emperor and his cronies. She nodded to Rand. Ayanokoji nodded back. More bloody echolalia. "Ah, you get my point, Charlotte. No need for me to elaborate."

His next comments—tangential, unforeseen—horrified her: "I have heard a Western expression, 'The sins of the fathers are visited on their children'. The Chinese have a similar adage. Unit 731 did not conduct research on children unless their parents were criminals. The parents would have expected it for their offspring. As for the criminals themselves, they knew the risk to themselves and their children of spying, subversion, sabotage, stealing military stores, and so on. Risk does not always pay. That is what risk means, *n'est ce pas?*"

Is this guy genius or lunatic? A scary mix of brilliant and absurd. "Back to Tojo, Hiroyuki. Your objections to dirty weaponry had a different premise to his. As a doctor you couldn't harm people deliberately and therefore could not work at Unit 731. Tojo, as general and erstwhile PM, didn't baulk at using plague and gas to kill foreigners, but for ethical reasons couldn't risk provoking foreigners to devastate his own people. Something like that?" Ayanokoji nodded, head still in Kawabata hands; no resemblance to the benign author in disposition or mood.

"Yes, a reasonable assessment of Tojo's motivation, if not necessarily the right assessment."

"Let me try again, Hiroyuki, in the spirit of the Tuol Sleng photographic analysis. Another guess, simpler, is that he applied common sense in a deluded attempt to save his own neck. Is that better?" *That's enough for the moment, Charlotte. Sit back a bit and let him run.* Rand eased his grip so she could lean back and sink deeper into the sofa.

Ayanokoji reacted at first with a twitch of his right eyebrow. A few seconds later, a wry smile, a slow nod. Trying to be Kawabata to me? Can't read his eyes. Behind them, Ayanokoji wondered how Peter Millar and Gamini Fonseka coped with her negativity and compulsion to say what she thought, so much unlike her efforts at dinner last night to mask her thoughts with smiles and words of opposite or innocuous meaning; weak camouflage, though—her inner meaning always in her eyes if not her words. High intellect, strong on logic, but her argument often cynical, with a sting in the tail. How could her pair of husbands cope with her anxiety, surely driven by impetuosity, and over-analysis of others but none of herself? Obsessive self-righteousness? Guile? Doesn't realise she twists her *hankechi* on the table instead of under it. Has her sensuality enticed them to cope? Probably.

From behind, Rand tapped her on the crown. *Take the good professor to lunch. You've done well not to let him bridle you with his constipated social graces. They're no more than a device to help him control everyone who intrudes on his stage.*

Ayanokoji lowered his palms from his cheeks onto the desk and pushed himself to his feet. He put his arms by his sides, fists against thighs, and bowed low to Charlotte; his nose almost on the desk, he held the bow: "I apologise for any emotional disturbance my tales of horror may have caused you. Your interest in my past required me to explain the works of my contemporaries in the context of war, which always generates horror. Of course, there are no excuses for creating and perpetuating it, unlike its opposite, Charlotte. Only reasons. They are hard to fathom for those of us who have participated directly in war. Perhaps even harder for other judges who must rely on hindsight into other people's history." Sure,

Professor. I'm a virgin, you're a veteran. Won't work. Sorry. He stood up and looked at her eyes to gauge his credibility; she would not look at him.

"Yes, Hiroyuki. Hard to fathom. But perhaps it's too easy to rework excuses as reasons, and reasons as justifications. If I had studied philosophy I might be able to expand on that line of thought." She stood and rubbed her eyes. "I don't know about you but I'm not up for lunch after Tuol Sleng and Unit 731, and Hiroshima. I do hope you understand."

"I do. The hunger pangs I noticed an hour ago have disappeared." They both forced grins, mere twitches at mouth corners. He said her mention of philosophy had caused him to wonder if they should get some fresh air along his favourite path in Kyoto. "As you know, I live in the Nanzenji district." Had she visited the temple of that name? No. He said they could walk a few hundred metres to Dimachiyangi railway station, ride a few stops, change to another line, and alight at Keage. "The temple is nearby, but I suspect you need a break from temples. Of more interest to me today, and perhaps to you, is *Tetsugaku-no-michi*, the Path of Philosophy, a kilometre or so to the north of the temple. Maybe it does not appeal to you. We philosophised ad nauseam this morning. Moralised. Semanticised. Quibbled but not quarrelled. Anyway, you decide.

"The name of the path derives from its use by Nishida Kitaro, a modern philosopher. He often walked that route in silence, frisking his brain for inspiration. Shall we follow his example, without the frisking? No deep discussion of human imperfection. No mention of the extent to which our moral reasoning may be a set of fabrications driven by our need to feel less disgusted with ourselves than with others. Then to my nearby home to look at photographs. My attempts at beauty as its own justification, no didactics, no moral lessons. No photographs of Tuol Sleng or war zones. No road carnage. No death masks or butchered animals. Most are about the idiosyncratic and collective beauty of people, perhaps my counter to horrors I have witnessed; my way of coping. We can snack at my home if our walk restores the appetite quelled by the foibles we discussed this morning. Shall we?" Foibles? Foibles? Christ! How does his head work? Precise grammar again. Another bloody shall, not will. Long lecture.

"Excellent suggestion, Hiroyuki. Shall we? We shall." *Fine, but pretend to forget the Tuol Sleng photo. Think interpretation of interpretation.* She nodded; Rand let go of her.

* * *

Ayanokoji praised her pace and fitness on their trudge in sunshine to Dimachiyangi station. "Remember you are not much more than half my age. But don't slow down. I'll manage." Nonsense. Fitter than she was. She laughed and told him she learned to walk hard on Bougainville administrative patrols with Peter Millar. "Did he tell you we lived there in the 60s?"

"No, he did not mention it. That island, Charlotte, has been and will continue to be a heart-rending place for Japanese families. And for my colleagues charged with doing the recovery work there that I did at Tarawa. Finding and cremating the remains of our soldiers. I have not been there but I know there is much evidence that Bougainville was hell for our troops. Especially late in the war when Macarthur severed supply lines as he pushed north and our navy weakened. You have heard about the mass deaths there?"

Charlotte said she had heard of the high Japanese toll, but no detail. Her husband knew a lot about the campaign but she did not encourage him to pass it on to her. She had not wanted historical reality to break the spell of her first exotic adventure. Deliberate naivety, she said. Another issue was Peter's nascent obsession with the fate of an Australian coast watcher whose body was never found. Had Peter mentioned the case to Ayanokoji in Tarawa?

"No, not that case, nor Bougainville itself. The chance did

not arise, owing to his redeployment on our first day of working together. However, I did encounter his somewhat emotive interest in coast watcher deaths in the Gilberts." *Here we go, Charlotte*. No hands on her. "As we stood on the very spot at Betio, Mr Millar told me of a tragedy, the deaths of 17 New Zealanders. You will perhaps understand, as he did not seem to do, that these people were spies from a Japanese point of view, in a war zone. Their activities led to the deaths of many Japanese, many more than 17." Sad, Professor, to say the least, she told herself. Right about Peter's disposition. Too much emotion, not enough common sense. Same imbalance led him to root every girl he could without considering the main game—our marriage. She waited for Rand to whisper support in her left ear; none.

"Charlotte, we shall reach the station in a few minutes. Once we get there, shall we agree to leave such matters for your next visit, or not ever talk about them again? Use the train trip and the Path of Philosophy, and our viewing of my photographs, as a purge? An escape? At least for today. Agreed?" She nodded. Rand dug her in the kidneys with both hands and whispered: *The professor is a tad ashamed of the Knights of Bushido, isn't he? As defeated victims, not butchers. Doesn't like the defeat at Bougainville, does he? Remember Bougainville? I sure do.*

At the station entrance Ayanokoji grasped her right elbow with gentle grip to stop her. He had one more point to make, not to excuse the horrors of war; rather to emphasise balance. He told her of Peter's account of the 80 Japanese soldiers shot in the head after surrender to the Americans on Betio. "The official version is that a mere 17 of our soldiers surrendered. A few Korean labourers. That the rest died because they would not surrender. It does not add up, does it, if Peter Millar was right? His source was strong, and I saw many helmets and skulls that suggested the Americans were perfect marksmen in chaotic conditions. Unlikely? Bullet holes all in the centre of the forehead?" Charlotte said she knew the story.

"Look, Charlotte, evil is rampant in war, and historical distortion, another evil in itself, follows on." He released her elbow and did not wait for a reply; conversation over. "So, we are at the station. I shall get our tickets."

No other European travelled in their carriage on either of the two trains that took them to Keage. No one seemed to see her or Ayanokoji. Too tempting to think about the things he might do to her at night? No one sat or stood with any hint of the normal slouch in Australia. No one talked. No one looked at anyone else. A few wore Walkman earphones, Charlotte thought more to cement their isolation than listen to music or radio programs. Many closed eyes. Inner demons twisting *hankechi*? Maybe within everyone. Maybe no one. Ayanokoji? She thought so. *You bet, Charlotte.*

From Keage station they strolled northward side by side, wordless for a kilometre; Charlotte calm; no sign of Hugh Rand, apart from her awareness of his absence, and so his de facto presence. Ayanokoji ruminated, as agreed. From time to time he pointed without explanation to things she could see for herself: temples, trees almost bare now, reduced from autumn glory to skeletons refusing to surrender their last scraps of sinew and skin. *Charlotte, are you grieving over....* Shut the fuck up! Her whisper to Rand was low but Ayanokoji must have heard it. Rand, shut up.

Ayanokoji broke his silence. "*Tetsugaku-no-michi* starts here. The Path of Philosophy. Let's follow it part-way as we contemplate nothing much. Then return the same way to here, then go to my house." He pointed. "See the roof 250 metres to the west? Okay with you?" She nodded.

They walked about 500 metres on a narrow path beside a canal a few metres wide; the canal lined with perfect basalt blocks and the path bordered with bushes, trees, and shrubs. Some flowering in the wrong season? A few strollers. The pair stood aside to let a geriatric man, lean as jerky, shuffle past in the opposite direction, led by a black, fat, arrogant cat, tail vertical, anus on parade. The cat's collar of chrysanthemum-yellow leather; a rope of red silk linked the man's right hand to the collar but probably not to the animal. The cat, as path's owner, strutted like a Chihuahua that thought itself a Doberman. The man bowed as he passed; the cat ignored them and did not permit him to hesitate.

Ayanokoji grabbed Charlotte's arm as she watched the cat over her shoulder and started to step back to the centre of the path. A snail silver-trailed where she was about to step. "Better not squash it, Charlotte. It has done us no harm." Her arm felt warm to his touch. He smiled at her. Is he worried about the snail or the septic mess I will make if I crush it on the path? Two minutes after freeing her arm he gave way to a lone cockroach that scampered across the path and over the top of the canal wall; a paranoiac chased by fear.

No traffic on this footpath but much noise from nearby roads. One of Kyoto's myriad refuges from the urban cancer attack. Look at him. Held my arm a fair while. What is he thinking? Not much, by the look of him, out of my eye's corner. Serene. Maybe. Some lip-quiver. *Twisting his* hankechi, *Charlotte?* You again. *I never really leave you.*

Ayanokoji suffered mute with his version of war history. Australian butchery of exhausted, starving Japanese troops on the New Guinea mainland: Kokoda, Buna, Gona, Popondetta, Salamaua. On Bougainville Island, 21,000 Japanese soldiers died; another 23,500 survived only because the war ended before they could be massacred. Western historians say the Japanese died there in suicidal battles against Allied forces, mainly Australian by then, towards the end. Lines of supply cut off. Many Japanese died fighting but most too weak to fight like Knights of Bushido. Starved to death; shot, blown apart and incinerated with ease by Australian heroes; minimal resistance, no mercy. She cannot know what it was like to lie in a foxhole, waiting to starve to death while you watch a harvest moon and listen through the breeze, ocean and wildlife for a human killer who might get you before the starvation. Starving men crazed enough to cannibalise anyone. Ate Indian carriers at Wewak and Aitape. Anyone. Sometimes skeletal Japanese corpses. This woman cannot imagine starved boys—friends—who watch one another as both predator and prey. They try to guess who will die first. Is such suffering heroic? Heroic sacrifice to be eaten so others may live? Did some die deliberately for that gastronomic purpose?

Brash Australians, plumper, better eating. Natives who strayed too far from Allied security. Dogs. Village and plantation cats much skinnier than the one we just saw. Earthworms. Snails. Cockroaches. Maggots. Rats fattened on soldiers' remains left to rot by troops too weak to bury them; too afraid to cremate them and reveal position with smoke; too wet anyway. Triumphant Allied photographs show dead Japanese without trousers; shit themselves to death, crying for their mothers. Why wear trousers if you shit every few minutes? Spies glorified and lamented by this woman's naïve husband. Killers by proxy. The 17 executed at Betio passed on information that killed Japanese men in their foxholes, far from home, their last meal a few maggots harvested from their own tropical ulcers and wounds. Temporary mutualism. Maggots eat man, man eats maggots. Not for long. Maggots the last diners.

Charlotte must speak. "Hiroyuki, there are so many pots, statues and artefacts left at hand's reach by the residents, right near the path. Unchained bicycles everywhere. Easy prey. They wouldn't last long in Sydney." No response after fifteen seconds. "Hiroyuki?"

"Sorry Charlotte. Student projects on my mind. The things wouldn't last long in Sydney? Nor in some parts of Tokyo, Osaka, maybe Hiroshima, Kobe. Elsewhere there are no petty thieves. The few thieves in Japan tend to wear collar and tie, and often have Korean affiliations. This is Japan, this is Kyoto. People respect one another. Petty theft is infra dig to us." How clever to throw in a bit of Latin, Professor. Theft of countries back a bit was okay? And now, their natural resources? Open slather as long as they aren't Japanese.

"Mutual respect and no theft. I've had that feeling since I arrived. It's sort of ... relaxing." Smug bastard. Don't dare cut down a Japanese tree. Fine to rip the guts out of anyone else's forests for chopsticks, paper and your bloody packaging fetish. Unit 731 savaged only non-Japanese logs. *Unfair, Charlotte? Too negative. Too extreme. Culture shock? Should have listened to Peter on that one.* No on all counts. Fuck off.

At 2pm Ayanokoji suggested they turn back; he was peckish. The return faster than the outward dawdle. Near their starting point they crossed a footbridge into Ayanokoji's street, at the opposite end to the taxi's entry from the main road the previous night. The footpath yet to be sterilised today. Fewer leaves now clinging to their birth-branches. Not much more Goldengrove to unleave.

PART SIX

Kyoto, Japan, 1982

The Second Gallery

Friday 17 December 1982. Kyoto. Afternoon. In the lobby of his house, Professor Hiroyuki Ayanokoji called out to his wife, Hitomi. No answer; the house cold. He took off his shoes, put on slippers and hung up his jacket. "Please wait a moment, Charlotte. I'll see where she is while you hang up your coat and don your slippers." Near the telephone he found a note to say Hitomi had gone with friends by train to shop in Osaka and would return at 8pm with takeaway dinner. He waved the note.

"Charlotte, Hitomi has gone out but will be home at ... 6pm. She has gone to see a friend who has fallen ill."

"Fallen?" On his or her arse? So clever, Professor.

He caught her meaning and pique. "My apologies, Charlotte. Unintentional. Our maid is away today, so let's repair to the kitchen and find a snack."

They chatted trivia while pork dumplings steamed and the house heating kicked in. They ate at the kitchen bench and took cups of green tea into the living room. Settled into familiar chairs. Did not speak until the cups were empty. Charlotte was relaxed; Ayonokoji more tense than she had seen before. He leaned back, stared at the ceiling for a minute; closed his eyes.

"Charlotte, we Japanese are not alone in playing down unfortunate aspects of our history or playing up heroic fantasies. Perhaps we play down more obviously than others because we don't try to substitute a fake history. We simply ignore the period or episode in question, out of shame rather than guilt. The former is strong in our culture; guilt is rare. We tend to regret an action only when it is noted by a respected Japanese source, which results in shame but not guilt." He paused for ten seconds. "At least we experience one of the two phenomena. I have met few Australians who appear to feel either guilt or shame about the history of contact with Aborigines, for instance."

She said she doubted shame and guilt were in tension for Westerners, unlike the Japanese. Rather, shame struggled with pride, and guilt fought innocence. Yet guilt might generate shame, and innocence might generate pride.

Sage nod, and "Maybe so. A little too deep for me, Dr Fonseka. I'm neither philosopher nor semanticist." Sarcastic bastard.

She agreed about Australian apathy in the case of Aborigines but denied equivalence with the deliberate Japanese suppression of facts, such as the doctoring of war history in school textbooks. *Good one*. What, Rand? *Doctoring*.

Ayanokoji not convinced. "In both cases the horror is ignored. Anyway, what would you have us do? Hamstring ourselves with shame and train our children to suffer guilt, surely a destructive path? Since the war we have not fired a shot at anyone, anywhere. Isn't that laden with a message? We know what we did. We shall not forget, whether or not we satisfy the foreign requirement for us to broadcast our guilt—I believe the Australian expressions are 'spill our guts in public' and 'wear sackcloth and ashes'. Our current behaviour, not platitudes and perpetual *mea culpa*, is what concerns us. This is not to deny history. As for doctoring history, even if you do not do it in textbooks you do it in other ways."

"Such as?"

"You and Australia's allies have your war mythology of doubtful tales and heroes. You have your mini-versions of our Yasukuni Shrine, scattered all over the Australian countryside. Also unequivocal heroism in books and movies. We have none of that for the last war. Perhaps it will come next century."

"Okay, war memorials." She thought of the Nyngan eyesore. "What books?" *Dumb reaction, Charlotte. Too defensive.*

"A few are on the shelves behind you." She did not turn. "My favourite, if that is the right word, is by a British aristocrat who plays at soldiering and has a deluded view of his performance.

Beyond the Chindwin by Major Bernard Fergusson." He went to the shelf, found the book and sat down again. "Shall I tell you about it, at some length? It is pertinent to our discussion."

"Please do. I haven't heard of it."

"Ah, yes. *Beyond the Chindwin: Being an Account of the Adventures of Number Five Column of the Wingate Expedition into Burma, 1943.* In essence, Charlotte, it is a born-to-rule account of a military farce. Fergusson reminds me of those who commanded the disastrous Allied campaigns of the First World War. We were allies then, did you know? At least he does not say he did much damage to the Japanese in Burma; but he could not make such a claim, as it was no secret that the Japanese harassed the British, not vice versa. Fergusson's occasional self-deprecation seems shallow, in particular his pangs of conscience about leaving half his force on a river sandbar, to be shot or captured because they couldn't swim and were too short to wade, while he made his own escape. A Japanese officer would have stayed on the sandbar or riverbank for at least a few more hours to encourage his men to cross."

"Encourage, Hiroyuki? Perhaps shoot them if they didn't try or couldn't make it?"

"Perhaps. I'll go on. Some of Fergusson's officers wanted to stay but he overruled them. Why? Perhaps they were of good British stock and might be needed for another glorious campaign. Perhaps Fergusson knew he would look bad if other officers could induce the men to cross the river or were captured with them. In his Boy's Own—note the book's subtitle—account of the mayhem, he depicts himself as an aristocrat showing pluck under duress while the rabble succumbs. It would be interesting to read accounts of Fergusson's role by his sub-officer ranks. I must search for any that the British would have been prepared to publish. Shall I go on?"

"Please do."

"I shall read a little section, bookmarked long ago. In what must be some of the most shameful writing in military history, Fergusson says:

> Before pushing on, we counted heads. Our strength was reduced to nine officers and sixty-five men; in other words, forty-six men had either been drowned or left on the sandbank. Of these the latter were certainly the vast majority. It is a matter of fact that those who had crossed and were with the column included all the best men, and the men whose behaviour throughout the expedition had been the most praiseworthy. It does not absolve me from my responsibility for the others to say so, but it was and is a comfort to me that among those whom I thus abandoned were few to whom our debt, and the debt of their nation, was outstanding. There were two or three whom I particularly regretted. There were two more who, had they got out, would have had to face charges at a court-martial.

"Let me find an author's endnote that I marked. Ah, yes. Here. It says more about Fergusson than he intended: 'Over 65 per cent of the force got out safely.' Charlotte, how about '35 per cent of the force did not get out safely'? Besides, he is referring to the 1943 Wingate Expedition overall. For his own peasant-class soldiers the figures were more like 50-50. Do you see my point about the universal mythology of heroism? Fergusson as hero. That is how the British still see him."

"I was born in England, and I lived with the British in Tarawa. I might not be an expert on heroism but I know a lot about British social class."

"Ahhh, the assumptions, self-deception and privilege of the British aristocracy. Would Fergusson himself have been court-martialled had it not been for his breeding and connections? He was protégé of Field-Marshall Wavell, Viceroy of India, a Viscount, who wrote the foreword to *Beyond the Chindwin*. Fergusson was promoted, then knighted a few years later. Regardless of class, we would have shot such a Japanese officer instead of rewarding him for his spurious heroics. Fergusson became Governor-General of New Zealand, like his Papa and Grandpapa before him. Became a lord; called himself Lord Ballantrae of Auchairne and the Bay of Islands. So inflated I wonder why he did not explode."

Ayanokoji scoffed at the lordly title. Clownish man, clownish title. Charlotte scoffed with him at the absurdity of Britain's aristocracy. "At that level, Hiroyuki, it's black comedy."

"Indeed absurd, Charlotte. Oh, look at what I've found here about Fergusson's monocle. I copied this section from an article I found last year in the *Geographical Journal*:

His father, a First World War General, had refused to allow Bernard to go to Sandhurst ["after Eton, Charlotte"] wearing spectacles and insisted that he joined ["should be 'join', right?"] that august Academy wearing a monocle. That monocle probably ranks as the most famous of its kind and, when he was serving with the Chindits in Burma, it was necessary to have an air drop of monocles to make good his supply.

"Preposterous mythology, is it not, Dr Fonseka? Spare me faux-eccentrics like Fergusson, and the military clown, Wingate, who strive to create heroic, plucky legends of themselves. Wingate, Fergusson's boss, also abandoned his men and flew to the safety of India when his legend was not enough to contain the Japanese advance. Wingate should have been shot too. It was perhaps justice that he died in a plane crash late in the war. So much for Allied heroes and honest history. And so much for bringing to justice everyone—not losers alone—who deserved prosecution. Do you agree, Charlotte?"

She said that one or two swallows did not make a summer. He gave another example—a book closer to home for her; it had been "swallowed whole, and therefore not digested well."

"*The Bridge on the River Kwai*. Dear to Australians. Am I right? Written by a Frenchman who was not there, then made into Hollywood glory, often wrong for dramatic and heroic effect. Or to propagate lies."

"Such as?"

"For a start, Japanese engineers and soldiers built the bridge, precisely to Japanese design and specifications. British officers had no role in it, were not drafted to design it or supervise construction. Nor did any hero blow it up. It was never blown up or bombed. Planes could not get a clear run at it."

Come on, Charlotte, quiz him about Australian prisoners on the Thai-Burma Railway.

"What about the thousands of Australian prisoners who died on the charming railway project associated with that bridge? Three thousand? Is that a lie too?"

"Some Europeans died, it's true. And it is true that our textbooks do not mention them. But most of the workers were paid labourers, mainly Tamils, Burmese and Thai."

"And the 3000 Australian deaths?"

"There were as many Dutch that don't get a mention on your Anzac Day. Twice that many British. Many more Tamils than the white men combined. How many Australian children know those facts and figures? Does your mythology make much of them? When you were at school did your history textbooks mention them? How many Australians would care if they did know? Do your histories tell the truth, that cholera killed most of them? They brought it with them. They infected our soldiers, many of whom died."

Ignore those questions, Charlotte. All rhetorical. He's on the offensive. Better put him on the defensive back foot.

She ignored the questions. "So, Hiroyuki, do Japanese histories say no prisoners died of starvation and overwork as slaves?" *That's it, Charlotte. Hang in. Stay calm.*

"Some died, as did our soldiers. There were no slaves. But your people did not work on the bridge itself. That's one of the lies. They helped build the railway, not the bridge."

Ignored your question. Sometimes he's thick for a smart man, isn't he? Maybe not as convincing as he thinks he is. She nodded to the unseen Rand, her nod again read by Ayanokoji as assent.

"Charlotte, I'm sure you know of a town called Cowra, in New South Wales. I went there on a war graves delegation eight years ago. Number 12 POW Compound was at Cowra, with a couple of thousand Japanese prisoners, plus a couple of thousand Italians and sundry others. In August 1944, 1104 Japanese tried to escape; 359 succeeded. Their weapons were mess knives and baseball bats. Over the next ten days all were shot or recaptured—231 killed, 108 wounded, 20 captured intact. Note the kill rate of 64 per cent. A lot more than the 25 per cent of Japanese soldiers killed for the entire war. Those baseball bats and butter-knives must have been so formidable that your heroic home guard had to fight to the death.

"Great heroes, the Australians, under such circumstances. Don't you think so, Charlotte? Just four managed to get themselves killed, two of them later awarded gallantry medals. Had to rescue the local farmers from the savage Japanese. Of course, the escapees terrified the local civilians—none of whom were harmed or coerced—so much that they invited them into their homes, fed and watered them. Apologised for not having Japanese tea.

"Shades of Tarawa, Charlotte. Many of the Japanese deaths were recorded as suicides. Mass *seppuku* with a few baseball bats and mess knives? Others fought to the death with those instruments of war. Either way, suicides, say your histories. Do you believe them? Have you been to the Japanese Garden at Cowra?"

She shook her head: "No, and I haven't read the histories yet."

"Well, Dr Fonseka, read them with a critical mind. Think of

Tuol Sleng. Think of Tarawa. And go to Cowra when you get a chance. Ask older local people about what I have said. Some will be honest, as they were to me. A few will say the prisoners were savages and the Australians heroes. And the garden itself? It has a long way to go. Not lush in that climate and soil, but serene nonetheless. See if you feel as I did, that it is founded at least as much on guilt for the massacre as on respect for the dead. Shame might also be an influence."

"I'll follow up. If your history is accurate, my visit there might cause me to question our earlier comparisons of Japanese and other people's attitudes to guilt and shame." *A bit touchy, Charlotte. Don't interrupt. I haven't finished.*

That quizzical eyebrow again, a little hesitant now; still the brow ripple, furrows less tight. "Because, Hiroyuki, if your account is right I would expect to find both guilt and shame in the Cowra community, in the same individuals, with variations in balance from one person to the next; not only guilt, without the shame you seem to think is a higher order of awareness that only Japanese experience. By the way, to deny guilt does not exclude or eliminate it from the denier's subconscious, does it? Or conscience? Sometimes to deny is to confirm. Ask any lawyer, even in Japan."

"Perhaps, Dr Fonseka. Anyway, ask the garden manager about the baseball bats and blunt dining knives, and the death-survival ratio. Go to the RSL for a drink and dinner. Ask the same questions of the old heroes who see you are attractive and offer to fund your night out. Their guilt, or guilt-shame, might make them hostile. Have dinner before you ask, and make sure you have an escape route. Park your car under a streetlight."

He had steered her away from the topic of shame and guilt; she had eased him back to it. She asked what engendered any shame— forget about guilt—the Japanese might now feel about the war, 40 years later. Was it Japan's savagery or the defeat? *You've got him there, Charlotte. Like one of those subtle barbs that impaled Peter.*

"Neither," said Ayanokoji. "It is more refined, more about misplaced loyalties and obedience to powerful people who tried to resurrect a dead nation. They invoked ancient pride and power structures, imbued with militarism and personal discipline. A return to cultural glory, to cultural and social superiority, would follow subordination of the self to national prosperity. We feel shame for allowing the elite to con us." Nice structure and vocab, Professor. Lecture's going well. Make a mistake, for Christ's sake.

"So, in 1916 Akutagawa saw the developing con-job and raised doubts about the resurgence of *bushido*? And no one listened to him."

Ayanokoji stared at her nose-tip for a few seconds, then turned his face back to the ceiling. "Pride and naïve nostalgia overwhelmed us, which made us easy to control to the point where all dissent was crushed. Communists and other dissenters who wanted more modern structures were culled long before the war."

"Was the culling like the Soviet revolution? Its ongoing purges?"

"No. Consider fundamental differences. The Soviet ideal was new, shallow, untested. Japan's *bushido* ethos was ancient and deep, even if diminished in recent times. A desirable recovery, in principle. Also, diverse Russia and its even more diverse satellites were scattered over a vast area. The Soviets tried to cook a casserole out of incompatible ingredients, many of them rotten. They created what you might call a dog's dinner. That was why their purges could never end, and why their system will soon collapse."

In contrast, he said, Japan was compact, confined; a refined monoculture, which made it easier to get rid of the few dissenters and stop others from replacing them. They had no significant support.

"We could eliminate them with confidence, with no risk of creating martyrs. The Soviets had to destroy history and culture and a few million people while they tried to cook the casserole. We destroyed nothing. Unlike the Soviets we glorified our roots, fell in love with them and therefore with ourselves. The Soviets had to learn to hate themselves and others for what they were. We reinforced what we already had, with a bit of tweaking. Nothing new. Old, proven ways applied to controlled modernisation." He had left plenty of gaps in his monologue for her to respond. Silence. "Charlotte, you are quiet. What are you thinking?" Silence.

Isn't it interesting that he says 'we' did this and 'we' did that? She agreed with Rand, but must he crowd her? She suggested he go back to the other side, leave her alone to live her life. *There is no 'other side', as you call it. It's all here, all the time. Don't dismiss Bos Simeon's unified world of* maselais, *ancestor spirits, and living people. No separate realms in time or place; a continuum, maybe, but no separation.* Disappear, for fuck's sake, Rand. You're not for real. *Not real? Created by your rampant imagination? I'll bet you think Bos's night visitor, the old bloke with her Mum's machete, was a figment of her head. Relax, Charlotte. I need a break anyway. Keep at him while I'm absent.* Rand, did you screw Bos? Again no reply to the question asked many times in the past decade.

When she noticed Ayanokoji's raised eyebrow and rippled forehead she retreated from Rand and Bos to the Soviet-Japan comparison. "Sorry, Hiroyuki. I needed time to think. I can appreciate your analysis but I also see other points of comparison and contrast. For instance, fear of violence. The Soviets used it as a means of control on a large scale at home and relatively minor scale elsewhere. The other way around for Japan. Agreed?" Silence. "Hiroyuki?"

He stared at the ceiling, exasperated. "We had no choice. We tried to help other Asians get rid of foreign exploiters. The colonial yoke. Local cultures had been corrupted, and ethnic groups fragmented to prevent cohesive opposition. We had to be harsh to rebuild them, consolidate them, rejuvenate them under Japanese tutelage; haul them out of subjugation, decadence, darkness."

"All for their own good. Sounds a bit Soviet. Nothing to do with controlling energy and other resources? Was Emperor Hirohito a more refined, less fist-in-the-face version of Stalin, even though one loved Communism and the other hated it?" The professor turned and stared into her brain.

Keep going, Charlotte, said Rand. Okay, she would. She told Ayanokoji the two leaders may have worked from different political and social bases, but they both took their nations and satellites along the path to Hell. Stalin as a cattle drover, Hirohito more of a pied piper—no, a deified hypnotist.

No reaction; no change of expression; not a blink. No apparent rumination. No sign of genuine doubt or a conscience. No sign of his *hankechi*. What moves this guy?

He shook his head for a nano-second and looked at his hands. "Food for thought, Charlotte. Let me pour us a bourbon, early as it may be, and go to my gallery. All beauty there, I hope you will agree. No past to disturb us. I am worn out with history and its horrors. We can sip as we stroll, against Japanese etiquette." She smiled and nodded. Right about the etiquette. She had never seen a Japanese person eat or drink on the move.

Keep at him, Charlotte. He's on the defensive. You can sense it. Don't chicken out now.

"Hiroyuki, one last thing. What do you think of the Santayana cliché about those who forget the past being destined to repeat it?" *Good one, Mrs Millar-Fonseka. Close to your marital experience.* You fucker, Rand.

Ayanokoji said Santayana's caution was a mere platitude to him and most Japanese intellectuals. "Those who remember too well, selectively or otherwise, and keep on telling the world not to forget, perpetuate the past by perpetuating revenge and hatred. Don't forget, I say, but don't rub it in at every opportunity. Let your identity evolve. Get on with it."

To her, no sense of personal or national responsibility tempered this apologist's resolve to play down Japan's havoc in the war. He went on: "If historians, religious leaders and politicians bombard us forever with tales of Nazism and Holocaust, how can anti-Semitism ever die, or even diminish? You did not react well when I mentioned the plight of your Aborigines this morning. If you constantly hear and read that you, as a white Australian, must inherit blame for the horrors your forbears inflicted on Aborigines, how can either party move on to a better life? Historical roles are projected onto white descendants, and politicised descendants of victims are disparaged for being anti-white racists. Each side takes offence at every perceived slight, and slights the other in return. A vicious spiral." Too slick, Professor. You were there when the horror originated and burgeoned in Asia. Did you inflict any of it? You suggest not. Your historical location for Japanese atrocities and mine for Aboriginal massacres are a lot different.

"I take your point, Hiroyuki. Neither guilt nor shame should be mine, personally. Shouldn't heap it on others, either, I suppose. Which is not to deny the past, however it might be interpreted." *Not bad*, said Rand. *But the professor was* there, *wasn't he? Remind him.*

"Hiroyuki, I wasn't there to do anything about it, but you were. Your biography says you were in various Asian countries, in the war zone." He smiled and reminded her that he served as a doctor and did much to ease the trauma of many civilians as well as soldiers from both sides in the Philippines and Indochina. Also Japan, after the Hiroshima blast.

Rand told her to back-pedal from the blame game for a while. Enough about the war. Try to be a social butterfly instead of one that flaps its wings in Argentina and generates an earthquake in Kyoto. Again she told him to fuck off. *Soon. Soon, and maybe forever.* Promise? *Like hell. I enjoy our relationship too much.*

"I still can't grasp your reasons for not practising medicine after the war. Medicine doesn't always involve blood and guts, does it? There's radiology, urology, endocrinology, psychiatry, and so on."

He said he had no philosophical reason, just did not want to be in a profession focused on human trauma; had seen too much of it.

"One thing to be clear about, Charlotte. The post-war medical world would not have excluded me if I had stayed on at Unit 731 or gone anywhere else to harm Chinese or other non-Japanese."

She would take Rand's advice. Enough about the war and the decision not to resume practice.

* * *

Charlotte went to the hi-tech toilet while her host half-filled glasses with bourbon and dropped an ice cube into each. He carried both glasses as the two philosopher-historians strolled down a corridor to a sliding door at the back of the house. They swapped house slippers for tougher versions; walked coatless for nine cold metres on stepping stones to a building of cypress and tile, in traditional design. He gave her the glasses, took a chunky key from under a mat and unlocked the door of honey-grained wood. She caressed it and sniffed chocolate on her fingertips. He bowed, ushered her in; breathed deep as he held the door open and she brushed past him. They again changed slippers.

Ayanokoji turned on a gas heater and a common switch for eight spotlights. The gallery was one rectangular room, 12 metres by 9 metres, furnished with three stools at the centre and a low table against the wall at the far end. Dark-green walls; a peaked ceiling of natural pine boards secured by parallel rafters of the same wood, wall-top to ridge; four adzed beams of caramel oak. The 31 photographs Ayanokoji had mentioned at dinner hung on the two long walls. Yes, a wider subject range than at the university gallery. At the far end, three *samurai* swords lay parallel across pairs of ornate wooden pegs attached to the wall above the table. On the table a squat rustic pot of yellow chrysanthemums; the arrangement flawless—of course, to her Western eye. Three cameras and a tripod on a wooden shelf to the right of the swords.

"The room will soon warm. My apologies for not getting your coat for you before we came out here, no matter how brief I expected the cold walk to be. Before we observe the photographs, please allow me to show you the camera that took most of the shots on these walls; also the disturbing group photograph you saw two days ago. Do you mind? I do not insist. Please decline if you prefer." No reply. He went on: "Your husband admired that camera. Held it, studied it with great interest at the Otintai Hotel."

She must see the camera up close, must hold it, so she nodded. He took his bourbon from her and sipped it as they padded across *tatami* mats to the shelf.

"Charlotte, please pick up the camera. It's the one in the middle." He took her glass. "A British Contax II from about 1935, favoured by war photographers during the Second World War, including Japanese if they could get one. This one is a rarity for that model, with a built-in timer, but no light-meter. Even so, much better than the Japanese Hansa Canon—copied from the German Leica III—issued to our military photographers. Please pick it up. Take off the cover. It's the original. Italian leather. The strap too. Please don't open the back. There's a fresh film in it. Twenty-five years ago a technician in New York told me it was one of the first designed for type 135 film canisters." She half-heard him. Feet tingled. Arms leaden by her sides, numb fingers pointed down. No life in them. She thought of Bos Simeon's mother, toes pointing at the earth below her tree gallows.

"Let me help you, Charlotte." Smug bastard. He put the glasses of bourbon on the shelf, picked up the camera and removed the cover; put the cover on the shelf and held the camera in his right hand; caressed the camera with his left; more a pet than a gadget to record light.

With his left hand he took Charlotte's right, lifted it gently to waist level and turned her palm up. "I'll put the camera in your hand, which does feel too chilly for this warm room. If you drop the camera, too bad." *Take it*, said Rand. She nodded to Ayanokoji and raised her left hand to pair with the right.

"I won't drop it." Warm to her cold touch. Weighed it, turned it one way and another to inspect it, as Peter would have done. Ayanokoji noticed a fleeting moment of distress in her. Nostalgia? Sorrow? Surely not guilt?

"Charlotte, this camera is significant beyond the connection with Mr Millar. The New York dealer who sold it to me in the 1950s said it belonged to Robert Capa and was almost certainly used to take his famous D-Day shots." No shit, Professor. Who cares right now?

"Thank you, Hiroyuki." With steady hands she returned the camera to the shelf, beside the cover and the glasses of bourbon.

"You may wonder about the other two cameras." Sure thing; excitement central. "They are much more modern but I prefer the Contax. I used it for most of the 31 shots on these walls." Really? Grabs me like a linguistics conference, Professor.

What do you think of the cutlery, Charlotte? She turned to the swords, all three a little over a metre long, with a mild curve that said 'slice'.

"These swords are beautiful, Hiroyuki. Not from a New York dealer, I assume."

"Indeed no. All acquired in Japan. The lower pair are simpler than the beauty at the top, in its rightful place. The drab two have simpler handles and are in well-crafted but dull scabbards. Mass produced *shin gunto*. Functional military swords issued in the 30s and 40s to junior and mid-ranking officers of low or mediocre pedigree." Low pedigree? Here boy! Fetch! Functional military swords? I can guess the function. *So can I.*

Ayanokoji said the brown and red tassels on the handle of the bottom one indicated it was issued to a field officer; the brown and blue on the middle one meant a warrant officer. Really, Professor?

Orgasmic.

"The two *shin gunto* have leather scabbards for use in battle. They attach to belts by the two brass rings. The bearers would have had ornate metal scabbards for ceremonial use, but I do not know what happened to them."

He said officers of higher pedigree usually had heirloom swords inherited from *samurai* ancestors. "Now we come to the third one, the beauty. Also with red and brown tassels to signify my wartime rank."

"It is beautiful. What is the hilt covering? The criss-cross?"

"Leather on ray skin, to ensure a tight grip. Cherry blossom designs on the hilt. The white and purple studs on the wooden scabbard are seashells. This sword is called *katana*. A little less curved than the other two. Over 300 years old. The steel is *tamahagane*—jewel steel—made from iron sand. Very heavy, this one, at 1.7 kilograms. Only *samurai* of high rank could bear this quality and style."

"An heirloom?"

"It is. Would you like to see the blade?" Before she could decline he took the exhibit off the rack with reverence and drew the sword from the scabbard. "Hear it ring? Like a tuning fork? Most don't ring loudly enough for the human ear, if at all." She had not heard it.

"Yes, Hiroyuki. A slightly flat C, I think." He said that was near enough.

A beautiful blade; frightening. Why did it seem to ripple silver in the spotlight? He said it had been beaten flat and broad, then heated and folded and rebeaten many times, perhaps 50 or more, until it came as close to perfection as any swordsmith dared go. Each fold and beating created a ripple, like annual rings in a tree trunk. He gripped the hilt with both hands; weighed the weapon, relished its balance, twisted it a few centimetres from side to side, poked its savage point at air. Slow, controlled, thoughtful. "Sharp and strong as the day it was finished." If Ayanokoji were to offer it to her to hold, she must refuse. Not sure why. All this should impress Rand. Where the fuck was he? Silent at last. Might buy a sword and hang it on my bedroom wall at home.

"You took it with you to war?"

"I did. In a standard military scabbard, not this work of art." More nostalgic poke and twist. "As a medical major. Middling rank but entitled to carry it by birth. In case you were wondering, which is how you looked when you asked the question, I used it for ceremonial purposes." *I'll bet*, Rand whispered.

"Doctors carried swords?"

"As an officer I had no choice. It was either this beauty or a *shin gunto*. The other two are with it on the wall to emphasise the difference in quality."

"Of the sword or the bearers?"

"Unkind, Charlotte. Don't forget Major Fergusson and his dead Chindits. But yes, and yes, in answer to your question. Now, that is all in the past in Japanese society, unlike British. Focus now on the beauty of this artefact. The exquisite workmanship applied to the blade and the hilt. The aesthetic merit of the scabbard. The vibrant colour of the tassels." Do go on, Professor. You are in love with this hunk of deadliness.

"Based on our discussion two nights ago about Japanese aesthetics and modesty, I assume this aristocratic exemplar has a deliberate flaw, discernible to expert eyes. Right or wrong?"

He said he had tried in vain for over 40 years to find a flaw in the sword and its scabbard. Nonetheless, both would have a flaw, even if only the maker knew what and where it was. "A bit late to ask him, Charlotte. It's 300 years old."

She feared he would offer it to her. "I would pass it to you to hold, but no woman has ever been permitted to touch it. That's a family tradition, not a universal rule. You will understand that I must uphold family tradition."

"I understand. Even so, I'm disappointed. What about women who may have upset your forbears? Might it have touched them?"

He shook his head; raised his eyebrow; ploughed furrows in his forehead. The family history did not include any evidence of the blade's use on any civilian, and therefore any woman. Nor had it been used in combat or to behead male criminals since he inherited it in 1936. Slid the sword back into the scabbard and lay it on the pegs with the care of a mother putting her new baby into a bassinet.

A bit touchy, isn't he? Butter him up a bit, I suggest.

"It's beautiful, Hiroyuki. Thank you for showing it to me. And the camera. You were kind to take my hand and guide me through all that. Not easy for me."

Ayanokoji bowed and thanked her. He took the glasses of bourbon from the shelf and gave one to her; put his hand on her back to ease her away from the swords and cameras. "Let's sip and look at the photographs to cheer ourselves up. Clockwise, shall we?" Such wit. Sarcasm? She grinned and agreed.

On the wall to their left as they had faced the swords hung 15 photographs separated into lots of seven and eight by a small window letting in afternoon glow, on the wane. On the opposite wall, an identical window split 16 prints into groups of eight and eight. All framed like those in the university gallery. Hung a few centimetres higher; an identification card below each. All monochrome.

They started to the right of the swords, at a portrait-oriented seascape: 'Squall, Gilbert Islands, 1971'. In English and Japanese. The photograph drew her in. At the top, rain plummeted from a storm cloud onto the sea horizon. Strong downward dynamics. The deluge drove waves onto a coral boulder worn to the shape of a black potato by aeons of surfwash and fishermen's feet; the boulder sitting solid and dominant at the base of the picture, and surrounded by a squabble of currents, foam-flecked. The format of the shot an elongated oval, its perimeter fuzzy, as if the moisture of sea and air had seeped into the margins of the white photographic paper.

The photograph ignored many guidelines for composition: it did not even hint at the Golden Mean; no diagonal forces; no use of the frame to create balance, completeness or unity. The downward forces threatened to wash the frame's contents over the bottom edge onto Charlotte's feet. *Strong metaphor, Charlotte. This morning the professor chose not to hold it all in. More beans to spill?*

Charlotte congratulated Ayanokoji on the transitional effect instead of sharp borders, as if he wanted to suggest the shot was a vignette of widespread turbulence in the region that day. He thanked her and explained the alchemy performed on the borders in his darkroom, a converted bathhouse in another annex.

Beside the seascape, an almost abstract shot in landscape orientation: 'Coconuts Out to Dry, Gilbert Islands, 1971'. A pretty pattern, fit for a happy dress, of 18 coconut halves; white flesh, succulent, still embedded in stringy husks—the farmer would rip them into shreds for coir or burn them after he sat cross-legged, buoyant on palm toddy, to gouge out the copra with a stumpy blade. A near perfect composition founded on a circle of five half-nuts around the top-left Golden Mean; the five held 13 others in orbit, trying to beat gravity, to fly out of the frame. Taken from above—he must have leaned over the nuts, just short of toppling onto them. Some held a spoonful of liquid. Coconut milk? No, water—a few blades of grass, rare in the Gilberts, captured a few drops of dew. Rain? Too rare. Dew.

"An early morning shot, Hiroyuki?"

"Indeed! About 7am. Ah, you see the dew." *Fuck you, Professor. Gotcha, didn't he? Reads your mind, like I do.* Fuck you too.

Ayanokoji put his left hand on Charlotte's right shoulder. "Charlotte, to ease any tension you might feel, there are no more shots of the Gilberts. The remainder will be easy on the emotions as well as the eye, I hope with due modesty. Ah, yes. Modesty." He hesitated. "Please hold my glass for a moment."

While she studied coconuts he crossed to the opposite wall,

removed a photograph, and rested it on the floor, face against wall. What in hell? He returned to her. "A figure study on the other wall might have been a trifle confronting. I have taken it down."

She said thanks, he need not have bothered. He said she would see another, less explicit figure study; a copy of an American torso she may have seen at the university gallery.

I wonder what he took down. Missed it when we came in from the cold. Too interested in the swords, which might not surprise you. Rand! You missed something, did you? Here I was, thinking you were omniscient. All-seeing. *Your turn to fuck off, Charlotte.*

Ayanokoji again wondered what and why she sometimes whispered to herself. Schizophrenia? No. A medieval familiar? An incubus that should fuck her in a nightmare and depart at dawn? Poe's raven in her head? A talking fox?

To the next shot: 'Thirteenth Century Sculpture, Angkor Wat, Cambodia, 1980'. A close shot of a stone face, fearful, no clue to dimensions. Sunlit from the left. Late afternoon? Female, weatherworn, cracked almost in half from crown to chin; patches of moss; face trapped in sunlit spider web. The woman drawn to the twilight, alive but doomed, trying in vain to evade oblivion. When did her face crack?

Stay alert, Charlotte. Tuol Sleng. There's always doubt. Big head? Small head? Natural forces cracked the skull over centuries? Smashed by a vandal? Executioner? Piss off, Rand. Go look for your face.

Ayanokoji misinterpreted her wince. "Ah, Cambodia. My apologies. I should have warned you. No more photographs will evoke the horrors of Tuol Sleng." She thanked him and gave him his glass. For fuck's sake stop the fake apologies.

They wandered and sipped for 15 minutes past the other 12 shots on the first wall, mainly portraits of Southeast Asian women; four Japanese landscapes. Ayanokoji said he took the three shots of Mount Fuji from what he judged to be the spot where Hokusai stood or sat to make the sketches for his series of *ukiyo-e* prints in the 1830s, 'Thirty-six Views of Mount Fuji'. "I did not try to replicate his 'Great Wave off Kanagawa'. Impossible. You know it, of course?" Sure do, Professor Capa. It's a calendar cliché throughout the world.

"Yes, Hiroyuki. It's much loved in Australia, like many things Japanese. Please don't think me flippant, but if you had tried to take it without a boat from the viewpoint suggested by Hokusai I might not have got to see the photograph of my husband with you at the Otintai Hotel. And I wouldn't have made such a fool of myself and put you and your wife to so much trouble. On the other hand, I would not have heard about Peter's last few days. Including the ones he had with you." The professor nods.

They crossed, past the door, to the left end of the other wall. Two Nevada desert-scapes did not interest her. She complimented him on their composition and technical finesse, and moved past the photograph on the floor to a copy of the American nude at the university gallery—'Young Woman #2, New York, USA, 1954.'

This shot, printed in much more detail than the shaded copy at the university, choked her. *Tuol Sleng, Charlotte. Tuol Sleng.* To Ayanokoji's dismay, she dropped her empty glass; it bounced off the *tatami* mat and shattered against the wall. She gasped and backed off, rubber knees about to collapse and dump her on the *tatami*. He put his glass on the floor, grabbed her left elbow with his left hand and wrapped his right arm around her back. To take her weight he lodged his hand in her armpit and reversed her to a stool. The room not warm enough to explain the sweat she left on his fingers.

"I should have removed that photograph from the wall. I did not think it would offend." She did not hear him. Four moles on the girl's right shoulder blade, little mesas casting shadows in the side-on light; the moles not visible in the darkness of the version at the university gallery. They formed a familiar cross. Two women with an identical, odd pattern of moles on the right shoulder blade?

Not likely.

Take it easy, Charlotte. Deep breaths. Cool head. Okay. I'm cool now.

"Don't worry, Hiroyuki. Artistic nudity doesn't offend. A mere swoon, out of the blue." He pushed a stool close to hers and sat. Had she been examined for epilepsy? No. She would have a check-up on her return to Sydney. No family history? None.

She regained the rhythm of her lungs and the strength of her muscles. "The photos are beautiful. Portraits. Seascapes. Jungle. Exotica. If you ever get a chance to visit Papua New Guinea you will find wonderful subjects there." *Brilliant but risky, Mrs Millar. Cool as an iceberg. Let's hope he doesn't see the submerged 90 per cent too soon.*

Ayanokoji's demeanour betrayed nothing. Did he twist his inner *hankechi*? Was he on to her? She could not know; he would make sure of that.

"To assure you I'm not offended, watch this." She stood on steady legs, too steady, kicked off her slippers and strode with unnatural stiffness on hard heels, in dark stockings, towards the photograph he took down earlier. As she leaned forward to pick it up she read the expected caption on the wall: 'Young Woman #1, New York, USA, 1954.' Picked up the photograph, did not look at it, and returned to her stool beside Ayanokoji's.

"Please don't look at it, Charlotte. It may offend you and embarrass me." A blush. He's human after all.

Turn it over. But stay iceberg in temperature and concealment. No matter what, don't falter. Rand, sometimes you make sense.

She turned it face up and rested the bottom edge on her knees. The other side of the same girl, probably; mid-thigh to neck. Well-lit all over. Thighs parted enough for a glimpse of labia through dense, curled hair; coal-black, shiny. A perfect navel. The generous breasts of a teenager; familiar zig-zag tattoos on each. She put the photograph face down on the floor at her feet.

"Love the shot, Hiroyuki. I didn't know the girls of New York were into breast tattoos." He grinned with relief. He said he did not know about the tattoos when he hired her from a modelling agency. "But I'm pleased she had them. They do give the girl individuality, do they not?"

Now, Charlotte, now! Get him.

"More than individuality. Identity. Do you remember her name?" He did not. She asked if both shots were of the same girl, and did he take them with the Capa camera. Yes and yes.

"Hiroyuki, I'm confused. Must be my epilepsy or whatever. My addled head told me the two photographs were of someone I met on Bougainville when she was much older. About 30 years older. Can't be so. You have never been there, in the war years or since. And I know you took the shots in New York. I met no American girl on Bougainville. The model's black skin must have misled me. Most Bougainvilleans are even darker—the blackest of black."

Not a flinch. "Charlotte, your perceptions of the subject, location and year are certainly misperceptions. But more than a little amusing. Our minds do sometimes lead us astray, do they not?"

"They do. It's happening to me a lot lately." *Try him on Capa.* "Here's another mental twist, pure fantasy for its own sake. The camera was Capa's. Even if the shots had been taken in, say, 1943 instead of 1980, he couldn't have taken them as he didn't go to Bougainville as far as I know. He would have had to lend the camera to someone else who did go there, then get it back in good condition for D-Day in June 1944, on the other side of the world. All a bit unlikely." *Did you see him blink when you said '1943'?*

"Charlotte, you seem to poke fun at me about the origins of the camera. The Australian sense of humour sometimes disconcerts others. In good spirit, I accept that the camera might not have been Capa's. Perhaps the dealer duped me. Who knows?" Silence. "Charlotte, your disposition concerns me. Are you annoyed about something? Perhaps trying to hide distress? You perspire in a mildly warm room on a cold day. I'm worried."

He sure is. Vigorous hankechi *twist. Jugular time!* Here I go, Rand.

"Two questions, Hiroyuki. Has your memory led you astray about buying the camera in New York? And does the name 'Bos Simeon' ring a bell?" Look at him. Raised eyebrow and forehead concertina; hands clenched; lip tremble, soon stifled; might not remember the name, probably didn't know it anyway, but knows who I mean.

"No, and no. Look, Charlotte. You seem to suggest I am dishonest in one or more ways. Hardly the way to treat a host and new friend. I shall try not to feel ashamed. Is this some sort of whimsical experiment? Does Japan bore you so much?"

Now for the big one. Carotid and jugular together. Now you're the expert samurai *wielding the cutlery. You know what I want you to say.*

She stared into Ayanokoji's eyes; his turn to enjoy the drill-bit in the brain. "Forget about the camera. I accept that you've forgotten Bos Simeon's name but not that you have never met her. How about 'Hugh Rand'?" *Perfect uppercut. Now Cool-San knows his script is a dud.*

Ayanokoji gripped his knees hard, fingertips bloodless; looked up at the roof, closed his eyes. Left heel tapped on the *tatami* mat—patter-patter-patter. Right heel joined in to form a duet out of control. The rhythm of lid-rattle on a kettle of boiling water.

Well done. Thanks for the mention. Let him cook hard for a while. Go for it when he goes off the boil and stops tapping his heels.

The heels tapped for ten seconds. When they stopped she put her hand on his shoulder and gave him what Peter would have called a shit sandwich. "I don't think you are fundamentally dishonest, but I doubt aspects of what you have told me about your wartime experience." No reaction; eyes blank. "I'm sympathetic, Hiroyuki, not stupid. We all have at least one skeleton in our cupboard and there's no law to say we have to tell the world about it. Some things are no one else's business, if you insist on that stance." Minute twinges of Ayanokoji's shoulders; staccato. Heels steady now from the force of hands on knees.

He turned from her to stare at the swords. She jerked her hand from his shoulder as if burned by it. Her turn to tremble. He noticed out of the corner of his eye, and raised his eyebrow.

Relax. He won't take the cutlery option, yet. He has an urge to distort the truth as a sort of compromise, because it's not feasible to totally cloak his past for another 40 years. He has to tell you— needs to tell you—some sort of truth about what he thinks you've more or less guessed already, whatever it might be, and trust you with it. It might be shameful but he can only entreat you to contain it, never let it out. To achieve that, he has to justify himself to you. If he can't, look out. Now you're giving speeches, Rand. Liked you better when you were pithy. *Please call me Hugh. We've known one another for ages.*

Why had Rand not mentioned Ayanokoji in the context of Bougainville? Still afraid of Ayanokoji, she was about to put the question to Rand when her host turned to her, calmer than she had ever seen him. He held his hands towards her, palms-up, not in submission but to ask where she wanted to take him from there.

"Charlotte, I need to talk if you will do me the honour of lending me your ears. You mastered the Tuol Sleng exercise too well, to my disadvantage."

"Maybe not to your disadvantage. I'm a good listener and not as judgemental as you might think. Bottled up people can pull the cork and trust me with the contents." *That should tenderise him.*

"Uncork the bottle, Charlotte? Perhaps smooth out the twisted *hankechi*?" Worried but affable.

Take it easy, Charlotte. Simmer him. If he goes back on the boil it's all over, one way or another. Rand behind her, physical in his grip on her shoulders but as usual neither his hands nor any other part visible. She asked him if he and Ayanokoji had come together anywhere other than Kyoto. No answer; grip released. Alone, now that she might need him for the first time.

Ayanokoji's hands now clenched in his lap. "Charlotte, you say I can trust you if I uncork the bottle. How can I be sure of your future behaviour in other circumstances, far from the man to whom you now give your assurance?"

Where are you, Rand? I detest you for the ruin you have done to me but I need you now. Ayanokoji about to retreat, to hide the bottle forever. Still has an occasional glance at the swords.

Still here. You're doing well. I'm backing off. Leaving it to you. But hear this. If you want him to open his bottle you'll have to spill some of your beans first. Give him something he knows he could hurt you with if you do the dirty on him ten years from now. Tit for tat. No hands on her shoulders; a pubescent whisper in her left ear.

"Hiroyuki, to prove I'm trustworthy, I'll open my cupboard and trust you with one of my skeletons, then maybe another, and another. Tit for tat. If that's not acceptable, let's erase today and forget we ever met."

Heard herself breathe as he pondered the swords again. He turned to her and nodded a few times; in slow motion, neck loose, as if about to fall asleep.

"Agreed, Dr Fonseka. Give and take. You give a little first, and if my take is adequate, I shall then give back in due proportion. Can you give me enough? You don't really have many strong cards, you know, no matter what you think you have deciphered. Kyoto is a long way from Sydney, especially for a lone woman. If you want to swim back to shore before the water gets too deep, now is your opportunity. If you take it, I shall agree to erase today's explorations, an option you have suggested. Erase the day itself. But if we proceed to deep water, neither a return to shore nor erasure will be feasible. Your choice. Your risk. Are your closeted skeletons sinister enough to destroy your life? As sinister as you think mine are? I doubt it. Think about it for a few minutes while I stroll around the gallery."

He stood, picked up the frontal nude and hung it back on the wall. Thrice he stepped back two metres to see if it was straight and returned to adjust it. After the third adjustment he moved on to another photograph, then returned to readjust the nude. To Charlotte it was in perfect place after the first adjustment.

Did you see that? Bos is a magnet to him. Must love it when he's alone with her in the gallery. More than speculation, Charlotte. Use what you've just seen.

She asked him how in hell she could use Ayanokoji's kink to her advantage.

Look, Charlotte. When I suggested you give him something he knows he could hurt you with, I should have said you might have to make something up. There's no skeleton in your cupboard. Screwing Aidan Conway while Peter was on tour? Peter's philandering caused it. His skeleton, not yours. Right? She nodded. *Of no interest to Ayanokoji. The same goes for telling him about the students you've laid. Nothing to him, probably. You could start with that to get the exchange rolling but it won't be enough. And you don't have anything else. Your closet doesn't make as much noise as a baby's rattle, does it?* She shook her head. Ayanokoji again sidled past the nude. *There's your way to loosen his tongue. Get it?* Not really. *You will. Here he comes. Dangerous to back out now. He's already got too much to lose if you opt to erase the day.*

Half a metre away, Ayanokoji stood to stare down at her on the stool. She could smell the dry-cleaning fluid in his suit, and his breath of bourbon. He smelled her fear, and saw it in her reluctance to look up at him.

She looked at his red slippers, an absurd mismatch with his buttoned-up suit of woollen twill; creaseless, dark grey. The back of her neck pale and beautiful to him; vulnerable. A whiff of shampoo. Unkempt wisps of fine hair at the border of her neck and scalp.

"Charlotte, what have you decided? Tit for tat, or erasure?"

As her gaze rose from slippers to head, for the first time she realised his physical power, unusual for his age and size. *Get up. Don't let him stand over you.*

"Tit for tat, Hiroyuki, if you promise I can trust you as much as you can trust me. That is, without reservation." She stood; he stepped back.

"You have my word." He bowed low. "Let's proceed. But wait. First I should go to the house to get the bourbon bottle and another glass." She asked him to bring a bucket of ice.

Alone with Rand, she sat on the stool in the warm gallery and shivered at what she had decided to do. In silence, he held her shoulders with a soft touch, not of a father, yet much softer than the usual grip of ice. *You've decided. What will you tell him?* Wait and see.

Ayanokoji had detected her disdain for the disharmony of his suit and slippers. When he returned seven minutes later with the bourbon, ice and a replacement glass, he wore a black kimono of fine cotton with narrow sash of grey, in the casual *yukata* style, a better match with the slippers. He put the ice bucket on the floor and the two glasses on a third stool; dropped ice into the glasses and poured a double shot of bourbon for her, a single for himself; put the bottle in the bucket as if it were champagne. The ice cracked as he handed a glass to her. He sat near her, his bourbon breath stronger than when he left to get the bottle.

"Well then, Charlotte. Let's click glasses, wish one another well, and proceed to spill our guts to mutual advantage. Cheers?"

"Cheers. I wish us well. I understand the arrangement is that I will tat and you will later tit. Ready, Hiroyuki? It's 4.15. Your wife will be home at 6."

"Yes, I'm ready. No, for Hitomi's return. We can take our time. She left a message on the answering machine after we came out here. She will get home at 8pm. Shopping late with a friend." His slow nod and wide eyes, quizzical, invited her to proceed.

She said he must think her mad for not taking the erasure option. Why should she want to hear his story? And compromise herself to hear it? He said perhaps because she was bored. Perhaps afraid not to proceed, given what he had already told her and what she already seemed to know.

"Go ahead, Charlotte. You cannot bore me, and I shall try not to bore you. Get on with it, please. Don't fear me."

"Okay. I have no closeted skeletons that can rattle me into trouble, so I must create one." He laughed; fiction would not do. This was not the Iowa Writers' Workshop.

"The skeleton doesn't exist yet but its creation will not involve fiction. Your Capa camera has a roll of film in it. I've noticed your taste for fine nudes. As security for your story—as my tit for your tat, so to speak—use the roll on me. You promise to keep it to yourself. After the shoot, you talk, I listen. Ten years from now I'll know you have the film. You will know I have your story."

Charlotte, what the fuck are you saying? Brilliant, though. He can't resist.

Ayanokoji wanted to swill his bourbon and pour another to celebrate his luck; sipped it instead, eyes closed, after some difficulty bringing glass to mouth, a delirium tremens patient who needed three tries to touch fingertip to nose. After the sip, a swill and refill. Then, a bow and, "I'll be back soon."

* * *

As soon as Ayanokoji left the gallery Charlotte slapped herself twice on each cheek and replenished her bourbon. What in hell was she doing? Where had he gone? Go now. Run if you have to. No. She said aloud, to the ceiling, "Be resigned. Be afraid but don't show it. Fuck him!"

That's the spirit, Charlotte. Even if you lose in one way you win in another. Do I? Can't get your point. What I do know is that I would have won more often over many years if you hadn't been dumb enough to lose your head. His hands released her shoulders.

Ayanokoji went to the house for five minutes and returned with a bundle of cloth held to his chest with both hands. Three metres from Charlotte he unfolded the bundle, smiled and held it up, a couturier tempting a rich client. A kimono of white silk with a few patches of luscious yellow, like maps of Alabama and Nevada; embroidered flowers of red and blue in studied scatter between and within the maps. Broad collar, loose sleeves wide open at the wrist, the shoulder seams well down the upper arms.

He bowed and asked her to please strip and put on the kimono; her youngish circulation and skin would soon erase the marks left by her underwear. "It would have been pointless to bring the *obi*— the sash, or cummerbund—which takes an age of gymnastics to secure; and, of course, to unfasten. You can hold the front together, and perhaps stroll around the rest of the photographs while your pulse smooths you out. I'll prepare the camera and tripod. No flash needed in this light if you can hold a steady pose."

Ayanokoji bowed and sauntered to the camera shelf. Conscious of Bos's display to the officer-thug at the stream, Charlotte stripped with her back to him. He blew dust off the lens and screwed the camera onto the tripod. Charlotte put on the kimono. Liquid sensuality. Camphor smell. Mothballs? She did not know if he had watched her strip. He had not.

She folded her clothes and put them on the floor beside her stool, then walked barefoot to the photographs; pretended to study them, saw only blurs with dark borders; calm on the outside, *hankechi* twisting in her gut. Rand whispered in her ear but she heard no words; the squeak of a rat, more nerve-wracking than her primary teacher's false talons grating the blackboard when her chalk wore short.

On this trip Rand had become a worse trespasser than usual;

not always sarcastic or argumentative, sometimes supportive, even wise, but to Charlotte he was an escalating form of migraine with no cure. She must find a way to neutralise him, otherwise he would needle and nettle and mock and torment her more than ever, and one purple day nudge her into the deep end of the pool. Why had he followed Peter and her to Tarawa? Why the fuck didn't he stay in Bougainville when they left? Why pursue her all over the world?

She returned to her stool and poured another bourbon. Ayanokoji heard the chatter of bottle against glass in nervous hands; looked back at her. Refill his glass and take it to him? *No, Dr Fonseka-the-Wise. He's too close to the swords. Keeps looking at them. When he comes back, ask him what his missus thinks of his photography.*

Ayanokoji walked towards her with camera on tripod. She held up the bottle; he nodded and smiled. He sat on his stool and told her they must be patient as her skin would not yet be smooth. Glasses clinked. They could chat, he said; she could ask questions that he would consider answering on credit.

Don't delay, but you'll have to give him something fast to get credit. Yes, Lieutenant Rand.

Ayanokoji took four minutes to explain the electronics and use of his modern light-meter.

"Hiroyuki, maybe the marks have gone." She stood in front of him and opened the kimono. The ice rattled in his glass; he dared not try to sip the bourbon. Feared his heels would again tap-dance their wild duet. The two tells she saw in his poker face were a twinge of the right eyebrow and a minute flicker of eyelids. She lifted the kimono to her waist and turned her back to him.

"Beautiful body, Charlotte. The marks have almost gone but wrap up and sit down for another twenty minutes or so. I want perfect photographs. I shall of course copy them for you so that you will know exactly what I hold in trust."

She closed the kimono and sat; asked him if his wife would

see the photographs. No. Would he tell her he had taken them? No. That Charlotte had been naked in his gallery? No. Did Hitomi approve of the nudes on his wall, in particular the explicit one? Yes. Did she think he took them in New York, while she was there with him? Yes; she thought the girl's tattoos were a symbolic attempt by a descendant of slaves to claim her African heritage, but not too much of it. Did he take the photographs of the black girl in New York? No. Bougainville? He hesitated, sipped his bourbon; stared at her over the glass, his breath fogging it. No, he didn't. Did you take them, wherever they were taken? Next question. Were they taken in New York? No, Counsellor Charlotte. Bougainville? He would get to that later.

"Did you serve in Bougainville?"

"Again, next question, Dr Fonseka, unless you think you have already asked too many."

He wants to look unfazed. His gut's churning. Check again for dints and grooves from the elastic. She put down her glass, turned on the stool to face Ayanokoji, opened the kimono, and separated her knees in the pose of Bos Simeon. He nodded and sipped: "Almost ready, Charlotte. Ten more minutes."

He's distracted from the swords, that's for sure. For the moment, anyway. Go back to Unit 731, then to Bougainville. Bougainville too soon will be Bougainville never. No, Rand. Bougainville now or never. I'll tell him he was there, not ask him.

She left the kimono open. "Hiroyuki, let's go back to Unit 731. How did you get from there to Bougainville?"

Beautiful, Charlotte. Nothing like the power of a body like yours. Still as good as when I watched you strip for Peter two nights after you screwed Aidan Conway. Drove me nuts. Fuck off.

Ayanokoji said he would answer her rhetorical question later. Now she was due to reciprocate, in good faith. How did she know the girl in the photographs? She told him about her meetings with Bos Simeon, and Peter's obsession with the case of Hugh Rand;

summarised Bos's notebooks.

"Please tell me more about the notebooks."

"Tell me more about Unit 731." He refilled his glass and hers; both drinkers mute for a minute, thoughtful.

You're as suspicious as I am. Ask him why he really left China. She moved her knees together and covered her breasts. He offered to turn up the heater. No need.

"Did you have sex with the Chinese girl at Unit 731?" He hesitated; she leaned forward and allowed the kimono to slip off her right nipple. Not enough to move him. She parted her knees a few centimetres. *You've almost got him. Wait ten seconds, then show him the other knocker.* Is this for him or you? *Him. I've seen it all more times that you want to know.*

Ayanokoji wondered again about her confidant, the target of her indistinct whispers, sometimes affable in delivery, sometimes spiteful. Interlocutor or mute listener? Poe would have adored this woman; her intelligence, complexity, strength, weakness, confidence, dependence on some dark other; also the power of her body.

"Shall we check the marks again?" Yes. She stood and repeated her earlier exposure. He said they could proceed. Smooth as the Korean comfort girl's belly.

He's had a hell of an eyeful. Enough for you to test his Unit 731 story. Magnificent, Charlotte. Aidan must still dream about his geography excursion every night. Not Peter, though. No dreams for him. You bastard, Rand.

"Hiroyuki, I can see a couple of dints that have almost disappeared. Let's wait a bit. I've earned a fair bit of credit already, don't you think? While we wait, let's revisit the story of you and Unit 731."

"Maybe. First, I need to walk a little and get my thoughts back together." He did not wait for an answer; poured another bourbon for both of them, stood up and walked towards the swords. *He has a sense of purpose. Get ready to bolt, Charlotte.* Her neck and fingers stiffened. Ayanokoji turned from the swords and ambled ten metres to the gallery door; strode back faster to the swords, stared at them for half a minute, and again ambled back to the door; then to the stool. His face taut, without malice.

Don't get demure. Keep a fair bit of skin exposed. Not too much. Don't show any shock or censure at what he tells you. He'll clam up if you do. Remember you want to steer him to Bougainville. He knows that. Let him go there at his own pace or he'll stop short.

Ayanokoji said he would elaborate on aspects of his experience at Unit 731, in wartime, when behaviour might not be consistent with civilised norms in times of peace, and soldiers in particular—not only soldiers—were disinclined to even think about moral categories of rightness and wrongness. Actions were judged by function, efficacy; by the call to survive and to assist allies to do so. Unit 731 sacrificed a few criminal lives to save and improve many others. Yes, Professor, you mentioned that.

Charlotte allowed him to go on for five minutes with his contextual justification, most of which she had already heard from him that day. *He's hesitating because he can't keep on pretending to ignore the view. He's turning on and on. Look at his eyes. Ask him again about the Chinese girl.*

"Hiroyuki, I accept there are things you might have done in wartime that you would not have done before the war and would not do after it. Sex life? A tough one for soldiers, tuned to harshness and function. The concept of cruelty becomes irrelevant, even meaningless. Does sex for a soldier become no more than another function, something you need to do? When soldiers are deprived of women, does sadism substitute for sex? Does sadism become sex? They learn to be like this? Then sometimes bring their learning back to sex with women? Rough sex?"

"Yes to all of that." Good, Professor. I'll use that later.

He's now watching your knees more than your eyes. Move your knees a bit and ask him the question he ignored before.

"Yes, I can understand the psychological deviance of that unfortunate time, and the problem of unlearning, of returning to normal. That considered, did you have sex with the Chinese girl at Unit 731? No judgement. Just asking. Probably for no reason other than prurience." She crossed her legs. He did not falter.

"She did not object as she seemed to think it was a condition of her release the next day, and she wanted to thank me for arranging it. Poor girl to think she needed to do that, I reflect now; not then. In that era, my soldier trumped my doctor." *Quick thinking with that last bit, Professor. Good anticipation, even though I wasn't going to mention Hippocrates. She uncrossed her legs.*

"Why didn't you refuse if the truth was that she didn't need to do it? Why deceive her? Is that soldierly?" *He blinked. Did you notice? Yes, Rand.*

"Consider the context, Charlotte. A rustic girl, simple in the head like most Chinese, then and now; but smart enough to understand women's instinctive use of sex as a pay-off for men, who all crave it. If I had declined she would have wondered why, and might have become suspicious about our plans for her. Perhaps doubt our intention to release her, and create enough trouble to get herself shot. We had put much effort into her preparation, and needed her next day. I was compelled to ensure she had another night of life." *Does he believe this crap? Does he think I believe it? His concentration has lapsed.*

"How was the experience for her?"

He made sure he gratified her, which gratified him because she deserved the pleasure he wanted to give her as a reward for her participation in the medical research that would save so many lives. "I could not reward her in any other way at Unit 731. Could I kiss her on the cheek, give her a bunch of chrysanthemums and escort her to the exit?"

Reward? He's crazy and still dangerous. Wound up by his

memory and getting an extra buzz from what's mostly under your kimono.

Charlotte tucked her feet under the stool to make the kimono slide further off her thighs. Easy to do with silk. "As you say, at that time and place you did the best you could for her. I do hope you were gentle with her. You said before that she was pregnant." She feigned the smuttiest grin of her life. *Perfect, Charlotte! Here he comes.*

"Not gentle. She demanded otherwise. I felt a duty to comply."

"Rough sex with a fit soldier. Every teenage girl's fantasy." His eyebrow questioned her.

Quick, Charlotte, said Rand.

"I'm serious, Hiroyuki. If she asked you to rough her up a bit you can be sure she enjoyed it. We all know about the fine line between pleasure and pain but most of us won't admit it." Eyebrow relaxed. He said he understood and agreed with the adage; unfortunately his wife did not.

Perfect. Now back off from sex for a bit. Not too far. Ayanokoji saw her mini-nod and knew it was not for him. That confidant in her head again. Evokes Faust: 'Who's this presumes to interfere? What means this forward fellow here?'

She asked Ayanokoji what happened to the girl the next day. At 8am he went to her room to check her condition. She sat clothed on the bed, a packed bag at her feet. In her hand a half-finished glass of water in which a sedative had been dissolved in the galley. She smiled at him; showed him bruises on her neck and arms; proud of them; gulped the drink. He watched her for two minutes until she stopped gabbling in Chinese; until she looked even vaguer than usual and loose of limb, but not sleepy. He turned to the open door and beckoned two research assistants; told them to strip her and take her to the operating theatre, 20 metres away. "The sedative did not work well. The *maruta* screamed as the men dragged her naked along the corridor. I followed. A robust girl. Bruises on her buttocks and scratches on her back reminded me of her passion the previous day. I also had bruises and scratches." *Maruta?* A passionate log?

Don't ask him why he lied about taking pills to make him ill so he'd get evacuated from Unit 731 and not have to cut up the girl. Maybe he's lying now, Einstein. *No, look at his glazed eyes and lips quivering. Delicious memories.*

The sedative took effect while Ayanokoji put on his smock and the research assistants strapped the girl to the operating table. She relaxed, as if bullet-stunned, a wounded soldier who has screamed himself to exhaustion, to silence. Good science, close to reality; especially when Dr Ayanokoji opened her body and modified the liver to mimic the effects of a bayonet or sword. Stab, twist and slash.

"We did not anaesthetise her. The girl must suffer as a soldier would, because emotion influences the outcomes of physical trauma. No sterile instruments or disinfectant. We needed to simulate the worst of battlefield conditions. She flinched and became exophthalmic at my surgical incision, but went to sleep, eyes still open, as I excised the liver portion. A privilege to work on the body of a lover. I noticed a strange thing—her erect nipples in a warm theatre."

Like yours, he wanted to say. Take it easy, Charlotte. He's fucking crazy. I am too, thanks to you, Rand, you bastard. Without you, none of this crap. *Work out how to get rid of me, Dr Millar, if I'm such a burden and you're so clever.* I have.

Ayanokoji, poker-faced, searched Charlotte's eyes for a tell—glaze, lid flutter, pupil constriction or dilation. Normal. No clenched fingers. No lip tremble. No whiff of sweat; the kimono dry at the armpits. Superficial calm. She's afraid to ask but yearning to know why my story has changed so much since this morning.

Charlotte had masked her rising fear; had hidden all evidence of her active *hankechi.* Ayanokoji now so open and unguarded he seemed to have discarded his. Her horror at his dispassionate tale of savagery was so extreme she wanted to dash from the gallery like a panicked soldier who deserts his post to shirk a looming battle. Too late for her to flee, so she must adopt the mental and physical control of a trapped soldier who will defy his enemy, not roll over like a terrified dog.

"Ah, Hiroyuki, such are the imposts and sacrifices of war. You're a brave man to tell me what you had to do. May I raise an issue of scientific method? A professional observation." His open palms invited her reasons. "A Chinese girl. Japanese soldiers were male. For a better simulation, why didn't you use a male ... *maruta*?"

"Charlotte, I wish I had not discussed the Tuol Sleng photograph with you. You will doubt me if I do not tell you the truth, or if I do tell it. I do not feel compelled to tell it. Yet I shall try, for reasons I do not understand. She had to participate because the senior surgeon who impregnated her did not want anyone to see her swell. Abortion, and saving her for another experiment, might have been an option but he preferred to get her off the list." A smirk.

Turn her into planks. Have a little laugh with him.

"He wanted to turn her into planks right away, Hiroyuki?" He chortled at her grin. *He is way off-guard now.* She asked him about the results of the experiment. It failed because the girl's heart stopped as he stitched her abdomen.

"We did not want to waste our efforts and her sacrifice, but we could not revive her. I closed her eyelids. Two attendants rolled her off the table, facedown onto a bare trolley. I gained some consolation on seeing again the marks of passion from our tryst. They threw a sheet over her and wheeled her out of the theatre to the crematorium." *Sleeping like a log, on the death trolley. This guy is a kink. Would have been into necrophilia if he got a chance. He's wondering if he's already said too much.*

Nice posture, Charlotte. Glimpses of your bits and the memory of his Chinese lover have really heated him up and loosened his tongue. End of chapter one. No more questions for a while. Time for photos! Show him what you're made of. Tell me what to do while you can, Rand. I've got a plan for you.

She stood in front of Ayanokoji, took off the kimono, dropped it on the floor, and put her hands on her hips. His face expressionless, his heels tapping the *tatami*. "No marks, Hiroyuki?"

"None. I'll take the full film—36 shots. The poses are up to you, apart from four. One of you in each of the two poses by the girl you call Bos Simeon. One from the back, one from the front. Two more, full length, both from the front, in which you rest my shots of that girl on your hip. Shall we proceed, in silence?"

Linking you to his gallery, Charlotte. No problem for me. *Maybe so.*

They worked for 18 minutes on a mix of demure and semi-pornographic shots, some in close to her body, a few taken from one end of the room, near the swords, while she leaned against the door at the other end, tempted to exit naked and run; would do so if he took a sword off the wall. More than half the shots included her face.

After the shoot she sat naked on the stool. He draped the kimono over her shoulders, gave her another bourbon, and sat beside her. "My wife thinks this kimono belonged to my mother." Don't explain, Professor. Who cares?

"It didn't? It's beautiful. Where did you get it?"

"Ah, we're back to questions. Tit for tat? I bought it during the war from a Korean girl. She was not entitled to wear this quality and pattern of Japanese kimono, so I insisted she sell it to me." He paid her well. Hitomi would not wear it because she and his mother were always distant, which meant they would never refer to it, let alone discuss its origins.

"You were based in Korea?"

"No. To anticipate your next question, she was on a visit to Rabaul, not far from a place that seems to be of inordinate interest to you. And your follow-up question: Why was she there? Charlotte, you have heard of comfort women?" She shook her head. He said they provided sexual services to soldiers. Most volunteers for this role were Korean. A few Dutch girls from the East Indies.

So, Charlotte, you're wearing a whore's kimono. He loves the idea. Loves his past. He's written you into his nostalgia script. By the way, a whore's kimono suits your history. Peter would agree. Your time is near, Rand. Exorcism coming up.

"You were in Rabaul on leave from Bougainville?"

He grinned, nodded, and shook his head. "The nod confirms your question about Bougainville. My head-shake responds to your asking about leave. It was work. The comfort woman made me work hard."

Charlotte complimented him on his humour and energy. Why did he go to Rabaul for sex when there were so many girls on Bougainville? Were there no native comfort women?

"Japanese soldiers were forbidden contact with natives so the latter would not interpret functional sex as acceptance of racial and cultural equality. Our authority might diminish, in their primitive judgement. And the Japanese soldiers would feel post-coital shame after contact with savages. Bad for morale." Comfort women did not visit Bougainville while he was there, so he had to find official reasons to go to Rabaul. Officers did turn a blind eye if junior ranks at Bougainville had occasional contact with local girls.

"Were you the commander that I told you Bos Simeon mentioned in her notebooks?"

"I do not remember her. Did she give a name?"

"No."

"Even so, it would have been me. For eight months I acted as commander of the Kieta garrison. A small contingent with a few isolated outposts until late in 1943, when our troop numbers escalated ahead of expected Allied landings. By then I was long gone." She did not need to know he was Kempeitai, always powerful, regardless of their formal rank; always in charge of interrogation when spies like Rand were to be drained of information and their spirit, and turned into compost or fish-food.

Go for it now Charlotte. Rand gripped her shoulders.

"Surely you had sex with her if you took the photographs I've seen today. Especially the explicit one. As promised, I'm not being judgemental. In your circumstances in that place it would have been entirely proper for any man to take up what looks like an offer to the photographer." She grinned and raised a quizzical eyebrow to mirror his. "Hell! Who am I to judge her or you, while I sit here like this?" He returned a lesser grin.

Ayanokoji reminded her that he had earlier told her he did not take the photographs. His deputy owned the camera. That officer had no authority to have one so Ayanokoji seized it and put it in his own kitbag, where it stayed for the rest of the war. He did not know what was on the film. Back in Japan he removed it and kept it until he set up his own darkroom in Kyoto. "In 1947 I developed the film. Two shots, and maybe a third, were of the girl I now assume is Bos Simeon, based on your assertion. You have seen two of them in my galleries."

"Did you see your deputy take the photos?"

Ayanokoji's right heel tapped twice. "Look, Charlotte. Did she say I was there? Did she say I took them? If not, did she say who did take them? Did she even mention the photographs?" *Relax, Professor. He's holding back.*

Yes or no. Toss a quick coin and sound confident when you give him the answers.

"No, Hiroyuki, she didn't. And no. No again, and another no."

She had guessed right. Ayanokoji was not there when the shots were taken, just as he had claimed earlier.

I know what you're about to say, Charlotte. A risky lie. If you're wrong, you lose all credibility with him. If you are right, you may be in big trouble. Don't do it. Here I go.

"She did say the garrison commander had sex with her. A powerful man, taller than most Japanese. If that was you, all fine. She was old enough, it was wartime, and she said she liked it. My immature husband lusted after her 30 years later, so I can understand how the young Bos would have appealed to you. The body in the photographs is strong, sensual, eager. Asking for it. A teenage tart."

She waited. He stared at her breasts and nodded, in slow rhythm, as if he were a judge who weighed the verdict of a capital case and would be mute until he was sure of his decision. This woman stretched his credibility. He must have her but at what cost to him? Surely more expensive than mere anecdotes about his wartime experience. Take the risk.

Say nothing, Charlotte. Sip your bourbon and look sympathetic.

"Charlotte, that girl was a black barbarian. If she had also been a trollop, an officer of my heritage could not have touched her without eternal shame." He fixed on Charlotte's nose-tip. "She was a virgin." He swilled his bourbon and poured another; topped up hers.

How about that, Charlotte? Not in the notebooks. What else isn't in there? How true is the stuff she did write? And Bos was a virgin, if you believe the professor. Professors don't lie, do they? So much for the old guys on the beach that she reckons took her cherry. You assumed they gave her the kid she buried in the bush. One of them, anyway. You're right, I hate to admit. But get back to being terse, or better still, shut up.

Her body and mind cramped in horror at Bos Simeon the girl, alone in the forest of fear as she dug a hole to conceal the foetus planted in her by this rapist, thief of her future. Charlotte wavered; could not go on with this game. Rand annoyed her back to it—the game he did not yet grasp.

Yep, so much for the notebooks. Especially the bits you added. The bits that destroyed Peter. Rand, you bastard. Get ready to disappear.

"Hiroyuki, I'm on your wavelength. My husband had sex with a few local girls in Bougainville. He said they liked it rough, and he taught me to like it that way too. A sort of war game. I'd resist—whack him, bite him, scratch him where his clothes would hide the damage from his work colleagues. He'd reciprocate. Ecstatic pain. Not every time. Now and again when we needed a bit more than usual. Anyway, how did Bos perform?"

"Let's say she was exuberant. Very physical. In contrast to her rough mind and disposition, skin like silk, except on her lower legs. Hands rough. Soles like elephant hide. Again, to anticipate the comment I believe is on the tip of your tongue, she was much like the non-virgin Chinese *maruta* but a lot stronger; better equipped to feign resistance. Neither girl wanted to yell, which surprised me. By the way, my wife is staid and knows nothing of this aspect of my past. Our sex life was humdrum compared with yours, long ago when we had one. We have not seen one another unclothed for almost 25 years. And your sex life with your current husband?"

Charlotte said Gamini was dull. She would rather read a linguistics article in bed. Rand told her to say she felt like a recidivist back in the prison of virginity.

"Since Peter died I've seen myself as pretty much a virgin. I guess that's the right label for a woman sexed by only two men. One a champion, the other not even an also-ran." Two? Rand called her a champion liar. She said it was in a good cause, namely getting rid of him. *Impossible, Dr Millar.* Wait a bit, you faceless moron.

Ayanokoji wanted this woman with a confidant in her head but did not trust her. Now she was calm and self-assured; 30 minutes ago he could see her apprehension and smell her fear. Now she had too much insight into his psyche; too much tolerance of his past; too much frankness about her sexual history and attitudes. Concocted for a purpose he did not understand? Too alluring; too ready to display her body, doubtless to seduce him; too ready to prostitute herself for his biography. Her eroticism had revised their game and its control—his at the outset but now hers. She had shepherded him to the point where he must have her, and she knew it; seemed to know he would divulge whatever she wanted to hear to get access to her. Why did she want his story as her price?

He could decide later what he had to do about her; perhaps nothing, considering the future deterrent power of her brewing infidelity with him, and the photographs he would possess after her departure for Sydney. The infidelity a lesser deterrent to breach of his trust than the photographs if, as he suspected, she would soon rid herself of her second husband.

"Charlotte, you signal sexual availability to me in exchange for wartime anecdotes. Am I presumptuous? Surely I cannot be so entertaining. Am I a fanciful geriatric? A cynic, perhaps? If any of those things, I apologise to you without reserve."

Hooked him, Charlotte. You might get time to wish I hadn't, Mr Rand.

She affected surprise, told Ayanokoji she expected the photography to secure his story. If he agreed to that as their original deal, she would consider sex with him but not to pay for his story; rather, to enjoy it with a man who preferred combat to nursing.

Too easy, Dr Fonseka. "Agreed, Charlotte. But you have asked me many questions. I have asked none of you. I have one, for now; perhaps no more than one. Why do you want to excavate my ancient history? Forty years have passed since the war."

He's got you there. It doesn't make sense. It does to me. I need to know if he had something to do with bumping you off. Did he? No answer. You say too much when I don't need your castrato squeaks, and nothing when you might be helpful. *Shut up. He's listening.*

"Hiroyuki, I'm mainly interested in Bos Simeon because I knew her many years after you did, and she gave me stories about the war. Hugh Rand, the spy? I have an unpleasant connection with his family. I will not elaborate, but if he was anything like the members who survived the war he deserved the chop."

You're a liar, Mrs Millar. You might as well disappear now, Rand. Your time's almost up. *Fantasy, Mrs Millar.*

"If you had anything to do with lopping Rand's head, I'll give you a prize—a gold medal. *Schadenfreude* for me."

Ayanokoji's heels tap-danced, hands not heavy enough on knees to choke the pitter-patter. Eyes wide, eyebrows arched high, tongue darts to lick lips twice; Adam's apple a buoy in waves; strands of hair shivered out of place. New *hankechi.* Got him.

"Charlotte, is the gold medal prize concealed, in part, beneath a comfort woman's kimono? My apologies for such directness. If I misunderstand you, I apologise and shall accept my shame as deserved." Comfort woman, you bastard? Comfort teenager, like Bos and the log.

"A real possibility, Hiroyuki. First, though, some tat before we consider tit, if you will forgive my Australian crudity."

Clipped laughter. "Forgiven. Ask and you shall receive."

"Let's leave Rand for later. If you didn't leave Unit 731 because you were ill, why did you leave? And you didn't end up in a medical role on Bougainville, if you were, as you have agreed, the garrison commander mentioned in Bos Simeon's notebooks. A non-medical commander, I presume."

Throat purge; buoy still bobbing, less agitated. Heels tap twice, then calm. "You presume well. I was an officer in the Kempeitai— military police, responsible for military discipline and intelligence gathering. Earlier today I said an excess of pills relieved me of my medical role at Unit 731. So far, so true. As you no doubt suspect, I told you a somewhat creative story. Let's cut to the chase. We experimented on logs with *shabu,* which we knew inflated the *banzai* syndrome in our soldiers. You look quizzical. *Shabu* is amphetamine, invented by a Japanese chemist in 1897. It enhances aggressiveness, energy, focus, physical strength, determination, clarity of mind. We overdosed *maruta* to work out the maximum our soldiers could take over a given period and maintain optimal efficiency."

A clue there, Mrs Millar. Bos's notebooks. The thug who bashed her and her mother. The pill-popper in the jungle, who apparently ignored Bos's bare arse at the stream. Thanks. I'd already twigged to that.

"I see. *Shabu* impelled the Japanese to fight to the death."

"Honour was the principal impulse, *shabu* a refining agent. We also introduced it to the German SS. Your Australian SAS used it in Vietnam, as did elite American forces. Green Berets."

"Chemical courage, bravery, heroism?"

"An enhancer, I suggest. Anyway, back to Unit 731. I could see no value in *shabu* experiments on non-combatant *maruta*, none of whom could have passed the fitness standards for the military. So I also tested it on myself, without higher approval. In short, I overtested it and became addicted within three weeks; became difficult for my superiors to manage, and for my subordinates to bear."

"Were you on *shabu* when you coupled with the Chinese girl— the *maruta*?" He was, which enriched her experience.

The senior surgeon and the Unit 731 pharmacist suspected Ayanokoji's self-experiment and told General Shiro Ishii, who confined him to the infirmary until he completed withdrawal, strapped to a bed like a *maruta*. Wretched. Then had him reposted to non-medical duties with a clean record apart from a statement that the officer material within a man of his fine heritage should be fostered in a combat role as a prelude to a senior appointment on return to Unit 731. In reality, he could never return as he had committed safety breaches by doing surgery on *maruta* while drugged, unforgivable in a medical environment. Even worse, he had overstated the dosages he gave to *maruta*, so he could take the unused amounts himself, and had therefore compromised the research.

"After Kempeitai training I went here and there as a major,

including Kieta. Eight months there. Now, Charlotte, I have told you all I know about Bos Simeon, whose name I had forgotten, if I ever knew it. Now you will want to know about Hugh Rand, whose name I did not forget."

Here I come! Rand, why the fuck didn't you tell me about this guy at the university gallery? Or at his house the other night? Rand silent.

"I do, Hiroyuki, but Rand can wait a bit. Tell me again how you acquired the photos of Bos Simeon if you didn't take them." *Another Tuol Sleng moment, Mrs Millar?*

"Allow me to modify my earlier explanation. The camera did belong to a subordinate officer, who carried it night and day. As I said, he must have taken the shots. I did not seize the camera from him. I acquired it when he died suddenly, and I put it in my pack, where I kept it until I returned to Japan. The rest of my earlier story is accurate. After the war, when I was living in Kyoto, I became interested in photography and remembered the camera. About to open it, I realised it had a film inside. I rewound it into its canister, took it out, and kept it in a dark cupboard until I learned how to develop and print film."

Bos didn't mention the thug officer's camera in her notebooks. Why not? Didn't know what it was, I suppose. Rare at that time in remote places. Use your brain, Rand. She might not have known what a camera was in 1943 but she would have seen a lot more of them in her adulthood, including Peter's, long before she wrote the notebooks. Didn't want to tell me or anyone else in 1971 that a Japanese officer took crutch-shots of her in 1943. Simple. Embarrassment. Reputation. *Get back to the professor, he's cooling.*

"Hiroyuki, why didn't you take the film to a professional photographer?" He's hesitant.

"My officer expended the film in wartime. All 24 frames. I did not know what might be on them. Discretion told me to destroy the film. Curiosity beat discretion, as still sometimes happens to me.

Today, for instance."

"Did you think Rand might be on it?"

"He was not on it. Twenty-one shots of birds and village life. And, of course, the two of Bos Simeon, whose body I recognised. He took them before I encountered her. You are thinking '21 plus 2 is 23'. The twenty-fourth shot was unclear. Probably a young woman pointing her rear at the camera in the jungle, beside a stream. Poorly lit. Impossible to print well enough to frame."

"The officer took those photographs before you met her, yet she was still a virgin?"

"No doubt. One does not have to be a doctor to interpret the reaction of a girl to her first penetration. I made love to her after he died. The officer was perhaps impotent, but I suspect he did not want to defile himself with a black girl. To anticipate your question, I had no such inhibition—regrets came later—once I was sure she had serviced no black man or that upstart Japanese; a low-life *burakumin*, descended from an outcaste butcher or undertaker. I still do not know how he came to be an officer."

"Perhaps queer, that officer? Homosexual. Bos wrote that she saw his erection at the stream. And that he bashed her when she tried to seduce him at the base camp. So, not impotent, but didn't like her enough to couple with her." After a few seconds she added, "Rough or otherwise."

Jesus, Charlotte! Look at his eyes. Hold back on sarcasm or he might drop you, in one way or another.

"A weak joke, Hiroyuki. Sorry." He nodded.

"There were no homosexuals in the Imperial Japanese Forces. I heard that some Australian and British prisoners in Singapore and Thailand were ... queer? Perhaps you have read about that in your uncensored history books and research articles. The one homosexual I met during the war was Hugh Rand."

Her jaw slackened. Ayanokoji smirked; raised eyebrow triggered forehead ruts. "Charlotte, your eyes and hands and slack jaw tell me I have shocked you for perhaps the first time today. A queer hero! Hard for you to imagine? When captured, Rand was naked, and had tried to sodomise the forward scout when he entered the cave to make the arrest. The soldier tried to fight him off but Rand stabbed him to death. He left a small semen stain on the soldier's clothes."

In Melbourne, Walter Brooksbank had told Peter of Rand's polite but distant attitude to women involved in his coast watcher induction course; his lack of response to their lusting after him.

Ask Rand. Rand, are you queer? Silence. Her shoulders no longer in his grip. Ayanokoji stared, puzzled again at her confidant. Who? What?

"Okay, Hiroyuki, back to the film. Did you think Rand *might* be on it? If so, why would that be a problem?"

"I did wonder. You must understand that spies like Rand had to be encouraged to divulge military intelligence. I led the interrogation, and always talked to Rand alone. The *burakumin* officer also dealt with him to prepare him for discussion with me, and I thought he might have taken photographs of the process when I was not present. He did not do so, as I discovered when I developed and printed the film. I wanted to know what was on the film but could not entrust it to anyone so soon after the war."

"Photographs that might incriminate you, indirectly, as Kieta commander, if they found their way into American hands?" His lips are sealed. More dart-licks. Question answered.

Come on, Rand. Tell me what happened. *Get back to the notebooks.* Hands clamp her shoulders. If her plan worked, those hands would soon release her for good.

"Hiroyuki, Bos said a shark ate the officer who executed Rand. This officer beat her and her mother. She said she told you so." *Good one, Charlotte.* Why so coy when I asked you why you had never mentioned this guy to me? Okay, ignore me again.

For want of other things to do, Ayanokoji had learned some

Pidgin, the only common language with Bos. She came to his house-cum-office late at night—"as I played the *shakuhachi* to myself and drank rum"—to complain to him about the violence, which was against the *bushido* code. "Of course, she did not know that. The officer had a reputation for brutality against his own men, let alone the natives." The brute difficult to control, unlike his tracker dogs, a superior species of brute. *Burakumin*. His behaviour unsurprising.

"Running on amphetamines rather than breeding?" *Charlotte! That got to him for some reason. Follow up.* Later.

"Hiroyuki, how did a shark get him?"

Ayanokoji silent for half a minute, eyes closed. Opened them and talked. "I intended to discipline the thug for his assaults on civilians. A shark got him off the hook, so to speak." Side-splitting, Professor.

Ayanokoji and the officer went fishing alone one night, well out to sea in a motorised whaleboat requisitioned from a German missionary. The *burakumin* baited the heavy line and dropped it overboard. They smoked but did not talk. A shark or some other monster took the bait and dragged the officer overboard. "The fool must have looped the line around his wrist. He surfaced twice; gurgled screams. A couple of weak splashes. That was all. We recovered no part of him despite a search that night and the next day by several boats. Three days later his cap washed up on the beach."

Look at him. He knows you don't believe him. Get your head working, Charlotte. Later. He can sweat on my blank look. I'll come back to the shark.

"Good riddance, I would guess. Bos said he beat hell out of her mother—almost killed her—and shot a lot of men who carried cargo for Rand. Told his men to hammer Rand when they captured him, according to Bos's observations of his condition when his men brought him down from his hideout, down to where the officer waited with Bos and her mother in the forest."

Did you see his eyes flash! You're cagier than I thought, Charlotte. Or did you make a happy mistake? Fuck off.

Ayanokoji confused and annoyed for ten seconds. Charlotte crossed and uncrossed her legs.

"He told me he captured Rand himself, in person. The truth emerges after forty years. A liar, Charlotte. He knew he would get away with it. No underling could dare contradict him to me or anyone else. A liar, a brute peasant devoid of principle."

"A low-life, no doubt. But why couldn't you control him? Wasn't he trained to take orders without question, like a dog? To defer to senior officers without condition, in the *bushido* tradition? Especially to a senior officer of your heritage. Never to deceive you. Something's missing. Remember our pact—tit for tat."

Brilliant again, Charlotte. But don't be too clever for your own good. Don't think he won't back off any second. And consider the cutlery. Droll advice from someone too dumb to take it himself. *Where's this going?* You'll find out pretty soon.

She sensed reticence. "Hiroyuki, all this talk of, shall we say, 'extreme physicality', is having a less than calming effect on me." He raised his eyebrow. She pulled her shoulders out of Rand's grip, stood, opened the kimono and took two short steps to where Ayanokoji sat; clasped the back of his head and pulled his face against her belly. Drenched on her doorstep with Aidan Conway. Erotic then, with a gentle man of high intelligence, but degrading now with a thug, delusional and brilliant; menacing in his lack of emotion. Degradation would be a trade-off, her means to end more than a decade of pain.

You're whoring yourself for a story? No, for deliverance. *From what?* You. *Pardon?*

She started to tell Ayanokoji to grip her buttocks harder, to dig his fingernails into her skin. No, too much too soon. Stay in control, pretend to be a bit unbridled now, much unbridled once you're sure he's smitten and his brain is slower.

Ayanokoji thought of the Korean girl who first occupied the kimono in Rabaul on her first assignment, the day she arrived from Japan with ten older comfort volunteers. His luck to be there on a visit from Bougainville, an officer of aristocratic origins that gave him first choice of the women. Chung-Cha, his first lover after the Chinese log, and his first virgin, not long before Bos Simeon. Unlike this Australian woman, all were young and naïve but lesser conquests than she would soon become. Less voluptuous for their inexperience with robust sex, which would be natural to this woman who had extolled it already. Between breaths he pushed his face hard into her belly. Twice the pubic hair of the log and Chung-Cha, and more curled, like Bos Simeon's; a little more hair than the barbarian but lighter in colour and with less sparkle.

Must think about this persistent woman. What did she want of him? Why whore herself for wartime anecdotes when she could not know if they were any more accurate than her first interpretation of the Tuol Sleng photograph? Maybe she wanted nothing more than vigorous sex. This revelation game might be a variation on a routine she devised for strangers, to garnish her copulation with fantasy. A twist to the Japanese tradition of old men in an elite club, all ears to a *geisha* as they try to have an erection they will use only in their minds.

His account of Unit 731 and the young *maruta* did seem to arouse her. A streak of sadomasochism? Ah, yes, and exhibitionism. She had soon needed to strip, to display herself; to suggest nude photography and sex as a way of gaining his trust. He now had the security of the photographs and would soon have much more in his care, hidden from her husband and colleagues.

Ayanokoji had never told his wife or anyone else what he had told Charlotte about his war, to feed her fantasy. To tell her more— even about the Rand story if she raised it again—would elevate her libido, already generous, to the point of a demand for sex as combat. His last such skirmish was eight years ago with a German student, unwilling at first to don the kimono. Now he was almost old but still strong, fit, eager, potent. They could achieve much in the hours before Hitomi arrived home from her Osaka lover, a pansy of a boy, so he has heard. She does not know her husband knows; nor can she know he does not object, that he feels pleased for her, the beloved wife he cannot gratify.

Enjoy the whoring-as-barter game with this Siren. Stay sharp, lead her on, maintain control. Don't let the emerald-and-shamrock eyes and pretty voice enchant you onto the rocks.

He let go of her buttocks; ran his hands along her sides and up to her breasts. Never suckled by a brat. Twice the measure of Chung-Cha's and the log's; as full as Bos Simeon's and still as firm. Hitomi's small apples with large cherry tips too sensitive to his touch; his type of touch.

Charlotte cringed as he twisted her nipples between fingertips and thumbs. She faked ecstasy, dropped to her knees and whacked her face on his forehead, the collision just hard enough to make her nose bleed. Painful, but perfect in timing and effect. Blood from the right nostril, the other clear. Like red ink on blotting paper, blood drops dyed new flowers on the kimono sleeve and revised the embroidered originals. Her boxer's forearm jammed against her nose as if to deflect a blow, she allowed blood to seep unchecked into the cloth; gurgled an apology and stood to remove the kimono to prevent further desecration of his prized garment. Ayanokoji transfixed, her blood's job done.

"Leave it on, Charlotte. It was a little stained when I bought it from the Korean woman in Rabaul. After the war I had a drycleaner work her wonders on it. I'm so sorry. Sit down and relax. Hold the sleeve beneath your nose while I stop the flow." Silent, he pinched the bridge for two minutes with the forefinger and thumb of his left hand while the right patted her breasts, infants due for slumber.

His gentleness with nose and breasts a setback. Now no sign of an erection beneath his kimono.

Theatrical manoeuvre, Charlotte. Would have been obvious to the good Dr Ayanokoji if he hadn't been navel-gazing. What was that all about? For me to know, for you to find out later. Tell me this, Rand. Is this the guy who cut off your head?

No reply.

Ayanokoji close enough to feel and savour her breath but could not decipher her whispers from a mouth held like an idiot paralysed of tongue; impossible to lip-read her. What society went on behind those eyes, closed now while she whispered to some entity within her head? Not introspection. No. Inclined to analysis of others—harsh analysis—but not of herself.

"The flow is stanched, madam, as a real medico might say to his patient. Shall we go back to the house for you to wash? Or I can bring water and a towel here."

"Later, Hiroyuki. Let's not lose any more momentum. I'm in a bit of pain but having a good time. We both need a rest. Let's stay on the stools, talk for a while, and decide where to go from there. Time for some tat, don't you think?"

He licked her blood from his finger and thumb; leaned forward, put his hands on her thighs and pecked a spot of blood from her cheek; kissed her mouth with the flutter of a dragonfly wing. She feared his gentleness.

Blood-smell in her right nostril, and in the bloodless left her own body scent from his face.

"Salty lips, Charlotte. Pleasantly so. Yes, let's talk. Which to you means 'Tell me what I want to know'. I still do not know why you want or expect me to purge myself to you. You want to justify something, I know not what, and you evade explanation. I'll talk anyway. That's our deal. Ask whatever you wish." That eyebrow raised again. Eyes quizzical, sceptical. Beware of this bastard. An emotional and intellectual deviant. Good that his back is to the swords.

I know how confused he feels. Come clean to both of us. Later, to him maybe. Nothing to explain to you.

"Hiroyuki, do you know you fathered Bos Simeon's baby?"

He took his hands from her legs, leaned back, stared at the ceiling, shook his head.

"You seem sure, Charlotte. Those notebooks again?"

"Yes. Bos said so, explicitly."

You're a better actress than I thought, Mrs Millar. A better liar. Bos said no such thing. Still editing her notebooks after all these years.

"What happened to the baby?" Shocked that he had not passed his life without spawning a replacement; disgusted at seeding a black womb.

"It died. She miscarried at ten weeks and buried the foetus in the forest near her village. She miscarried in horror because her mother hanged herself after your officer bashed her."

"It died? It? Of course, too young to distinguish boy or girl. Much too young, but a human being nevertheless. Of sorts." He looked at her for a few seconds, and closed his eyes. She saw his lips quiver; a micro-quiver, soon quashed.

"That officer. That peasant. That basher of women. Ask me to revise my earlier story about what happened to him. Go ahead, Charlotte. First ask me if I executed Rand." His heels pitter-pattered; he did not try to stop them.

"Did you execute Rand?"

"No. I interrogated him, as I told you already. He had to be executed, so I ordered the officer to behead him. I was briefly tempted to do the job myself but I had given up on beheadings as they gave me no satisfaction. I preferred to trap people into making capital admissions and have someone else administer the penalty. Anyway, I had a wrist injury and could no longer wield the sword well enough to even practise on banana trunks.

"Twenty minutes before the execution the officer came to my house and said he had damaged his sword while sharpening it. Two non-commissioned officers had swords but it would take an hour to hone them well enough for a clean beheading. He asked to use mine to avoid delay or the shame of a botched execution. He bowed and said he was sure a garrison commander would keep his sword well-honed as an example to his subordinates. I doubted his story and despised his style but agreed to his request." Ayanokoji pointed back over his shoulder.

"The treasure behind you on the wall?" asked Charlotte.

"Indeed. But in a standard military scabbard, not in that heirloom beauty, which has never left Japan. I allowed a peasant to use the sword—an upstart, a thug—and therefore abused the *samurai* tradition; betrayed my ancestry. When he was about to behead Rand I became nauseous, not for the inevitable gore, of which I had seen plenty, especially at Unit 731. No, not gore. Shame at my betrayal of heritage made me forgo the execution. I marched to the beach and vomited in the shallows, which were fouled with the excrement of natives. Disgusting. Why did they not use the nearby latrines?

"Charlotte, you might not understand why the gore worried me less than misuse of the sword that created it. Japanese society embodies a tension between simultaneous refinement and savagery. My superbly crafted heirloom, with a deliberate but hidden flaw— to you the ultimate conceit—had to be used to slice off a head in the right way; that is, the right combination of user, victim, attitude and expertise. The writer Yukio Mishima called the tension a clash between elegance and brutality. Think of the rustic crockery we discussed at dinner. The American anthropologist Ruth Benedict explored the principle in her book *The Chrysanthemum and the Sword*. It's all about irreconcilable contradictions in the culture that imprisons us Japanese; like yours imprisons you, albeit with a little more flexibility than we have. I allowed the element of savagery to dominate refinement, and associated honour, by allowing that *burakumin* to use the sword. Do you follow me? I'll come back to

Mishima. He and Rand had a specific, somewhat quirky interest in common.

"First, more about the officer. A smug animal. Full of veiled insolence. That evening, when he returned my sword, he asked me if I still felt unwell. He said some troops and villagers saw me vomit. Suggested I take extra *shabu*; smirked.

"Two days later I went fishing with him at night, as I already told you, well out on a calm sea in pitch dark. I hit him on the head with my revolver and dumped him overboard. Held him by the hair until almost drowned, cut his throat, washed the knife, sipped rum from a bottle and waited until I heard the sharks do their work."

"Good riddance to scum, Hiroyuki." Charlotte moved her legs until he could see as much as Bos displayed in her frontal nude. He grabbed his knees; heels clattered for a few seconds.

Rand gripped her shoulders. *Dr Charlotte the Harlot, ask him why that particular scumbag of an officer would smirk and suggest a* shabu *fix. Your quips and grips are numbered, Rand.*

"Hiroyuki, I've lost something here. Why would the *burakumin* suggest a *shabu* fix, and smirk?"

"Ahh! I should never have discussed the Tuol Sleng photograph with you. You have guessed there is more than culture-based shame to my contempt for that vermin. He was an officer of guards at Unit 731 when Surgeon General Ishii removed me, and was already on Bougainville when I arrived at Kieta. We never talked about Harbin but it was always in the air.

"So, I had more than one reason to eliminate him. At that point our supply lines were threatened and we already doubted we could win the war. Retribution would follow—victor's privilege. This animal had bashed and murdered civilians for no good reason when he was under my command, and therefore I would be held responsible, as well as him. He executed Rand under my orders. I destroyed all relevant records, of those that I did make; but he knew too much and would take his chance to whitewash his own behaviour and compromise an aristocrat to the Allies after the war. By then, my leadership at Kieta might be called a war crime, yet my brief stint at Unit 731 might not be considered significant, or even noticed. I expected the victors to be more concerned with the fate of one white spy than that of many Chinese.

"On a more social and personal level, he would spread the word among the lower classes at home about my *shabu* habit and my removal from the medical corps. Worst of all, he had allowed me to shame myself by letting him use my heritage sword. I could read his stunted mind. He knew I would not want to lend him the sword. But if I did not, I sensed he would tell the soldiers at Bougainville about my disgrace at Unit 731. He might tell them anyway, if he had not done so already. He deserved to disappear. You understand, Charlotte? The honour of my family, my class. Those were different times."

"Of course. As I said a minute ago, good riddance to scum. Let's get back to Rand. You said you interrogated him, talked to him. Did you torture him? What did he divulge? Don't hold back. I've obviously never met him but I despise him by reputation."

He would go into the Rand case. First he needed to answer questions she had not asked, and he would otherwise wonder later why she had not thought to ask them. About other witnesses to Rand's execution—soldiers and villagers who could point the finger at him. "In short, Charlotte, they could point all they liked. There is no proof I was at Bougainville. Not long after the war, when I heard about the immunity deal being canvassed with Ishii and his team at Harbin, and I still worried about my role at Bougainville, I used my father's connections to have my military record laundered. It came to exclude my removal from Unit 731, and to place me there and in other medical roles for the whole of my military service. My Kempeitai stint in Bougainville and elsewhere disappeared. Why should I hang for ordering the execution of a spy when Ishii was going to get a life pension for what he ordered and supervised?

When the most junior of the Emperor's worshippers were more likely to hang than the politicians and heroic military leaders who forced their subordinates to kill and kill and kill without demur.

"On the official record, I trained in Japanese military hospitals after my first few months at Harbin, and went on to a few brief medical administrative postings in Asia for a while. Returned to Harbin for the rest of the war. Therefore I was forgiven by Macarthur, along with everyone else at Unit 731. No pension though, unlike Ishii and his senior colleagues. No one ever raised our role in public, but our past was no secret in higher society. For many years we were the *kuroko* in *kabuki* drama. Stage attendants, dressed in black, obvious to the audience but also invisible, easy for them to ignore at will. Ah, the contradictions in us Japanese. Ubiquitous.

"No villager in Bougainville would have known my name, and almost every soldier at Rand's execution was bones by the end of the war, including two junior officers and a couple of NCOs. My immediate successor, a Kempeitai major, did not stay long, and anyway I didn't mention the Rand case to him during our half-day handover. Nor, of course, was there any record for him to see. If he did hear about the execution and survived the war, he would not have implicated me, a fellow Kempeitai officer.

"There was safety for me in my compatriots' obliteration, sad to say. Those who left before the late-war massacres, mainly by Australians, would have been untraceable after the war, if anyone had an interest in me, which no one did seem to have, despite my worry until 1948. By then the victors had lost interest in further charges, and General MacArthur had freed the last 42 untried suspects, all national leaders in wartime—Class A suspects, war instigators and promoters. No chance of my being charged after that.

"I did worry in the meantime that Rand's Australian superiors would investigate and find out enough to point to me. It seemed they gave up, or did not try at all. By 1947, I was sure no Japanese soldier of any rank had been prosecuted for executing a coast watcher. That is, a spy. In anyone's military system in a war zone, spies get executed, summarily." She listens to me, she nods. No reply to my long speech. Whispers again to her inner confidant, animus—whatever.

Charlotte asked Rand: Did he torture you? I almost hope so, considering the hell you've given me. What did you give away? Were you hero or chicken? *Fuck you, Mrs Millar. Ask the guru.*

"Tell me about Rand, Hiroyuki. I hope you gave him hell." He studies the blood on my face and sleeve, then whatever else he can see of me, then back to the blood; only his eyes move—a cat and its target bird.

"We used standard interrogation techniques, no doubt unpleasant, but perhaps not much more uncomfortable for him than his festered hand." He awaited her question.

"Festered hand?"

"When Rand tried to sodomise him, the soldier stabbed him through the hand before succumbing. The hand festered quickly after he reached Kieta and we had no medical way of treating it. Just splashes of young coconut water—Do you know it is sterile?— and a bandage. We did not even have stitches. It needed many. Rand lost a lot of blood before and after we captured him, and began to hallucinate after a couple of days. He could never have survived, so his execution was at worst unnecessary, at best a relief for him. It was hardly a war crime to put a homosexual rapist out of his misery; to award him an easier death. Hardly a war crime to execute a spy, certainly not by Allied standards. Hardly a war crime to execute someone who murdered a village headman, if the rumour I heard about his murder was more credible than the story his villagers told about his loss at sea on a fishing trip."

"The rumour you heard was correct, according to his daughter, Bos Simeon. She said he was powerful but not the village head." A slow nod by Ayanokoji. "As I said, Hiroyuki, no sympathy for

Rand from me. What did you do to him? What did he tell you? Can you remember much about him?" Have to stir up his blood-lust again. Rand, not much to say, have you? This is all about you.

"He does invade my memory from time to time, an occasional crass intruder. He was and is a passing nuisance. Do not misunderstand me. He generates no shame and certainly no guilt. Mainly annoyance. Well, I admit to a touch of shame because he fooled me." Fooled you, did he? I'll come back to that.

Charlotte here, Rand. Where are you? 'Nuisance' sounds familiar, doesn't it? Nothing from you? Silence.

Ayanokoji sighed. "I have slain Rand several times in my dreams since I ordered his execution. Here is an imperfect analogy. I am caught in a cycle a bit like Yoeman in the *kabuki* dance, *Kasane*. I am harassed a little by Rand, but not as disturbed by him as Yoeman is by Kasane, his lover, who transforms into the ugly form of a woman Yoeman murdered in a former life. He slashes at her to kill her again and she falls dead after they struggle. Yoeman departs the stage, thinking he is in the clear. The stage lights are dimmed, but the drama is not over. In the weak light the woman's hand rises from death and reaches towards Yoeman's exit point. Her power pulls him back. I am Yoeman; Kasane is Rand, a damned cyclic nuisance. Do you understand me, Charlotte?"

"More than you might realise." He sure gets at you more than you admitted at first.

"Rand? Who was he? Who cares? Is he really such a mystery man that you need to bother about him at all? Have you created a mystery of him because you need one? Is he a proxy for something else that bothers you? A scapegoat, perhaps? A substitute for the comfort of lost religion? Filling some gap?" Too much theology and psychoanalysis, Professor.

"Hiroyuki, you ask 'Who was he?' He was at least someone whose family suffered because you had to kill him. Drove some of them to madness, suicide. Not all your fault, though."

"Charlotte, I am not perfect. Don't we all have contradictions and hypocrisies in our normal lives, let alone during wartime? Well, maybe wartime is less contradictory, clearer. Kill or be killed. Rand knew it. He knew his family would suffer if he were a victim, and rejoice if he were a killer who made it home. Life is all contradictions and hypocrisies. Do all Buddhists live like the Buddha? Devout Christians live as Jesus demands? I suspect that you, although from a Christian tradition, if not faith, think adultery is unwholesome. And yet, here we are." Ah, he's refocused on what he's about to get. Move legs.

"Hiroyuki, I want to come back to what you did to him, but first tell me what you meant a few minutes ago when you said he fooled you?"

"His fooling me was one of the reasons he deserved to die. And it was not an honourable death, to us. It is a myth that execution by sword is always a gesture of honour. In his case it was convenient, and didactic theatre for the natives, whose own traditions tell them violence is sometimes a necessary tool to impose order on chaos, or prevent chaos in the first place.

"Beheading is the most feared death for non-Japanese, therefore the best deterrent for observers. There is also the fear of a lonely death, a fear that crosses cultural borders. I have never seen a man look as lonely as when he is about to lose his head. Shooting seems more social for the condemned man as well as for observers and the shooter or shooters. Rand certainly looked lonely. Yes, a strong deterrent.

"His execution was justified under our code. He spied for the Allies, our enemy. Like the spies in Tarawa, he intended to pass on information about us that would kill our men and destroy our equipment. I judged that he did not have the time or capacity to pass on anything before his capture. That is beside the point. Intention matters—the intention to kill and destroy." This fucking scholarly innocent has no sense of hypocrisy.

Charlotte again asked how Rand fooled him.

"He lied. He lied to me about Allied plans. I believed him and passed the information to our Pacific command. To my shame they immediately dismissed the information as nonsense, as counter to intelligence from various sources, all reliable. Anyway, for pretending to divulge secrets to save his head he deserved to die as a coward. I also decided he should die because he gave false information through me that might have been credible to our intelligence people. We might have moved troops and equipment. Well after I left, the Allies invaded Bougainville and other islands, and massacred us at weakened places that might have been even weaker if we had believed Rand's lies. Some men might have died because of them. So, the execution was justified by more than the cowardice of confessing."

Hang on, Professor. Your logic is a bit off. Rand! Listen to me. Was he right about any or all of that? No answer; then *Maybe, Dr Tuol Sleng, the lies were not intended to save my skin. Tell him.*

"Hiroyuki, how do you know he confessed—told the lies—to try to save his skin? He would have known you would kill him anyway, so why not go out with a deception that might confuse the Japanese command and save allied lives? Maybe Bougainvillean lives?"

"I made my judgement at the time. Anyway, no Japanese soldier would want to be perceived as yielding, regardless of motivation. Unambiguous honour must prevail. I understood shame; he did not. As I have said, those were different times."

He saw her scepticism. "Charlotte, you think he is my eternal *hankechi* because he got the better of me." She ignored him.

"Charlotte, you may be right about the personal need for revenge. Whether Rand lied or not, he had to disappear, like his executioner, because he annoyed me, goaded me, insulted me, would not let me dominate him, shamed me to my superiors. But there was always more to it than that.

"Here is another twist to the tale. My decision to have him executed was justified in hindsight for another reason. Back in Japan, war news from the Pacific revealed to me that some—not all—of the intelligence our Pacific command dismissed as lies may have been accurate. In which case Rand may have been a traitor to his own people. There we are, Charlotte. Rand as my *hankechi*? Perhaps, but not out of guilt."

Rand, where are you? Silence.

"Ah, Charlotte, let's move on. Oh, another relevant point, which might mitigate the brute you perhaps see in me. At first, before the extent of his wickedness became clear to me, I did not intend to have him executed. Once I got the information I wanted from him, had wrung him dry, I would ship him to a POW camp in Southeast Asia or Japan. Then I realised he might survive there, at least long enough to tell others what I and my subordinates did to him.

"As I have said, we already sensed we could not win the war and victor's revenge would follow, dressed up as legal process. I might be prosecuted and jailed, or worse, merely for torturing Rand. At first I was prepared to take my chances. After his true nature emerged I had no qualms about relegating him to permanent silence. I already planned to have my record altered but could not know if I would succeed, and a living Rand would not help my cause. Of course, I did succeed and became a paragon. That is how I came to be appointed many years later as a collector of war remains in countries sensitive to former Japanese officers with a questionable history, such as Kempeitai membership."

All over the place. Boggles the mind. Bring him back to where I want him to focus his emotions. Evoke his wartime learning about functional sex, rough stuff. "How did you torture him?"

"With words, apart from one burn to his forehead, with a cigarette I first offered to him, then withdrew as he tried to take it in his lips. A mean-spirited act, I know. Of all my wartime behaviour, apart from lending my sword to the *burakumin* thug, it brings me closest to shame at my loss of dignity; closer than the *shabu* aberration, even though the latter met the requisite of a witness and the cigarette incident did not—apart from Rand himself.

"Otherwise I tried to talk down to him, to break his spirit in the hope of getting information that would save lives. My approach did not work well, so I ordered others to do the usual things. It was my duty, no matter how unpleasant. Beatings. Hot iron applied to the skin. Withholding food. Sleep deprivation. Bastinado. Kicks and *kendo* strikes to the testicles. Fingernail removal. Various techniques with water poured on the face and hosed into the gut. Then a punch or kick in the swollen stomach. His defiance tired me. At night I would play the *shakuhachi* to relax after suffering his nonsense all day. He did get to me. Even now the *shakuhachi* reminds me of his bastardry and his victory over me, much to my shame. Yet I love to hear and play it. As you see, another contradiction."

His eyes are fuzzy, and he suppressed a grin. Nostalgia. Time to make a move, Dr Fanny Hill-Millar. Soon. And you'll move too. Sure I will. Ask him what he thinks I have in common with Mishima. It had better be erotic or you'll lose him.

She stood in front of Ayanokoji with her hands on his shoulders, the kimono open. "Hiroyuki. You said Rand and Mishima had something in common. What?" He put his hands on her hips and drew a deep breath; exhaled hard onto her belly.

"More than a passing interest in St Sebastian, as painted by El Greco, Rubens, Botticelli, Mantegna and a few others. I had seen reproductions, and since then have seen some originals. The homoerotic martyr, ecstatic, orgasmic, tied to a tree or pillar; full of misaimed arrows, like an archery target for beginners. Rand talked about the paintings when he was semiconscious or hallucinatory. A sodomite under stress. The festered hand got to his brain, I suspect. Made him let down his guard." *Mishima homoerotic? The Siren will pick up on that, you fool. You have already denied Japanese homosexuality.*

She spoke to his crown. "The link with Mishima? Oh, yes, I've seen the self-portrait. Mishima looking like a porcupine in orgasm. A homoerotic Japanese? You said Japanese were not homosexual."

Got him.

Peter told you all about Mishima? Right? Fuck off.

"No, Charlotte. I said no Japanese soldiers were homosexual. Mishima formed his own militia after the war but was not a soldier. A mad fascist. I knew him. Not well. He certainly did not have the respect of the armed forces. They laughed at him in 1970 when he tried to inspire a military coup and restore imperial authority. So he committed *seppuku*—suicide by ritual disembowelment. As you know, I suspect Rand's homosexuality, in contrast to Mishima's in Japan, would not have been an aberration among Australians on the Thai-Burma Railway project, or in Changi."

She fondled his earlobes. "Did Rand agree that he attempted to sodomise the soldier?" Ayanokoji said he denied it, which did not matter because his references to the paintings of St Sebastian indicted him. He refused to give any other explanation for his nudity and sexual semi-arousal when captured.

"Fair enough, Hiroyuki. All in all, I guess he had to go. Did he behave well at his execution?"

"Well enough until the girl you know as Bos, and her mother, approached him near the end as he knelt for execution. The mother shoved the girl's face close to his and spat at him, presumably because the rumour was true that he shot her husband, the girl's father. Then I wondered if he had defiled the girl, or the mother, or both—but the mother was much too old for him, and had told us she had no success when she tried to entice him to have sex with her in his cave so that our soldiers could capture him at a weak moment. Then I remembered his homosexuality. Later, as you know, I discovered the girl was intact. For whatever reasons, the pair accosted him on the point of death but their behaviour did not interest me enough to follow up. My focus was on my sword and

430

the *burakumin* officer."

She felt Rand's grip on her shoulders. *All bullshit, Charlotte. He's eloquent for someone with his eyes less than half a metre from the main course. Get back on track. The suspense is a killer.*

Ayanokoji's grip like horse-bites on her hips. Nails well-manicured but sharp. Good. He looked up at her, his eyes eager. "You whispered to me, Charlotte?"

"Yes. I said your hands are strong." He gripped harder.

Quicker thinking than usual, Mrs Millar. You've primed him, that's for sure. His blood-lust is back. I still don't know why you're doing this. Rand, you're too dumb to realise I'm giving you the eternal exit we both need. Any New Guinean villager would understand what I mean. You didn't learn much there, did you?

"Charlotte, I can't hear you well." *Why and what does she whisper? Now to me or still to the overworked confidant in her skull? She knows she kindles me; pretends attraction to me. Wants to couple rough with a war criminal she thinks is a devil, an incubus, a nightmare in daylight? In exchange for pointless anecdote? Shows fake sympathy for me and other men at war. Contrivance imbues her, even ritual. And some fetish too deep for me to fathom. Decide now.*

Ayanokoji slid his hands from hips to buttocks and dug his nails into her skin. As she flinched in pain and fear, and he cut deeper, she saw him try to turn his gaze from her belly to the wall almost behind him.

Make your move pronto, Dr Geisha, or you are history.

She grabbed Ayanokoji's head and pulled his face to her groin; let go of his head when he did not try to pull back; dug her fingers into the softness behind his collarbone, enough to hurt him; wrapped her hands around his throat and squeezed hard to contuse his skin. Not a wince.

No light through the windows now, which magnified her isolation from the rest of the world, and added to her fear at not being able to turn back time, to quit when she had the chance. The time now? Dark outside. Her watch with her clothes.

He stood up fast, threw off his kimono and kicked away his slippers. She had expected boxer shorts of bland American design, or nothing; instead, his erection tented a loose white cloth tied into jocks in the Japanese traditional style. He untied the garment and took it off. Wisps of straight black pubic hair; no hair elsewhere on his torso or legs.

He saw her surprise. "*Rokushaku fundoshi*. You seem nonplussed." She knew he meant the underwear; told him every erection intrigued her but none surprised.

Come now, Professor, don't waste an invitation to diminish me a little, to feel more in control. Ayanokoji converted an incipient sneer into a smirk. "I meant the underwear. Erect penis is *bokki inkei*. After today I do not think you will confuse the two."

Ayanokoji, a priapic waiter preparing a table napkin for a diner in a nudist club, folded the *fundoshi* and placed it with reverence on the mat near his kimono; picked up the crumpled latter, folded it flawless and laid it beside the *fundoshi*. Paired the separated slippers.

Ah, Professor Nostalgia, a traditional nappy under your work suit, that tailored veneer of post-feudalism. Mangled Japanese soldiers of the emperor wear the nappy in victors' photographs and documentary films.

His body remarkable for a man of his age. Peter had told her Mishima was a bodybuilder. "Hiroyuki, like Rand you have something in common with Mishima. A strong, fit body. Beautiful. Honed in a gymnasium, like his?"

"Take off the kimono." No 'please', Professor? The Kempeitai major is back? She threw it aside. He told her to spread it out and lie on it.

That got to him, Mrs Conway. He doesn't like the comparison with Mishima or, by association, with St Sebastian and me. Trying to goad him into proving he's not a pansy? *That he's not into* *homoerotic sadism? Better action for you?* That and more. You'll see, and thank me for it when you head off, so to speak, for where you know you need to go. *Pardon?*

She pulled her shoulders from Rand's grip and lay on her back on the kimono, knees together, demure right hand on the right breast of Botticelli's Venus; left hand not guarding her groin like Venus but lying in open invitation beside her hip.

So far her script had developed well, with a few glitches to which she had adjusted with ease; and if the play developed as she intended, that might be the last of Rand's grip on her. Now the penultimate act, the trigger for the highpoint of her script.

Ayanokoji stood at her feet and stared down at her, his eyes wary as those of a yard-dog whistled by an intruder armed with a brick.

"You refused before but as a gentleman I must ask again. May I fetch water to wash the blood from your face? Some also on your left breast."

"No, Hiroyuki. Don't make me wait."

"Much of the ice in the bucket has melted. Perhaps a little chilly. Cold water is best for blood."

Too hesitant, Charlotte. He's a fox. Your script is almost in *the shredder, and you are in deep shit if he takes another look at* *the swords. Move all his brainpower to his groin, fast.* No grip on shoulders—Rand would grip her only when she sat or stood.

"Since when did blood turn you off, Hiroyuki? I don't mind it. Quite the opposite."

Move now. She solicited with both hands palms-up beside her hips, raised her knees, parted them even wider than for the American boy in New Orleans, the one whose mother had told him to concentrate on the woman; that his pleasure would take care of itself. Ayanokoji dropped to his knees for a few seconds, fell on her with the full weight and strength of his body, and started to pound her as if propelled from behind by a force she could not see. Unusual for men, his slow breathing did not match his physical rhythm.

Such a subtle gesture, Professor Bulldozer, to drop like a sack of rice, to tell me wordless that you are now the director of the play. I made you do it, so who's the scriptwriter and director?

His face over her left shoulder, against her cheek. He smells no commercial perfume. Whiff of shampoo and ear wax. The intimacy of ears. Studs of pearl-drops stab her lobes. Gift from her husband? Millar or Fonseka? Another lover? Buy expensive ear-rings for her later. Jade or emerald. She can tell her husband she bought them herself, if he cares.

He stood up and went to the camera on its tripod; wound the film on, focused on Charlotte, set the timer button and remounted her. "Look at the camera." She gulped in pain as his right hand seized the hair at the back of her head and pushed her face hard over his left shoulder, her nose spurting blood as the shutter clacked. "A little more insurance, Charlotte. Pity the film is monochrome, not Ektachrome. It would have been perfect for your bloody nose and emerald eyes, so wide and eager." He kept her neck bent and held her chin against his shoulder, smeared with her blood, until she stopped trying to pull away. As he relaxed his hand she bit into the shoulder, which made him pound her harder; the same when she scored her fingernails across his back to draw blood.

After his first peak he ordered her to lie still while he pinched her nose for three minutes with a mother's tenderness, to stop the minor bleed. All he said in that time was, "Your nose isn't damaged. No swelling. No one but you and I shall know about it." A whiff of rice and sweat rushed up her clear nostril when he released the pinch. Didn't Bos say in her notes that Japanese soldiers smelt like their food, different to Bougainvilleans, whose skin and breath presumably emitted their own diet of fish, coconut and yams? White people's sweat stank of beer and canned bully beef.

A rest of three minutes for Ayanokoji was too long for her

script. She must tire him much more than he tire her, and so begged him to remount her, not let her lose the level of ecstasy to which he had stimulated her.

For the next half hour he seemed to have no rules about what pain she could inflict on him, and where, apart from his head, upper neck and hands, which he would not let her touch. She bit into the mobile skin over his collarbones, and scratched his chest when he raised himself to change position.

After 16 minutes. "Rough enough for you, Charlotte? Into that grey zone of pleasure and pain?"

Ask him if it has ever occurred to his brilliant mind that debauchery and butchery are almost homonyms. In his head, maybe synonyms? Back off, Rand. I'm preparing your ticket for a long journey. *Get him to strangle you, give you a purple collar.*

She had done almost enough damage to Ayanokoji; he had not done enough to her. Nor did she think him tired enough for her endgame.

"Not quite rough enough, Hiroyuki. Not quite in the zone. Why do you ignore my breasts? I thought men were never weaned."

She held his head hard against her while he bit her breasts and upper arms, and again dug his fingernails hard into her buttocks. She grieved and cried within, not for her own pain or predicament, but for the Chinese *maruta*, the log whose name she did not know; for Chung-Cha the Korean comfort girl, and for Bos Simeon, whose notebooks did not mention the suffering this bastard must have inflicted on her.

And inflicted on Hugh Rand, the intrusive, a malevolent wanderer, a spirit unable to free himself and not yet freed from the grey realm by anyone else; and now, owing to an improbable sequence of events in Kyoto—from a boring linguistics conference to a fortuitous sign placed outside an obscure gallery, to discussion of the Pacific war with a refined thug—she could now free Rand and therefore rid herself and Bos Simeon of his harassment, while avenging Ayanokoji's cruelty to girls who liked it rough.

Easy to read your mind. Are you sure your crusade is well-founded? A bit deluded, maybe? Lots of unchallenged assumptions. For a start, I feel free now, thank you. And in her notebooks, does Bos say I did anything to her, other than make her carry a bag of spuds? She remembers me, that's all. Tell me if I'm wrong—you're the expert editor of her tale. If you remember Peter and Aidan, does that mean they abused and exploited you? Any doubts? None.

Charlotte could not know that Rand had not bothered Bos Simeon's mind since 28 February 1973.

Rand was right sometimes—she needed evidence of attempted strangulation; a purple collar. Ayanokoji struggles for breath. The unseen force behind him weaker now.

"Hiroyuki! Go for my throat. Not long to go. Nearly there. High collared dress for me tomorrow." He gripped her lower neck with both hands, not the tender hands that had patted her breasts as a mother pats her baby. Dug his thumbs into her thyroid gland, compressed her trachea and carotid artery; squeezed tighter as she faked orgasm after 30 seconds, not far short of blackout; both she and Ayanokoji right in assuming her extreme pain and pleasure would trigger his second peak. Again the whiff of rice from his sweat, bourbon in his groan. She saw ferrets at war in a Nyngan farmer's cage.

He rolled off her, hard onto his back; a sweat-slap on the *tatami*. Eyes closed, hands under head, prolonged gasps of a turtle sucking air. Don't let him sleep. She sat up, crawled over to the bourbon bottle and poured two glasses; one a triple shot, the other a half; with the tongs, dropped two much-shrunken ice cubes in the former and topped up the latter with some of the ice water that might have doused her face before the coupling. Like rum, watered-down bourbon holds its colour. The glasses identical to the eye if not the nose.

"Hiroyuki? Cheers." Knelt beside him, rattled the ice in his glass. He sat up and reached for it. Still breathing hard, looking like an antique *oni* she had seen in a travel guide; the horned mask of a red-eyed, sunburnt devil who creates disasters and, consistent with the incongruities of Japan, wards off evil spirits. Complementarities?

"Cheers, Charlotte. The last of the bourbon? You pour monster shots." Cannot smell her fear above the fumes of the bourbon. Eyes troubled but demeanour confident. A novice high-diver at the edge of a cliff, resolved to leap.

She nodded, tried to smile; failed; feigned exhaustion. Now full of energy for the final act. Gulped her drink in three draughts, five seconds apart. Ayanokoji laughed and followed suit.

This woman, gratified as she might be, still holds back on something. "Charlotte, look at you. Did you fall off your bicycle?" Ah, see her laugh, but those eyes, ice emeralds now, speak another language.

The geriatric professor's better at photography and rough stuff than Ironman Peter, don't you think? Shuts up and goes for it. And Aidan the Linguistic Geographer looks like a pansy now, with his little torch and clever repartee. What about the mummy's boy in New Orleans? Go get your passport, Rand. *A shame the gold medallist let go of your neck so soon.*

* * *

Hands clenched behind back, shoes shrouded in blue cotton covers, charcoal suit impeccable, Inspector Tsuneo Yagashita of the Kyoto Prefectural Police walks clockwise around the body twice, then thrice anticlockwise. He stands in one spot for ten minutes and contemplates the corpse. His team of two men and one woman wait at the door of Professor Ayanokoji's home gallery. The men want to get closer to a couple of nude photographs visible from the door; the woman pretends she does not see the shots of the black girl. A fourth officer, her hands holding the patient's, is in the back of an ambulance on the way to the Takeda General Hospital.

Although Inspector Yagashita, 37 years old, plans not to touch anything or anyone, he wears sterile white gloves; also a surgical mask, perhaps to reduce the risk of inhaling evidence or contaminating it with his breath.

He beckons the officer with the camera. She wears similar facial protection, and a white boiler-suit over her uniform. 'Forensic' is on the back, in English capitals and Japanese characters. Inspector Yagashita tells her to take 25 photographs from all angles, some in close, especially where the sword has entered and exited. Minimal bleeding. Would have been more if the sword were pulled out right after the stab. That's why you don't pull a knife out of a live victim. Also need a shot of the bite on his face and the scratches on his chest. The rape victim fought hard. Had him by the neck, like he had her. Photograph that injury too.

The room does not stink as in other cases of death by sword in the gut. The difference is the entry wound, a stab no broader than the blade, not the usual stab and twist and slice that oozes blood and entrails into the lap of the victim, and begets an overflow of shit and gore onto the floor.

While the photographer works, the Inspector looks at the empty bourbon bottle and glasses, and the ice bucket with cold water but no ice. Near a blood smear on the *tatami* is a pair of small slippers, one upside down, and a scatter of women's clothes in Western style. Discarded in panic, under duress? Also a woman's watch. Beside them a man's informal *yukata* kimono and *obi*, folded with perfection. A neat pair of slippers. No loss of composure by the savage who took these things off. The rapist.

Professor Ayanokoji wears only a watch and a *rokushaku fundoshi*. He sits almost cross-legged as his eyes wonder at another world, distant from this gallery. Arms and hands flopped at his sides, his palms upward, knuckles on the floor; back straight. Sword through his torso. Halfway up to the hilt near his left rib-cage, medial position.

Strong lady, thinks Yagashita. Stabbed him through stomach and pancreas, for sure; a cut across the transverse colon; probably nicked the duodenum, missed the liver; well above the right kidney; about 15 centimetres of the blade sticks out of his back between the broken 7th and 8th right ribs. Fast death—face says it—so probably not much internal bleeding, unless the blade nicked the abdominal aorta. Right eyebrow raised frozen, forehead corrugated with sudden worry.

How can he hold this pose? They often do. But most don't still have a skewer in them. Almost enough blade and hilt hanging out of him at the front to topple him on his face.

Inspector Yagashita tells the photographer to take shots of the items on the floor, and walks careful as a cat to the wall to inspect the two swords still on their pegs. He stands over an ornate scabbard on the floor. Old. Worth mega-yen, even without the *katana*. On a shelf are three cameras, one attached to a collapsible tripod. His team will bag them for scientific examination; also develop the film he sees is in one of them—the one on the tripod—when he breaks his no touch rule and picks it up with gloved fingertips.

Inspector Yagashita cannot know it yet, but the film is blank. He will wonder why; will not be able to attribute its condition to anyone other than Ayanokoji.

Charlotte Fonseka, now on her way to hospital with the devoted policewoman who holds her hands, has opened the camera with a clean section of the Korean whore's kimono and exposed the bare film to a nearby spotlight for a minute, enough to ensure overexposure beyond recovery. The ray more than strong enough to penetrate the thickness of the roll. Peter ruined one of his half-used rolls that way, in much weaker light.

Leave the film in the camera and close the back. Don't take it out and put it in her bag for later disposal. Police might find it there and ask difficult questions about why she has it. Also suspicious to pull the film out of the camera, expose it, leave it on the shelf or floor. No. Best to open, expose, close.

Shuts the camera, still attached to the tripod, and puts it back on the shelf. No bloodied fingerprints. Just Ayanokoji's and her clean ones will be there, deposited when he gave her the camera to hold at the outset of their afternoon and evening together. His prints overlap hers, a significant observation that Yagashita and the forensics team will make. Ayanokoji must have been the last person to handle the camera, so the lady cannot be suspected of damage to the film after his death to hide anything relevant, whatever it might have been. A fanciful prospect anyway. Not worth thinking about any motive she might have had for obliterating any images. No sense in it.

Inspector Yagashita will ask her a few days later why her prints were on the camera. She will say Ayanokoji was proud of it. He bought it in New York a few years after his war service as a military doctor. It belonged to Robert Capa. Yagashita nods. Ayanokoji asked her to pick it up, to feel the weight that made it easy to hold steady for sharp shots at low shutter speeds. All fine, Dr Fonseka. Merely something we needed to clarify.

Yagashita contemplates the body. The woman has clear motives for obliterating the Professor. Much evidence supports her claim of rape and self-preservation. What a fighter. Yet a sense of ritual about all this. Semi-ritualistic, assisted *seppuku*? Assisted without her knowing it? A mere hunch. No suggestion from her, or any other evidence. Inspector Yagashita guides his sharpness away from speculation on the Professor's motivation and modus operandi.

Ah, our land of anomalies. What are we to make of a professor seated in his underwear like a benign Buddha, with a sword though his guts. That sword is antique *samurai*; must have a story. Yagashita cannot know it sings to some ears, not to others; that the person who knows most about its history is the *gaijin* who was stupid enough to get herself raped by a geriatric.

Minimal bleeding from his wound. A fair bit on the *tatami*, where he raped her. Her blood, not his—she said he head-butted her nose. Cleaners tomorrow. New *tatami*? Depends how far down it seeped into the 6 centimetre thickness.

Inspector Yagashita has come across this sort of scenario five times in Kyoto with aging Knights of Bushido. Unlike this one—with its perhaps fanciful feel of ritual—all were obvious suicides. Two formal *seppuku*, one of them assisted, both with disembowelment and beheading; one hanging in a garage, inefficient, purple tongue of strangulation, no neck-break; one efficient hanging, jumped from a tree near the Imperial Palace; one beheading by a train at Kyoto Station, most efficient of all. One day the cork pops and they go crazy. Nostalgia for clear rules made for young men and enforced by older, loftier others? Who knows? None left a reliable note or gave a warning to anyone. One note, credible to his family and mistress, blamed the war; really embezzlement sniffed out by an auditor the previous week. Ah, how could a wife, a son, a daughter, a colleague, not see the reality, the difference between war trauma and embezzlement? See but not see.

This case weirder than most. How did the *gaijin* woman fall for the rape? Smart enough to be an academic linguist. Studies what people say without a clue about body language? Regardless, a lovely woman. Tragedy. Attacked her, then out of remorse gave her the *katana* to kill him? No, far-fetched. Not least because remorse is un-Japanese. Planned like a *kabuki* plot? No. What does his wife know? Rape victim expected her home at 8pm; 7.33 now.

Inspector Yagashita cannot know how close he is to the truth when he asks himself if Ayanokoji gave her the *katana* to kill him. He did not give it to her but stared at the weapon again and again over his shoulder to frighten her into his preferred resolution of the play. She must get in first. No rush by her; an eventual stroll to the sword, to take it off the wall behind him and use it; to think him too exhausted to get to it first or restrain her. Thus Ayanokoji writes some of the script she thinks she writes and directs. She does not know he grasps much of her game, different to his. He knows part of her game is forensics.

To Ayanokoji, the assisted suicide is not so much about what he could or could not get away with if he were to kill Charlotte Fonseka, which he could do with ease despite her rash assessment of his physical condition. More a question of what he now can or cannot live with; what he needs to do, must do, about himself. For reasons he cannot come to understand in the last few minutes of life, she has worked hard to best him—play him like a doomed Spanish bull, not easy for anyone to do to him. She has shamed him; and he has exposed and shamed himself, pushed himself to the abyss by telling her too much in return for venting his lust in a style learned at war, and applied since then with various degrees of roughness— according to his situational power—with the other women in his life; apart from Hitomi, who will not miss him for long and will have a better life without his moods and enigmatic history, always present, never broached. He is perplexed that Charlotte Fonseka does not seem to respect him for having gratified her libido in her preferred style, so much attuned to his own.

Where is she? He hears the *katana* grate from the scabbard and sing the song to which she is deaf. He instructs her: "Not from behind, Charlotte. Face me."

She arcs a wide semi-circle until she faces him. He sits naked. "Charlotte, it's too hard for me to cope with knowing what you know, and how you made me talk, even if I believe, as I do, that you would not betray me, nude photographs or not." He is perhaps wrong on that point but she does not tell him. "I am too tired to struggle. Too ashamed. Too tired of a secret life history known to how many? Too tired of hiding its facts and effects from Hitomi, my life's love." Asks Charlotte to give him the *rokushaku fundoshi*, for the sake of his dignity and therefore his wife's. He dons it, seated.

He pushes a fingertip hard onto a yielding spot halfway between the bottom of the sternum and the left medial curve of the ribcage. Ahh, he says, only Botticelli, Rubens and El Greco put an arrow there in St Sebastian. Mishima did not, in his self-portrait as the saint.

He mocks Charlotte: "You are the first female to hold that sword. Try to strike an accurate blow for women."

"Anything else?" she taunts.

"Yes. Remember Tuol Sleng. Photographic analysis in our case has turned out to be at least as dangerous as warfare. By the way, I truly did not want to resume medicine. But, also in truth, an inner voice may have warned me that, even though the medical world would have cared nought for my possible harm to participants at Unit 731, they would have cared about the indignity of my *shabu* addiction, regardless of whether or not I still had it. And they would have cared about my loss of credibility in research; my betrayal of science and my colleagues by causing invalid experimental findings through flawed process. Lying. Not discussable or even mentionable, yet unforgiveable. That is why I was never invited to join the *Seikonkai*, the association of Unit 731 science veterans."

"I feel so, so sad for you. A final question, Hiroyuki. Has all this shit ever worried you at night?"

"The past has rarely stopped me from going to sleep. It has sometimes woken me. Not for long. You might take barbiturates for insomnia. My method has been to remind myself that we did what we did because we had been moulded to fit an ideology—one that would free us and others from Western oppression. The moulding gave us power as individuals and a group; it also dominated us, gave us no choice. Another Japanese paradox for you to grapple with."

She does not reply. He takes his fingertip off his torso. Waits, hands on hips.

As she focuses on the fingered blotch she snaps at him: "Hiroyuki, this is for Bos Simeon, for the teenage *maruta*, for

Chung-Cha, for and because of Hugh Rand." No, he says, it's for you.

Charlotte, what the fuck are you doing? Rand tries to grip her shoulders. She shrugs hard; he cannot get purchase. I'm doing you, Rand, that's what I'm doing. No more from you. This is the payback. Off you go. *Like hell!*

Ayanokoji watches past her to the infinity of nothingness that he believes in, and longs for. No need for belief in an afterlife to camouflage the normal human dread of oblivion. He sniffs hard for his last scent of a woman in fear. Again he hears her whisper to her confidant.

She grips the hilt and pistons the blade into the finger blotch with the smooth swing of a Nyngan farmer heaving a dead sheep onto a bonfire. The stab-sound an apple whacked with a cricket bat. Hands slide off his hips; knuckles smack the *tatami*. The eyebrow lifts quizzical, less steady than usual. Lips quiver. Brow-waves, an electric ripple fired into the forehead by migraine or a shrill soprano. Exhales once, a howl cut short; no other sound. Goggle eyes take a few seconds to close—a dying chicken—then reopen, sightless, with enlarged pupils. Eyebrow still arched and corrugation frozen.

Dr Fonseka, head cool, goes behind Professor Ayanokoji, seated in surprised nirvana. She inspects the steel that sticks out of his back at the angle of an erection. She does not want or need to pull out the sword, starved of blood for 40 years after it killed Rand. Wipes the protruding part with the comfort girl's kimono, gets onto her knees, leans her marble throat on the point and breaks skin; bleeds enough to prove he menaced her with the blade she used to neutralise him after he exhausted himself with rape. Goes back to the front of body, breathes deep, glares at its face, bites hard on the left cheek, thinks she feels it cringe; scratches both cheeks to ensure plenty of evidence of her struggle is on his face and lodged under her fingernails. Lifts the body's hands, one at a time; scratches her face, not too hard—incriminating skin and blood from her buttocks are already wedged in his nails.

Again she bashes her nose on the body's forehead, ensures blood trickles over the face. Bleeds into her cupped hands; grabs the sword-hilt to leave bloodied prints as evidence the rapist injured her before she stabbed him to save her life. She finger-paints more smears on the *tatami* where they coupled.

She invites Rand to applaud or decry her work. Repeats the invitation many times during the next twenty minutes. As she expects, he does not oblige because he cannot do so. Inspired by Bos Simeon's thinking in Notebook Three, Charlotte has neutralised him with ritual; has forced on him a benign character and driven him into a higher realm by fulfilling a task impossible after the war for Bos or her mother. A shark ate the pig-officer who killed Rand; but, as inferred by Bos, the intrepid coast watcher also required vengeance against the instigator, the Kieta garrison commander. With the sword that killed Rand, Charlotte has despatched the Kempeitai major who ordered the pig-officer to conduct the beheading. Payback accomplished. Exit Rand.

* * *

Inspector Yagashita will take a day or so to review her account from the night of the rape. Right now he has no reason to disbelieve she was there because of an interest in Ayanokoji's photography; that she walked the Path of Philosophy with him after discussion at his office; that she dined in splendour at the house the previous night, and got on well with Mrs Ayanokoji, who had been so kind to her when she fainted; and that she expected the lady to arrive home tonight at 8pm.

Yagashita will not detect her forensic manipulation, and will, in company with the Australian Consul, put her on a plane from Osaka to Australia within a week. The medical and forensic examinations of Dr Fonseka and the rapist will support Yagashita's preliminary hunches and observations. The rapist's blood alcohol content is much higher than hers. Her pubic hair is on him and his on her. There is semen; also bruising of the mons pubis, internal haematoma, and abrasions to her inner thighs. Deep scratches and gouges to her buttocks, breasts, face, arms and back. Bites to arms and breasts. Left nipple bleeds. Almost broken nose. Lucky her hands are uncut by the sword she grabbed from the floor near the rapist after he put on his *rokushaku fundoshi* and sat exhausted from his savagery. No doubt she had to take the opportunity as he intended to kill her after he rested. He told her so. What else could she do?

The victim is distressed but lucid. In the house, where they found her lying on the foyer floor near the telephone, she has answered Yagashita's questions and displayed her most intimate injuries with an endearing mix of embarrassment and courage, in the presence of a female ambulance officer. The inspector has made three trips to the gallery and back from the house, where she sits on a plastic sheet over the Professor's armchair. Yagashita is sure she replies with consistent truth to complex questions he asks in the strong English he learned as the son of a diplomat in Canada.

* * *

The photography done, Inspector Yagashita beckons the other two policemen and points to the things he wants bagged. They reach the body via the photographs of Bos Simeon. Why take a diversion to those photographs, he asks them. Irrelevant to the case. Concentrate on your job here, and porn at home.

To one of them: "Let your companion bag other things while you get prints off the hilt."

Two men arrive with a trolley and a body bag, olive-green plastic, zippered, to collect the Professor. Not yet. Wait at the door until the hilt prints are taken and the bagging done.

Okay, done. Come in. Wait. Inspector Yagashita takes an eraser-tipped pencil out of his notebook, which he rarely needs to use, and with the eraser closes Professor Hiroyuki Ayanokoji's eyes for the last time. Face grey now. Lips purple-blue. Right eyebrow locked in an arch. Mortician's job to shove that and his forehead creases back into place for Mrs Ayanokoji. Women's cosmetics on the scratches and cheek-bite. Forensics people already told to get skin and blood samples from Dr Fonseka's fingernails. Routine. I know what happened. Brave lady. Stupid though, despite her IQ. Must move him out before his wife gets home.

Inspector Yagashita knows his scenario is a reconstruction that relies, until the forensics are complete, on the *gaijin's* account. Ayanokoji might tell another story, probably much less truthful, if he could do so. Over the next few days the inspector will discover that Mrs Ayanokoji knows nothing negative about her husband, as expected from a loyal Japanese wife. She will refuse to even reflect on the possibility that her husband raped the *gaijin* woman, the murderer. Staged *seppuku*? Absurd. Never a smidgeon of shame, or any reason for it, in the decades she has known him. Yagashita's search of Ayanokoji's pre-marital history will support her claim that he spent the war as a doctor and had nothing shameful to hide.

Tonight in Ninzenji the inspector realises but prefers not to dwell on the slim chance that Dr Fonseka, now Charlotte to him— and he Tsuneo to her—has outwitted him. He cannot know she is elated at the script writing and direction that have promised her a freer life, have ticketed Rand against his will to his next destination, beyond the grey zone; have avenged Ayanokoji's teenage victims of long ago; have freed Hitomi, *hankechi*-twisting bitch that she may be, from the talons of the sadomasochistic tyrant who must have tormented her for decades.

The two corpse collectors, male, dressed sterile like their boss, stare at the sword and wonder aloud how they will get this human scabbard into the body-bag. Pull out the damned *katana* first, suggests the inspector. If a motorist kills himself do you wonder how to fit the car into the bag with him? They look at him to do it. Not me. He nods to the stronger man, knowing the sword is jammed fast between ribs at the rapist's back and will be hard to extract.

Take care. You could shave with it. Kintaro, mythical child of superhuman strength, is Yagashita's nickname for this man of light sumo proportions. A hand gloved in rubber tests the sword and finds that extraction will require both hands on the hilt, and a foot on the stiff's chest to stop him from nose-diving.

Yagashita wonders. The ritual beheading of assisted *seppuku* impossible because she couldn't withdraw the sword? Fantasy. Forget it.

The photographer takes three quick shots to record the extraction. Ribs crunch at the back as the sword withdraws into the body. Nothing much comes from that wound, which closes fast and tight. At the front, the chest farts rotten seaweed as the sword slurps out. Pressure within the chest forces a spurt of crimson onto Kintaro's gloves and sterile suit. Wound closes tight. Only one spurt. No heartbeat to pump more, thinks Yagashita. Looks as if she did get the abdominal aorta. Almost instant death. Lucky for her, with this guy. When Kintaro withdrew the sword the body didn't fall. Expected it to tumble back. Good timing to take off the foot pressure as the *katana* came out.

Don't wipe the *katana*. Put it in the scabbard and give it to one of the evidence baggers, instructs Inspector Yagashita. Your gloves and suit are a mess. Don't let onlookers see you like that. Take your gear off in the garden. Tells Kintaro's colleague to get him a replacement suit from the body van.

Good, he's in the bag. Wait. Don't close the zipper yet. The inspector again breaks his no-touch rule and removes the watch from Ayanokoji's left wrist. Sees the watch is old, much older than its webbing strap; nickel casing; black face with white, luminescent numbers and hands; the second hand dead. No maker's name or logo on the front. He turns it over and reads the back: Type A-11 at the top, Bulova Watchco at the bottom; in between are specification, serial and order numbers. American manufacturer. Looks functional, not dressy. Military. I wonder where he got it. Wartime souvenir? Checks the time against his own watch. Perfect. He calls for an evidence bag and drops in the watch. Clean that up for his wife, he orders. Not relevant to this case.

* * *

At 7.58pm Hitomi Ayanokoji gets out of the taxi, blocked at the entrance to her street by two police cars nose-to-nose, flashing red-blue lights. Thirty-three casual spectators and five journalists crowd the intersection. Her driver ignores what does not concern him; opens her door and bows low. She gets out with a small parcel from Osaka and the takeaway dinner; bows back, three times. Her afternoon in Osaka with Kazuo has been exquisite, muscular. She feels more indulged and fulfilled than ever before in her adult life. Looks forward to dining with her husband.

Police? A robbery? Not likely here. An accident further down her street? In the street lights and others—steady, flashing, white, coloured—she sees and scoffs at a few fallen leaves strewn on the path and road, and in the gutter. She will complain tomorrow to municipal authorities.

Four police block her path as she starts to walk the 64 metres to her house. Parked there she sees three patrol cars and an enclosed van; red and blue lights flash off the van's white duco. No, she tells herself, they are parked well beyond my house. No ambulance. There was one; she cannot know it came at all; came empty and left with a passenger familiar to her.

I am Mrs Ayanokoji. I live in this street, this side of the cars and van. A policeman in uniform bows to her; there is some trouble and madam must wait for a few minutes. Please relax in our car until Inspector Yagashita Tsuneo comes out to see you. She bows twice. Allows a policewoman to escort her and her packages to the car. The two women sit mute, stomachs tight. To distract herself, Hitomi thinks of the discussion at dinner about Akutagawa's story.

After 17 minutes they see the driver in white uniform open the back of the van that reflects the carnival of lights. The policewoman grips Hitomi's hands, clenched on her knees. Two other men in white wheel a trolley to the van, collapse the trolley legs and slide the bagged body of Hiroyuki Ayanokoji inside; the driver slams the door. She knows whose body it is. Why at the neighbour's house? The policewoman helps her out of the car. Hitomi, the police, the spectators and the journalists hold a low bow as the van drives her familiar way of life out of her street. She and the policewoman get back into the car.

Inspector Tsuneo Yagashita, madam. The policewoman gets out. The inspector and Mrs Ayanokoji now sit together in the car. Your husband the Professor has left us, I am sorry to report, Ayanokoji-san. Perhaps by his own choice, it seems. Yes, most likely suicide, he lies. A form of *seppuku*, madam, as far as we can tell at this stage of the investigation. She shakes her head, sobs a little, bows mini-bows to the back of the front seat; bumps her head on the first bow; does not speak; cannot. He says they will interview her tomorrow. Sorry to say she may not go home tonight. Forensic reasons. An excellent hotel booked for her at police expense. Everything she needs will be provided, apart from clothes and any prescribed medication. Please tell the policewoman where to find them in your house. A police counsellor will stay at the hotel in an adjoining room. Police will arrange cleaners to prepare the gallery for her homecoming tomorrow.

Shall we call friends or family to come to the hotel tonight or tomorrow? Ah, she tries to speak now. No, Inspector. Then yes, a friend of her husband. Dr Charlotte Fonseka, Australian linguist staying at the such-and-such hotel on Karasuma Street. Will try to contact her, Ayanokoji-san. Thank you, Inspector. Please ask her to call me at my hotel. Do not say why. I do not wish to shock her as she is emotionally delicate. I shall advise her of the tragedy. As you wish, madam.

Why cleaners, Inspector? Fool to have told her. The *tatami* soiled a little by our chemicals, Ayanokoji-san. She knows he lies. He knows she knows.

At 11.07pm Inspector Yagashita calls Charlotte's hotel from his office. He speaks to the same receptionist who called the police earlier that night to say a foreign guest had telephoned from the Ayanokoji house to request an ambulance and an English-speaking policeman. Yes, Miss, Dr Fonseka is in good health after an unfortunate incident but will spend a couple of days in hospital for observation. She will then return to the hotel. Please extend her room booking for a week at police expense. "*Hai! Hai!*"

He calls the Australian Consulate in Osaka and gets an answering machine; leaves a request for an Australian official to come to his Kyoto office the next morning to discuss the case of Dr Charlotte Fonseka, of Sydney University. She is fine after an ordeal but a consular visit to the police and to her, under observation in a world-class hospital, is advisable.

Now to deal with my dear husband, Charlotte tells herself as she lies in hospital next day, after the consul's visit. Gamini has called her, not out of concern for her; to tell her the Australian media are onto her story and have mentioned him, asked to interview him. Has she orchestrated this out of jealousy, to destroy his career? She will deal with him soon to her satisfaction, if not his. After Ayanokoji, Gamini is no challenge. Also, she must deal with her Dean, who has not called her, and the colleagues who have not tried to find out why she did not join them on the *Shinkansen* to Hiroshima that morning. Who needs such colleagues? Who cares about them as friends? She will find better ones.

The colleagues are about to enter her ward after waiting five hours for permission to see her. They cancelled the trip to Hiroshima when she did not meet them in the hotel foyer as planned, and the receptionist said she was in hospital. They carry a bunch of perfect chrysanthemums.

* * *

In Charlotte's bed in Sydney, on the night of the murder in Kyoto, the teenage daughter of the British Consul works hard for an A-plus from Professor Gamini Fonseka to replace her Fail in his end of year examination. His conscience is clear. She is another of his routine post-exam conquests, symbolic recompense for colonial horrors that have disrupted his heritage and his country, the erstwhile paradise of Serendipity.

While Charlotte is on her way to hospital by ambulance in Kyoto, Aidan Conway is soon to make a similar journey 3000 kilometres away in Manila. Now in the wrong place to lure schoolgirls with an apple and a can of Coke, he is about to fall off a stool in the bar of a down-market brothel; rather, to be bludgeoned off with a chunk of Macassar ebony—density 68 pounds per cubic foot—by the husband of a young wife enticed three times over the past month with a few US dollars converted from a Sterling pension, known to British ex-colonials as the Brass Handshake. Aidan cannot afford to pay the husband an inflated agency fee in arrears and has therefore refused to do so. The husband will not negotiate. Not one of the 67 barflies, whores, pimps, barmaids and gangsters will see the clubbing. As he sinks into a coma on the floor he will think of Charlotte; his piss and the floor-slops will seep into his clothes. He will name her when he wakes up in the Makati Hospital a week later, tubed like a chemistry lab, and stares into the green eyes of the comely British Consul. Her eyes will soon return to brown.

At his desk in Paris on a cold morning, while Charlotte rides in the Kyoto ambulance, and his old friend Aidan is bludgeoned in Manila, Alastair Todd-Willox wears sandals with green socks; a red *agbada*—Nigerian cloak—over Levi jeans and black rollneck jumper. As he prepares to write the first paragraph of his third novel in the style of P. G. Wodehouse he sips Vietnamese weasel coffee—US$800 per kilo—and puffs a Gauloises, a post-Tarawa habit. This novel, like the other two, no publisher will read. He cares not—his new wife is a rich Nigerian 'princess', half his age and almost twice his weight, whom he loves without reserve. She is pretty enough and adores him. For three years Alastair has not lusted over Charlotte's wet dress in the beam of his torch.

Tema the Air Pacific flirt from Tarawa, now based in Fiji as general manager of another airline, drives home after work to her French-American husband, a professor of anthropology at the University of the South Pacific; and to her toddler, Pierre, dusky and winsome as Peter Millar would have fathered him.

A little under six nautical miles to the west of Numatong, 2018 kilometres north of Tema and her family, Peter Millar's gold marital ring hides 1254 metres deep in black brine; always black, day and night. The ring has been engorged and disgorged or crapped nine times over the past eleven years, first on a reef by the anxious shadow, now five years dead at 24, old for a shark; later by a series of territorial reef-cod, and a barracuda that snatched the brilliance from the sand beside a coral head a month ago and bolted for the open sea with the indigestible prize.

Dusk cloaks Bougainville. Beside a once-beloved garden near the forest of dread, the bones of Bos Simeon will not stir in her grave of almost ten years when the Fearful Owl laments again tonight on the mountain for cancered daughter and hanged mother, both still trapped in the temporal zone, awaiting release by ritual that no one plans to perform. The village is poor and the pair, in death-life as in life, have not been nasty enough compel the ritual. Far within the forest a crow caws down from a tree through fireflied mist that stinks of plant and animal fester. Alive and anxious as the Numatong shadow, the mist murmurs evil as it swirls through this banyan on the grave of a half-Japanese foetus, not sniffed out by pigs 40 years ago; the foetus still honoured by the descendants of the crow that watched the girl bury it, and witnessed its rebirth as a sapling through the forest mulch. Professor Hiroyuki Ayanokoji will never know he fathered a tree.

* * *

Dr Charlotte Millar, formerly Fonseka, now the icon of a senior group of female lunchers at Sydney University, all divorced or never married, is promoted while on stress leave to acting Associate Professor for her courage in Kyoto. Even if she is still on leave, she is assured of confirmation at the next promotional round if she can publish a journal article in the meantime, her first for five years. One regular luncher, a journal editor, has two PhD candidates who have already conducted suitable research and will draft an article for Charlotte to edit. The data and findings will require minimal massage. She will be the lead author.

As a condition of her indefinite paid leave, granted from the day of her return to Australia from Japan, Human Resources appoint a psychiatrist to counsel her. After four months of twice-a-week counselling, the blue-stocking psychiatrist, Dr Abigail Ashkenazy, 71 years old—who gets to hear only what suits her client but extrapolates and surmises as shrinks must do—deduces from Charlotte's cursory asides to her story that a confidant, perhaps a tormenter, used to sojourn in her head. Such a visitor is one of several symptoms of the schizophrenia she has diagnosed in the patient but not named to her; a milder case than it must have been when the sojourner, absent from her head since the shock of Kyoto, was still a frequent resident. Reduced alcohol intake a factor? Always a mild drinker, she says.

A confidant? Ah, yes. The former Dean of Social Sciences, a friend of Dr Ashkenazy's husband, told him six months before the Kyoto incident that one of her staff, Dr Charlotte Fonseka, had an amusing tendency to soliloquise from time to time, usually in a whisper.

The patient is highly intelligent and strong on analysing other people as gremlins in her life; weak on introspection behind those green eyes, almost always cool and alert even when she brings a tear to them. Almost devoid of honest self-criticism. Quick to form opinions and expert at eloquent defence of them; disinclined to reconsider even when it makes obvious sense to do so. Continually tries to steer the consultation back to her grit during the rape and in the face of death as threatened by Ayanokoji, closet war criminal, demented attacker, and fake friend. Every session she displays the neck nick of the *samurai* sword. Don't feel sure of much beyond her stated reason for being at the professor's house, to view his fine art photography.

Dr Ashkenazy sees evidence of fundamental attribution error. Whenever the patient makes a rare slip, and realises she imparts a hint of her own questionable behaviour, usually towards her first husband—whom she declines to discuss in any detail—she tends to present herself as driven by external factors that she has tried to control. She has tried to do the right thing, consistent with her innate, worthy disposition. If other people in her life have screwed up, or caused her to screw up, she attributes their behaviour to innate rather than external factors; to the perpetrators' flawed character. Mr Millar the main culprit before the mad Japanese professor?

Dr Ashkenazy tends to scepticism. The patient is too controlled—no, controlling. Ringmaster. Ship's captain. Wants to direct the information nature and flow. Time to walk on eggs, to steer her closer to the less delusional reality of most people's lives.

"Charlotte, my apologies if I am wrong. Although we are progressing well, I wonder if you have inadvertently suppressed information vital to our understanding of your trauma, and therefore your recovery from it. Am I right?"

"Right? I wonder. Perhaps. You could be right," admits Charlotte, with vigilance and tactical pause. Think fast, stay nimble, but look a bit sleepy.

"I wonder if you have had a long term tormenter, perhaps not a normal human being. Don't hesitate. Say what comes to mind."

Dr Freud is onto me. While you ward her off, tell her enough to satisfy her she's a brilliant analyst. "Okay. An occasional nuisance. Not really a tormenter. His name was Hugh Rand. He no longer exists in my life. He has gone elsewhere since the rape."

With strategic omissions and adjustments, to ensure she does not incriminate herself or reveal the extent of Rand's erstwhile hold over her, she tells his story, first as live coast watcher, then as her faceless, occasional, disembodied pest, a wimp with a girlish voice; forever young because he died young, like dead soldiers named on monuments. They shall not grow old, and so on. She recounts his relationship to Ayanokoji, parts of whose story she has already told from various self-serving perspectives; her coming together with him in Kyoto, against all odds; her discovery of his wartime cruelty, the psychosis evidenced in his attack on her without provocation; a passing mention of her first husband as someone who once met Ayanokoji, also against all odds.

"Did Ayanokoji and Rand seem to communicate with one another in Kyoto?"

"No. Rand saw and heard Ayanokoji but not vice versa."

"How do you know Rand saw and heard Ayanokoji?"

"He commented to me about him. Said Ayanokoji noticed my whispers to Rand. Advised me how to deal with him. Berated me for not taking his absurd advice." Where is this boiler going?

The chook in blue stockings eases back in her armchair behind Charlotte's *chaise longue*. "Please close your eyes. Tell me in detail, fine detail if you please, about your interactions with Rand. What did he say about you, about himself, about the rapist? Please be full and precise. Take all the time you need. I have no other client this morning." She has already told the receptionist to cancel other appointments as she will spend the whole morning with this patient.

"Charlotte, I will try not to interrupt, except to have our coffee and cake served at 10.30. Let your thoughts and words flow as you wish. Say what comes into your head." Look, Dr Freud, no stream of consciousness from me. No self-dobbing by mindless association of words and random ideas. I've read most of Freud and Jung, and a bit less than half of Ulysses. Here we go, as you wish. No, as I wish but you think you wish. I'm the scriptwriter.

Charlotte meanders her tale with purpose for 65 minutes; takes two breaks, one to sip coffee and guzzle cakes, and the other to take a needless pee so she can luxuriate on cool marble and assess her act.

She finishes her performance with panache: "So, that's it, Abigail. A fortuitous but inexplicable effect of my defeat of Ayanokoji was Rand's full retreat. Something about my self-defence gratified him and in return he freed me from his crap. Maybe shamed him as a not-so-macho male. Weird." I've done well. Tell me I haven't, boiler chook in De Beauvoir uniform.

Dr Ashkenazy has listened to Charlotte for 34 hours over four months. She takes 15 minutes to try to convince Charlotte that Hugh Rand was not an invader, and has had no independent reality since his beheading in 1943; that Charlotte's version of what Ayanokoji told her about Rand and Bougainville is enough to prove Rand a figment. If he were an entity external to her mind, he would have told Charlotte obvious things about Ayanokoji and wartime Bougainville. For instance, that the rapist lied at first, and maybe later, about his war record and postings; about never having been to Bougainville. Charlotte fears she has divulged too much despite her expertise as game master.

"An independent Rand would have known such things,"

cackles the Freudian boiler, "and would have identified Ayanokoji, and told you of his record, pronto. Not waited for you to squeeze the past out of the thug."

"Unless Rand's pettiness caused him to hold back, to keep me on a path to suffering," says Charlotte.

"Keep you on a path to suffering? Do you suggest he led you to Ayanokoji, all the way from Bougainville to Tarawa to Sydney, and to Kyoto? Did you ever suspect as much? Did he tell you as much?"

"No, no, and bloody no. He was not that influential. He was an aside in my life." You fuckwit, Dr Jung. He was real for a lot of years, and independent of me.

"Maybe he was an aside. What about this woman, Beth Simon, who wrote to you about Rand? Sorry, let's look at my notes. Bos Simeon. Rand knew her but it seems he told you nothing about her, himself or Ayanokoji that you did not already know from her notebooks and your own meetings with her in Bougainville.

"And so on, Dr Fonseka. Sorry—Dr Millar now. We have come at these matters from many angles over the past months, during which you have changed your name back to Millar, pending divorce from Professor Fonseka. Please do not take offence, but I surmise that Hugh Rand has never existed outside your mind since his death. That is not an existential or religious opinion. Rather, a professional one about your relationship with a likely figment that you interpret as an independent entity, a nuisance if not a tormenter. From what you have told me, he never once revealed anything that you did not deduce already or could not have deduced. There is also the problem, which we need not pursue today, of his being faceless, disembodied, yet still capable of speech.

"Regardless, some clouds have a silver lining. If your mind creates something, your mind can destroy it. The appalling rape has somehow empowered your mind to purge itself of this annoying phantom, this figment. Excellent outcome. Yet it might be in your best interests for us to further explore Mr Rand in later sessions.

For example, I wonder why you speak of him as if the rape and its immediate aftermath have somehow exorcised him, forcibly. Don't answer now, but please think about my observation before our next chat."

This chook is smarter than she looks. No next chat, old girl.

"Dr Millar, I admit to a personal interest in the possibility of a link—merely of theoretical interest—between your experience and the way native peoples in the Pacific Islands and Southeast Asia perform ritual to rid themselves of malignant spirits, which cannot resist the ritual if it is performed correctly. My husband, a retired anthropologist, conducted lengthy fieldwork on such ritual in Borneo; and in the Western Highlands of Papua New Guinea, where he also studied its connection with serial payback murders. Someone is murdered; his or her spirit wanders around doing dirty deeds until the murder is avenged, and that killing requires reciprocal revenge, ad infinitum. Perhaps you encountered something similar in Bougainville? Anyway, time's up, so let's bring it up next week, in passing, and only if you raise the matter. In the meantime I'll get a briefing from my husband. Of course, without any mention of you. Agreed?"

Charlotte nods, says nothing. Dangerous boiler. My intellect sometimes suggested Rand was a figment; experience says he was a real *maselais* or wandering soul, even though he didn't stink. Never been off your own dunghill, have you, Dr Abigail? She does not know her therapist survived Belsen. We could all spend our lives in a library. Whatever he was, I purged him with a powerful script and impeccable stage direction.

"So far, so good, Charlotte. But we have a fair way to go. Oh, by the way. There is another matter we need to canvass, if you agree. I refer to your first husband. You have hinted that he did not treat you well. At my seven attempts to discuss him I have let you steer me elsewhere. Not so with your soon-to-be ex-husband. You have truly done him over, we must agree. The process seems to have given you some cheer. All I know is that Peter Millar drowned many years ago, and that you now use his surname. If we are to get you back to excellent psychological health we should at least consider the possibility that talking about his misdeeds will give you even greater cheer and therefore improve your chances of relegating the Kyoto horror to history. Don't tell me now what you think of my suggestion. Next time."

Take control. Unexpected contextual factors. Rewrite the script. New counsellor coming up next week, if HR say I must continue to have one to get my salary and hold my rank. Prefer not to have one if I can swing it. No problem.

After the union representative and Charlotte's luncheon colleagues put pressure on HR, it is agreed that further therapy will not be required. On the advice of her husband, who thinks she works too hard for ungrateful patients, Dr Ashkenazy has chosen to submit a letter to say her patient has recovered as well as can be expected from her trauma and is fit for work, but not too much of it for a few weeks. Please refer her back to me if she regains confidence in me and feels further need of my professional services, or the services of someone else whom I might recommend.

To close, Dr Ashkenazy writes a file note to say her former patient seems to assume, without saying so directly, that the Papua New Guinean payback phenomenon is not bound by cultural or national borders. If she does think that way, which is an untested inference at this stage, it appears not to have dawned on her that by her own logic she is vulnerable to retribution by her rapist's relatives. This fantasy should not be discussed with her unless she brings it up, as the resulting anxiety might trigger a worse disorder than her current paranoid schizophrenia.

* * *

Ten weeks after the killing, when Charlotte is settled into stress leave and thinks she controls her therapist, Hitomi Ayanokoji and her effete but cherished lover, Kazuo, the devoted boy from Osaka, ride 76 kilometres by winter train on the Tokaido line from Kyoto to Hikone, on the eastern shore of Lake Biwa; from there another 14 kilometres on the Hokiriku line to Nagahama, and a five kilometre taxi ride to their rented cabin at Minamihama beach.

Kazuo knows she is likely to suicide, perhaps best for her—if not for his finances—given the shame of her husband's death by the hand of the whore who cried rape; and given the snippets of his wartime history murmured in Kyoto and Osaka bars, restaurants, offices, hospitals, art galleries, brothels, universities and homes since the media laundered his passing. The finding of the Japanese variation on a coronial inquest, controlled by the police, is inconclusive.

On their second night at Minamihama, the Osaka lover sleeps off dinner, love-making, and an afternoon in which he has soaked himself in *sake* while she has had her hair and makeup done at nearby Nagahama; done in the Western way, with a touch of traditional style, at which he has laughed; for which he is ashamed and has apologised. To repent he has made careful love to her after dinner, her mood intense. At her insistence, their coupling is protracted, energetic, wordless, almost formal.

At 11pm she rises from their bed and puts on her finest kimono, created at Kyoto by the ancient firm of Chiso. Luscious indigo silk clustered with blue hydrangea and imperial orange chrysanthemums. The *obi* sash of yellow spots on orange silk is 30 centimetres wide, as worn by younger women. Her mother gave her the kimono and *obi* for her 18th birthday. She takes nine minutes to wrap the three metre sash; to tie the bow to perfection in front and slide it clockwise around her body to the back. Should she reach back and kink it a little? No one else will see it tonight but that is irrelevant. She leaves it alone; it would not be perfect to an expert eye.

Mrs Ayanokoji puts on toed white socks, thrice bows low to

her snoring boyfriend, whom she knows loves her and whom she loves; switches off the bed-lamp, and shuffles across the *tatami* to the door. In dull light from some outside source, she puts on her *geta*—formal sandals with wooden sole and fabric thong.

The air temperature outside is 1.2 degrees Celsius; her face stings when the air attacks it but she does not shiver. Town lights guide her as she clacks 125 metres across a carless road, and on stepping stones through scattered pines to a small *torii* gate.

She passes onto the beach, where intermittent mist embraces her; it smells of stale fish. Pebbles wrack her arches when she steps out of the *geta*. She puts them back on and hobbles into the water with tiny steps. Sobs a little as she thinks of Kazuo in mourning, and of her beloved husband and his assassin, whom she disdains for her barbarian reaction to Hiroyuki's rebuff; for her too-clever mouth and bad manners at dinner ten weeks earlier.

Despite sexual incompatibility, the mutual love of Hitomi and Hiroyuki has never waned. For over 30 years she has enjoyed his company and has shared and tried to mollify his mental torment. Without any detailed knowledge of his war service, she knows he has suffered for it, and for the serial veto of his attempts to join his old colleagues as a member of the *Seikonkai*.

As she wades deeper, she berates herself for not going to Kazuo's bed in Osaka instead of caretaking Hiroyuki's exhibition on the day Dr Fonseka wandered in, bored and edgy.

Hitomi does not shiver until the water of early winter, 6 degrees warmer than the night air, rises to her chest. A small creature nibbles her left little toe. Carp? Frog? Mullet? She stops, untwists her inner *hankechi* and yells in English, because Japanese is inadequate for her mindset: "Fuck this! I refuse to comply!" She yells it to the firmament and to the *kappa*—the water demon about to drag her deeper in an embrace of long arms, elastic and slimy. The *kappa*? The fishy whiff on the mist? She turns with petite steps to avoid a stumble back to her aborted drowning; refuses to become bride of the *kappa* or feast for a school of giant Lake Biwa catfish, *silurus biwaensis*, led by Namazu, creator of earthquakes.

With the kimono a sopped burden soon to be discarded outside the cabin and never worn again, the professor's wife shuffles back through the water to the beach. She shivers out of control, gasps, and drips rivulets that try to freeze on her feet as she clacks her way on wooden soles to the cabin. Twitching from the icicle stabs of air, she discards the kimono on the outside step—to protect the *tatami*—and hobbles inside on numb legs. Her lover still snores and reeks of *sake*. He dreams of the mother he adores as if she were here, seven years since her ashing.

In the warmth of the bathroom, Mrs Ayanokoji, for several minutes a Picasso blue nude in the fluorescent light, dries and massages herself with a towel. Then she goes thawed to lie on the *futon* mattress beside Kazuo's warmth and his filial dream. Still shivering, she contemplates the puzzle of her husband's life and death; in particular, a matter they have never discussed—his reluctance to couple, despite a tender attitude to her that did not waver, and his genuine love for her; despite his need for occasional relief outside the marriage. Kazuo feels her presence, clings to his mother.

Hitomi hopes someone will steal the kimono during the night; knows it will not happen in Japan. How will Kazuo react when he finds it on the step?

* * *

A month after her return to work, Associate Professor Charlotte Millar goes with elevated morale to a conference at the Sheraton Hotel in Singapore. At the bar on the first evening, she is calm on diazepam and alcohol when a Japanese delegate cuts her out of a group of colleagues. He buys her a gin-tonic and lauds his *shakuhachi* prowess; bows low and offers to play his flute in her room, the most polite offer ever made to her at a conference. Thanks for the drink but please go away. No? "Fuck off then," she purrs, tempted to say she is not Millar but Fonseka, a name he might recognise from the Japanese press of not so long ago. No need. He bows twice and heads for three female groupies, all recent and aspiring PhD graduates, who have harried and adored him all day. He is a journal editor.

She slumbers after her day of academic tedium. No dinner, five gin-tonics instead; two at the bar and three in her room. A late call from her lawyer in Sydney; bravo, the divorce is through. New life, here I come.

At 1.03am a pubescent voice, silent since Kyoto, pipes in her left ear: *Wake up, Charlotte. Hiroyuki wants you to join us at the pool for a chat and a swim. Wants to discuss the infinite payback chain of New Guinea. Peter's with him.*